SINS OF THE FIVE FATHERS

JAMES H. DRURY

BLAKE ATWOOD

Copyright © 2017 by James H. Drury and Blake Atwood

All rights reserved.

No part of this book may be reproduced in any form or by any electronic or mechanical means, including information storage and retrieval systems, without written permission from the author, except for the use of brief quotations in a book review.

ISBN 978-0989777384

AtWords Press

❦ Created with Vellum

For Linda

"The past is a pebble in my shoe."

— Edgar Allan Poe

NOTE TO THE READER

Sins of the Five Fathers is a work of fiction.

Engelmann County, Utah, is the product of my left-handed, right-brained imagination. While I have attempted to make the general geologic descriptions as accurate as possible, readers should not try to place Engelmann County in a particular spot within Utah. Southeast central Utah, especially Carbon and Emery Counties, were touchstones for the setting, but all locales described in this story are fictional.

I have also attempted to be true to Norwegian traditions, Lutheranism, the Roman Catholic Church, and the Church of Jesus Christ of Latter-day Saints. Each of those faiths is represented, I hope, with sensitivity and respect. Any resemblance to actual events, church leaders, or other incidents is coincidental. Any resemblance between one of my characters and any actual persons, living or dead, is also completely coincidental.

— James Hugh Drury

I
BY NO MEANS

I

"Seth. You up? Let's get going." I pounded on his first-floor back entrance steel door.

In the silence that followed, I realized it'd been ninety-three days since I'd moved back home to Rosemont, Utah, to begin my retirement. My former boss, the Chief of Detectives at the Louisville Metro Police Department, had encouraged me to retire. That was the nice way of describing it.

"Seth, our coffee's getting cold."

For nearly every one of those ninety-three days, my childhood best friend had met me at Heavenly Grounds. Every day except for this one.

A reluctant November morning sun revealed a dark gleam, guiding my eyes upward toward something trailing down between the deck boards. I duck-walked under the stairway to follow a blood trail. Decades of homicide work had prepared me for moments like this—but not moments like *this*.

I didn't believe in premonitions, but my lungs felt tight, like the last time I had pneumonia, when every breath I'd tried to take fought back.

I whacked my right shin on the first stair tread and cursed just beneath my breath as a bright spot of pain bloomed along my leg, but I managed to take the rest of the steps two at a time up to the apartment, to another locked door. I peered through the side double-slider window. Even with my blue safety team ball cap, I had to shade my eyes with my right hand to block the sunlight shining straight across the deck, bouncing off the windowpane.

Seth lay sprawled on the old, blue-patterned linoleum floor in his kitchen. Blood pooled beneath his head and ran down the couple of degrees of pitch, creating the dripping trail under the stairs. A darkening ache drew me toward a conclusion I did not want to reach. The growing certainty threw off icy splinters that stabbed my lungs. I'd seen too many bodies and too much blood at too many crime scenes—but never someone I'd known so well and for so long.

Blood pressure pushed a hot flush immediately around my neck. I tried to pull a pair of black Nitrile gloves out of my back pocket, promptly dropped them, and had to wait until my hands stopped shaking to slide them over my fingers.

Seven deep breaths later, I untangled myself from my leather jacket, wrapped it around my elbow, broke the glass over the latch, unhooked it, slid the window back, and reached around to unlock the door.

I stopped counting my breaths. As long as I had to work around Seth's body, I'd be struggling for air no matter what. The left side of my brain reached for my notebook. The right side spiraled off into shards and sparks, lighting up childhood memories of us playing cops and robbers with me chasing him while wailing like a police cruiser and him wailing back, "You ain't gonna catch me, copper!"

I was always the cop. Funny how that worked out.

Left brain won the argument. I needed to get words on paper, every observation from when Seth hadn't shown up, map what I saw right now—blood, drops and pools, floor, Seth, furniture, hundreds of yellowed newspapers, some now splattered in red—everything drawn and noted so I could reconstruct the scene later for reports and make sure any investigator worth his or her salt would be able to see the room with as much clarity as did I in this moment.

My pen bore into the paper, quick notes forcefully written. The familiar act staunched the deep anger I feared would overtake me. Allowing myself to feel what had just transpired would have to come later. It always did.

Once satisfied that I'd done the scene justice, I stepped into the room, avoiding the blood trail.

The faint but unmistakable sharpness of gunshot residue made my nose itch. Twenty years on homicide detail had left me with a host of unintended sense memories. Seth lay on the floor like a gingerbread man. A single gunshot wound had left a hole in the middle of his forehead, point blank from the stellate pattern of burns and residue, but I didn't see a weapon nearby.

I needed Nick to bring me the department's camera, fingerprint kit, evidence collection baggies, and the thick manila envelopes we used to hold said evidence. I reached up to key my mike then hesitated.

Rosemont has its fair share of nosy parkers scanning our frequencies for entertainment. One of our good citizens could easily pass on assumption as fact, igniting a gossip wildfire. Few things burned me—and *had* burned me—more than unfounded gossip. The blaze would eventually alight no matter how hard I tried to control this news, and I wanted time to get out in front of the potential conflagration. Get a backfire started, or least construct a rudimentary firebreak. With this job, there was always more to consider than just what—or who—lay before you.

I scratched down my list:

Nov. 14, 2001, Seth Ramsey residence

1. *Get Nick.*
2. *Call Emilio Consolves, Engelmann County Sheriff. Ask for an investigator. Find out if the county has appointed a new medical examiner.*
3. *Call the acting county attorney. Better yet, talk to him in person. Optimum, get a reading on the lawyer from the Sheriff's investigator.*

I could get away with running downstairs and around to the storefront nearby since I wasn't technically leaving the crime scene. As I did so, I nearly ran over Freda Jacobson, her hair buns as tightly wound as she was. Then again, I was fairly certain her job was harder than mine most days.

"Whoa, Tomas."

"Sorry, Freda. Didn't signal my turn, did I?"

She laughed. "Good morning to you. How's the day treating you so far?"

I hesitated two beats too long, just enough for Freda to know that whatever I was about to say wasn't the truth. As the boss lady of Rosemont Normal School for the past thirty years, she knew how to spot a liar.

I refrained from saying the day was treating me like three-day-old grits. "You on the way to school?"

Left eyebrow cocked, twirling a strand of luxurious white hair I'd knocked loose from one of her two buns, she smiled and let me off the hook. "I am indeed. For some odd reason, my students and staff rather expect me to drop by the office now and again. Helps keep the morale up you know."

Well, not totally off the hook.

"I'm having trouble with my radio." I shrugged. "And—" I tried to make the pause and my expression as sheepish as possible. "I forgot to charge my cell phone last night. I need to borrow Nick for a while. Could you ask him to meet me around back of Seth's store, bring the camera, the fingerprint kit and our evidence collection folders? As soon as he can?"

Her left eyebrow arched higher, which I didn't think was possible.

I plowed on. "Looks like we had some vandalism last night around back. I'll have him back in the classroom, well, by noon, maybe."

"Afternoon or not, back at all is more likely, Tomas. However, we scheduled three of the classes he teaches for health checkups with Nathan and the county health nurse. That gives him more free time, doesn't it? Works out fine for you, Chief."

"Yes'm, just fine."

"When you can, you might let me in on what's going on here, as a member of the City Council and your friend. Your daddy said you never could tell a lie without your neck getting red. Looks like a fire engine from where I'm standing."

"When I can, Freda. When I can."

She smiled, patted me on the shoulder, and walked down the street toward the school. When she was well out of earshot, I pulled out my cellphone and dialed Sheriff Consolves. "I need your best investigator ASAP. Possible murder. Make that a highly likely murder."

Ever the pro, Emilio curtly responded, "Dispatching my best right now. Detective Yorke will be there shortly." He hung up.

In my haste, I'd forgotten to ask about the county's M.E. Guess that'd have to wait.

As I walked back up to the apartment, I pushed away a discomforting thought. It pushed right back. I am the first Rosemont city official who will write the word *homicide* in our town journal. We haven't had a murder in the 120 years since those first seven Norwegian Lutheran families and three Latter Day Saint families settled Rosemont.

Twenty years writing reports as a homicide cop had rather emptied these hard words of meaning—until now.

2

True to Freda's word, Nick Lowrance showed up in less than ten minutes with our supplies. I led him to the back of the store. As a spry twenty-three-year-old, Nick bounded behind me like a puppy ready for a walk.

"Seth's dead up there." To divert Nick away from how my voice had cracked, I pointed to the apartment. "Shot once in the forehead. Point blank. Look down at your feet."

Nick stared back at me. He didn't look around. He didn't look down at his feet. When he spoke, he choked. "Freda said vandalism back here. She didn't say anything about a murder." He didn't look away, but I don't think he was seeing me at all.

"Because that's the white lie I told her. We need to keep this tight."

"Seth? Dead?" Nick shook his head and his ball cap almost came off.

"Seth is dead." Repeating this fact a second time, out loud, did absolutely nothing to help obliterate the black hole still trying to extract my senses from the present moment. I waited for another few seconds then touched his shoulder. Nick twitched and pushed my hand away. Now he saw me.

"Look down."

This time he looked down.

We didn't have those fancy, plastic, yellow numbered markers. I'd used sheets from a sticky pad grabbed off Seth's desk, some advertising gimmick all shaped like cowboy boots.

"Everywhere you see a paper boot, photograph it and the area around it. Multiple angles, close-ups, long shots. Got it?"

"Yessir."

"Walk carefully around the apartment. Don't touch anything. Think about everything you see through the lens."

"How many photos you want me to take, Chief?"

"Just fill up the damn card's memory and get another one if you have to."

"Sure." Nick stepped back.

I reached out and tapped his arm. "Sorry, son. Didn't mean to take it out on you."

"No sweat, Chief. You and Seth were pretty tight. Even with all those murders you investigated in Louisville. Guess a close friend does up the ante." Nick's shoulders dropped a few inches, but he wasn't relaxed.

When I touched him he was taut, like a bowstring halfway to full draw weight. Was this his first time to see a dead body so soon after the fact? Or was it because he'd known Seth too? Whatever it was, I felt bad for the kid, but I needed his help. Plus, in this business, we all have to pay our dues, eventually.

Nick started taking pictures. I went to work with my elementary fingerprint kit, checking surfaces, looking for smears and smudges. If I thought it was a fingerprint, I dusted and taped and transferred, mostly smudges, to a card. I picked up several good prints. Figured most of them would be Seth's, customers' perhaps, although most didn't come up here to the apartment. Maybe even some of his late wife's were still here.

"You gettin' any good prints, Chief?"

"Nah. Smudges and probably a ton of Seth's prints."

"Yeah, probably a ton of his since he lived here." Reflective listening. Carl Rogers would have been proud.

"Nick, when you get the photos done, check the railing outside and the stairs for any more blood smears or fingerprints."

"Will do, Chief."

I continued drawing more maps of the scene, outlining the body's position, angles, placement in the room, everything I could write down. The photos would be useful, but I trusted my brain to hold these images a bit more tightly. Drawing them seemed to cement them in long-term memory.

Back downstairs in the office, I shuffled through more of Seth's papers. Was there a clue hidden in his invoice stacks or correspondence files? I kept wishing we'd be so fortunate. I lost track of time as I scanned for any surprising or unusual keywords. Alas, fortune did not reveal herself.

"Hey, Chief. Deputy's here."

I nearly fell off the chair. Took a deep breath. An Engelmann County Deputy stood next to him. Both of their eyes flickered to my neck, where the flush ran up into my cheeks. Eyes bug-eye open so wide even I could see them.

"Sergeant Trooper Yorke." He walked in and held out his hand. We shook. His grip was firm, not trying to prove anything. He was my height, give or take an inch or two shorter. Dark hair, thinning at the temples, and eyes I remembered from school days. Not gray, not blue, but so nearly colorless they took on the hues of his surroundings. The first time you met him, you knew those eyes did not miss very much at all. He stared back at me, and I suspected he was paging through those same high school yearbook images to locate me.

"Bet I know why you introduce yourself that way," Nick said.

Yorke cast a sidelong glance at Nick. "Why?"

Nick rattled on. "John Wayne movie. Can't remember the title."

"Rio Grande. Wayne is the Commanding Officer. His son enlists as a Trooper."

Nick laughed. "Your dad liked John Wayne movies so you got the reminder."

"I did. Sergeant Trooper Jefferson Yorke, that's me." Yorke placed his hands on his hips, bowed out his chest, and flashed a half-smile in his best imitation of The Duke.

Nick smiled back. "You kinda look like one of those characters in the movie. All you need are cavalry boots."

I stepped in to keep my earnest assistant from adding a review. "Nick, you get the photos completed? Find anything on the railing or the steps?"

"Photos are all right here." He held up the SD card. "It's pretty much full up like you said. Found a couple good prints on the railing, took samples of the blood from underneath, what you spotted. Nothing else I could see out there at all."

"OK. Before you copy the pictures to our computer, take some more close-ups of the ground around the bottom of the stairs. Light is still good, so clear close-ups of the gravel and the dust might show up something."

Nick gave me that annoyed "Haven't I done enough already?" teenage look but said, "Roger that. Anything else?"

I tapped the camera. "Remember to save a full set in a different file. Make sure your report is as detailed as possible. How you took the photos. Angles, everything. Where you found the fingerprints. Write down every detail you remember, no matter how small or insignificant, from the moment I brought you upstairs till now. I know the deputy here will want to look at them and read our reports once he's had a chance to walk the crime scene. Make sure you print the evidence notes on the bags and envelopes. Your handwriting is worse than mine. Case number will be R-H-O-M-one."

I rubbed my eyes again to try to make Seth's ash gray face go away. It didn't. Yorke started to say something, but his fan cut in and said what we were all thinking.

"Hell of a thing. Pardon my French." Nick made the Sign of the Cross, good Catholic boy that he was, although I doubted he'd been to Mass at Our Lady of the Canyons Mission in Rosemont more than four or five times in his adult life. Father Swarez had once told me he'd invite Nick every month, and every month Nick would smile, shake the old priest's frail, age-spotted hand and say, "Sure will give it a try this month, Padre, sure will try."

I thought about making the Sign of the Cross with him but didn't.

Us Norwegian Lutherans, well, we just aren't that demonstrative with our faith. That five-hundred-year-old Protestant Reformation, anti-Catholic sentiment still seeped through our heritage. Lots of interesting religious ideas and attitudes had traveled to Utah along with those Latter Day Saint pioneer families.

"Yeah, Nick. You're absolutely right. Helluva thing." I patted his shoulder, hoping he'd shut up.

The kid didn't take my hint. He kept talking.

"What a mess, Chief. You're going to have to tell folks something soon. That yellow tape outside is creating a buzz. If they ask me, what do I say? Kirsten will need to know as well. It's going to mess up everyone's morning routines, I know that."

I shook my head, hard. "Tell them nothing. Refer them to me, at the office, in person. Nothing more and nothing less. I told Freda we were looking at vandalism back here behind Seth's store. Let's leave it at that for now. We'll get information out when we know something specific. Now get working on those photos and your notes. Scoot, son." I grabbed his shoulders, resisted the temptation to kick him in the butt, and aimed him out the apartment door. With Nick out of the way, I got back to business with Yorke.

I led him out the back and walked him through every step of my morning, from the coffee shop to the moment I knocked on the locked front door of Ramsey's Used Clothing and Treasure Emporium. Upstairs, I stepped back and let him go to work. He surveyed the room from the doorway and didn't move. From behind, I watched as his head slowly moved from left to right then back again. He gazed up, then down, then heaved a professional sigh.

Yorke turned around and ran his left hand through his barely there hair. "You know the victim?" He pulled a grimace as he asked the question, then answered it. "Small town. Your home town. Everyone knows everyone. You knew the victim. Sorry about that."

I stayed quiet for a second too long.

He frowned. "Ah. Good friend."

"Best. We grew up together. Families connected way back. Yeah."

I appreciated his silence. He let the weight of my grief settle. In that moment, I wasn't sure if I was more thankful that he seemed to understand my loss or that he appeared to very much know what he was doing. Either way, I sent a silent thanksgiving up county. Thank you, Sheriff.

"Glad you're here, Yorke."

"Glad to help. Sorry for your loss though."

We both turned back to the room and surveyed it again. The tears that'd been threatening to break through my professional facade welled upon my eyes. *Get it together, Tomas. Investigate now. Arrest soon. Grieve later.* If there's one thing I'd learned on the force, action almost always numbed feelings.

"We need to do something with the body, right soon. Who do we call, and what about the Medical Examiner?"

Yorke answered, "I'll call Southern Memorial Funeral Home, Welling office. We have an agreement with them. As to the M.E., we're in between at the moment. Doc Cassidy retired, and the state M.E. hasn't gotten with the county commissioners to get a new Deputy Medical Examiner appointed. Dr. Grey approved having me stand in as the county's lead investigator. Sheriff signed off as well. Although I've had some basic training, given what I see here, the body will go straight to Salt Lake. And I hate to ask you, but you're right—we do need to move Seth to that cold storage unit ASAP. Got everything you need from the scene?"

I nodded. Wordlessly, we moved Seth's body, just two professionals at another day on the job. If I would have paused and realized for one minute that I was actually moving the *body* of my one true friend in Rosemont . . . Thank God for training, right? I looked at Yorke while we moved Seth, unwilling to make eye contact with my dead friend. I didn't want to remember him that way. I wanted to remember our talks over coffee, our constant conversations about the women who'd come into and gone out of our lives, our stupid games as kids.

Job done, I turned to walk down the stairs, another welling of emotion forcing me to hide.

"Oh, one more thing." I paused on the steps but didn't look back.

Yorke continued, "I had the Sheriff call our acting county attorney. Figured he'd need to know. He's on his way, oddly enough, riding with the mortuary crew. Too cheap to drive his own car or something, or too lazy or savvy enough he wants to save the taxpayers a few bucks. I will be more than happy to let you deal with him."

Check off another item on the list. I'd just gotten my reading on the county attorney.

3

Downstairs again, sitting in Seth's office, I stared through the picture window into the main store space, racks of second-hand clothes everywhere and the biggest bin of used gloves I'd ever seen. Our Norwegian ancestors had made a huge splash in the deep end of our gene pool: never waste anything. If it's still serviceable, share it. If it still runs, keep it running. "Applies to people and machinery equally," Seth used to say.

"Rosemont One, Rosemont Dispatch."

I almost tipped over backwards in the chair as the radio squawked at me. "Go ahead, Dispatch."

"Chief, I have a relayed radio call for Sergeant Yorke. County Dispatch in Welling can't reach his radio or his cell phone."

The good deputy was still upstairs walking the crime scene for the fifth or sixth time, at least, taking his own photos, jotting more notes on his tablet. He hummed, knelt down every once in a while like he was reading trail, an old cowboy tracker sniffing horse dung and rolling a couple of broken twigs with his fingertips.

I walked up, waved him over to me, handed him my mike, and stood next to him. "Our dispatcher is relaying a call from County."

Yorke answered, "Engelmann two."

"Sheriff Consolves needs you in Springwell. Copy, Engelmann two?"

"What's up?"

"State Senator Ian McAuliffe's plane crashed at thirteen fifty near Springwell. Five dead. Senator, his wife, an aide, and two Citation Oil and Gas Corporation execs he was courting. NTSB, Secret Service, Homeland Security, ATF, FBI—who knows what other feds are on the way. Sheriff wants the department front and center on this investigation, even if the big boys take it away from us. Our own BCI folks are already there. Apologies to Chief Arnesen as well. Engelmann Dispatch, out."

"Ten-four. Engelmann two out."

Yorke turned to me and shrugged his shoulders.

"We've had you here for what, a couple of hours?"

"Chief Arnesen, I don't have a choice. I'm senior investigator. He wants me in Springwell, I drive to Springwell." Yorke frowned, looked over the crime scene, and typed a few more notes in his notebook computer. "I sent you my notes." He turned the tablet off and walked out the door to the stairs.

I asked, "Terrorism?"

"Don't know what they're thinking. You heard Dispatch. Who knows how many federal agencies will end up messing this around. Shove all of us, state and county to the side, that's for dang sure." Yorke shrugged his shoulders and slid behind the open door of his Dodge Durango.

Yorke ordered, "Seal your evidence and send it up with the body. I'll ask the Sheriff to call Steve Ritter at the state crime lab and let the M.E. know the score. I'll do my best to get up there for the autopsy. If I can't, the Sheriff will let me assign a deputy to stand in for us. If that happens, I'll make sure she's got experience. I'll be back to help you once all the fuss clears the fan from the senator's crash."

Yorke's Durango rolled down Main. I didn't envy him the long drive past the county seat and on out to Springwell. Gorgeous country, but he wouldn't have time or attention to enjoy the vistas.

On the way out of town, Yorke flashed his lights at the Southern

Memorial Funeral Home's dark blue Dodge Magnum coming into town. I liked their sense of style. Just because you're dead doesn't mean your last ride out of town has to be in a white Chevy cargo van.

4

I'd known Boyd Patrick since our days at Welling Middle and High Schools. We voted him "Most Likely to Leave Utah." He surprised us all by becoming a mortician, winding up as one of the main funeral directors at Southern Memorial Funeral Home. I was glad to see him, impressed that he made the trip with an assistant rather than sending other staff to take care of Seth's body.

The man in the pale brown suit and bright red tie had to be acting county attorney Emery Burchfield. He wasted no time getting out and around the car in front of Boyd.

"Jeez Louise, Arnesen. You guys got my first murder as acting county attorney." The short man bristled with energy. My bet was Type A, all the way.

"Our first as well, Burchfield." I held up a hand to forestall his response. "Can we hold off the rest of this conversation just a bit, 'til we can get Seth's body settled?" I didn't wait for an answer. I shook his hand, limp and damp, said thanks, the stepped around him to greet the funeral director.

"Glad to see you, Boyd. Appreciate you coming out here yourself."

"Tough times in Rosemont, Tomas?"

"Very."

"You sure this is a murder? Not suicide? Not an accident?"

My eyes flared at Boyd, then relaxed. Had to remind myself that he doesn't know Seth like I do . . . did. "Seth didn't like guns. Didn't own a gun. Wouldn't take any kind of weapon in trade at the Emporium." I paused and rubbed my eyes again. Seth's face still wouldn't disappear. "Murder. I hate that word, now more than I ever did when I worked homicide. It's sitting there on that new page in the town journal, glaring at me, all green and bloody with Seth's name attached."

"Understand that. Rosemont's been a model of consistency all these years, no big ups or downs, no crime waves. Mostly accidental deaths from farm machinery, the occasional dumb tourist drowning or falling off a cliff or folks finally letting go due to extreme age. You Norwegians do have that longevity gene going for you."

I tried to smile. Guess that gene had skipped Seth. Selfishly, I hoped it wouldn't skip me. I like the idea of being around for another forty or even fifty years. I wanted to make it to one hundred. I didn't like the idea of not being here at all. Guess I'd better come to grips with that notion one of these days.

Boyd tapped my arm and motioned toward the young man standing at the passenger side of the Dodge. "This is Joseph. He just got his mortuary science degree. Can't you tell?"

I waved a greeting. "Thanks for helping us out here, Joseph."

Joseph seemed downright respectful of the work he was about to do, a notable difference from another young professional-in-training I knew. Joseph unloaded the gurney and equipment. I waited until they were ready then led them to Seth's body. Coldness creeped through me before we even opened the cold storage unit. Burchfield tagged along behind us, and every thirty seconds or so he coughed, grunted, or sneezed—hard to tell exactly what he did to produce the noise, but I knew what it meant: first-timer.

Boyd and Joseph were efficient and thorough. Boyd let Joseph do most of the physical work handling the body. The young man worked deferentially to get Seth into their extra-thick body bag, zipped it shut, ran the tamper-proof lock through the zipper holes, and clicked it shut. I noted the serial number of the lock and wrote it down on the evidence summary sheet.

Patrick waved me over to the side of the Magnum. "Seth's body will arrive at the Medical Examiner in good shape for the autopsy. We'll do everything we can."

"I understand, Patrick. Believe me, I understand. Thanks for helping us."

"You have any idea what the family wants to do with the remains once the examiner completes the autopsy?"

"His wife Dorothy died last year. They didn't have kids. I'll check his papers to see if he made any notes about that. Suspect he'd want to be buried there." I pointed down the block toward the small white steeple and cross gracing the front of Augustana Lutheran Mission. We'd never had enough folks to grow it up to adulthood. This part of Utah isn't exactly flush with new Lutherans, but we do have a solid handful of old Lutherans getting older.

Ten years ago, an already ancient retired pastor from Norway shuffled our way once or twice a year to administer the sacraments. After he died, the good Father Swarez let us know that when he came to hold Mass at Our Lady of the Canyons Mission, we were all welcome. We still have these joint services today. Father shares his one and only homily and gives us all communion. No one asked permission from any official church judicatories to do this. If we'd asked, they would have all said no. Which we would have promptly ignored and gone ahead with our joint, shared worship. Might have gotten Father in trouble, but then he didn't seem to care either. For ten years we've shared the meal, held hands, and prayed the Lord's Prayer. We'll keep on doing it, of that I'm sure.

Nick handed the evidence box to Joseph, likewise sealed with red tamper-proof tape with a clear mailing pocket where I inserted the summary page, dated, with time of day, list of contents, and three signatures: mine, Nick's, and Yorke's. Now Patrick added his signature. They'd drop Burchfield off in Welling, then Patrick would deliver Seth to the medical examiner and the evidence box to the crime lab. At Seth's next-to-last resting place, someone from the ME's office would sign the papers and the evidence chain would be complete. Boyd shook my hand and then nodded to Burchfield. "We'll wait for you, Mr. Burchfield."

"Finally." Burchfield stood next to me, hands held waist high, fists lightly closed, rather like a fighter. The top of his head would fit under my armpit. He made Sergeant Yorke look tall. He meant the stance to portray strength. His eyes scanned the horizon, like he was ready to bolt.

"Look, Chief Arnesen, I want to help, but how about we let the Sheriff's office run point?"

I thought about asking him why he rode out here just to tell me he didn't want to be involved. But it was his first murder scene. Ignoring it likely wouldn't do his budding political career much good. "So you have no objections if the deputy works the case straight up with us and Salt Lake?"

"That's exactly what I'm telling you. You got email out here in the boondocks?"

I let that dig pass. You could probably apply Burchfield's description of Rosemont to 90 percent of Engelmann County. "You should have my email in your files."

Burchfield laughed and rubbed his thumb all over his smart phone. "Yep, there you are, email, badge number, all your identification." He tapped, tapped, and tapped some more on the phone's keyboard. He stopped talking while he typed, and his lips moved as well. Seemed to demand a little too much of him to multitask.

"Hang on. There. Done. Sent. Check your email when you get a chance. I sent you permission to keep me informed of the investigation at all points, but you don't need to directly involve my office. Unless I decide, from your reports, that I need to be more engaged."

I took out my iPhone as his email popped up. "Works for me." I showed him my email screen.

Burchfield frowned.

"By the way, where was the deputy heading?" Burchfield shaded his eyes and looked down the street.

"You'll probably get a call very soon. State Senator McAuliffe's plane crashed at thirteen fifty near Springwell. Going to be a lot of important people in that little burg in short order."

"When did you know this?"

"Fifteen minutes ago."

Burchfield's eyes went wide and his volume increased. He may have even gotten on his tip-toes to get moderately closer to my eye level. "And you're just now telling me about it?" He was done with me, that much was clear as he scuttled around the car, bounced into the passenger seat and yelled at Boyd. "Hey. Let's get going. I need to be back in Welling ASAP. You got that?"

Boyd waved at me and leaned his head out of the window. "I'll make sure Joseph gets the signatures in Salt Lake."

He put the Magnum into gear and pulled very slowly out onto Main Street. Acting Engelmann County Prosecuting Attorney Emery Burchfield had his phone out and the little man's high-pitched, wheezy voice carried all the way back down the street to where I stood. Bigger fish to fry, I guess.

The late morning sun highlighted the eastern slopes of the forest watching over us, guarding us, or so I used to think. I watched the light scramble all over the slopes above me, hoping the light, however fractured, might illuminate more than rocks or the scrub cedars clinging to the slopes of our deep ravines.

I stepped off into uncertainty for a long walk around downtown, wishing those mountain slopes could tell me who had killed my oldest friend. I'd visit with folks, answer questions, try to keep things calm, try to keep the rumor mill slowed down to a fast canter, and wind up at The Cliff to relax.

If I could.

5

Calling 911 in Rosemont works the same as calling 911 in Salt Lake City. Well, almost the same. When you call 911 in Rosemont, we like to think one of us will *always* show up to see what's wrong and show up in a timely manner. Unlike first responders in the big city, it's 90 percent likely everyone at the scene will know everyone else at the scene. The only thing that monkey wrenches that equation are the tourists who come down and get lost or hurt doing things they don't know how to do and going places they don't have any business going.

So there I was, retired part-time Chief of Public Safety, pulling down the princely stipend of five hundred dollars a month, along with my vehicle, gas, and basic expenses. I had a modest budget with which I ran my department—me and three part-time Safety Team members: Nick Lowrance, patrol officer and full-time elementary school teacher, Nathan Bronstad, paramedic, SAR Team leader, and full-time physician's assistant who managed our two-bed clinic, and Kirsten Dyrdahl, our dispatcher and night bookkeeper for Parkin's, our main grocery store.

By almost any way you measure it, Kirsten was the most valuable team member. Where she went, Dispatch went with her. New technology enabled her to be mobile, always in touch via radio, cell phone, satellite phone, and her new wireless tablet for full access to state and federal data banks. She knew CPR, knew everyone in town, knew the quickest way to get to everyone's house, ranch, or business, and had extensive GPS data on all our recreational cabins.

So what exactly was I thinking when I waved at Kirsten on the way to The Cliff? I wasn't. Thinking. My still visceral reaction to her presence, even with her presence across the street, threatened to overwhelm that part of my brain that should have been paying attention to the murder at hand.

I thought about slapping myself on the back of the head but that would only add to the way I was making a fool of myself, flirting with this dark-haired, dark-eyed, beautiful young lady, a mere twenty years my junior. I tried to keep that thought in mind but couldn't see anything except that long, braided black hair swinging down off her right shoulder, those incredible eyes flashing as she drew closer to me.

"Hey, Chief. How's it going?"

At least five very cool and confident responses surged toward my mouth. "Um, not bad."

"Except for poor old Seth zip-locked in that cold body bag riding north with a hole in his head."

"Yeah. That too, Kirsten." Saying her name out loud created the same long-forgotten adolescent tingling sensations in my body that seeing her walk toward me did, or seeing her walk away from me, for that matter.

"You feeling OK? You look kinda funny."

Honesty spewed forcefully, an involuntary reaction. "My best friend was just murdered, Kirsten. How am I supposed to feel?" I looked down at my feet. *She knows that, and she's the last person you want to push away.* "I'm sorry. It's just . . . ."

"It's OK to be angry, Tomas. Just be sure to be angry at the right people."

"That's partly why I'm angry. I don't know who the right people are yet. And I know weird things are going to happen when your town has its first murder."

She studied me a few more seconds. I tried to keep the blush—part seething anger, part not-so-hidden attraction—down inside my uniform collar.

"Heading to The Cliff?"

I nodded. "Nick's coming over later. Handling evidence, that sort of stuff." *Stuff? Smooth, Arnesen. Way to dazzle her with your intellect.*

She laughed. "Gotcha. Cop talk *stuff*. I talked to a lot of them while I was in school." She giggled. "Dated a trooper and then a lab assistant at Forensic Services. Good guys."

My heart sank a little. No reason her dating habits should mean anything to me, except, of course, they did.

She raised her left hand and started to count off each slender finger on her right one-by-one. "But I finished school, got my degree, extra EMT and rescue training so I could come home and be useful in Rosemont, the best place on earth to live. Those city boys would laugh at me. I flipped the trooper candidate onto his head one night when he wouldn't take no for my answer. When that word got out, they left me alone. No more dates, no more little boys chasing me around bedrooms, or pools, or restaurants. No more distractions. Just me, my books, my internships, training classes and now, here I am. Here we are."

She reached over and took my arm.

I felt like someone'd plugged that arm into a wall socket.

"Chief? You're shaking. When's the last time you had something to eat?"

"Lunch, yesterday, I think."

"OK. You. Me. Nick when he comes. Dinner. Now. Gotta keep you healthy for all our sakes."

She squeezed my arm, nestled a little closer to me, close enough I could feel the side of her left breast pressing the outside of my right arm. Close enough I could not misread her signals, assuming she was sending signals. And, since I haven't dated in, like, twelve years since divorce number two, I'm not sure I'd recognize signals. She was comfortable with me. Guess that was enough.

I let her lead me down the block, past Wangaard's Pharmacy, then past Wood & Wire, our one hardware store. I swear everyone on the street or in the stores shot multiple double and triple takes in our direction.

I shut off the introvert and let my intuitive personality take over. That character tuned in sight, smell, touch: the sight of her profile when I glanced over at her, that clean, lilac-scented fragrance drifting up from her hair, the warmth and texture of her hand on my forearm, her breast against my arm.

The remainder of the walk turned out to be quite invigorating, for me at least.

❦ 6 ❦

The Cliff Cafe runs a steady business, hard not to when you're one of two decent eateries in town and the only one featuring excellently brewed micro-beers. Utah's liquor laws have always been strict. When Tony Weiggand applied for his license, he made sure he talked to Colin Parkin, President of the Rosemont Branch of The Church of Jesus Christ of Latter Day Saints. The town register lists two of the three families who constituted the Branch as members of the original ten pioneer families. Those ten families still figure prominently in our daily lives. That's one of the many traits I appreciated about Tony—his sense of community, how to be a good neighbor. On days like this, I knew this particular restaurateur's character would help refresh my spirit.

When you walk in, you smell French onion soup made fresh daily, homemade rolls, all topped with the yeasty, hoppy bouquet of Tony's amber drifting in from the brewery rooms next door to the restaurant. The décor was what I'd call mid-America rustic: stained concrete floor, white oak paneling, split-log tables and benches, booths with red vinyl cushions, dark gray laminate table tops with a miniature juke box perched at the end. They still worked, but Tony hadn't updated the music selections since 1969. When the occasional tourist complained that the music was woefully out of date, Tony sniffed and walked away without comment.

"Hm. I love the way it smells when I walk in here." Kirsten stopped just inside the front door.

I'd have bet she never intended to make an entrance, probably never crossed her mind. It was just part of what happened when a beautiful woman walked into a room and changed the atmosphere. Every male head in the room, all four of them, turned our direction. The women looked too, but sideways, that certain glance that admired and envied Kirsten's natural grace, and every one of those sideways glances glowed a jealous green.

"Hey, Chief. What's going on over at Seth's?" Tony "Wiggy" Weiggand popped out from behind the counter and walked over to us, smiling at Kirsten even though speaking to me.

If there was one place that a fast-moving gossip conflagration would begin, it was Wiggy's restaurant. "Not here in the doorway, Tony. OK?" I didn't blame him. It's what we do in small towns: eat too much and talk too much.

"Back booth as usual?"

"As usual."

He turned to Kirsten and held out his hand. She took it but held on to my arm as well.

"So, you finally decided to be seen in public holding hands with Tomas?" He laughed.

I could have sworn I saw a legitimate sparkle in her eye.

"I've waited the last three months for him to make a move on me. Nothing. So I decided to take matters, and him, into my own hands." She laughed. They walked away.

Someone nailed my boots to the floor. I also did not let go of Kirsten's arm as the distance stretched out between us.

"Either let go of the lady's arm so she can come with me or get your feet moving there, Chief."

Nonchalance was not one of my strengths. I grinned, looked down at the floor, and consciously willed my boots to move. One step at a time. Good advice for whatever was coming—Seth, Kirsten, and all those unknowns waiting in the dark.

"Open-faced roast beef sandwich with Mom's brown gravy, coleslaw, and apple pie?" Tony finally looked directly at me.

"Yep."

"Chef salad, hold the bacon bits, light on the ranch for you, my dear?"

"And two Mountain Lights, Tony."

"You got ID?"

Tony had been asking for Kirsten's ID since she turned twenty-one. It was a game and she loved it. I expected people would be carding her when she's fifty-nine.

I settled into the booth with my back against the rock wall. I could see 95 percent of the restaurant's main dining floor from this vantage point. I could also see the kitchen through the half door and the hallway to the bathrooms to my right. The booth's wall extended two feet out so I would see anyone coming out of the bathrooms before they saw me.

"Gunfighter syndrome still operative." Kirsten looked at Tony as she nodded her head toward me. "Can't get rid of his old Louisville PD days, even here in what used to be quiet Rosemont." She smiled, then slid into the booth for six and kept right on sliding around the end and down the back length until her thigh touched mine under the table.

Tony watched the proceedings, his eyes widening a fraction, enough so I noticed. "Well, well, well." Then he knelt down, put his elbows on the table, and stared at me until I told him what he wanted to hear.

"Seth Ramsey's dead. Someone came into the shop last night and shot him."

Tony's jovial restaurant-manager smile quickly faded. "Who'd want to kill Seth?"

"I don't know."

"So you think it was murder? Not suicide? I know he's been a little lost without Dorothy but never thought he'd be the suicide type."

"Hard to know if anyone is the suicide type, Tony. Hard to judge that. I know. But I agree with you."

Kirsten stared at me and came to Seth's defense. "I talked to Seth two, three times a day. We had him out to our place for family dinners every Sunday afternoon after Dorothy died. It was hard, he said. Seth always told me he would keep the Ramsey Used Clothing and Treasure Emporium open, that he'd go on with his life, for her sake. Suicide never entered the conversations. Just the opposite."

"So. Someone killed him. First murder in Rosemont's history?"

I nodded.

"Doesn't help much to know but better than nothing at this point. I'll get your dinners going. Is Nick joining you?"

"Eventually. Oh, Tony, this is not for public consumption yet, although we both know speculation is running up and down both sides of Escalante and back over to Main Street."

"Got it." Tony walked away mumbling to himself. "Blue cheese cheeseburger, steak fries, and a Dr Pepper for Nick."

"This is nice, sitting here with you." Kirsten slid back away from me so she could turn and look at me. "Isn't it?"

"Yes. It is." I'd be an idiot if I said anything else. I'd also been an idiot in my big city life. I knew the territory. Two marriages gone south, second one took less than a year. Mostly my fault. I liked being on patrol, then working, studying to become a detective, getting that gold badge. Too much time away from home. Not enough time paying attention. And that other issue I never really wanted to confront. If I'd applied my investigative skills to my two marriages, I might have discovered the exact moment when each relationship turned over and died—for all the good that would have done.

"And?"

That one little word snapped me right back to this moment.

"I want to do it again. This, sitting with you in here, everyone watching us like turkey buzzards circling a fresh-dead coyote kill."

"Ew. That's nasty." Then she laughed. "But I understand the sentiment."

"And?" I thought it was endearing to turn the question back on her in fine rabbinical fashion, question for question.

"I want more than sitting in The Cliff Cafe with everyone watching us like turkey buzzards circling a fresh-dead coyote."

Now. Time to get up and run. Ohio River flood waters running under the

Fourteenth Street Bridge between Clarkesville and Louisville had somehow rolled down into Utah. Breathe, Tomas. This is real, right?

"Tomas. Talk to me."

"I don't know what to say, Kirsten. I'm twenty years older than you. I knew you when you were a little girl. I have a hard time getting rid of the image of a pig-tailed urchin trailing me all over town."

"I'm grown up now. Maybe I can give you a new image, replace that old one." She sat up straighter, arched her back, and let her breasts press against her shirt.

I swallowed a bubble, started choking on my own spit.

She kept slapping me on the back while I coughed it out.

"Yes, you certainly are. Grown up, that is."

"Got the new image snapped onto your memory card?"

All I could do was nod and blush.

I tested another direction. "OK. I'm divorced. Twice. Turns out I'm great at living alone, pretty good at being a cop, and pretty much a walking disaster when it comes to the ladies in my life."

She didn't take the turn with me. "I've always liked cops, and I've never considered myself a lady." She raised her left eyebrow and stared straight into my eyes.

I flinched but didn't look away.

"You noticed me the first day you came home, didn't you?"

I could see my only way through this was to be completely honest. "Who wouldn't notice you? Every man in this town, single and married, notices you. The wonderful, lovely fact is that when you notice them noticing you, you don't play it up. So. Yes. I noticed you. It's a good thing we had already worked out my contract details before you walked into the council room. Otherwise I'd be working for a dollar a day. Or less."

"You are so sweet." She leaned in and kissed me, not on the cheek, but on the lips, a light exploration, a question, less-than-confident, a kiss that asked if I was going to be worth the risk.

My investigative skills told me this was the moment. Unlike the ones I'd missed, this time I was in front of the curve. I took her face in my hands and kissed her back, with a little more force while trying to remember what tender felt like.

"Wow. Hand-holding to kissing in less time than it takes for me to get your orders going. What will the good citizens of Rosemont say?" Tony set our beers down and slid a bowl of popcorn to us.

"Most of them have known our families for generations. I hope they say, 'Hurray! Kirsten finally made Tomas see the light.'" Kirsten placed her hands on the tabletop and came up off the bench. "In this moment, you, Mr. Tony 'Wiggy' Weiggand, my good friend, have me confused with someone who gives a damn about what the citizens of Rosemont may or may not think about Tomas and me."

I had trouble adding anything to her commentary, savoring the taste of her raspberry lip gloss, so I kept my mouth shut, put my hand on her shoulder ,and guided her back down. The smile she turned on me made me almost forget the world outside. Almost. For the first time in years, I felt like things might be turning around for me.

Aside from the murder of my best friend, that is.

7

Nick rounded the corner and walked past the picture window with Nels Anderson, editor of the grandly named *Rosemont Republic* right on his heels. The city's chief newshound wasn't going to be an easy sell for keeping a citizen murder quiet. Big news like that came along once every few generations in Rosemont.

Nick waved to us and nodded over his shoulder. Nels brushed past Nick and hurried right to us. Kirsten made room for our inquisitive interloper and slid to the other end of the booth.

"Young Lowrance here is giving me absolutely nothing about what's going on. I expect more from you, Chief Arnesen. Much more."

"Tony. Bring Nels whatever he wants to drink." I turned back to Nels. "You want something to eat?"

"I want you to tell me what the hell is going on. What happened to Seth Ramsey?"

"Sit. Sit."

He sat down opposite me, got out his pad and pencil, and set a voice recorder on the table between us.

"Nice try." I took all three items and slid them to Kirsten.

Nels tried to grab them but she beat him.

"Off the record. Completely off the record. That's the only way you get information from me right now." I held out my hand.

Our editor did not look happy. Most of the time, it was hard to tell if Nels was happy, sad, frustrated, or angry. You didn't want to play Five-Card Stud with Nels Anderson. I'd learned that the hard way, to the tune of a hundred dollars. Must have been that quadruple-both-sides-of-the-family Norwegian heritage of his.

"Agreed. I don't know why, and I don't like this, but OK. Off the record."

"Thank you." We shook hands. "I want to keep as much of this private for now as I can. A person or persons unknown entered Seth's store last night, after hours, placed a large caliber weapon against his forehead and pulled the trigger."

Nels twisted in his seat. "Damnation. Who'd want to kill Seth?"

"Same question we've been asking."

"First murder in Rosemont's history." Nels paused to let the city's new reality sink in, then splayed his hands wide a few inches from his face. "Banner headlines, front page, above and below the fold." He dropped his hands and dead-eyed Tomas. "And I can't write it. Newspaper man's worst nightmare."

"Exactly. I wrote that nasty word in the journal this morning. Every time I close my eyes I see that word floating like a green aurora over Seth's body."

Ever the inquirer, Nels pressed. "So what's next?"

"Not another murder, I hope and pray." Kirsten slid back closer to me and pushed the editor's press instruments back to him.

To his credit, he put them away. Nels took three long swallows of the iced tea Tony had brought him. I left him alone. He looked at me, at Kirsten, then back to me. A glimmer of a smile touched his face, then disappeared. Even though he couldn't write what he wanted, it seemed he had enough information now for his next "About Town" gossip column.

"So? Again I ask what's next? What are you doing?"

"Working with the Sheriff's Department and running our investigation. Seth's body is on the way to the State Medical Examiner along with the evidence, also headed north to the State Forensics Lab. If we need them, BCI is waiting in the wings. They know what we have down here. That's what we've done. As to what we're doing? Not much at the moment, except trying to enjoy the end of a lousy twenty-four hours in Rosemont, Utah."

Dinner arrived and cut my tantrum short. I waved at Nick to sit down when he started to walk away. We didn't talk much. The food was excellent, as always. The beer better than usual, at least it tasted that way to me. Might have something to do with Kirsten's nearness, the fact that we kept brushing each other's hands and arms, hips, and thighs.

Nick would take a bite; look at her, look at me, and then grimace. Every bite got more ferocious than the previous. The sandwich didn't stand a chance. Finally, with the last bit of roast beef heading south, his face getting redder as he tried, and failed, to turn the grimace into a grin, Nick said, "Something seems to have changed this afternoon, eh, Chief?"

"You could say that, Nick. Yes, you could say that something's changed this afternoon, for all of us."

In the silence that followed, Seth's absence had finally and fully sat down with us. We finished eating without speaking, restrained and honorable, providing space for our grief to begin to take shape. These quiet moments had a growing sharpness, grief honed against the whetstone of an unknown danger.

Tony joined us at the end of the meal, stepping deftly into our stillness without creating one ripple.

I glanced at Tony and Nels, then looked at the two people I trusted most and addressed them all. "Whatever comes, we'll face it together, as a community, as citizens of Rosemont. We will do the best we can."

"Amen." Nels, Tony, and Kirsten capped my almost-prayer.

Sometimes-Catholic Nick remained silent.

8

I walked Kirsten to the door, watched her walk across the street to her car, then ambled back toward the table. I stopped my approach when I heard low voices. Neither Nels nor Nick realized I was close enough to hear them.

"Having trouble figuring those two out?" The editor asked Nick.

"Nah. He's the big city boy, seen and done a lot. She's the small-town girl, went to the big city, or what passes for that here in Utah, and came home. Life's been pretty tame and quiet for her."

"So you think Kirsten is something like, what, starstruck?" Nels laughed.

"Why else is she climbing the age ladder and leaving her own behind?"

Nels sat back, took another taste of his very sweet tea. "Sonny, that girl had eyes on Tomas ever since she was old enough to follow him around. I honestly think she's been waiting for him to come home just for her."

"I don't understand that, Mr. Anderson. I simply do not get it."

"What's to understand? She's a young lady, smart, beautiful, and what or who she wants is completely unfathomable. Trying to figure this out would be like dropping a rock into that far back shaft they finally boarded up at Angel Point Mine. You'd never hear it hit the bottom."

Nick didn't move, didn't laugh, didn't say anything. He turned his gaze back to the door, like he was trying to see through the wood, and saw me standing there. His face reddened immediately.

I pretended I hadn't heard a thing. "Come on, boys. I've got an idea," I said to him.

Nick didn't respond, so Nels tapped him lightly on the shoulder. Nick swung his head around, eyes wide open. He came up out of his seat and his thighs hit the table bottom.

"Whoa, there, Nick. Just me, Editor Anderson."

"Sorry, sir. Guess I got a little lost in my thoughts. What did you say?"

"I didn't say anything. Tomas did. He's got a suggestion for us." Nels got up from the booth and stepped away from Nick, two steps. Nick noticed and looked down at the floor.

"Jeez, Mr. Anderson. I'm sorry. Don't know what came over me."

Nels relaxed a bit. "I do, sonny-boy. I surely do. Same problem all the rest of us males in town confront when Kirsten walks down the street or into the store."

I shouldn't have thought it, but I did. *Suspicions of Kirsten's desirability: check. Luck-level of city sheriff: rising.*

Nels continued, "So, let that go for now and come with us."

"Where to?" Nick finally looked at me, likely wondering why Nels was giving him orders.

I rejoined the conversation. "Newspaper office. I've been thinking here it might not be a bad idea to go through back issues of the *Republic*, look for stories, gossip, anything that might throw some light on Seth's murder. You remember the scene, Nick?"

"I remember blood."

"Me too, but you recall all those old newspapers? They didn't seem like a casual consequence of what happened."

Nels asked, "Off the record, of course, but what does that mean?"

I paused. "Either Seth was reading 'em before he got shot, or the suspect wanted to clue us into something."

"You think there may have been a boundary dispute, getting crossways with someone here, something like that?" Nick asked, now paying full attention.

"Wouldn't be the first time in our fair city that a supposedly buried hatchet has been unearthed."

Nick nodded. "But it'd be the first time in a long time it's killed someone."

"Not just someone, Nick. Seth." I felt foolish for reminding them of my loss, but it was getting increasingly more difficult to separate the personal from the professional. I offered a quick amends by asking for help.

"Come with us to the *Republic*. Three sets of eyes will make a tedious job only slightly less tedious. We've been well-fed, well-watered, and rather than go home and fall asleep, why not give this search a shot, try to find something that might help us sort out this case."

"Let's go, then. Be a fun kind of tedious. Maybe learn more about our fair little principality here." Nick got up and headed for the door.

Nels trailed us both by three steps.

9

Nels unlocked the side door to the office, entering the press room. "Quite the odor, huh?"

"Your press room smells like you handwrite the paper with a thousand black Sharpie pens and you left a cardboard pizza box warming in the oven three minutes too long." Nick wasted no time sharing his observation.

Nels stood in the middle of the room, caressing his single-color printing press engraved with *Autoprint 1501 Colt*. Guess that was the make and model. I remembered when he'd first bought it, one of his first official actions as Rosemont's Editor-in-Chief. He'd told everyone about his pride and joy. He'd spent a lot of his own money to bring the small press to our city so he could immerse himself in the paper. Report, write, edit, print, distribute. Like the small Public Safety Team, Nels did it all. For the less than 966 residents in Rosemont—plus the two hundred or so on the surrounding ranches—once-a-week printings were perfect.

Nels took a huge breath, savoring the air sweeping into his lungs. "By golly, young Mr. Teacher Deputy Nicholas Lowrance, I think you nailed it." Nels pulled out a reporter's notepad and made some notes.

"Every day for the last twenty-two years, I've worked, sweated, shivered and cursed each piece of machinery in this room, every story that didn't want to get written or edited, every hung-up, misfed, ripped-up page, every edition that came out with not one hitch, and I never thought once about the weight of this history. It was always the next event, the newest council person, the latest innovation in cell phone service." Nels took another step backwards and bumped the press, but he could see the entire collection. He swept his arm toward the stacks. "Five thousand plus issues of the *Rosemont Republic* right there."

"Where do we start?" I asked.

"Twenty-five years ago, I'm thinking?" Nels walked down the line of shelves. "Ah. Here 'tis. Nineteen seventy six. How 'bout we take four months at a time, cover one year. I'll take January to April, Nick takes May to August, Tomas, you take September to December. If you find something, sing out and we'll make a note: date, storyline, names, anything we think will be useful."

"Got it. Where's September?" I asked.

"Right there. Second shelf to your left, up one." Nels pointed over my shoulder.

Twilight outside passed into night then full dark after the moon went down. We searched 1976 to 1990. Nothing showed up. Not one mention of Seth Ramsey, except a picture of him and Dorothy when they opened the Clothing Emporium in 1980.

"I'm beginning to wonder if this was such a good idea after all, my young friends." Nels stretched and walked up and down in front of the archive shelves.

"You want to stop now, sir?" Nick asked.

"Do you?"

"I could go a few more years with something to eat and drink."

"Ah, yes. Youthful metabolism at work."

Got anything in the fridge?" Nick looked across the room at the twenty-five-year-old Amana.

"Frozen burritos, ancient ice cream, Mountain Amber, and some off-brand fizzy water."

Nick's expression revealed a rethinking of the food equation.

I had no scruples at all. "My metabolism is working just fine, for all my advanced age, thank you very much, Mr. Editor. I'll have a burrito and an Amber. Neither one, I hope, will dull my senses too much."

"Coming up in five, Tomas. Gotta plug in the microwave. You sure you don't want something, Nick?" Nels held open the refrigerator door.

"Got any chips or pretzels, something crunchy? An Amber, if nothing else."

Ten minutes later, burritos gone, beers half-gone, stale pretzels sitting in the bowl staring up at Nick, we got back to shifting through the papers. This time, we each took a whole year.

Nels flipped through July of 1994 and noticed that Nick had stopped and was sitting very still, staring down at the paper. "Find something?"

Nick didn't answer right away. Nels rolled his chair close to Nick.

I walked over behind the editor.

Nick turned around again, a slightly bewildered and wild look in his eyes that passed quickly into a nod. The expression in his eyes sent a shiver up the back of my head, the same feeling that presaged my infrequent migraines.

"Yeah." Nick recovered his composure and let the page fall back open to the one he'd been reading.

We read the headline: PROMINENT ROSEMONTER COMMITS SUICIDE.

Nels sighed and placed his left hand on his forehead and his right on Nick's shoulder. "Damn, son. I'm sorry. I should have remembered. I should have taken that year."

"It's OK, Mr. Anderson. Just surprised me, that's all. Whole weeks and months go by when I don't think about Papa Lowrance, how he killed himself."

"Again, really sorry, Nick. I surely didn't mean for you to have to face that again." I'd read the story soon after the event. My mail subscription to the *Republic* always came in handy, keeping me in touch with my hometown.

Nick didn't seem to hear me, stared off as though through a

window. "One day I think I know why he did it. The next, I don't have a clue. Sure do miss you, Papa L." Nick shook his head to clear his thoughts, got up and started to walk around the room. He blinked several times as though startled to realize where he was and who was with him.

"Think it's time to quit, Nick. We're finished here for now. Bet you need to get an early start on the day, get your classroom ready. And here us two old men keep you up all night."

I coughed. "Speak for yourself, Nels. Only one of us in this room falls into that category."

"I do need to work some at school tomorrow. Still lots left to do." Nick yawned, first one of the evening. A second one followed hard on the heels of the first, then a third, by which time the yawn was so deep it brought tears to his eyes.

"Yep. You need to pack it in, young man. Go. Shoo. Tomas and I will stay and sift through a few more years." Nels grinned at me, ignoring my prior comment. "We fogies don't need much sleep anymore. Go, go, go." Nels pushed Nick toward the side door.

I held it open and we both gently shoved him out into the cooler night air. "Make it home alright from here?"

"No sweat. I can find my way around this whole town in the dark."

We laughed. Nels slapped Nick on the back to get him going again. "Well, now's your chance to test that theory. If we find anything, we'll let you know tomorrow or Friday."

"Thanks, Mr. Anderson, Chief. I appreciate it. Sorry we didn't find anything tonight."

"Probably nothing to find but it's still worth the effort. At least we thought so yesterday at the restaurant, didn't we?" I chuckled.

Nick didn't. He looked at me exactly as though Kirsten was standing next to me, holding my hand, that squint and frown he'd given us at the restaurant when he thought I wasn't paying attention, the look that said he really didn't like what he was looking at.

"Good night, sirs."

"Night. Be safe."

"Do my best."

We watched until the young man disappeared around the corner of the newspaper building, smiled, waved into the dark, then went back inside, found where Nick had left off, and continued our black-and-white scavenger hunt.

10

Nels jerked awake. "Let's take a break, shall we? I need to splash some water on my face, get my eyes opened wider."

I didn't let on that I'd known he'd been sleeping for the last two hours. "Sounds like a plan. You go splash yourself. I'll get some air." At that hour, he looked as old as I felt.

Outside, I saw the office lights on at Parkin's Store and looked at my watch: 0:25. Had to be Kirsten working on the books. I walked over and knocked on the window.

She looked up, smiled, then frowned a little as she opened the door. "The door was locked. I have all the lights on. I've done this a thousand nights, you know."

"And during one of those thousand nights a friend was murdered around the corner." I didn't give her a chance to reply but plowed on. "We're driving home. Now. No arguments."

No arguments.

We walked back to my truck. I got her in the passenger seat, closed and locked the doors.

"Nels," I yelled through the office door. "I'm taking Kirsten home then I'll come back."

I didn't wait for a response but went back out, unlocked the doors, and sat down in the driver's seat of my almost brand new Special Service black Chevy Tahoe 4WD. "At least the good citizens of Rosemont saw fit to make sure their Public Safety Chief has good wheels." I patted the steering wheel, put the key in the ignition but didn't start it up. "I don't know what your expectations are for the rest of this evening but mine are simple—take you home, make sure you're safe with all your doors and windows locked, and drive back to the office and crash on the bunk there."

"You could crash in my guest room."

My face reddened and reminded me how bad I was at playing poker. "I could. I want to at this moment. But we both know that's a bad idea."

"Is it?"

"It is."

"Why?"

"Kirsten." I turned in my seat and took both her hands in my rough, calloused ones. "You're the brightest thing that's happened to me, in, like, well, forever. Right now, I'm experiencing waves of cognitive dissonance, stuck between Seth's murder and your smile. I can't do anything yet about Seth, and now's not the time for us." The words came out more forcefully than gracefully.

Kirsten blinked back a tear.

My heart hit two beats, one premature and one totally out of rhythm.

She squeezed my hand but didn't say anything.

I had to fill the silence that grew between us. "If I ever get married again, it'll be for all the right reasons. I won't be in a hurry. The two people at the altar marrying each other will be two human beings who know love and want to be known in love, not marrying some idea of love or an image of the other person. Does that make sense?"

"Perfect sense. That's what I want as well. But you're wrong at one point."

"What's that?"

"When. Not if. I can absolutely one hundred percent guarantee that I will be the bride standing opposite you. Remember that, Tomas

Arnesen. You remember that, whatever happens. When. Not if. Never if."

I saluted her, grinning like the idiot I knew I was, the tension of trying to figure out where this relationship was going drained away.

"Now. Fulfill your expectations. Take me home, get me safely locked up in my little house. You'll be up a while longer, won't you?"

"Look through some more back issues with the good editor then crash at my office. So, yes. Probably."

"I'll be able to help you with that problem, one of these days."

"Which problem is that?"

"Not sleeping well."

Seems she was ready to go all in. So was I, in a matter of speaking. Even stoic Norwegians have feelings—and needs.

For our sakes, I couldn't bet the house. Not yet. I left her advance alone as we pulled into the driveway of her tiny adobe house. Her grandparents had owned it and willed it to her. She divided her time between it and the family ranch thirty minutes out of town, which put her thirty minutes from my homestead. I wanted nothing more than to drive her on out there and tuck both of us into the ancient, worn-out, and immeasurably comfortable feather bed in which three generations of Arnesens had slept. Back to the paper to turn pages for a while longer, then to the office. I still wanted to look over Nick's report, Yorke's documents, go over my notes and crime scene maps, peer at photographs, and fall asleep about 03:30 on the lumpy, Mission-style futon that was probably older than my bed at home.

"So? Do I walk to the door by myself and hope there's no one lurking behind the rosebush?"

"Caught me. Give me your house key and sit tight."

She tossed it to me without a word.

I got out, walked around the front yard, opened the door, turned on the inside lights and the outside perimeter landscape spots. I took two steps toward the Tahoe, but she was already out, heading up the walk.

"I know, I know. You were planning to continue your gentlemanly service by opening the door for me."

"Let's get you inside."

She cocked her head and raised an eyebrow. "You're nervous, aren't you?"

"Well, yes. You're with me, and I have a murder I can't explain. Yet. Yes, I'm nervous. I will continue to be nervous for all of us until we solve this case. OK?"

"OK." She stepped up onto the porch landing, leaned over, kissed me lightly on the lips, went inside and shut the door, almost in my face. I heard the locks click.

"You OK in there?"

"Fine. Now, get back to the office and get your thinking done for the night. Call me in the morning, around seven. If I don't hear from you, I'll call you on the way to work. Got it?"

"Got it."

I drove left-handed, my right hand fingering my lips where I could still feel her, taste her. *Not smart*, I thought, *leaving her alone in that house*. Maybe someone was already in there waiting for her. I hit speed dial: 02.

"Tomas. You going to call me every hour?"

"Guess not. Sleep well, Kirsten."

"You too, Tomas. Sleep well."

Not bloody likely. To sleep at all I'd have to figure out the best way to ignore every sensation Kirsten had left on me.

11

I drove back to the newspaper office but sat in the truck for a long time, headlights off, engine off, driver's window half down, listening to the night, peering into the shadows around the office, the darkness of the alley between Wangaard's Pharmacy and Sonny's Machine Shop. *Cautious. It pays to be cautious.*

Something skirted past my rearview mirror then sidled up next to my car. "Hey, Chief."

"Jesus, Nels." *But it's a heart attack to be too cautious.*

Nels stood in the office doorway, surveyed me sitting in my Tahoe, streetlights half a block away, and assessed the shadowy effects waving up and down Main Street.

"Thought someone was sneaking up on you, eh?"

"Idea crossed my mind, yes."

"Yeah. Guess I goofed there, Tomas. Sorry."

"Nels, I don't think I can look at another line of print. No offense."

"None taken. I feel the same way. Cold and hot water did nothing to open my eyes any wider than they are now."

"Don't know that I can get to sleep any time soon."

Nels giggled. It didn't seem right, that kind of sound coming out of a grown man. "Yeah, she has that effect on us all."

But now her cause is me. I chose to remain silent and leave that blisteringly jealous and honestly prideful retort where it belonged.

"Wanna come down to the Safety Office? Chat a little?"

"Or we could just sit and stare at each other until one of us implodes from exhaustion."

"There's that too."

Inside our tidy and tight Public Safety space, I wandered over to our ancient Bunn brand coffee pot that I now only used for hot water. I filled one of the decaf pots halfway, poured it in, and let it go to work. I grabbed two used tea bags off the back of the sink. Brewing a fresh pot would take too long.

"That's going to be bad, you know." Nels rummaged for clean mugs in the kitchenette. Failing to find even one, he picked two semi-clean ones and rinsed them out in the sink. Eying the tea bags, he chuckled. "Long way from your granddaddy's egg coffee, eh?"

"I hear ya. Those old Norwegians who settled this place, and God knows why they settled this place, liked, nay, enjoyed their coffee stiff, black, and damn near undrinkable."

We laughed. I thought of Grandpa Arnesen sitting on the long front porch on the log cabin he'd built with his own hands, sipping from his tin coffee cup, holding it in both hands, letting the warmth bleed into his gnarled and broken fingers, savoring that black, stiff brew. He'd smile after three sips—always three sips—look up at me when I was around, and say, "*Nektar av gudene*, Tomas. Nectar of the gods."

We sat there, sipping, grimacing, then sipping some more. We'd known each other a long time. Nels kept track of me from the day I'd left Rosemont to the day I'd returned. One of the few men I'd ever confided in. I trusted him with my life. He was chewing on something other than the coffee. I knew not to rush it; he'd get to it when he was ready. Exactly like my father and grandfather. More tendrils of that Norwegian DNA.

"Wanted to chat about what happened with young Nick going through those back issues."

"Yeah, I hear you. I'd forgotten all about his grandfather's suicide until he picked the stack with that issue in it. Really threw him for a loop."

"He drifted off, that vacant look you get when your brain is watching an old film, totally lost in the experience." Nels slurped his tea, grimaced and barked like a small fish slapping pond water, twice. "Takes three to get past the taste, doesn't it?" He laughed.

"Refresh me on the story, Nels."

"Nick found Averil. Nine years old and he's the one who walks in to the cabin and finds his grandfather dead on the floor, blood everywhere. Those two were, as they say, 'thick as thieves,' always together whenever possible. Whatever else the old man was or did, he loved Nick. That's gotta be hard."

"He snapped out of it pretty quick, though. Laughed about how old stories sometimes get a hold of you and surprise you." I tried to get my third swallow to go down and barely made it.

Nels nodded. "Well, young Nick has always bounced well. Remember how he'd dive for every baseball coming his way, even if he didn't need to dive at it, grab it, bounce up, and throw to first? Sometimes he even got the ball close to the first baseman's mitt. I just think he liked bouncing and getting dirty."

We sipped. Nels stayed ahead of me. I finally stopped trying to taste the brew, letting silence fill the room. Nick's reaction to Averil's suicide article wasn't the whole story. There was more. Nels knew I knew that much.

Nels pulled a piece of copy paper out of his inside jacket pocket. "I found this after you left. You know, one more year. Don't know if it means anything or not, but it is connected to Seth."

He handed me the copy. I scanned it, a short article from the *Republic's* back page, dated August 15, 1991. "So. Seth had a business disagreement with Mathiesen and the Carlson sisters, eight hundred dollars of ruined merchandise. No one claimed responsibility and all parties agreed to split the loss three ways."

"Ten years ago and every once in a while, when Gregory Mathiesen has too much to drink—"

"—which is too damn much lately."

Nels nodded. "He complains about that incident. Seems like Seth took all the heat for being the bad guy by insisting they split the loss. Apparently Gregory thought Seth should have paid the whole thing, that he didn't have anything to do with the mess."

"Not much of a motive, a twenty-year-old minor business dispute. I mean, eight hundred is a tidy sum, but murder for God's sake?" I rocked back in my chair. "I should talk with the sisters. Don't want to give Deputy Yorke or any state SIS investigators that might wander this way thinking I've forgotten how to be a good detective."

Nels grinned. "Cross the I. Dot the T."

I replied with my best TV cop impression, monotone and without expression. "Just the facts. Get the information. Collect the data. Tie up loose ends if and when you find them."

"Connect the dots. Fill in the blanks."

"Enough." I laughed. "Enough. We could do this until dawn."

"Let's not," Nels answered. "We've already spent one night together."

My left eyebrow arched.

"Don't worry, that'll always be off the record." He heaved himself up out of his chair, shook my hand, and headed for the door.

"You want an escort home?"

"No thanks. Going to crash at the office. Too late to go home and too early to get up. Split the difference and wake up right where I need to be, next to my press and ready for this morning's labors of love." He saluted me with his coffee cup. "Here's to discovering useful information tomorrow, I mean today."

"Good night. Good morning." I returned the salute.

"And peace at the last." Nels laughed.

I was not going to let him walk to the paper alone so I drove the Tahoe slowly down the street behind him. I waited until the office lights flicked on and off a couple of times.

"OK. Sleep and rest. That's the ticket." I looked at my watch. Three hours would be about right.

12

My normal pattern has been four to five hours sleep and get up at five a.m. before the alarm goes off because I decide to quit trying to fall back asleep. The three hours did help, and I felt good enough to hit the ground running, trotting, well, a leisurely stroll from the office to Heavenly Grounds, for that one cup of coffee and scones. Sarah O'Reilly Jordahl makes the best scones I've ever tasted.

Sarah didn't let me down, and by the time I walked back to the truck, I was feeling very good about life, Rosemont, Kirsten, everything going on around me—except for the murder. The scene sat on an easel at the back of my mind, vivid colors, sharp, almost 3-D renderings, depth, texture, odor, and sound. Everything about Seth's murder, everything we had mapped and catalogued, not an iota drifted away from my awareness.

The unmistakable double-squeak of two rockers woke me from my remembrance of things—people—recently passed.

"Morning, ladies." I tipped my hat toward the Carlson sisters, old and gray as the day felt, but none the worse for having gained so much wisdom and Rosemont goodwill during their lives.

"*God morgen*, Chief Arnesen." Anna and Petra answered in unison.

"Mind if I sit up there on that porch with the two loveliest pillars of our community?" Years ago but for many years, these spinster sisters had fostered dozens of children. Many of those same children, now grown up and making their ways in the world, returned often to visit the best parents they'd ever known.

Anna patted the cushion next to her on the porch settee. Turning toward her sister, she giggled. "At least he didn't call us pillars of salt."

I took the stairs two at a time, bowed to Petra, then sat down next to Anna. I held out my hand.

She took it and giggled again, a soft whisper that belied a deep humor, held tightly in check.

Well into their eighties, their vibrant eyes belied their age. If I believed in auras, theirs would be deep gold shot through with streaks of royal blue.

"Would you care for a cup of tea? We just brewed a fresh pot. I think it is a lavender blend."

"Delighted, Miss Petra. *Takk*."

Both of them giggled again. "*Du er velkommen.*"

I knew exactly four phrases in Norwegian. I'd already used one, understood the second, 'You are welcome,' and decided to try the third: 'How are you?'

"*Er du foler?*"

"Spoken almost like a true Norwegian, wouldn't you say, Anna my dear?"

"Very close, Petra. Very close." Anna smiled at me. "We are both doing as well as can be expected for spinster community pillars attempting to age gracefully. Very well indeed. Thank you, *takk*, for asking."

Petra must have noticed the slight coloring rising from my collar. "Oh my, sister dear. We have embarrassed the good Mr. Arnesen."

"Oh my, yes. We are spinsters, don't you know? Don't mind the description at all." Anna laughed this time, hearty and welling up from depths of character.

"Then I must commend you for wearing the title with such grace and dignity."

They may have been spinsters, but they'd had no shortage of suitors in their time, from all over Utah and from as far West as Hawaii. Not one of the suitors proved suitable in the end. The problem? Each suitor who mounted the steps holding flowers only had eyes for Petra. No one stepped up on the porch of their modest home and asked for Anna.

I'd heard the story from my grandfather, Aksel, about the one that almost got to the altar with Petra. A doctor from Ogden, proverbial tall, dark, and handsome. Petra loved him deeply but refused his marriage proposal when she discovered he wanted her to move to Ogden with him but would not make room in his Ogden home for Anna.

After that, Petra and Anna enjoyed each other's company, worked hard, made bundles and bundles of money, then donated much of it back to the children and young people of Rosemont, the county, and the state. Then they fostered, then they aged, then they kept watch over Rosemont, our graying guardian angels.

Likely knowing I'd wandered into their past, Petra lifted the Royal Norwegian Navy teapot as Anna lifted my matching cup and saucer, both beckoning me closer. Practiced, unconscious, synchronized as perfectly as any Olympic tandem divers I'd ever seen. Cleanly poured, the pot went back onto the rosemaled trivet, cup and saucer set down on the table in front of me. I'd asked once about the china, so simple and so elegant.

Petra sipped, sighed with pleasure, then spoke. "Papa served Norway as Ambassador to the United States. That's how we came to America. The diplomatic corps gave him a place setting for eight, plus accessory pieces, when he retired."

We sipped the lavender blend, strong and hot, letting the early November morning's stillness surround us. They did not mind the cold, wrapped in lap robes and shawls. Everyone who drove down Escalante waved at them. They sat on the porch until 10:00 a.m. when they got to work on their daily chores: quilting, rosemaling—painting wood signs with those intricate folk-art-based patterns which they mostly gave away to local families and sent an occasional one on consignment to the Hummingbird Gallery. Break at one for lunch, walk downtown for light shopping, more visiting than shopping, then back to work until supper, six on the dot.

"You will doubtless want to know about our business dealings with Seth and Gregory, won't you?" Anna, first to break the silence, patted me on the arm.

"Yes, I will. I do." The Carlson sisters, ever the wise investors, owned the building that housed Thoresen's Office Supply, The Hummingbird Art Gallery, Pine Creek RV Rentals and Tours, and the River Runners Outpost.

"Don't look surprised, Tomas. We're old. We're not deaf—"

"—and we certainly aren't stupid."

When Petra started, Anna finished. I loved hearing their long-practiced cadence, an endless Möbius strip of words falling into words.

"We knew you would be looking into Seth's background—"

"—and business history in Rosemont."

"We knew you would find the record of our disagreement—"

"—our three-way mess with Gregory and with Seth."

I smiled. "Neither deaf nor stupid. Rather, insightful and very wise."

"Comes from living with the same person—"

"—for a long, long, belovedly long time."

"Can you tell me what the disagreement was about?"

"Nothing worth killing—"

"—another human being over."

Petra looked across me at Anna. "Dearest, why don't you give Chief Arnesen the details? You remember things so much better than I do these days."

Anna cupped her hand to her mouth and whispered to me. "Petra has Alzheimer's. Today's a good day and everything is clear. Tomorrow she might not even remember you were here."

"Sorry to hear that, Miss Carlson. I cannot imagine either of you not being able to remember every day of your exceptional lives."

Anna leaned out of her chair, patted me on the knee, and spoke more loudly. "We'll be just fine, young Mr. Arnesen. I do my best to take good care of her and Community Services is setting up home health visits. We are getting the house redone for her too."

"Now, enough about me. You go ahead and tell Tomas the story." Petra settled back into her rocker and sipped her tea.

Anna took up the tale as requested. But I saw the look she gave her sister as she turned to face me, a glance filled with such sorrow and love I had to look away for a moment and fight back a tear that threatened to break free.

"You know we own the building where Seth's clothing store is. Gregory Mathiesen owned Wood & Wire, which was also in our building then. Gregory wanted to expand into the space where the Hummingbird is located now. Looking at the plans, Seth saw a way to also add space for a small office on his side. We all agreed. We were going to take bids, but Gregory insisted we hire Deckard Construction out of Welling, a friend of his. Old man Cable at Canyon Construction wasn't too thrilled with that, but he had the job rebuilding The Cliff Cafe—enough on his plate with a small crew. About halfway through the job, the Deckard boys left one day and never came back. Two days later, we got copies of bills for supplies, lumber, electrical, and plumbing, a little over twenty-four hundred dollars. We tried to find Deckard, but he'd just disappeared. We'd paid him for the first half. Everything had been going smoothly. Work looked good, passed inspections. Then they left, out of the blue. Nothing."

"Who suggested you split the bills?"

"Seth did. But Gregory said we should pay the whole thing since it was our building after all."

"Somewhere along the line Gregory must have forgotten the plan was his idea." I laughed.

"Exactly right. He talked like we had forced him into this remodeling and expansion. Refused to talk to us about it. Got very angry at Seth one night when Seth told him to shut up, stop acting like a baby, and pay his share."

"What happened?"

Anna shifted in her seat, visibly uncomfortable. "We weren't there, Tomas. But Seth told us later that he thought Gregory was going to take a swing at him at one point. Seth stood his ground, he said, and Gregory backed down, with a lot of fussing and cussing. Seth kept at him, however, until Gregory came up to the house one morning and threw eight hundred dollars, cash money, onto the porch and stalked away. Two months later he'd sold Wood and Wire and went to work for the gas company, some sort of inventory management job."

We sat there for a while. I held out my cup and Anna filled it. Three or four more sips later, I asked Anna, "Is there anything else you remember?"

Petra's eyes came alive. She answered. "This I do remember. Gregory refused to talk to us for almost two years. We felt badly for a while but then realized there was nothing we could do about his bad behavior. We let it go. Seth took over managing the building for us. But I do remember one night, should be in the town ledger, look a couple of years after the entry about our little construction dust-up. Seth had to stop a very drunken Gregory Mathiesen from setting fire to the building. At least Seth said that's what it looked like Gregory was trying to do, but Gregory disputed that. The Sheriff's office investigated and nothing ever came of it. But Gregory never talked to Seth again. Would cross the street to the other side if he saw Seth coming his direction. You think that helps, Tomas?"

"I don't know. It fits Greg's character, sounds like something he might do. I know he can hold a grudge for a long time."

Anna nodded. "Even with a name like Mathiesen, a long-time Rosemont family has to have some Norwegian in it. Stubborn, prideful, willful, with long memories for the good and even longer memories for the bad."

I held up my cup. The ladies raised theirs to a delicate clink and toast to our forefathers and foremothers. "Here's to the homeland."

All the way home, I thought about that last remembrance Petra had tossed on the table. Attempted arson? Or maybe just too drunk to know what he was doing? Knowing Greg, even money on arson or intoxication wouldn't be a bad bet.

13

Nick's report. Yorke's files. My crime-scene maps laid out in a grid across the conference room table. Third time, fourth time through them and the words blurred out on me. I rubbed my eyes. Closed them for a second. Then jerked awake, feeling like I was underwater, trying to reorient myself. Short naps make me feel stupid, more tired than when I fell asleep, and completely confused.

Where am I?
Office.
Why do my butt and hips hurt?
You fell asleep in your chair. And you're old.

I loved how my body constantly reminded me of my age. As if I needed internal proof of that external reality.

"Earl Grey." Kirsten stood behind me and held a car-proof driving mug bearing the distinctive red and gold logo of Heavenly Grounds. I turned. Seeing her was better external proof of a growing internal reality for both of us. Or so I hoped.

I took the mug, flipped the cap off, and one large gulp scalded my throat and the back of my tongue, but I did not care. Full awareness resurfaced as caffeine primed my engine. Maybe it was a placebo effect, but my chassis stopped creaking as my mind began firing on all pistons.

"Thank you."

"You are welcome. Now, pay attention. We have work to do."

I must have raised my left eyebrow question mark. "What's up?"

"Estella Mathiesen called. She can't find Emily. Wandered off. Again. Estella sounded panicked."

"To say the least." Now was not the time to dawdle. "Damn. How does a five-year-old get away with no one noticing? This is the third time since I've been back. My patience for this is about as thin as that Rider Back ace-of-spades over there. This time they get a citation and I call DCFS to get someone down here for interviews." I savored another blister-forming hot cascade of tea and sighed. "You call the troops?"

"Nah. Figured we should handle this quietly, so to speak. Nick and Nathan are meeting us at the Temco Station."

"Gregory making a scene yet?"

"Wife said he was sick last night, that he's sleeping, doesn't want to wake him up."

I got up to get going. "Drunk-as-a-skunk-hung-over-disease and poisonous as a scorpion." I almost ran into Kirsten in the hallway, had to hold on to her to keep her from hitting the floor. Not the worst way to get close to beauty.

"Whoa. We're in a hurry, but at least we can do this on the way out to the trucks." She leaned back into me, put her left arm around my waist, pushed my tea mug away with her right hand, then kissed me, hard.

I was giving in and falling down when she laughed and pulled away. Talk about revving your engines.

"Let's go. Boys are waiting. If we aren't there in five minutes, not only are they going to wonder what we've been up to, they're going to think you aren't serious about watching out for our children."

"They know that's not true."

Kirsten cast a question-mark eyebrow back at me. "True. They know that's not true, but they'd have some fun at your expense, wouldn't they?"

"At *our* expense. Let's go."

I picked up my manliness from where it had fallen at her feet, pushed her gently on the butt to get her out the door, enjoying that brief contact even through the fabric of her jeans, paying for it with a singular bemused glance back over her shoulder.

Nick and Nathan had a county map spread out on the hood of Nick's Jeep Wrangler when I drove up to the building. Kirsten pulled in right next to my Tahoe.

"Where do we start?" I asked Nick. He knew the county land around Rosemont as well as anyone of any age, of any length of residence. There's not a road, four-wheel track, game trail or hiking trail he doesn't know. I'd been out with him many times in the last six months to relearn my home territory.

"Estella Mathiesen does not know when Emily got out of the yard. She has no idea which way she might have gone."

"So twenty minutes to six hours for a head start. Not helpful. That little dickens can step it out as we all know. Did Estella know what she was wearing?"

Kirsten answered. "Pink jumper, pink snow boots, and a dark blue jacket with a white fur hood. I've started calling folks along Pine Canyon Road, telling them to watch for her. That's where we found her last time. So far, no one has seen her." She held her phone up, more calls in the queue.

Nick looked up at me, had his finger on the map. "Start calling along Ridgeway as well. Unlikely she'd get up there, but let's cover up there."

"Good call, Nick. Higher ground with views back down to town. Someone up there could spot her."

"Nick and I will head out to Rosemont highway and check all the side roads. Nathan will take Pine Canyon Road to the Nordheim's place."

"OK. Let's go."

Took about thirty seconds for Nathan to rev up and blow out of town. Nick had his Wrangler purring and the passenger door open, waiting for me. Kirsten sent me a dazzling smile and a thumbs up. She had the earpiece microphone in her left ear, had been talking steadily since we'd arrived.

As I climbed in, Nick hesitated, then spoke. "Chief, I got a feeling, don't know why, but I think we need to leave the highway alone for a bit and run over toward Walker Mountain. We took the school kids over there last year. Showed them those three dinosaur tracks on that shelf just off the track."

"Something happen that makes you want to go there first?" I asked.

"As soon as she saw them and knew what they were, Emily started walking back and forth in them. Kids and teachers tried to get her to stop walking on them. She did *not* want to leave." Nick got quiet as something popped up in his memory. "I started to pick her up, was real gentle, told her what I was doing, and she freaked out. Started screaming, fell down, and curled up in a fetal position. Christina Amsler finally got her calmed down enough to get her back on the bus."

"I've been wondering about that family. Estella seems likable but hangs back when Greg's around. Emily's always behind her mom too. DCFS caseworker seems like a better call now that you've told me this."

We drove in silence out of town, turned off onto the dirt road to the Red Cliffs.

"How far out is it?"

"Eight miles."

"A five-year-old child not only remembers the way to go, but she decides to walk there by herself? Does that scare you as much as it scares me?" I looked at Nick.

"Same. More. Bad news is, Greg's somehow a distant relative of mine. We haven't figured it out, but there must have been a couple of brothers in the old country who got separated when they came to the United States. Way back in our family tree. I don't think much of it, but Greg does. Keeps hassling me about how I should always cut him some slack since we're relatives. How he got on the town council is beyond me."

I must have arched that left eyebrow again.

"Chief. I never have given Greg, or anyone else in town for that matter, any special consideration."

"Nick, I know. Rosemont's the kind of place where if you did it once, I'd know about it in, oh, say, maybe five minutes, don't you think?" I slapped him on the shoulder. He jerked the wheel a little and the Jeep swerved onto the shoulder.

"Sorry. Didn't mean to startle you."

"No problem."

I looked down at the sandy shoulder. The county plows had come through recently and left a foot-high berm when they'd smoothed out, or tried to smooth out, the late fall rain washboard. Beyond the berm, the soil was softer, studded with green-and-purple table cliff milkvetch and the occasional Payson's daisy. Today felt like a suddenly premature spring afternoon. I liked it.

"Nick. Stop. STOP." The wilderness I'd been admiring had suddenly revealed tracks that could belong to only one type of animal: the small bipedal kind.

Nick slammed on the brakes in response to my second stop.

I got out and knelt down on the vehicle side of the berm. I heard the driver door open. Nick came around and knelt beside me. I pointed. "See those?"

He leaned over to get a closer look. "Footprints. Small ones."

"Not old ones. High winds and rain last couple of nights would have blown them over."

"Emily."

"I hope so. Looks like you were right on the money. Let's go."

Back in the Jeep, I keyed the radio. "Rosemont One to Dispatch. Copy?"

"Copy, Rosemont One. Dispatch."

I glanced at Nick. "Damnation, but she is fast. Barely enough time for the electronics to get the signal to her."

"I think she has a sixth or seventh sense about these things. She was probably picking up the mike before you called."

"Dispatch. Get Nathan moving to Red Cliffs Road with his full kit. We found fresh footprints that look like Emily's. We'll be ten-twenty-three in about five minutes. Rosemont One, Out."

"Copy that Rosemont One."

"As I recall, the road takes a sharp bend about a quarter-mile from the shelf. Let's stop there and walk in. Don't want to scare her into taking off again."

Five more minutes to the curve. Five more minutes hurrying and walking up the road, then about a hundred steps up the trail to the top of the shelf with the dinosaur tracks at the far end, up against the Walker Mountains vertical bookshelf red rocks. Neither of us spoke. I hated this kind of necessary work. And though it wasn't that hot, I was sweating. *Where are you Emily, and why'd you leave this time?*

We paused at the top and scanned the shelf.

"Go back to the car, Nick. Call Kirsten, tell her we found Emily. Have her call Estella as well. Give Nathan our ten-twenty and to step on it. We don't know what shape she's in."

He nodded, asked no more questions, made his way quietly down the trail. At the bottom, I heard his boots crunching into a run to the car.

I walked up and knelt beside the tiny pink and blue bundle. I watched her for what felt like an hour. Chest rising and falling, nice and even. She'd fallen asleep, exhausted by her adventure. I could see the dirt stirred up around and over the tracks. She had indeed come to walk with her Cretaceous hadrosaurids.

"Emily. Wake up. It's time to go home."

Her blonde hair was caked in dirt, her tiny face just as browned. Still, she shivered awake with a hint of a smile, as if waking up in the middle of nowhere and sleeping with dinosaur tracks was her normal naptime routine.

"Hi." She pointed to the tracks. "Did you see those dinosaurs?"

"Yes. I know. You walked all the way here by yourself?"

She nodded and licked her lips. "I'm cold."

"Can you walk with me?"

Another nod. She got up but fell back and bumped her elbow on the rocks. She started to tear up.

"It's OK. Want me to carry you?"

She held out her arms to me so I scooped her up. "Can we walk by the dinosaurs, please?"

I held her so she could see the tracks, then walked next to them, back and forth, twice.

"Okay." She nestled her head against my shoulder, ready to leave.

I met Nick going back down the trail.

"She all right?"

"Think so. Tough little cookie. Dehydration, exposure, some scrapes and bruises. Looks like that's all. Nathan can give us a better picture. Where is he?"

"He'll be at the junction with Cold Creek Canyon Road in five. If we hustle we'll be right behind him."

We did and we were.

Nathan gave her a quick going-over and gave me a thumbs up. He had her wrapped up in a heated blanket, light antiseptic ointment on her scrapes, sipping water.

On the way back, the radio squawked at me.

"Dispatch to Rosemont One."

"One here."

"Be prepared for an angry father when you get back. Although I don't know why he's so angry at you. He's the one who lost his kid. Over."

"Ten-four. Rosemont One. Out."

14

I sent Emily on down into town with Nathan. He'd take her straight to our little frontier clinic and wouldn't take any crap from her father. But I'd have to face the man sooner or later and let that ox have his say. Part of me relished the confrontation, especially when I'd have to hand him his summons to appear in family court in Welling. Part of me knew it was going to get ugly.

Since coming back, Gregory had not missed an opportunity to tell anyone who'd listen that he had not voted for me as Chief, that he thought I was absolutely the wrong person for the job, and that he intended to exercise his authority as a member of the town council to get rid of me. Yep. It was already ugly. Later today it was going to start getting worse. In about twenty minutes, he'd be swearing and posturing.

The reptilian part of me, which is why I let the boys take Emily on with them, wanted to drop Mr. Gregory Mathiesen with one sharp uppercut and leave him lying on the street. That angry creature needed leveling. My second wife had sent me and my creature into "time outs."

Nick dropped me off at my mailbox. From there it was a two-mile walk back into the mostly evergreen forest that surrounded Arnesen Ranch. In the late 1930s, my grandfather worked a deal with the Forest

Service when they consolidated four National Forests into the aptly named two-million-acre Engelmann National Forrest. Grandfather gave up the back three hundred acres of the homestead in return for five hundred additional acres adjacent to the original holdings.

The Arnesen Ranch, now shaped like an upside-down capital T, set into and bordered on three sides by the Engelmann National Forest, continued to prosper. The streams that ran through our landscape provided a steady water supply. Grandfather made sure the family also received water shares as part of the settlement and got the government to drill three good wells. They drilled five to get those three. Grandfather Aksel was a smart man.

Early fall now, our aspens had begun to change colors, the palette of light yellow with bright gold on the way. I'd walked this road most of my life so I could look at the slopes running up and away from me, the growing yellow-gold streams of those aspens glowing in stark contrast to the conifer green, that more solid, unchanging rusty earth tone that seemed to hold my mountain home together.

One mile in, I decided to take the old Ford across the stream instead of crossing the bridge my father built in 1972, over my grandfather's protests. "Too dang convenient. Now everyone in the county be parkin' here and raisin' dust."

Grandfather was smart, like I said, but he wasn't always right. Neighbors stayed away like they always had, coming over when invited or when there was trouble. All of us here in this little valley stuck together. Well, most of us. I guess there was some truth about heredity, things in our DNA, because those damn Mathiesens didn't like anyone in the valley since showing up late in 1904 to homestead the least desirable parcel of land left in the valley. The homestead didn't last long, and the family moved into town to try its hand at a long string of failed business enterprises.

I continued walking west into the setting sun, the stream cutting through the rocks and tumbling down to the slough where the second stream met it. Only one flowed on out and down toward the Sevier River.

"Hey, Mr. Arnesen. You want a ride? We got a spare horse here." Martin Thiele, our squat and weathered foreman, along with Bud

Holly and Charlie Dupree, both hardened though kind cowboys themselves, were moving stock out to the eastern flats, better wintering for the cattle.

"No thanks, Martin. I need to walk."

"Suit yourself." He waved and rejoined the other two.

I walked about five steps around the bend in the dirt road, saw Mabel standing on the porch, shading her eyes with her right hand. Mabel had been a fixture in my life from since I was born. Strong, still spry at her age, which no one knew for certain, sharp-tongued, Mabel was Spirit Mother to a constant parade of children, cowboys, cousins, and friends. She always knew when I was lying. She always knew when I was telling the truth. Given my current mood, she was the last person I wanted to see at the moment. Spirit Women have that effect on people.

I turned around and whistled.

Martin reined up, looked at me, then waved at Bud. No words, no shouts, no wild hand-waving in the air saying, "Bring me the horse!" Just silent attention and awareness.

I'd known Martin most of my life, Bud and Charlie for about half of that.

Bud rode up to me, leaned down in the saddle and handed me Chance's reins. "Horse worked hard already today. Ride easy then cool 'im off when you get home. Grain 'im with a good rubdown."

Bud, always close-spoken, didn't wait for a reply. He trusted me to take care of Chance and to do it right. I'd cleaned out some incredibly messy stalls for not learning that lesson quickly enough.

Mounted, I sat there looking out over the property, my land, Arnesen land. I could see the long downslope to the southern boundary. The northern property lines were hidden behind the long ridge that ran from just below the stream to disappear into the mountains and forest above and west of us. Chance did not move until I tapped him slightly with my right boot heel. He stepped off and I laid the left rein easy on his neck so we headed north and away from the house.

My radio burped static at me. "Dispatch to Rosemont One."

"This is One. Go ahead."

"Emily is just fine. Exposure. Her core temp was going down

though, so it's good you found her when you did. All in all, good shape and the little dickens seems quite pleased with herself."

"That's good news. How are the parents?"

"Mom was relieved but very quiet, stayed in the background."

"I take it Daddy Mathiesen was not helpful or polite?"

"Not even close. You'd be proud of Nathan. He didn't let Greg get to him. But you are not a popular person right now."

"I've been unpopular before. Kirsten, I'll be ten-seven. SAT phone is charged. I'll keep that handy. Just need to wander around the ranch a bit."

"Am I going to get a personalized tour of special places out there one of these days?"

"You probably know this place as well as I do. You've been out here before, lots of times."

"Not with you, I haven't. Dispatch out."

I didn't even get to reply, "Rosemont One, out." I could tell she'd turned the radio off on her end. I did the same, but likely with more frustration than she did.

Without my attention to the reins, Chance had decided to go his own way. When I looked around, I saw the edge of the Russian sage garden my grandfather had planted. His favorite plant by a landslide, we had Russian sage gardens all over the property. The purple-leafed long stems bloomed for a long time. Grandfather said, "It adds a splash of color to this green-toned, cedar-brown landscape of ours."

He'd also planted several acres of sunflowers. And he always made sure no one dug up, ran stock over, or drove over the creosote, cholla, or sand sagebrush. Most of the trails on the ranch followed game trails. A few had been widened for convenience when trucks and four-wheelers became popular and useful. I liked my grandfather's sense of protecting plants and animals way before it became more popular. Forty years ago, he'd been more than politically correct on environmental issues. My father and I both followed his lead.

I knew where I needed to go so I tapped Chance into a light trot. We headed up into the forest. I let him pick his way as long as we stayed on the track I wanted to follow. He knew where to put his hooves better than I did.

Course, the way I felt about Seth's case made me feel like Chance also knew more about the murder than I did. A long, frustrated sigh escaped me. Chance echoed it with a neigh. I chose to translate that as, "It'll be all right, boss. The world has a way of rectifying itself. Your break'll come soon, just like night always descends and eventually gives way to that supreme morning light where all is clear and right."

I patted Chance's neck. "Thanks for the encouragement, friend. You have quite a way with words, you know that?"

Chance neighed again.

15

This high desert landscape carries a stark beauty that's hard to explain. Even the tourists who drive through Arches, Canyonlands National Parks, or Bryce seem mostly to drive through. Sure, campers bring tents or drive motor homes that costs tens of thousands of dollars or arrive in a thirty-year-old classic Airstream fifth wheel. They park, hook up to electric meters and water lines, relax in their made-in-China camp chairs, drink a beer, and talk about how incredible the scenery is. Then they go inside and turn on the generator so they can watch satellite TV or get on the internet. Roughing it for sure.

I loved being out here, alone, in wild country. No way to see it except on horseback, at least on this part of my ranch. I also, and I've been called strange and peculiar for speaking this observation out loud, enjoyed the cognitive dissonance when wilderness met civilization.

Half-an-hour careful riding, I dismounted near a very small spring at the back of the property. Like my destination, you had to know where it was to find it. Generations of this steady flow had scooped out a basin in the broken boulder out of which it ran, forming a pool about the size of one of my hands before disappearing back into cracks in the boulder, down into a subterranean chamber or river, or simply filtering its way through the sand until it was gone.

Standing with the spring at my back, looking a few degrees south by southeast, I could see the Orange-painted top of the tipple at the Cold Creek mine. Shut down in 1994 after a disastrous fire, much of the above-ground skeleton remains. Gated, fenced, and protected most of the time by a security company out of Wyoming, hired by the parent company, Engelmann County teenagers still used the site as a rite of passage. More got in and escaped with proof of their trespassing than got caught. It was about twelve hundred yards away, but you couldn't get there from this spot unless you were a raven. I'd have to ride at least five miles up and down and around several deep gullies and ridges to hit the mine road. But there it was, sticking up like a broken finger in a splint, and all I could see around me was cliff, Evergreen forest, Navajo Sandstone, and about five other strata of ancient formations.

Yep, cognitive dissonance was exactly the right term for what I felt when I looked up.

Clear, cold, and dependable, I'd been taking sips here since discovering it when I was ten. I know now that Grandfather and my Dad were aware of the spring's location, but when I rode home that special night, as excited as a ten-year-old can be, thinking he'd discovered something amazing that no one else knew about, both of them clapped me on the back, pumped my hand, and made a big deal of my discovery.

My father also quietly brought me back down to earth. "Tomas, you discovered an amazing gift on our ranch. But your excitement is no excuse for nearly running that pony of yours so hard. You weren't thinking about him, were you?"

"No, sir. I guess I wasn't."

He nodded, rubbed my head, and smiled. "Damn, but you look like your mother when you get that hang-dog, mopey look on your face. She was an incredible woman. Now, go take care of that pony. You know what to do."

I did know and went out to the barn and followed my dad's suggestion.

That was also the last time I ever asked him about Mother.

I snapped back to the present. For reasons unknown, I'd been taking nostalgia trips much more often lately. Guess that's what happens when you get old. You start thinking your better days are behind you. But it's those past days that often make the present ones better, if only we can remember and see the connections. Then again, I'd dealt with enough lawbreakers to know that one's history could just as well lead to anger boiling for decades.

Geez, Arnesen. Get out of your head. Shut off your mental motor for one second and take in what's around you right now.

The force that had broken this piece of our land had done a magnificent job. Boulders the size of station wagons littered the ground, smaller pieces, fractured, split, hammered by wind and rain, made the walking difficult.

Chance watched me walk carefully over the rocks, staying in his place at the spring under the Douglas firs. He was ground-tied, trained to stay in one place when the reins hung down to the earth. Martin had trained every saddle horse on the ranch that way.

Ten more minutes of relatively hard scrabbling over what I always imagined to be a lunar landscape, I stood in front of a solid cliff, a few evergreens clamped in, on, and around its face.

No place to go, you'd think, dead end for sure. *Kind of like your case, Arnesen.*

I stepped up onto a small ledge, then onto the top of an ochre-streaked boulder, then let myself slide down the back side into a dark declivity. A second ledge, formed when a slice of granite caved off the cliff face and came to rest on the boulders below, hid the opening I knew was there, the one I'd found when I was twelve and never told anyone about. This was *my* place.

In all the years I'd been coming here, looking carefully at my back trail, checking the hundred or so yards of rock-strewn carapace leading to the boulder for signs of another's presence, I'd never seen so much as a single footprint, bootprint, hoofprint, not even animal tracks. If someone else had found this and knew about it, they were better at hiding signs than I was.

Now sitting down, I pushed myself beneath the second ledge,

scooted down, hunched over, and popped out into my private slot canyon, which I had proudly named *Invisible Canyon* in my youthful enthusiasm. Narrow, water-stained walls, sharp-curved and carved into tall partitions at least a hundred feet high, ran back into the cliff face for at least a mile. I hadn't explored all of it. The front half had kept me busy for years until I started high school. After that, schoolwork, athletics, ranch chores, and socializing had severely reduced my canyon visits.

Shafts of sunlight illuminated and colorized the sands, while pebbles and stones the size of fists scattered across the little canyon's floor. Three hundred or so steps in, I came to my cold camp. I never made a fire here for fear someone would see the smoke and my invisible canyon would become visible.

Noise disappeared in this place. The wind that rushed over the tabletop mesa above never descended to stir the dust or scrape itself against the knife edges of the angled walls.

Though I'd argue hard and long that I'd always come here to escape others, deep down I knew that I really came here to escape myself. When I slid into this place, I dropped my past under the first hole in the rock, shed it like a snakeskin. But it wrapped itself around that boulder and waited for me to come out. And as soon as I relaxed, it hissed at me.

I heard the crackle of Kirsten's radio in my mind. "Am I going to get a personalized tour of special places out there one of these days?"

When I climbed out, I pulled that snakeskin right back onto me. If I wanted her, wanted to marry her, I'd have to take care of some serious business first.

16

There were two ways to get to my log cabin nestled behind the main house in a two-acre stand of Douglas fir my father and grandfather had refused to cut. You could walk through the main entrance, turn right and go out through the two-story, windowed breezeway that connects to my deck. Or you could use the 99-percent private entrance hidden behind the garden trellis, also to the right of the double-paneled, White Oak front door.

For a long time, when I came home from college or on vacation from Louisville, I'd stop at Grandpa Aksel's room just off the breezeway. With Dad gone, Aksel was always the first person I wanted to see. In those last years, he'd put away his book or writing papers, pull himself up out of that ancient rocker, shuffle his feet across the braided rug, and shake my hand.

"Good to see you, boy. *Kommer i. Hva skjer?*"

I'd sit down on the edge of his bed and we'd talk for hours. I'd tell him what was happening in my life, where I was with which wife, what cold case details I was working at the time, and he'd bring me up to speed on doings at the ranch.

Since his death, I avoided the breezeway.

The door to his room had never been locked, just kept closed.

Mabel didn't even go in there anymore. The dear old woman hated dust with a passion, so I found it fascinating that she didn't clean his room. She used to clean it once a week, so I suspected the entropy of the universe was doing its spiraling downward work in the dust and spider-web collection and who knew what else growing in the darkness.

My modest split-rail door faced away from the main house. There was no way anyone in any part of the homestead could see me come and go or know when I was there. Yet, when I woke up and walked out to stand on the porch, there sat the stained cedar breakfast tray my grandfather had made, which my grandmother had covered in her rosemaling, a delicate, intricate and hard-to-master form of Norwegian folk art. The tray held scalding hot morning tea in my father's heavy white porcelain mug, cherry yogurt, a banana, and two pieces of lightly buttered whole wheat toast. Mabel's omnipresence hovered over me, as did the presences of everyone who'd ever worked on the ranch and set foot on our land.

From this vantage point, I enjoyed the breakfast offering, more quickly than I liked, knowing I needed to get rolling on back into town, though I did not relish the coming confrontation with Greg Mathiesen. I keyed my mike.

"Dispatch, this is Rosemont One. Ten-eight at the ranch."

I think the girl slept with those telephones and the radio. It was 0630 and she sounded as bright and chipper as a person could over a police radio frequency.

"One. Ten-twenty-one, Dispatch."

"Ten-four, Dispatch."

"Morning, Chief." Kirsten answered on the half ring. "You on the way to the office?"

"Finishing up breakfast, then yes."

"Mathiesen is waiting for you."

"In the office?"

"No, sir. He's sitting on the front porch of Wangaard's, looking up and down the street. Nick stopped by to talk to him, but Greg waved him away. He wants you."

"Thanks, Kirsten." I looked at my watch. "Be there in twenty minutes."

"Copy that. Anything else?"

"Yes. You stay away from Mathiesen. If he's been drinking, which probability is around ninety percent, he's not going to be fun. So, stay away, but have Nick keep an eye on him, from a distance."

"Got it."

"Bye."

I took the banana with me, closed the door to the cabin, and locked it. We had some pretty smart little critters that had learned to open unlocked doors and wreak havoc on the insides of a room—though it seemed they were just as scared to go into Grandpa Aksel's room as I was.

My grandfather's '47 Chevy, 324,258 miles on it and still running, keys always in it for anyone and everyone who needed it, had also been at my disposal since I had turned thirteen. I drove it around the ranch until I could take my driving test in it. Only took me three times to pass. I'd forget I wasn't on the ranch. Driving instructors always seemed a bit put out with my tactics.

Bud or Charlie would take it back to the ranch for me when or if they had a good reason to come into town. Feed store runs were a good reason. For Charlie, Silje Erickson was an even better reason.

I stopped the truck at the corner of Fifth and Main street, opposite the Carlson building, a block and a half from Wangaard's. Greg apparently hadn't moved.

"So, let's get this over with or get the next lesson started," I muttered out loud, dropped the truck into first gear without using the clutch, and rolled onto Main.

The grinding turned Greg's wild-haired head for sure. He stood up, shaded his eyes against the morning sun and watched me drive down the street and pull into the space next to my truck. Stood there, watching, not moving, watching. But I could see him biting his lips, like he was generating venom.

I resisted the temptation to wave at him, unlocked the door, opened the blinds on the front window, walked behind the counter, started making coffee, then sat down and waited. Next move belonged to Greg.

Lumbering over, he didn't hesitate to make his case known. "You know I had DFYS calling yesterday. Caseworker on the way down here to little ole Rosemont."

"And good morning to you too, Mr. Mathiesen. How may I help you?"

"Call DFYS and tell them to hold off on the caseworker, that there's nothing here they need to check out. That's what you can do."

"Actually, I can't do. That. The state's wheels are rolling. We'll just have to ride them along, see where things go."

Greg spit on the floor because he knew he couldn't spit on me. In rapid succession, he balled his hands into fists three times. I could smell his breath from across the counter, sour whiskey tinged with sweat-soaked fear.

"If you're going to do something, Greg, do something. It won't be my first rodeo."

He turned completely around, like a dog trying to get settled into position, but just once, then leaned over the counter and gestured toward the electronic latch. His eyes told me that whatever had just come over him had passed. I hit the switch on my desk. The latch buzzed and clicked open.

He pushed through and sat down in the swivel chair opposite me.

I got up and poured a cup of tea. Handed it to him.

He held it in both hands. Both hands trembled. He tasted it, grimaced, set it down on the desk. "That's bad."

By that time, I had my own cup ready to go and swigged more of my special morning blend. "Just the way I like it."

"Look, Tomas, Chief, I don't need this aggravation right now."

"By aggravation, you mean that which has been caused by yours and Estella's inattention to Emily, so much so she manages to walk out of your house, out of your yard, not once, but three times, the last time getting more than five miles away from here? You mean that aggravation?"

Greg glared at me. "I don't need this right now, not with the gas company execs coming next week."

"Ah. Business before family."

"A lot of business for a lot of Rosemont's families, you arrogant bastard."

I wanted to laugh. *Arrogant? Me? Well. Maybe a little.* But Greg sitting over there all red in the face won that prize from way out in front.

"Potential business, Greg. You've been trying to sell this deal at city council for what? Six months at least? Long as I've been back home. Maybe the fact that no one else on the council thinks it's as good a deal as you do ought to tell you something."

Greg pounded his fist on my desk. It made me jump inside, but I was a trained professional. The tea in my hand stayed steady as a morning lake.

He looked at me straight on. "Tells me they're all idiots who wouldn't know a good deal if it ran out from under the porch and bit them, that they don't care to help boost our economy, just want to keep this damn place small, backward, provincial . . . ." His voice tailed off as he slumped back into the chair.

I set my tea down and stared right back. Sometimes silence was the next best question.

"Tomas, can't you do something here, give me a little break? If not for my sake, for the town's sake?"

"I notice you haven't said anything about Emily's or Estella's sakes."

"Well sure, I'm concerned about them, about how this might affect them. Estella's not well, you know. She has those fainting spells. Sometimes I think we need to get her checked for MS or something, the way she keeps getting hurt."

Beneath my desk, now I balled my fists in quick succession. *The way you keep abusing her*, I thought. *When I can prove it, I will nail your sorry hide to a wall in this office or maybe the front wall facing the street. But we can't do that anymore, can't we?* "Yeah. Guess something like MS would explain how those bruises keep moving up and down her body. Emily must have a touch of that as well."

Greg's eyes narrowed to slits. He stood up, stabbed the top of my desk with his fists, knuckles on the top like a gorilla. "We have medical evidence. Even Nathan said there was something going on with Estella he couldn't figure out. Let's leave it at that."

"Leaving it at that. For now, Mathiesen."

"So you're not going to help me out? My vote swung things your way at council, you know." He wrapped his third approach in attempted guilt.

"As I recall, the vote to offer me the job was unanimous."

"Wouldn't have been if I hadn't stepped up first."

"Hmm. Explains why you've been so nasty lately at council meetings. Wishing you'd changed your vote perhaps?"

Ignoring me, he plowed on with this approach. "So, when the deal falls through that means a loss of hundreds of thousands of dollars for folks here in Rosemont, I tell them you're the one who messed it up? Is that what you want me to say?"

"Doesn't matter what you say, Greg. Not one whittled stick's difference. Right now, there's no deal to fall through so you might need to rethink your approach."

Nick opened the office door and stuck his head in. "Sorry, Chief. Didn't know you had company."

"Company's just leaving." I pointed at Greg, then at the door, which Nick held open for him.

"Don't forget what I said, Arnesen. This falls on you."

I gave Greg a mock salute while he shoved past Nick.

He tried to slam the door but since the heavy metal frame has hydraulic hinges, his temper tantrum exit amounted to the door swinging in two inches until the cylinder pressure caught up and held it back.

"Excitable, isn't he?" Nick laughed.

I nodded and took two more sips of coffee. "What you got there?" I saw the manila mailer under his arm.

"Preliminary reports from the lab and a note from Deputy Yorke."

I held out my hand and he tossed the package at me over the counter.

"Check with you later. Need to get over to school for the afternoon in-service. But holler if you need me."

"Will do."

I was already opening the envelopes, Yorke's note first.

17

ey, Tomas. Thought you'd like to know what happened with the senator's plane crash. No terrorism. Nothing out of the ordinary except all those people died. Guess that's not too ordinary, is it?

He wrote just like he talked.

Anyhoo, NTSB preliminary ruling is instrumentation malfunction compounded by pilot error. Then there's a lot of federal aviation double-speak jargon. I asked our county copter pilot to translate for me. Upshot is some instrument reading got out of whack and the pilot overcorrected, causing the plane to stall and then go into a spin. He couldn't recover from the spin. Sorry I got pulled away but now everything's copacetic. I'll be back that way in three days.

The radio on the countertop crackled and I nearly hit the ceiling.

"Rescue One to Rosemont One."

"Go ahead, Rescue One."

I heard what sounded like Nathan taking a big breath with the mike open.

"We have a ten-thirty-five at Thoresen's."

Major crime at the hardware store? What kind of major crime could—oh, damn.

"Rescue One, ten-twenty-one, Rosemont One."

"Ten-four."

My cell phone beeped right away. Nathan must have had his thumb on my speed dial number.

"Chief, Tate's dead. Been shot. Same damn scene as Seth's. Same exact scene. What the hell's going on?"

Somehow, blood rushed to my face and just as quickly disappeared. Light-headed, I said, "Sit tight, Nathan. I'm headed there now."

"Should I call it in to Kirsten and Nick?"

"Not yet. I want to look at the scene myself before anyone else gets there. You copy?"

"Copy. Just get here, Chief. I don't like this."

"I hear ya, Nathan. I hear ya."

I grabbed the keys to my truck off the wall, pulled on my leather jacket, and dialed another number on my phone as I walked to the truck.

"Trooper Yorke here."

"Yorke. Tomas Arnesen in Rosemont."

"Yo, Tomas. What's up?"

"Can you ask the Sheriff to skip the three-day wait and send you back here, now?"

"Not another murder, I hope." Yorke's voice took on that official tone we all get at times in the line of duty.

"Your hope is in vain, Deputy."

"Damnation. When?"

"Just got the call from my paramedic."

"Similar to the other?"

"I'm on the way there now. But Nathan said it was spot-on the same. Pretty shook up about it too."

"OK. You keep the scene clean, start cataloguing, mapping. I'll talk to the Sheriff. Get his official okey-dokey so we can do this right."

"What about the funeral home guys?"

"Go ahead and call. No way they can get there before I do. OK?"

"OK. See you."

"I'll call back with my ETA as soon as I check with Sheriff Consolves. Damn, Arnesen. What you all got going on down there?"

"I wish I knew, Yorke. I wish I knew."

❧ 18 ☙

I made the sign of the cross as I stood on the loading dock behind Thoresen's Office Supply. Norwegian Lutheran roots from my great grandmother's side, Church of England from my great grandfather's clan. No one in the family now remembers that story, but it must have been fascinating.

Nathan, pale-faced as I felt, waited for me. "This creeps me out, Tomas."

I grunted. "You found him exactly like this?"

"Yessir. Haven't touched anything. Soon as I saw Mr. Thoresen lying here in that pool of blood, I called you."

"What don't you see here, Nathan? What's missing?"

"Don't follow you?"

"What's missing?"

He looked puzzled. I decided to help him out. After all, he'd never trained for this.

"No defensive wounds on his hands or arms. No powder burns, like he threw his arms up to protect his face. Look around the dock. Nothing knocked over—"

"—no signs of a struggle. What's *not* here. I get you, Chief."

I picked my way closer to the body, making sure I didn't step in any blood or otherwise disturb the floor, snapping on black latex gloves as I went. You can never have too many. I always have ten or eleven stuck in various pockets.

Squatting on my haunches, I stared down at Tate. Stellate pattern from the gunshot, again, up close. Had to be personal. I resisted the temptation to close his eyelids. *Leave everything alone.* I looked carefully at his hands. Nothing there. The lab might discover something but I doubted it.

I looked up from Tate's body to consider the next move. About twenty feet away, a newspaper flapped against a chain-link fence.

"Call Kirsten. Have her call Boyd Patrick at Southern Memorial Funeral Home. Tell him we have another body for transport to Salt Lake and then get an ETA from him." I ticked off the list for him. "Then have her call the state medical office, alert them that we're sending up victim number two. Tell her to patch Deputy Yorke straight through to me if he calls her first."

"What about Nick?"

I considered things for a moment. Seth's death had seemed to unseat Nick for a while. I wasn't sure how he'd handle a second murder in so short a time. But I needed him, so his actions or reactions would have to wait.

"Have Kirsten call Nick first and get him over here. Then work on that list."

"Got it." He turned away and keyed his mike.

"Phone, Nathan!" I shouted. "Use the phone. I don't want this out over the radio. Too many listening ears out there."

Too late. Kirsten had heard the electronic click of a mike being keyed. "Dispatch."

I waved Nathan off and replied, "Rosemont One. Dispatch. Sorry. I bumped my mike button. Rosemont One. Out."

I heard a quick squelch as she keyed her mike to acknowledge.

"Now. Use the phone."

While Nathan talked with Kirsten, I stepped back to survey the scene and tried to get a map going in my head first before I started sketching it. I was drawing it out when my phone rang.

"Arnesen."

"Deputy Yorke. ETA twenty-five minutes. Chief said I could use the lights and siren for this one, at least until I hit the city limits. What's your twenty?"

"Alley behind Thoresen's Hardware, two-fifty-five Halberg Street. Left on Forsberg. Alley is halfway down the block on the right. You'll see my truck."

"Ten-four."

Nathan walked back toward me, his call to Kirsten completed.

"Did you check the store?"

"Not thoroughly. Walked around to see if doors and windows were locked." He snapped his fingers. "Crap. Didn't check the registers or the office safe."

"It's OK. Do that now. If anything is out of place, if it looks like robbery too, write it down, leave a marker or something at the location so Nick can take photos when he arrives. Then come back here."

Nathan could have swept the floor with his goatee, his head was so low.

"Keep your head up, Nathan. Remember. You're not a cop or a detective. You're a physician's assistant, fireman, paramedic, and search-and-rescue expert—all the things I'm not. You've already been a big help."

His head came up, eyes brightened, and he smiled. "Thanks, Chief. Be back in a bit."

"Take your time. Do your best."

He disappeared into the store. I *was* grateful for guys like Nathan and Nick. They didn't have to help, but they did, because they knew Rosemont needed it. But still, help from a professional was needed, and soon, especially now that we may have a serial killer and zero leads.

I walked back out onto the loading dock apron to watch for Nick. I didn't have to watch for too long.

Nick came trotting around the corner, panting. "What's happened? Why didn't you call me sooner?"

"Tate's been shot."

"Shot . . . wounded?"

"Shot dead. Exactly like Seth."

Nick sat down on the loading dock overhang and took three deep breaths. "Exactly?"

"Exactly."

Nathan hollered at me from the doorway, "Nothing missing, Chief. Safe is closed and locked. Far as I can see none of the cash registers have been tampered with and there's no sign anything else has been touched. Anything else?"

"Make sure the front doors are all locked. Get the crime scene tape around the entrance and around the loading dock. I don't want anyone here who doesn't need to be here."

"Tape is in my truck. I'll have to go get it."

"Supply in the office is closer. Use that first."

"Once I get that done?"

"I'll let you know. Right now, get these areas sealed off. I'm waiting for Deputy Yorke to arrive."

"Yessir."

Nick stood up, recovering his equilibrium. "What do you want me to do?"

"Start photographing. You know the drill."

I know time doesn't speed up or slow down according to scientific theories, but I suspect there are at least two occurrences when time does actually slow down: when you're bleeding all over the emergency room floor and the nurse has just told you the doctor will see you shortly, and when you're sitting on a murder scene waiting for your backup investigator to arrive.

Five minutes stretched to seven, then almost reached eight, when Deputy Sheriff Yorke's cruiser nosed around the corner and rolled down the alley toward me. We shook hands and I showed him to where Tate lay on the floor.

Yorke walked around the body, cataloguing the setting, stopping every fourth or fifth step to survey that area in front and all around him.

"What's missing?"

"Yeah. I did that lesson plan with my young paramedic."

"So? How'd he do with the test?"

"Not bad. No defensive wounds on Tate's, um, on the victim's hands. No powder burns on his forearms. No signs of struggle at all. Here or in the store."

"Money missing? Guns? Ammo?"

"Nothing missing."

We stood there in the silence. The rusty, ripping sound of Nathan pulling the yellow crime scene tape off the roll set my teeth on edge.

19

Yorke walked around Tate's body again until he stood opposite me. "Close range. All those signs that aren't there. I've got pretty much only one way to go here, Arnesen."

"Me too. I don't like the destination."

"One of your own." Yorke pointed down at Tate's face.

"One of our own is a stone-cold-blooded killer and I don't know why."

Yorke nodded. "Usually hard to answer the *why* question, most of the time. This time, we find an answer to why, we more than likely find the killer." He paused and looked across the body at me. "What connects Tate Thoresen to Seth Ramsey?"

"You mean other than they both lived here their whole lives, knew each other well, families knew each other, both served on the town council at different times, helped with every volunteer event we ever held, and knew everyone in this whole area? You mean those connections?"

Yorke held up his hand. "Whoa, Arnesen. No need to hit me with the sarcasm round. I get all that. Hard to live here in Rosemont for any length of time and not discover you know more about your neighbors than you might want to know."

"Sorry. But two murders in less than a week? Getting me frazzled."

"Has a way of doing that to you. Haven't had many of these in the county, but we've had a few where the body count added up to serious numbers. Quiet place like Rosemont, well, I guess you were due, or something like that, and this much death in a small place in a short time has to leave its mark somewhere."

"Wish the killer had left a mark somewhere."

"Maybe he or she did. Maybe that clue is here, or over at Ramsey's. Maybe we just need to look harder."

My phone started playing Roy Orbison's "Pretty Woman." If Kirsten ever called me from across the same room, one of us was going to be mighty embarrassed. I knew it wouldn't be her.

Kirsten's voice was more urgent than usual. "Tomas. The esteemed editor of the *Rosemont Republic* just accosted Nathan pulling the tape across the front of Tate's store. I bet he's on his way around to you now. You going to tell me what's happening?"

"Thanks for the heads up. Info coming your way soon."

Sure enough, Nels came fuming around the corner, saw the official vehicles parked in the alley, and steamed up to me. "What's happened, Tomas? Nathan wouldn't tell me a damn thing."

"Tate's been murdered, exactly the same way as Seth. And if you print a word of any of this before I give you the go-ahead I will have your hide on the side of my office, right next to Greg Mathiesen, when I get him for spousal or child abuse."

Nels the friend gave way to Nels the professional journalist. He pointed at me. "You can't threaten me like that, Tomas Arnesen. Chief of Rosemont's Public Safety Team or not, I know my rights."

I pointed right back. "You know your rights well enough, Editor Anderson. You also know any premature leakage could ruin our chances for finding this killer." Then I started counting off. "One murder is messy. Two homicides sporting the exact same MO, and I mean exactly, does not engender a sense of well-being. If there's a third, God help us, then we're looking at a serial killer in Rosemont."

Nels stopped marching in on me and stood still. He looked at Deputy Yorke, back to me, back to Yorke, then sat down on the loading dock. "My God, man, do you know what you're implying?"

"I'm not implying anything, Nels. I'm telling you that based on two crime scenes, even without the evidence reports from Salt Lake, you and I know the killer. One of our own is doing this."

"Why?"

Deputy Yorke stepped over and into our conversation. "This could easily wind up with us doing an Abbott and Costello routine. Who? Why? I don't know. I don't care and he's our shortstop." Yorke's laugh was short and sharp, not much humor in it, but Nels got the point.

"I won't write anything. Yet. But folks are going to ask questions, lots of questions. You think you had it rough after Seth's death, well, it's going to get tougher. I followed your lead after Seth. Now, Tate. You're not going to be able to keep this very quiet much longer."

I thought about that and then keyed my mike. "Rosemont One to Dispatch."

"Dispatch. Go ahead, One."

"Start getting the word out. Town meeting tonight, seven p.m. One. Out."

"Ten-four. Dispatch out."

"You OK to stay for a couple of days?" I asked Yorke.

"Sheriff turned me loose for the rest of the week. I'm yours for now."

"Thanks. What about your family?"

"Wife and kids visiting the relatives in Logan. Won't be back until next Tuesday."

"You mind bunking with me at the office? Plenty of room there."

"Figured that. You got someone to sit on the scene until the mortuary troops arrive?"

"Figured we'll take turns. Two deep at a minimum from here on out. Nick and Nathan can take the first shift. You and me take the next."

I keyed again. "One to Dispatch. You have an ETA for Southern Utah Funeral Home?"

"Dispatch to One. Three hours. Thirteen-thirty."

"Copy that."

I keyed for one last need before we left the scene. "Rosemont One to Rescue One and Rosemont Seven. Meet us behind the store ASAP."

Once all four of us were together, we divvied up the three hours so Tate would have company, two of us at all times, until Boyd and probably Joseph arrived. Nathan and Nick took the first shift so Yorke and I could eat. I needed to clean up a little.

"No one goes into the store. No one loiters around the store. You answer no questions. All questions come to me. If someone does come up, tell them about the town meeting tonight at seven. Check in with each other every fifteen minutes and with Kirsten every half hour. Got it?"

"Got it, Chief," they answered. Nick and Nathan headed to the front of the store. Yorke and I walked to my truck.

Wanting to solve these cases but not wanting to face the reality of what was happening in Rosemont, I asked Yorke, "How about we drive around for a bit? I can show you the rest of the town. Don't feel much like eating, but we can grab something to go. Might as well keep our strength up."

"Lead on, Chief. Lead on."

20

One thing about Engelmann County Deputy Sheriff Trooper Yorke: he was not the least bit shy. Yorke talked to anyone, anyplace, anytime, about anything. Religion, politics, small-town life, the staggering variety of plant, animal, and human life that call Engelmann County home.

I drove through most of downtown, then drove out and around Rosemont to give him a sense of the landscape, pointing out who owned which store, who lived where, trying to help him connect the few dots we had on the cases. In the first hour, he covered Utah politics, what Senator McAuliffe's death meant for the legislature and especially for Engelmann County, and had just launched into intense speculation about our own acting prosecuting attorney, Emery Burchfield.

"I know he's going to run for the office. Everyone knows he'll run."

"He won't get my vote."

"Don't know that I'll vote for him either. I mean, he's a smart guy, maybe too smart, if you know what I mean. He's looking up higher, and this is the first rung on the ladder. Overheard him trying to convince Sheriff Consolves to come on board with him in some way, cooperate, help each other out, and when the time came, Burchfield would take him on up to the state house. They didn't need to stay stuck in this Podunk county."

"Wouldn't help him much if that little tidbit somehow started circulating."

"Thought about it. But his job performance right now is halfway decent. All the courthouse denizens think he's all right, not good, not terrible. And we have had some, shall we say, interesting prosecuting attorneys. Most of us, when we talk about him at all, are willing to let him get his term under his belt, then move on to the big city life he wants."

"Think the Sheriff will sign on with him?"

"Not a chance. Emilio's roots are here. Three generations at least. Just like ours."

We drove another ten minutes to complete the town circuit. I was ready to head back to the office when Yorke surprised me.

"Got time to show me your place? My grandpa knew yours. I think he and Aksel actually got into some trouble when they were in school together."

I laughed. "Robby Yorke was your grandpa?"

Yorke grinned. "Small county. Small world."

"Yeah. Grandpa Aksel told me a couple of stories, ones he said a youngster could hear and not get ideas about trying to do himself."

"Tell you about taking apart their gym teacher's old Ford while he was on vacation?"

"I love that one. Put it back together in his apartment."

We both started laughing. Apparently, Aksel and Robby had been the ringleaders of the plot against an extremely unpopular teacher.

"Your grandpa ever say what happened? Mine never would." Yorke looked over at me.

"The teacher left. Spent over two hundred dollars to get the car torn down and reassembled outside again. Said the fella loaded up his clothes and drove the car right out of Erik's Auto Repair, got on the highway, and never looked back. If he had looked back, he'd have seen all those kids dancing in the streets."

"That was one of the tamer stories. Those other outings must have made for some interesting times around Rosemont." Yorke laughed.

"Interesting," I said. "But not as interesting as the times we're in right now." Neither of us said much until I rounded the corner and Yorke saw the huge, carved, cedar arch entrance to the Arnesen Ranch.

"You'd have thought in a county with such a small population, the way so many families are related to each other, driving under that arch wouldn't be a surprise for me today," Yorke said.

"Well, you come from up-country as we say, city boy. I spent my first eighteen years working on this ranch, attending Rosemont Unified School, then Welling High. Soon as I graduated, Dad sent me to live with my Uncle Thomas in Richmond, Kentucky. Two criminal justice degrees later from Eastern Kentucky University, I went to work for the Louisville Police Department. Stayed there for the next eighteen years. Came home three times in those years. Not surprising we never met until now, even though our grandfathers knew each other well."

I parked the truck in the front yard, hard-packed from decades of wagons, then cars, parking on this spot, once scrub grass and dirt, then gravel, now blacktop ringed with small stone cairns overflowing with more Russian sage.

"Come on up to the main house. Mabel will have some light refreshments set out on the porch table."

"How would she know? You didn't call her or anything. Did you?"

"Don't have to call. Mabel knows everything that's going on around here. She saw us turn off the road back there, started the tea kettle before we drove under the sign, and pulled the cookies out of the oven when we parked. Warm sugar cookies await right next to the teapot."

"Teapot?"

I nodded. "Not very typical on a Utah ranch. Grandfather Aksel met an English lady during that first Great War, fell in love, and learned to drink tea. When she died in a bombing raid in London in, oh, I think nineteen sixteen, in the fall, he decided to drink tea in her memory. But for that German bombing raid, I think *she* would have been my grandmother rather than Ingrid."

"So the Arnesen Ranch is a tea drinker's paradise?" Yorke asked.

I gestured to the table as we walked up onto the wide porch that stretched completely around the house. Yorke whistled and took the last four steps two at a time.

"Teapot. Steaming. Sugar cookies, still warm. A selection of tea bags and loose tea." He took inventory, then turned to me and bowed, which small honor I returned in kind. "So what kind of teas are these?"

I knew without looking. "Afternoon teas."

"You mean there are different teas for different times of the day? How funny."

"My grandfather didn't think it was funny. He returned home a serious tea connoisseur and made damn sure everyone who lived and worked on this ranch either learned to love drinking tea or learned to tolerate it without letting on they didn't much care for it." I sat down in one chair and gestured at Yorke to take the one next to me, both on the back side of the table so we could look out over the ranch.

"So what do we have here?"

I gave him the menu. "Loose teas are Vanilla, Darjeeling, and Earl Grey. Tea bags are Lapsang, Souchong, Jasmine, and Blackcurrant Herbal. Which would you like?"

"What are you having?" Yorke seemed like he was leaning on an oak bar in an old Helper, Utah, saloon, elbow-to-elbow with soot-blackened railroad workers and miners.

"I mix Vanilla with Darjeeling, perfect complement to warm sugar cookies."

"Then set one up for me, pardner. Who knows? Maybe two."

I mixed, poured, steeped, then re-poured the afternoon concoctions into our large white Arnesen Ranch ceramic mugs.

Yorke, to his credit, held the mug in his hands and let the steamy odor rise under his nose. He sniffed it and smiled. "Smells terrific."

"Taste it carefully. It's very hot."

He blew on the edge of the mug, then took a careful swallow. I watched his eyes widen as he experienced his first custom-mixed mug-o-tea.

He started to say something but I held up my hand. "Taste the cookie now, while that sensation remains in your mouth."

He did that, savored the tastes, gave me a thumbs-up, and went back to his tea and cookie. By the time sunset colored the far ridge from the backside, orange and red highlights on the few clouds lingering before dark, we'd both gone through three mugs and a dozen cookies.

"Think that'll hold you until supper?"

"That'll do just fine. I might even skip dinner tonight."

"Nah. You won't. One of the benefits, or drawbacks, depending on your perspective, is this blend works on your system somehow, and in about an hour you're going to be hungry. Won't matter what you eat either. The leftover taste in your mouth will make that meal taste better than anything you've had in a long time."

"After today, I think I can stop being skeptical about anything you tell me, Mr. Chief Arnesen, sir."

"Smart man, Deputy Sheriff Trooper Yorke. You ready to head back to town?"

"Can we sit here and watch the sun get down behind the mountains?"

"Sit and watch to your heart's content, if that's what you want to do. My porch and God's view are all yours."

21

Yorke and I sat there for a while. I suspected he had something more on his mind. In my previous detective life in Louisville, I had learned to wait, to hold off comment, to resist the temptation to fill in the silences that cropped up in a conversation. Sitting in an interrogation room across from a suspect, silence could occasionally be a powerful weapon. I'd listened to a lot of criminals who liked to talk, mostly about themselves, who did not like me sitting across the table from them, listening and watching.

"So, Tomas, what do you think is going on here in Rosemont?"

"If I knew, I'd have solved two murders by now and wouldn't be sitting here chatting with you."

"But you have thought about this."

"Sure. How could I not be thinking about what's happened? I came home to start a new semi-retired, quiet life on my family's ranch. Kentucky was good for me. I learned a lot about people being a detective. A lot of what I learned I don't like, but there it is. We're messy folks, unholy disasters. Leave us to our own ends and we'll screw up sideways, backwards, forwards, and every other way you can think possible, maybe foul up in impossible ways as well. I've seen circumstances where I wondered, how in the hell did they get that truck on top of that building without a crane? Messiness has always made me feel unsettled, not at ease, ever. All those years on the force, walking a beat, then making detective, I never, for one day, felt at ease in my own skin."

Yorke looked at me. "I'm not sure I follow you, Tomas."

"How many times have you been outside Engelmann County, Yorke? In your whole life?"

Yorke paused. "Geez, Tomas, I don't know. Maybe three or four times."

"Where'd you go? Nevada? Colorado? Arizona?"

"Two trips to Vegas, one to Four Corners so I could touch four states at once." He scratched his head. "Another one down to the Grand Canyon on a family vacation."

"So, in twenty-eight years, you've been out of Engelmann County four times. Right?"

"Far as I can remember."

"You've never been away from home for more than a week, at most. You've never had to find a strange address in the dark in a city you didn't know, asking directions from people who looked at you like you had AIDS or leprosy. You've never had to figure out what it means to look around and not find landmarks or familiar street numbering. None of the faces you see every morning as you drive to work are familiar either. You've always had home, right here. You've always *been* home. That condition, whether you know it or not, whether you acknowledge it or not, leaves you settled, comfortable in your own skin, aware of how and where you fit into this world. I'm twenty years older than you. I lived more than half of my life away from here. That's what I mean about being at ease in my skin."

Yorke brushed his left forearm and looked at me. "You came back to find your skin."

"Exactly. I came back to find my skin. I found some of it, but I couldn't find a chunk of whatever I'd shed leaving Rosemont and the ranch. I feel like I'm starting over, growing new skin. Taking the Public Safety Chief's position was not on my radar when I moved back to the ranch. I took it, hoping it would help me find or regrow one or two more missing pieces."

"Did it? Has it helped?" Yorke leaned forward.

"I think so. Maybe. I don't know. Yet." My notion that we might be on the verge of cementing a friendship deepened.

"Unexpected as these murders are, they're helping you find yourself, aren't they?"

I let his insight settle into the space between us. "Astute observation, Deputy Yorke. Very astute. I wouldn't have phrased it that way but yeah, you're right."

"Scares you just a wee bit, doesn't it?"

"It scares me. A lot. Now, can I take you back to town?"

"Let's go. Probably enough cop-talk-pseudo-psycho-babble for one late afternoon."

We didn't talk for the first few miles. Rode along in a comfortable silence neither one of us seemed to want to break. When we passed the sign and entrance for Liberty Estates, a newly opened planned community, I cracked the quiet first. "I sense anger in these murders, Yorke. But it's cold, specific. The killer had a reason for shooting Seth and Tate. I think they were shot in order, like whoever it is has a list. They're working down it, putting a check in a little box next to each name."

"You need to answer two tough questions," Yorke said. "One: Are there more names on the list? Two: Whose names are there?"

"Find the list. We'd know who's next and maybe also have the killer."

Yorke didn't respond to that observation. I looked over at him and followed the direction his head was turned.

"Ah. Estella Mathiesen and her daughter Emily."

I slowed down.

Yorke stared at Estella, playing with Emily in their front yard, mother and daughter lost in their dancing game, oblivious to everything and everyone around them.

I envy children when they play like that, wishing I could recapture the barest fraction of a child's ability to disappear into the illusion of their make-believe worlds. I honked the horn, startling the girls, who stopped their game and looked over at us. There was nothing between Estella and Yorke but eight feet and a pane of car window glass.

Twenty seconds, thirty seconds, could have been a minute or more if Emily hadn't pulled on her mother's skirt to break the connection between Estella and the deputy.

Yorke looked over at me with that *I've just seen a face I can't forget* expression. Trust me. I know that look. I've seen it too many times too. Kirsten produces that expression on my face, and she doesn't even have to be around.

"Well, that was a nice moment. She's married, by the way, to a member of the town council. Name's Gregory Mathiesen, just so you know. Not a particularly nice guy either."

I parked the truck at the office, got out, unlocked the office door, and was behind the counter at my desk before Yorke got out of the truck.

Still looking back up the street—I know he was hoping to catch another glimpse of Estella, even Emily—he walked right into the almost-closed office door.

22

I watched our citizens gathering for the town meeting. Usually, clumps of families would meet on the street and visit with one another for fifteen to twenty minutes. Their catching up with one another would fill the storefronts and sidewalks with an excited buzz of conversation and laughter. Well, tonight they jumped out of their vehicles and scurried into the auditorium. Tonight I watched them, every one of them, look over their shoulders several times on their way into what they hoped was a safe place. Family after family, individuals, groups of three or four, all of them exhibited this same protective behavior.

By five minutes 'til seven, I figured most of those who planned to come were inside, so I walked across the street and swung open the doors to the auditorium. I'd never heard the place so quiet. Ever. Maybe it had been quieter for some reason at some point while I'd been gone, but I doubt it. The room was full, probably three hundred plus of our citizen roster and no one talked, no one even whispered. Every face turned back toward the door. Every person in the room watched me walk down the center aisle toward the stage where the mayor and council members sat. I nodded to folks sitting close to the aisle. Most nodded back, but it was like their neck muscles had tightened up so much their heads could only deflect a couple of inches.

Emma Fosberg, Rosemont's third lady Mayor, waved at me to hurry up. So I took the steps two at a time to stand at the end of the chair line next to Deputy Yorke. We shook hands.

"Pretty quiet tonight," he said.

"Damn quiet tonight. These are scared people." I nodded to the members of the council. Fear had pulled their nerves tight like drawstrings cinching down a sleeping bag.

Greg Mathiesen watched me come down the aisle, pretending he wasn't watching me. He had his hands on Lukas Sogard's shoulders, keeping Lukas facing him and away from me. Greg's monologue seemed very heated.

The remaining three members, Freda Jacobsen, Reinert Tonnessen, and Anborg Laake, had formed a semicircle behind their chairs. The short arc they formed allowed them to see anyone coming close to them from any direction.

The mayor stepped to the podium. "Everyone? Everyone. Take a seat. Please. Let's quiet down now." Emma seemed not to notice they were already so quiet you could hear several people's heavy breathing. "Deputy Sheriff Trooper Yorke, from the Engelmann County Sheriff's Department is here with us tonight. Deputy Yorke?" She gestured to Yorke, inviting him to the center microphone.

He muttered as he stepped past me, "You're next, like right now."

"Thank you, Mayor. But the person you need to listen to is your Chief of Public Safety, Tomas Arnesen."

As I walked over to center stage, someone on stage spoke *sotto voce*, "Not keeping us very safe at the moment."

I ignored Mathiesen and took the proffered mike from Yorke. "Folks, I'll get right to the point so there's no room for doubt or rumor. Three days ago, someone murdered Seth Ramsey. This morning we found Tate Thoresen's body. Someone murdered him as well. We've sent both bodies to the State Medical Examiner for autopsies. The forensics lab in Salt Lake has all the evidence we collected at both crime scenes. No results or reports yet, from either of those offices. That's where we are as of tonight."

Someone shouted from the back of the room. "Have you heard from the forensics lab?"

"Not yet." I decided not to point out that I'd just answered that question because the hum had started. The room felt like we were meeting inside Parkin's industrial freezer set at five degrees above zero. More questions started popping.

"You have any ideas or suspects, Chief?"

"No ideas. No suspects."

"Who would want to kill Seth? Or Tate for that matter? Why them?"

"We don't know."

"You think there'll be more murders?" Councilwoman Laake stepped out from behind her chair.

"Frankly, Anborg, I don't know what to think. I'd hoped Seth's murder was it."

"You hoped wrong then, Chief Arnesen." Gregory Mathiesen also stepped out from behind his chair's scant protection. The next question he aimed at me but faced the audience. "Since you missed that *hopeful* call about Seth's murder, why, exactly, should we trust you now?"

"Yeah, Arnesen. What are you doing to keep the rest of us safe?" That same belligerent voice came from the back of the room. I recognized the brawny and aptly named Burley Wilkes. He and Greg had become Siamese twins working on the oil project.

"So? What are you doing, Tomas? What exactly are you going to do?" Greg stepped way into my personal space, so I put my palm on his chest and held him away. And waited. Stood there holding him back—and waited.

Greg saw the look in my eyes and kept his mouth shut.

"Are you finished interrupting me? Good." I pressed on, giving him a taste of his own sour milk and Jim Beam.

"Trooper Yorke, Nathan, Kirsten, Nick, and myself will be patrolling Rosemont for the next few days, twenty-four hours a day, seven days a week. We'll pull in extra teams of Search and Rescue volunteers. Anyone who'd like to add to those numbers is more than welcome."

"Welcome to go out there and get killed is more likely." Greg was not going to let this go. He had his audience, his moment. He couldn't resist pushing.

"We don't know that at all, Mr. Mathiesen. If we stay in teams, at least three and four deep at all times, I think we'll be all right." *Better than you'll be once I find proof of what you do to your wife and kid.*

"You *think* we'll be all right? You think?"

"You're not sure of anything are you, Arnesen?" Someone shouted from the back of the room.

"Burley, we hear you just fine. Why don't you get out of the shadows and join your buddies in the open?" I didn't have to raise my voice too much to be heard throughout the hall.

Heads turned toward the back of the room where Burley did step out of the doorway shadow but came no further.

"Thought so. Listen. I can tell you, without damaging the investigation, that both murders happened when the victims were alone. Stay in teams, stay connected, stay in communication. That's the key."

"What about nighttime?" Anborg asked.

It was subtle but unmistakable. Shifting seats and lowered murmurs were slowly increasing the decibel level.

"Keep your houses locked, as unusual as that will feel. Don't let anyone in during the night. Right now, we probably need to err on the side of safety rather than friendship."

"Hard on friends we've trusted all these years."

"Burley, don't you think I know that?"

Greg turned away from me completely now and addressed the other council members on the stage, loud enough that everyone in the auditorium could hear him. "Funny, though, isn't it? We've had no violent crime here for more than a hundred years. Six months after we hire our homegrown city-boy detective, we have not one but two murders. God knows how many more there might be."

I was impressed by his likely drunken eloquence. The man could make a point when he wanted to, even if that point was devoid of fact. I surveyed the room and saw more nodding heads than I would have liked. The volume rose another couple of notches.

Mayor Fosberg fired right back at Mathiesen. "Are you accusing Tomas?"

Mathiesen, ever the actor, shrugged his shoulders. "I'm not accusing anyone, Mayor. Not suggesting anything either, Emma. Just pointing out something I find interesting." Now Greg turned back to face me, raising his hand slowly, like he was holding a revolver, pointing it at me. "Can you verify *your* whereabouts when Seth and Tate were killed?"

At least three women audibly gasped. Whether out of shock that Greg would ask such a question of me or delight that they were witnessing a daytime drama live at night, I don't know.

"You've been watching too many bad television courtroom dramas, Greg. Of course I can *verify my whereabouts* when both men were killed. We'll work backwards. Last night, I was out at the ranch. Mabel made me breakfast. You want to try to impeach Mabel's character, go right ahead. I'll stand by and watch her fillet you. After breakfast, I drove into town where I spent some time in the office. Let me see." I made a small show of trying to remember. "What did I need to do at the office?" I snapped my fingers. "Oh, right. You were waiting for me, Greg. We had a nice little chat about some project or other you're not having much luck getting going. You left. Nick stuck his head in there as well. Soon after that Nathan called to say he'd just found Tate murdered."

Quiet returned as our town's new reality made itself far too clear.

I continued. "As to Seth's killing, I was three days hunting with Stig Tandberg and his boys. I can show you the deer tags. Stig has the maps with the positions marked where we shot each critter. Jeremy got a very nice six-pointer, didn't you, Jer?" I pointed to him in the crowd.

He smiled, nodded, but was not as enthusiastic as I could have used.

"Pretty hard to get into town, shoot Seth, get back out to Stig's place, and do all that unnoticed."

Stig shouted from the floor. "Arnesen was with us all three days, just like he says, Mathiesen. You need to look somewhere else for the killer cause it sure as hell ain't Tomas Arnesen."

"Here, here!" someone shouted.

Deputy Yorke settled himself next to Greg, thumbs looped in his belt. "Mr. Mathiesen, you've been trying to get a little fire going here tonight. Makes me kinda wonder. You know, how smoke and fire go together? Where exactly where you last night?"

Those same three ladies gasped again.

Greg lost a little of his puffiness right then and took a step back away from both of us. "I was home. Estella can verify that. I have an alibi." Mathiesen, discovering he'd lost this battle, withdrew, literally, to construct his next attempt to get at me.

I let him go.

"Don't think I won't be watching you, Arnesen. Don't think I won't."

I tipped my Stetson at him. "Likewise, Mathiesen, likewise."

The murmuring behind swelled in volume, a three-foot wave perilously close to becoming a ten-foot tidal wave.

"Folks! Calm down a little." The Mayor raised her school tone a notch or three.

"How do we calm down? There's a killer out there!"

She took a slightly different tack, illustrating why Rosemont citizens keep electing her as our Mayor. She raised both hands in the air and waited until she could be heard, the same gesture she'd use at school to make the kids quiet. "OK. How about we try to calm down in here, where we're safe? Whoever is doing this has a reason or reasons. He or she seeks people out when they're alone, conducts some sort of transaction with them, at the end of which, well, people wind up dead."

I nodded toward Emma. "Thanks, Mayor. Folks, as I've been telling you, as long as you stay together in large groups, you'll be fine. Just don't go out alone for any reason, even if you think it's safe. Do everything you normally do every day, but just do it with three or four more people. The more people in your group, the better, safer you'll probably be."

"Probably? That's not helpful, Arnesen." Greg gave me a parting shot before walking off the stage to confer with Burley, Reinert, and Lukas.

"There's something you aren't telling us, isn't there Chief? Something you don't want us to know." Anborg asked the one question I'd been dreading all evening.

I took a deep breath, let it all out slowly. I can do that without moving my shoulders, drop my diaphragm and my lungs fill up. All those years in college choir pay off in certain circumstances. "Yes. Deputy Yorke and I agree. Whoever killed Seth Ramsey and Tate Thoresen is one of us. Someone who lives here among us in Rosemont is a cold-blooded killer."

If there had been silence at the beginning of the meeting, my stone-cold declaration crushed the humming back into silence, then into less than silence. Not one noise. Not one cough, nervous laugh, heavy breathing, no surprised intake of air, nothing out there among the people to cause my ear drum to vibrate and send a signal to my brain. Those three ladies had run out of air too.

All weatherman love to go stand on a tan sandy beach on the East coast of the USA a few hours before the hurricane arrives. In great and colorful detail, they describe the calm before the storm. Then, when the storm hits, they go out and try to stand up in gale force winds to describe the reality.

But my fellow citizens surprised me, again, and in particular, one Karl Iversen, a stout, bald man who I'm pretty sure you'd never want to cross. I thought he was another of Greg's boys. When he took the microphone off the stand and stepped out front, right to the edge of the stage, I knew better.

"OK, folks. We know this is bad. But we have been through bad times before. Yes, maybe one of us is a murderer. If Tomas thinks that might be the case, then that's enough for me. I want the search-and-rescue team leaders to report to me here at center stage. Nathan, you take the volunteer fire crews on out to the lobby. Stig, you still out there?"

"Yep." Stig Tandberg, my recent hunting buddy and owner of the second largest ranch around Rosemont, stood up.

"You round up, sorry about the pun there, any of the ranch hands that can be spared for a while."

Stig asked. "What do you want us to do in our groups, Karl?"

"Create three-person teams, look at schedules to see who can work when. Write it down and give it to Tomas so he can coordinate the next few days."

I held up my hand. "Give the info to Kirsten. She handles that better than I do." I spotted Tollef Varland near the front of the stage and leaned over to talk to him. "Can you spare Kirsten for the next three or four days?"

"Sure can. Longer if you need her. Rather have her working on this full time than adding up my register totals."

"Thanks, Tollef."

I looked over the whole crowd, tried to capture one inclusive image with every upturned face in it. "Folks. We will do the best we can. I promise you that. Any time you have questions, if you think you see something or someone and it doesn't seem right to you, do not hesitate. Call me. Call Kirsten. Call Deputy Yorke. Don't try to do anything on your own."

Yorke and I met Kirsten on the right side of the stage. The phrase "sight for sore eyes" never meant more to me than in that moment. In that far-too-brief time between stepping off the stage and knowing we had work to do, I'm pretty sure I saw my next forty years just within her irises. It was enough to make me pause and consider bolting then and there, Kirsten's hand in mine, Rosemont receding into the distance. But she was wearing her professional face, and just as soon as I'd thought about leaving, I was pretty sure I felt Seth's blood dripping on me. So I left my love in that moment to focus on what had to happen now. Plus, who's to say she wasn't a target also?

"You can get a patrol schedule set up, town mostly, and both highways in and out of town?" I asked her, knowing the answer.

"Already have the town divided into patrol grids. Did that a long time ago as an exercise for my urban disaster response class. Won't take long to update it and add the road sections to it. Soon as I get the notes from our teams, I can have something ready to go first thing in the morning."

"Thanks."

"Last thing, folks." I shouted to be heard over the growing conversations.

"Each group needs to select someone to bring information to

Kirsten. Team leaders meet us at the office tomorrow morning at seven."

"What about tonight?" Greg Mathiesen still had his two-cent ante on the table.

"Go home in groups. Stay with one another. Keep the lights on and keep someone alert. We'll meet in the morning and do what we can to protect ourselves. An official presence will remain on the streets of Rosemont tonight."

I turned back to my future. "Come on, let's get back to the office. I want to call the lab and see if they've turned up anything at all." I grabbed Kirsten by the arm. Yorke followed us as we walked down the aisle.

Before we stepped into the street, I looked both ways, as did Yorke.

23

The town fell into a routine, business-as-modified. Groups of every size roamed downtown as well as the three neighborhoods of Rosemont's "suburbs" and patrolled around the school. Members of the Rosemont Safety team worked twelve on, twelve off. One of us was always reachable by radio or phone. I wasn't sure when Kirsten slept, catnaps here and there perhaps, but her presence hovered just behind the curtain of white noise generated by our conversations ratcheting around in the ether.

For the first six days, our schedules didn't overlap. On the seventh day, the one when God rested from creation, our twelve-off matched up, in daytime no less. I wasted no time in answering her summons. I pulled up to her house just as she exited.

She waved, grinned, and then tried to open the passenger door of my truck. "Today I get the ranch tour you promised." She fidgeted with the handle.

I was going to point out that I had never truly "promised" her the tour but decided that would only prolong getting out onto the ranch with a beautiful girl. I kept my mouth shut, grinned right back, and slowly reached across to unlock and open the passenger side of my truck. She hopped in and we hit the road.

Forty-five minutes later, we were mounted and riding up into the foothills behind the main house. Neither one of us had spoken a word. I felt at ease in our silence, no need to fill in the spaces, for the first time in a long time.

"Listen." I reined in Chance and held up my hand.

Kirsten pulled up beside me on her buckskin mare with no name. We hadn't had her long enough to know her temperament. Another couple of weeks and she'd get a name that suited her.

"What—?"

"Listen. Just listen. Close your eyes."

I closed my eyes and tilted my head back, hoping she'd follow my lead.

The aspens we'd been riding through had color-shifted from their fiery, fall, bright gold into the only slightly less impressive golden brown, like they had been lightly baked in an oven, the edges all crispy and dark.

It took only the slightest breeze to set them shaking, making music —*quaking* was the word most people used to describe the sound. For others, *rustling* served. For ranch-obvious reasons I didn't like the word *rustling* in any context.

"Hear it now?"

"The leaves?"

"The music. This light wind plays the trees, here and now, for the two of us." I opened my eyes to find Kirsten staring at me, a half-smile on her lips.

"A poet as well. My, my, what hidden depths I keep discovering in my Tomas."

The possessive startled me.

She caught the reaction. "Get used to it. You are *my* Tomas. Period. Now, before you decide to spur Chance into a gallop and head back toward the ranch without me, show me something spectacular. I know it's out here. How can a land this rough and beautiful not harbor a surprise?"

"You mind a few more miles riding, followed by a longish hike, then a couple of tight corners?"

"Not a bit."

We left the horses tied up a half mile short of the hidden canyon entrance. I used five different spots to leave my horse, never used the same one twice in a row.

"Now we walk." I held out my hand.

Kirsten took it and we started walking.

"Watch your steps as we go over these rocks. Try to walk lightly, not disturb things too much."

She didn't ask questions. She walked lightly, carefully, and kept up with me. She did stumble, twice, and both times said sorry in a soft voice.

"It's worth the effort. Trust me," I told her after the second stumble.

"I do." Then she laughed.

I knew exactly what she was thinking in that instant. I could see the scene play out in her eyes. White dress, long, black, western frock coats, hats and boots, the pastor from the Community Lutheran Church in Welling, both of us repeating, "I do." I understood my future with those two words and decided it might not be too bad at that.

"I might," I said, just to keep her a little off-balance.

"OK. I can let you think that, for now."

Took my lumps and kept going, which is what I did, with Kirsten in tow.

When we got to the entrance to my invisible canyon, I stopped to let her absorb the view, cliff walls of gray-pink Navajo Sandstone rising two hundred feet above us.

I heard a sharp intake of breath, just enough to make the wind stop. "This is surprising. It's beautiful, Tomas. Spectacular, even. But why bring me to a dead end?"

I climbed up onto step one of the entrance, the massive tabletop basalt formations that crumbled off the cliffs a few million years ago. "Come up here with me."

She scrambled up like a mountain goat, nimble and sure-footed. "A better view of the dead end?" She was looking up, not down.

I suspect anyone I brought here would probably do the same. This ancient lava-flow area and subsequent erosion had cut long, narrow lava ridges and old heights, again in the long frame of geologic time, became new valleys in these rocks of ages. One of them became my cleft in the rock.

Out of the corner of my eye, I could see Kirsten still looking up, taking in the vertical power of the long wall in front of her. She seemed completely lost in the view, her neck as far back as she could get it, left foot a good giant step back to hold her balance.

I slipped down into the passageway as quietly as possible and slid through to the other side. Then I waited.

"Tomas? Tomas?" She didn't sound frightened.

"Look down, Kirsten. Slide down off the rock into the declivity you see. Then sit down and push yourself through the hole down here."

I saw her feet, then her legs, then she popped up out of the slide, grinning like the preacher had just pronounced us husband and wife. Yeah, OK. Sue me. I couldn't go two thoughts away now without that image running through my head.

"Welcome to my—"

"Shush. Let me enjoy this for a second." Now she inhaled, deeply.

A storm could have been assaulting us and I wouldn't have noticed. In that moment, the radius of my world was about four feet wide. Anything beyond ceased to exist. At least for that moment.

I shushed and let her enjoy the view for more than a second.

After about a minute or two or fifteen, since I lost all track of time in this place and always resisted the temptation to look at my watch, she threw her arms around me, kissed me rather fiercely, then put her hands on the sides of my head, pulling me down close to her face.

"Thank you."

"You're welcome." I knew what her thank you meant and chose to leave further explanations for another time.

24

"Come on in to my invisible canyon." I took her hand and led her several hundred yards into the slot, crossing the little stream, always dry in the fall, several times until we came to my cold campsite.

"I discovered this when I was a teenager. I come up here every so often to collect myself, to think, to relax, to pray, question, wonder, worry over whatever it is or was bugging me at the moment."

"Did you ever get answers?"

"No. But after a while it never matters. I leave the nonsense heaped up in here like that terrace gravel in the stream bed. Let time roll it around and smooth the edges."

We could hear the aspens still singing, a slight echo running down off the canyon walls. The same wind tossed an occasional leaf into the opening above us.

"Did you bring a blanket with you?" Kirsten took my backpack and started rummaging through it. Water, dried fruit, energy bars, a small bag of oats for the horses, spare socks, two plastic ponchos. No blanket. "You obviously didn't think this through very well." She frowned.

"Yes, Kirsten, I did. I thought this through completely."

She stared up at me, her lower lip turning out and down the tiniest fraction.

I'd seen her pout like this when things weren't going well at the store. I took her hands and almost crumbled right then. The pout deepened and her eyes grew misty. "Kirsten. I am not ready for anything more than what we have right now."

"What, exactly, do we have? Right now?"

I took a deep breath. It was getting harder to look at her so I put my arms around her and drew her close so I could whisper. "We have an excellent professional relationship. We have a developing friendship. And," I held her back at arm's length to make sure she could read my expression and hear my words, "I have told you I want much more out of our relationship."

She started to speak, but I put my right thumb on her lips.

"You have to remember three facts here: I am twenty years older than you. I have two ex-wives, each of whom told me I didn't know how to love them. I am totally blown away by the fact that you are in any way interested in having anything to do with me other than work."

Kirsten burst into tears and launched herself back into my arms.

I lifted her off the ground and held on tight. Her tears and her fierce bear hug meant either good-bye or hello. I prayed for hello.

I'd learned at least one lesson from two ex-wives: when you're holding a crying woman, hold her, keep your mouth shut, hold her tight, hold on for dear life and wait. I held her and waited.

She let go and pushed herself gently away from me and walked all the way to the end of the canyon.

I let her go. She would get the next word, whatever it was. I watched her.

She touched the rock wall, ran her hands over the rough-smooth, pinkish texture. She kept one hand on the wall and walked back and forth. A gust up top rattled off the upper formations and dust sifted down.

I looked up, got dust all over my glasses. When I wiped them off, she was gone. "Kirsten? Kirsten!"

"Up here."

"Up where?"

"Come to the back wall, look left."

I did. More walls.

"Look around the edge, silly."

"Holy smokes."

"You never explored this back wall, did you?"

"Nope."

"Can you squeeze in? It's tight for the first two or three feet. Then it opens up a lot."

I took a deep breath, sucked in my stomach, and tried to push myself up into the notch, a belt buckle too wide. I took my belt off, pushed myself up again, felt some skin abrade under my shirt but kept pushing up until the chimney widened and came up with Kirsten's boots next to my face.

"Now. Look up," she said.

I did. I could see that the chimney went all the way up to the top of the canyon wall, narrow all the way but no narrower than the wedged entrance from the base. Crumbled rocks, erosion, and time had created a natural stairway of sorts. If one went carefully, you could climb all the way out.

"So? Do we go up or back down?"

"Back down, I think."

She looked at me and laughed. "How about I go up first, see where this comes out, and put a marker up there, something unobtrusive so we could find it from topside. You have a general idea of where this is on the ranch, don't you?"

"Yep. It'll be a long ride though. Long way around the base, then up onto the plateau, then up and down and over several ridges. But, yeah, I can find the top of this ridge."

"OK. Toss me a water bottle and one of those bars. Won't take me long to get up there and get down. Be nice to know where the bottom and top of your invisible canyon are, won't it?"

It took her a little longer than I thought it would, but an hour and fifteen minutes later she emerged from the back wall wedge, panting slightly, a sheen of perspiration covering her face, arms, a few damp spots showing on her top.

"Got it. Three small stones, one of them as black and round as a marble, set in a triangle five feet west of the opening. If you can get us up on the ridge, I can find the spot."

"Nice to know I can learn something new." I laughed.

Kirsten cocked her head sideways. "There's a lot of *new* you can learn, Tomas Arnesen." Without waiting for the retort forming on my lips, she walked down the canyon toward the hidden front door.

I followed. Outside, we held hands as we walked back out of the trees to the horses. Chance looked up at me expectantly. I pulled the bag of oats out of the pack back and fed him. The mare nickered, so I handed the bag to Kirsten, who fed the mare.

"Why doesn't she have a name?"

"She's too new. Two weeks on the ranch. We're weird, I know, but we like to live with our horses for a while, get to know them, then we name them."

"That is weird, definitely weird. But I understand it. Look at her, though. Did you see how calm she was when we walked out of the trees toward them? Didn't move, didn't make a sound, just watched us. Very patient, I'd say."

"Then you just named her, didn't you?"

Kirsten smiled. "Guess I did." She rubbed the mare's nose and scratched her ears. "So, tell me, Patience, how does it feel to finally have your name?"

Patience nickered softly and blew oat chaff off Kirsten's hand.

"She likes her name."

The angelic tender look on Kirsten's face, her eyes moist, alight with surprise and passion, made me begin to truly regret that I had not brought the blanket with me.

"She's yours now, you know. Any time you come to the ranch, Patience is yours to ride."

She gave me a look that both buckled my knees and swelled my pride. "So I'll be coming to the ranch more often?"

"Yes. You will."

We mounted and rode back to the ranch. The morning had become late afternoon. We had not slept. We both had twelve-hour shifts staring down at us. But I knew the energy our time together had generated would see me through the night. A buzz like three cups of my office coffee had just hit my system, coupled with some blanket regret and a little leftover lust.

In the truck, driving back to town, Kirsten put her hand on my arm. "You will let me know when you're ready to put the blanket in the backpack, won't you."

Not a question. "I promise. I will tell you."

"Make me one more promise. No. Two more promises."

Still not a question in there. I raised my right hand. The truck lurched to the left a little before I straightened out. "I promise. I do solemnly promise." I put my hand down and grinned at her. "What exactly did I promise?"

No smile or laugh. "You promised to pay attention to us, and you promised to wear your vest from now on."

"I will keep my promises. I always do my best to keep promises."

There are moments in life when you know, before the words come out of your mouth, they are exactly the wrong words to speak, yet you speak them anyway. "Not sure if the vest will stop a bullet to my forehead, but I'll wear it."

Kirsten went silent. The warmth we'd been generating for hours quickly dissipated. She stared straight ahead. In a low and deadly serious voice, she professed her love for this buffoon. "Don't you dare make light of this, Tomas Arnesen. Don't you dare joke about this. Seth and Tate are dead. No, a vest wouldn't have changed things. But maybe the killer has other ideas. Maybe the next victim won't be shot up close and personal. Maybe the damn vest could save your life."

I held out my hand. "Deal."

She shook my hand, but the glare she gave me made me feel like I was ten years old again and Mom had just decided I was the worst son she'd ever brought into the world. Neither of us spoke for the remainder of the drive, each of us lost in thought over what was and what could be—for better or for worse.

25

We were about a mile from town when Kirsten's radio squawked. Good thing we were together since I'd turned my radio off at the house before we left.

"Dispatch. This is Nathan. You got a twenty on the Chief?"

"He's right here, Nathan. Hang on a sec."

"O-kay?"

I could hear his eyebrows going up with the second syllable of his reply. I took Kirsten's radio and keyed the mike. "What's up, Nathan?"

"Harriet Stein, that DFYS child welfare caseworker, is here to interview the Mathiesens."

"That's good. Tell her to stop by the office when she's done so we can talk."

"Uh. Might be a while."

Sometimes I wanted to smack Nathan on the back of the head for the way he skated around, leaving little bits of information on the ice for me to find each time he passed me.

"Nathan. Tell me what's going on over there."

"Emily is gone. Estella is totally distraught. Mr. Mathiesen may be passed-out drunk at home. Mrs. Stein is kinda pissed. You need to get over here."

"Ten-four." I reverted to formal radio speak, or as formal as we get around here. "Rosemont One to Rescue One: call your troops out and get them looking for Emily. Dispatch will let the rest of our folks know to watch for her. Rosemont One, out."

"Rescue One, copy. Out."

"Damn, damn, triple damn! How in the hell does a five-year-old go missing in a town where everyone is looking out for everyone else? We've got small clumps of people walking all over this place, and Emily walks out of the yard and off to God knows where. Damn it. Greg's probably drunk again and Estella is too embarrassed, again, to do anything about it." I handed the radio to Kirsten. "Start running down your call list. Let folks know that Emily is out and we need to find her. Fast."

"Drop me at the office. I'll work from there, phones and radio. You get on over to the Mathiesen's." Kirsten put her hand on my arm. "Remember, stay calm. We have a caseworker here now and she can handle things."

"Stay calm? Why, Kirsten, what makes you think I won't stay calm?" I laughed.

She didn't. "Turn your radio back on so I can keep you in the loop, Rosemont One."

"Ten-four, Dispatch. Radio turning on . . . now." I turned it on, set the squelch, and smiled at her. She didn't smile back and made me wonder if she'd ever played poker.

I stopped the truck on the street in front of the office.

Kirsten opened the door, started to get out, then turned back to me. "Thanks for a terrific day, Tomas."

"You're welcome, Kirsten Dyrdahl. Hope we can do it again. Soon."

She made sure the door shut firmly, maybe a little more firmly than usual, and ran into the office. I drove to the Mathiesens.

Estella sat on the top step of their porch, heaving. Nathan and Mrs. Stein were standing in the front yard talking with each other. Their conversation stopped when I drove up and got out.

With his hand behind her back, Nathan escorted Mrs. Stein toward me. "Chief, this is Harriet Stein, DFYS."

"Good to meet you, Mrs. Stein."

"You as well, Chief Arnesen. Although the circumstances leave much to be desired. It's a pretty stiff drive down here you know."

"Yes, ma'am. I know. Made that trip more than once myself. Did up and back in one day and don't think I'd do that again." I turned to Estella. "When did you see Emily last?"

She twisted her long skirt in her hands, taking a few moments to gather herself. Her red face looked up at me, intermittent tears still falling into a small pool by her feet. "About an hour ago. Honestly, Tomas, I don't know what to do. We were playing in the backyard when the phone rang. I told Em to stay there while I answered the phone. I ran inside, answered it, came back out. She was gone. The gate was open." She brought her skirt to her eyes and wiped.

"What did you do then?"

"I ran out in the field to look for her. She couldn't have gone far. I wasn't on the phone that long."

"Who was on the phone?"

"Cathrine, over at Parkin's. My order was in."

"Nathan. Stay with Estella. Mrs. Stein, would you excuse me for a moment?"

"Certainly, Mr. Arnesen."

I must have fallen in rank a bit. No more Chief. I stepped away and dialed Parkin's. Cathrine answered on the third ring.

"Parkin's Store. Cathrine Varland speaking. How may I help you?"

"Cathrine. This is Tomas."

"Hi, Tomas. What can I do for you?"

"You called Estella a while ago. Her order was in?"

"Yes, I did. I called her at ten forty-five."

I glanced at my watch: 13:15, two-and-a-half hours gone. "Do you remember how long you talked with Estella? Short call? Your order is in, talk-to-you-later call? Or more along the lines of 'How are you today, Estella? How's Emily? What's going on at the school? Oh, by the way, your order is in'?"

"Second one, Tomas. We probably talked about ten minutes. Things were slow here so we just kept on gabbing. Why?"

"Well, while you two were talking, you-know-Houdini pulled

another disappearing act. Only this time she got away right before the DFYS caseworker arrived."

"Oh, dear. What can I do?"

"Let all your folks at the store know Emily's out again. Tell any customers who come in that she's missing and to keep their eyes open. If anyone finds her, let me know immediately."

"Roger that, Chief. I'll let our people know right now. Bye."

I like people who spring into action like Cathrine, and, let's be honest, who still respect me enough to call me Chief. The list of people she knew included most everyone in town and around town. Between her network and Kirsten's, the entire population of Rosemont would be searching for Emily soon enough.

"Chief Arnesen. Time for a word or two now?" Mrs. Stein approached me as soon as I flipped my phone shut.

"At your service. How can I help you?"

"This does not look good at all for this family. I see from my notes that this isn't the first time Emily has disappeared, run away, escaped, whatever you choose to call it."

"Third time gone for over two hours. Several other times, when she was younger, she'd get out for fifteen minutes or less. Too small to get too far. But she's amazing at five. Loves the challenge, I think. Loves being outdoors. She's fascinated with all things dinosaur and rocks."

She smiled, briefly, but I couldn't tell why. Didn't seem right to me for a child welfare caseworker to ever smile.

"Will you go on the record with your observations, Chief?"

Ah. My words could help her build a solid case. "I have to, don't I? I reported this to your office because I want Emily to be safe, to be able to grow up. I don't want to find her body out there, mauled, broken, dead from exposure. If Estella, as much as she loves her daughter, cannot keep track of her, well, Emily needs to be protected."

"What about Mr. Mathiesen?"

I had another opportunity to give Greg a break but didn't take it. Couldn't take it. Emily's welfare trumped the whole situation.

"If I could prove it, I'd arrest him for domestic violence. I know he's beaten Estella. I suspect he's hit Emily. But even sporting Class-A shiners, bruises on her arms and neck, Estella will not, and has not, pressed charges."

Mrs. Stein scribbled notes in her folder. Her quick smile disappeared just as fast as Emily had. She looked up at me and now she looked like, well, a child welfare caseworker. She spoke what I already knew.

"This is not going to go well."

II
CLEAR THE GUILTY

26

"Dispatch to Rosemont One."

"Rosemont One. Deputy Yorke found Emily walking along the Old Benchland Road. He's bringing her to the house now."

"Ten-four, Dispatch. Call off the search if you haven't already done that. One, out."

"Done. I called Cathrine as well to let her know. Dispatch, out."

Estella wept as the dam that had been holding back her true emotions finally gave way to too much stress held onto for far too long.

Mrs. Stein pulled a tissue from her purse, dabbed her eyes, then walked up the steps and sat down. Awkwardly, she placed one arm around Estella's shoulders and rocked her from side to side.

At the moment, not knowing exactly what to do to comfort a lady in distress, I was more than inclined to give the caseworker the benefit of the doubt. "Well, at least this time she didn't get very far," I said to no one in particular.

Nathan had his phone out, updating his SAR folks with the news, calling them to stand down from the search. Last call completed, he waved at me, then walked to his Jeep to get his medical kit just in case

Emily needed tending again. He sat on the bottom of the porch steps and stared into the distance.

We heard Yorke's Durango before we saw it. When he rounded the corner at Sevier and New Lake, he had the siren and lights going.

Estella stood.

Yorke stopped about three feet from me, shut it all down, and sat there in the driver's seat, grinning like he'd just been kissed. He got out, walked around to the passenger side, opened the door, and a small, bright, weather-coated pink jumpsuit leaped into his arms. He carried her to the front walk and stood there looking at Mrs. Stein and Estella.

I was looking at Estella and watched her eyes widen a bit, exactly as they had when we drove past them on our first rounds about the town.

"Here's your daughter, Mrs. Mathiesen. Safe and sound." He glanced at Nathan. "Not one scratch. Not one bruise. She was thirsty so I gave her a bottle of water."

Nathan nodded. "That's good. Maybe I can take a look at her in a bit, just to be on the safe side."

Yorke took Emily out of his embrace, held her steady until her little white tennis shoes touched the ground, then turned her loose.

She ran halfway to her mother, stopped, looked back at Yorke with a tiny grin, then ran on up to her mother's arms. "He's nice, Mommy. I like him."

"That's good, dear. I'm glad you like him." Although Estella's face was already reddened from the trial of her day, I was fairly certain it went a few shades darker.

Yorke looked like he'd run smack into my office door again. I don't think he was aware of anyone but Estella.

"Thank you, Deputy Yorke, for finding my daughter, for bringing her back."

An almost imperceptible tremor ran through Yorke's body. I was close enough to see it. I knew why. Estella's voice, low, warm, and raspy, came straight out of a smoke-filled blues bar, where she'd sang for years, leaning on the piano, wearing a low-cut, black velvet evening gown and black, arm-length gloves.

Their reverie ended quickly.

"What the hell's going on here? Can't get to sleep with all this racket."

Greg Mathiesen had finally made his appearance. Disheveled? An understatement. Unshaven, hair a mess, no shoes or slippers, raggedy, frayed fleece gym pants, topped by a tattered, paint-splattered University of Utah T-shirt. I could smell him from fifteen feet away, two parts sweat and two parts of the cheapest rum he could find, mixed with cola syrup.

Mrs. Stein started to move toward him, but he ignored her and staggered toward Estella and Emily. "What the hell is going on here?"

Estella backed away, but he grabbed her arm and held her.

I moved to the bottom step of the stairs. Yorke stood next to me. I spoke as matter-of-factly as I could to Greg. "Emily ran away again. The deputy brought her back." Figured the fewer the words I had to say to him the better for both of us.

Greg leaned down and put his face as close to Emily's face as he could. With his right hand, he grabbed her wrist a little too tightly. "So, you little brat. You escaped again, eh?"

Emily winced. From his breath or his hold, I couldn't tell. Probably both. Seemed like a well-rehearsed reaction to me too. As if she knew her daddy was only good at two things: drinkin' and hittin', and in that order.

I saw it coming and knew I wasn't going to get there in time.

Greg raised his left hand to his right ear in what looked like a well-rehearsed prep for the delivery of a backhand slap. But some small part of his inebriated mind must've kicked some sense into his mulebrain a split second before he brought that backhand down on his only daughter's face. With his hand still by his ear, he glanced at me and the Deputy. As he stared, he scratched his right ear with that left hand. He smiled at us, as if he knew something we didn't. As if he'd just outwitted us in some way.

In a way, he had. We couldn't arrest him for seeming to almost hit his daughter. But Greg Mathiesen was a drunk and an abuser, and drunk abusers tend to always see their day in court in due time.

"Greg, stop, please." Estella pleaded, her eyes tearing up again.

"I ain't doing nothing, Stel. You hush your mouth. It's your fault we're in this mess again."

I rolled my eyes.

"Greg, you're hurting her. Please, stop." Estella tried to wrest Emily out of Greg's grip.

He wouldn't let go.

Emily sobbed.

I stepped to.

Greg pushed me away, or tried to push. "My wife. My brat. My porch. My private property. All of it. So get lost."

Yorke stepped to next. Without a word, he pried Greg's hand from Emily's wrist. Yorke glanced at Mrs. Stein, who'd been scribbling notes so fast I thought I saw smoke, then he spoke directly to Greg. "I think we've seen enough here, Greg. We're going to take Estella and Emily with us. They need to answer some questions for Mrs. Stein. And since this is your private property, maybe you need some privacy for a while. Why don't you dry out before we all talk again?"

Greg wiped his nose with the back of his hand. "Fine. Leave. Allofya."

I nodded a silent thanks to Yorke. As he led Estella and Emily to his car, I followed a few steps behind. Then I smelled all four parts of Greg Mathiesen behind me.

"Hey, Sheriff!"

I turned.

He decked me, a glancing blow off the jaw. The hit surprised the hell out of me, but his aim didn't. He probably saw two of me right then. I should have known his anger might boil over. I staggered back. Crouched low and feeling my jaw, I said, "Assaulting an officer, Mathiesen? That's about the dumbest damn thing you could do today, and you've done a lot of damn dumb things already."

After I came back up to face him, Greg swung at me again, kinda what I was hoping he'd do.

I raised my left hand to my right ear and smiled at Greg, but I completed the motion he'd been too timid to do before. I slapped him in the face with the back of my hand. "Hurts, doesn't it?" I slapped him again, open-handed.

Arnesen, this is a pretty damn dumb thing to do too.

"I'll have your job for this, you son-of-a-bitch." He tried to hit me again.

This time I took his arm, pulled him around, and dropped him onto the porch deck. He hit hard. "I already have your job, Mr. Mathiesen." I slammed his head against the wood, twice, then a third time.

"Tomas. Stop. Stop it!"

Kirsten's voice cut through the growing red behind my eyes. I blinked and looked up. She was standing on the bottom step. If I'd been drunk, the look on her face would have sobered me up in an instant. In that instant, I figured I'd just lost everything worth having in this place. Namely her.

I cuffed him, stood him up, faced him, and read him his rights. "Greg Mathiesen, I'm arresting you for assault on a police officer. You have the right to remain silent . . . ." I read him the rest of his rights.

"You bet your ass I'll get you for this." Greg tried to spit at me, but most of it dribbled down his chin.

"Do you understand these rights?"

"I understand your day is coming."

"Do you understand these rights as I have read them to you?"

The message finally leaked through into some still functioning part of his brain. "I understand. But that ain't gonna change anything when I get you in court."

"Nathan, can you take Mr. Mathiesen here to our holding cell? Clean him up a little?"

"No problem, Chief."

Nathan led a now docile Mathiesen back toward his Jeep, got him in the back seat, and drove off.

I looked up at Estella, Emily, and Mrs. Stein, all huddled together by Yorke's Durango. I spied a small, smug smile on Estella. Emily clapped. Mrs. Stein stopped writing in her notebook and stared at me, mouth agape.

"Sorry, Estella, Emily. But I don't want him hurting anyone. Mrs. Stein, would you mind staying with Emily and her mother for a while? Maybe now's not the time for a formal interview, but you two have some work to do to protect Emily."

"I can do that, Chief Arnesen. But I will also have to file a report about this to my superiors."

"I understand completely, Mrs. Stein. I apologize for my behavior."

I walked down the steps past Yorke.

He looked up at Estella, tipped his hat, then turned and walked to his Durango. As he passed me, he said, "Shit, Tomas. Why'd you go and do that? Now I gotta file a report too. Damnation. This just isn't good."

"Do what you need to do, Yorke. Believe me, I understand. But no one threatens to hurt a child or a woman if I'm around. Ever. Plus, he swung first." I turned my swelling jaw toward him.

"I'll be sure to note that, Tomas, but I still have to report everything else. You know the drill."

"And you know what really happened here."

"Don't worry, Tomas. I'll do right by you." He climbed into his Durango and drove off.

Part of me knew his word would be true because I trusted Yorke. The other part of me knew it would be true because I'd bet my job that Yorke more wanted to do right by Estella.

Bet my job? Didn't I just do that because I let my anger—righteous as it was—take precedence over procedure? Even worse, I'd humiliated a drunk in front of his wife and child. Even if that drunk was Greg Mathiesen, no man deserves that kind of disrespect.

And then Kirsten. Why'd she have to show up just then?

I needed a drink. I needed space. I needed something I probably had just lost. I left my cruiser sitting in front of the Mathiesen's and started walking the six blocks to the safety office. The bottle in the bottom desk drawer. A wee touch o' the dram might taste good, at least for the moment.

I heard Kirsten's footsteps behind me but didn't look back. I did not want to see that expression on her face again. I kept walking.

She followed me all six blocks.

27

I unlocked the office door, resisting the temptation to kick it open, and went straight to my desk for the Glenlivet single malt I'd been saving for a special occasion. This seemed to qualify. I knew I wasn't going to take the time to brew a cup of Silver Needle or Lavender Tea.

When the door slammed shut about as hard as I'd ever heard it, I resisted the temptation to turn around. I still did not want to see Kirsten. I had a good idea what she was going to say and wanted to delay the inevitable for as long as possible. I sat down in my chair, took the bottle out of the bottom drawer, opened it, and poured a shot into my dirty tea mug. It tasted like summer fruit, smooth and warm, exactly what I needed. Then I looked up.

"Was it worth it?"

"Was what worth what?"

"Let me rephrase the question. Were a few good punches on a drunk worth losing your job?"

"If you're going to say good-bye, do it now, please."

"Don't change the subject. You might have played that 'I'm not worth the trouble' card for your ex-wives, but it won't work with me—

at least not today. Now. Let me rephrase the question for the last time. Was it worth it?"

More smoothness sliding down the back of my throat as I resisted the impulse to offer Kirsten a drink. Third taste down, I unclipped my key ring, found the small silver file cabinet key, swiveled in my chair, unlocked the bottom drawer, took out the single manila file envelope, and tossed it onto the desk in front of Kirsten. "Why I did what I did is in there."

She pulled a chair over and sat down. She opened the envelope, took out a manila folder about a half-inch thick, flipped it open, and scanned the cover page. "I see key words here: *suspension, reduced in rank, probation*. But that doesn't tell me what *that* was about with Greg."

I took two more large sips to steady my nerves.

"Tomas. Look at me. Look at me."

I looked at her.

"I know what you're thinking. You're thinking that when you tell me this story, I'll get up and run out of this office, run away from you as fast as I can run and never look back. Am I right?"

I nodded, not trusting myself to speak.

"OK. I get that. You've been hurt before. Well, so have we all. But love means trusting each other for better and for worse."

Did she just say . . . ? Not the time, Arnesen. Focus. She may have said it, but she just saw the worst part of you on display for near about the whole town to see. And word will get out about that fight. Will she stay then? She can talk of love all she wants, but I've been down this path before. Truth arrives and wives depart.

I thought about reminding this incredibly beautiful, angry young woman sitting across from me that the longer she stayed the more trouble she might find.

"But—"

"Butt's the south end of a northbound horse. Something happened to you in Kentucky on that big city police force."

We are our stories. Some of our stories mark us for life. When we are given the opportunity to tell a story, the more powerful it is, positive or negative, the odds increase that singular tale is the one we tell.

We repeat it. How often we repeat is a function of its power over our psyches. Too often, the story becomes a large chunk of our self-definition, whether we understand this or not.

"I could have saved a kid, a nine-year-old boy. I didn't. I suspected his dad abused him. The whole damn department suspected. We did have proof the bastard beat his wife. When the whole thing ended, we found out there were three hospitals, two clinics, two police precincts in two states with open files on this guy, pictures of horrible bruises, cigarette burns, broken bones, ugliness that made me want to throw up. But no one shared the information. No one made the one call or forwarded the one report that might have stopped what happened. No one paid attention." I grabbed the nearest pile of folders on my desk and threw them across the room.

"Feel better?" she asked, lips thin and eyes narrow.

"Not really."

"Go on, then."

"We answered multiple disturbance calls to their house. His wife never pressed charges. Just wanted us to talk to her husband. Help him understand. So we talked. He never understood."

I stopped, took a deep breath, and poured another half inch of the Glenlivet into my mug. Telling this truth was going to get harder. I was fairly certain of her love, but she didn't know this part of me, and everything within told me to stop talking. But the words of my past floated to the surface, buoyed by the rising tide of whiskey in my system. To her credit, she didn't say anything. She sat there and watched me lift the mug.

"It started as a ten-sixteen, domestic disturbance. My partner and I were on shift for the Domestic and Sexual Assault Unit. I recognized the address from previous visits. We were turned around and headed that way when we heard their ten-fifty-two. Dispatch rolled the ambulance, and within two minutes we heard the ten-seventy-nine. When you call in to notify the coroner, a domestic disturbance has escalated past violence to murder."

"What were you thinking on the way to the house?"

"Honestly? That the wife had finally had enough and shot, stabbed, or beat her husband to death with a baseball bat."

"But he wasn't the victim, was he?"

"The patrol officers had the husband in custody and were sitting on him on the ground. He was not cooperating. Wife sat on the porch, watching everything, seeing nothing. You could see she had checked out. I walked into the house. Our Sergeant knelt by the boy's side. There was blood everywhere. Looked like the kid's head had been caved in. I could hear the father screaming outside, kept shouting, 'It was an accident. Ask my wife. She'll tell you it was an accident. Let me go, you sons of bitches. It was an accident!'"

I drained the rest of the whiskey in one toss and managed not to choke. But it made my eyes tear up a little, covering the tears already forming. I looked up at Kirsten, looked her right in the eyes. If she stayed through what was coming, well, I'd know more about her than perhaps anyone else in this county.

"I walked out to the lawn, told the officers to stand him up. I looked at him, blood everywhere, on his hands, on his face, his shirt. I listened to him screaming that word *accident* like it was a talisman to ward off responsibility for his actions. I don't remember anything else until I looked up from the grass into the face of my Sergeant, two of the paramedics, and two more patrol officers. I remember the lights flaring around me, the murmuring in the distance, people buzzing like bees at the edge of the yard and street, the taste in my mouth, how the mother stared at me then looked away. All of it is right here and right here." I tapped my forehead and touched the tip of my tongue. "Lying on the ground, staring up at my patrol Sergeant." I began to sob.

Kirsten placed her hand on my leg. In that brief moment, I recalled everything, every word the Sergeant said to me.

"Balaam's ass, Arnesen. What in Sheol was that about? You damn near killed him. We got people all over the place, cameras, cell phones, WAVE3 and WHAS crews pulled up just in time to film you beating the devil out of a handcuffed suspect."

Good Kentucky Missionary Baptist that he was, Sarge had found a way to express himself rather vividly, replacing the usual curse words with biblical terminology.

"Did I hurt him, Sarge?"

"Busted his jaw, probably right orbital socket, broke his nose, more than likely a couple or three ribs, maybe punctured a lung. Medics got him in the ambulance now. He's going to Chandler ER ASAP. You better hope he doesn't enter the Holy of Holies for the last time."

"Too bad," I mumbled.

"Asps in a basket, Arnesen. This is going to cost you, but I'll do what I can. You know I know what really happened, but we can't all be Angels of Vengeance, even if it's called for. There's procedure. And there were cameras, Arnesen."

"Sorry, Sarge. You have me confused with a detective who gives a damn."

"You've never been out of control before tonight."

"Go back inside. Take a good look at what used to be a kid, had nothing but crap his whole short life. But hey, look on the bright side, he doesn't have to put up with any more violence and ugliness, doesn't have to put up with life at all."

He stood up and gestured to the patrolmen still holding me. "Take him to Rescue Two and let them take a look at his hands. Keep him away from Rescue One. When he's cleaned up, take him home. Make sure he stays there. That's your assignment for the rest of this shift. I'll clear it with your Watch Commander. Now get him away from these cameras."

They lifted me up and carried me to their patrol car, kept me on my tiptoes the whole way.

Sarge yelled at my back. "See you at the disciplinary hearings, Arnesen. I'll see if I can't help you in some way, but this is going to be a tough road to walk. You know how long Moses roamed the desert?"

I knew.

As I came to, I saw that Kirsten had been flipping through the file folder, likely scanning everything I'd just been reliving. I let the memory float away, my guilt keeping it tethered to me, as vivid as ever, and leaned back in my chair.

Kirsten and I wiped tears off our cheeks at the same instant, left hand, then right hand. The tiniest smile creased Kirsten's lips and cheek and then faded.

"The disciplinary hearings were short and sweet. I declined legal advice, admitted my guilt, did not plead extenuating circumstances like temporary stupidity or job-induced-being-with-bad-people-all-day insanity. I stood in front of the boards and took what they handed out: a hundred and twenty hours suspension without pay, retraining in ethics and conduct, probation for six months when I returned to the department, if I wanted to return. Both civilian and departmental review boards made it crystal clear I was perfectly free to walk away, take my retirement with me since I was vested, and say good-bye."

"That was harsh," Kirsten said.

"At least it wasn't a forty-year suspension."

Kirsten cast a strange look at me.

A wry laugh escaped through a sob. "Department guidelines for a Category C violation. I think I got the lesser punishment because this was my only blemish, big and ugly as it was. But the Citizens for Better Policing kept trying to make a commotion, that my punishment was too light. I hadn't paid my full debt to society and the victim, kept calling for my immediate termination. That all changed eventually."

"What happened?"

"Outside the hearing room, end of my last appearance, the Captain in charge and the Mayor's civilian representative went on record with my punishment. They were just getting to the apology to the victim when his lawyer barged into the conference. Made an ass of himself, threatening more legal actions, criminal charges, civil rights violations. He had several folks from the CBP behind him. Some of their signs were pretty offensive to me, considering no one was mentioning the dead kid. My bosses closed the press conference down right then and started to leave the building. Right outside the Police Center front doors, the supposed victim showed up, not wearing his neck brace or the cast on his hand, not rolling around in his wheelchair. His lawyer saw him and tried to stop the guy but failed. The rest, well, it all got filmed, just like they filmed me the night he killed his son."

"He went after you with a baseball bat, just like he did to his kid," Kirsten said.

"Yep. Cameras going, microphones hot. Called me names you wouldn't believe and swung the bat at me. I stepped back. He hit the Mayor's representative in the face, then broke an officer's arm, got another one across the knees, all this in vivid close-up color, before a

Bailiff tasered him. Even then it took two more of our guys to take him down."

Kirsten got up and walked around my desk. She stood behind me and began massaging my shoulders.

I kept talking. "Review Board met again, upheld the previous suspension but dropped the probation. They apologized, even tried to take back their comments about my retirement. They said they'd welcome me back, no more questions asked, bury this hearing judgment in the back of my file. That's what they told me. It sounded pretty hollow."

"You were already planning to come home, weren't you?"

"I was. I did. I am. Home."

"How did it turn out for the father?"

"He, notice I did not call him names—I should get points for that—was convicted of manslaughter for his son's death, two counts of felony assault with a deadly weapon on police officers, another felony count assault on a city official. He'll be in prison for a very long time."

"The mother?"

"She disappeared. Left everything in the house except some clothes. Gone. Vanished. Neighbors didn't see or hear anything."

"But you still see that boy's face, don't you? The before and after images are still there. They still haunt you, don't they? That's what the hell happened with Greg and Emily."

I nodded.

She wrapped her arms around me and let me cry the story away.

28

My mornings in the office usually feature a preset routine. After last night's introspection with Kirsten, this morning's schedule was critical for the rest of the day. I filled up my fancy electric teapot, flipped the switch, and listened as the entire bottom surface of the teapot holder heated up. Hot water in three minutes. Once poured, I let my special breakfast blend steep three minutes longer—that slight deviation from the timetable gets more caffeine into the brew, and I needed that. The office filled with peppermint-scented steam.

Five sips. Then and only then did I sit down, open the large brown manila folder with the state crime lab seal, pull out the autopsy and forensic reports, and begin reading. It didn't take me long to see that the Salt Lake crews had done their customary thorough work. I'd read the details later because you never knew what might be hiding in the open. But the cover letter intrigued me. Staff had summarized both reports in the letter rather than writing down two separate ones on each final report.

Both of Rosemont's latest murder victims had died in identical manners: contact gunshot wounds to the forehead, massive trauma to the brain causing instant or near-instant death. Residue identified as black powder, modern mixture. Projectile recovered from both victims: .44 caliber round ball, metallurgy consistent with Civil War era. Suspected weapon? A .44 caliber percussion pistol.

Black powder? Cap-and-ball revolver? Great. Every second man in Rosemont—and every third woman—is a hunter, and almost every Rosemont hunter hunts the muzzle-loader season. Most of them have multiple black powder weapons, including pistols, and including me.

I have an antique 1860 Colt Army Percussion Revolver, .44 caliber, passed down from my great grandfather, a drummer boy in the Twentieth Maine when he was fifteen. He took the gun from a fallen officer at Gettysburg. It's been in the family ever since.

My radio killed my reverie. "Dispatch to Rosemont One."

Even though her tone was all business, I couldn't help but think of the night before. I'd told her more than I'd told anyone in a long, long time. But she hadn't left. Then again, that was part of her job. Before I could make a fool of myself by asking how she felt about us right then, she went right on through with procedure. *No time for pleasure, Tomas. It's all business for now.*

"You copy, Rosemont One? What's your Twenty?"

"I'm at the office. What's up?"

"Stig and Tollef Varland think they found something while they were out walking the north side of town."

"Did they say what it is?"

"No. They called me and said I should call you and Deputy Yorke. He's next."

"Roger that. Where are the boys?"

"Off Escalante, just past where it crosses the creek behind the Broken Bow Trailer Park."

"Ten-four. I'm on my way." I paused. *Not the right time, Chief.* "One, out."

Kirsten clicked her mike to acknowledge. I figured Yorke would meet me there once she told him where to go.

Sure enough, Yorke was talking with Stig and Tollef. They were pointing toward the ridge that ran for about five hundred yards along and above the stream. I'd been up there a lot as a boy. You could see almost all of the north end of town from the vantage point.

"What's up, guys?" I asked as I walked up to them.

"We tried to keep it clean up, not mess it up if it's, like, ya' know, a crime scene or something like that." Stig had lived in Rosemont all his life, but when he got the least bit excited he sounded like he'd just stepped off the boat from Trondheim.

I looked at Tollef. "Tell me what you saw before we go up there. Describe it for me."

He nodded. "We hadn't walked this way and thought maybe we should. You know, cover all the bases. Well, we found a spot, right there on that hump, looked like somebody's been lying there, either for a long time or coming and going and lying on that spot more than once. Thought we saw bootprints on the back side and there was some paper-looking thing stuck in the bushes across from the spot."

Stig chimed back in. "That's a real good spot ta' watch folks from. Clear view down ta' Main Street. Can see Seth's place. Tate's too. Better with binoculars." He stopped, gulped, and went on. "Tomas, Deputy, you think the killer was up there?"

I shrugged my shoulders.

Yorke raised his hands. "Hard to tell, Mr. Tandberg, until we look at the spot and maybe get some samples, might be trace evidence that will help us." Yorke motioned to me. "After you, Chief Arnesen. After you."

We walked down the trail about two hundred paces, then climbed up the side of the ridge, trying to stay away from walking over potential track evidence. At the top, we walked carefully along the ridge peak, probably ten feet across at its widest point.

As we got closer, Stig yelled up at us. "You're three or four feet away now, straight out front there."

"Thanks."

I walked two more steps, stood on my boot toes, and peered down ahead of me. Nothing showed so I took one more step, then two, then stopped.

"You got it?" Yorke asked from behind me.

"Got it. Hand me the camera."

I took pictures of the depression. Course, I was on alert for something strange, and this spot looked like someone had indeed scooped out a wide spot to settle down into, stretched out, maybe even like Stig said: with binoculars focused on Main Street. Almost nothing of the person would be visible, only the top of a head, binoculars, that's about it. I edged over to the back side of the ridge and saw there were indeed faint bootprints in the softer dirt at the top edge, tracks which disappeared on the harder rocky surface down the side away from town.

Yorke handed an evidence bag over my shoulder. "On the ground, to your left, about seven o'clock."

I looked where he called out and saw a slip of paper, stuck in the thistles, pulled one of my black latex gloves out of my back pocket, bent down, retrieved it, and dropped it into the baggie.

Yorke sealed it, then wrote the date, time, and place on the front panel. Once done, he held it up to the light. "Chewing gum wrapper. Dentine brand."

"Could have blown there from any trash can in town. From the dump. Doesn't have to belong to the killer," I said.

"Well, maybe true, maybe not. Won't hurt to have the lab run tests, maybe get some DNA from it? Who knows. Might be a break in the making?"

"You are an incurable optimist, Deputy Sheriff Trooper Yorke."

He nodded in total agreement. "Thanks, I am indeed. Only way to go through this life as far as I'm concerned. What we see on the job these days, well, I guess being positive, wanting and hoping for the best, is the way I balance the wicked with the good."

We walked back down the ridge to our cars, where Tollef and Stig stood.

"Good call, you two. Someone was there, likely watching the town. We don't know if it was the killer or not, but chances are good it was. We have boot tracks to try and match and we have an old gum wrapper for a DNA test. So, good job you two."

We shook hands all around. I asked Yorke to hang around for a bit and sent the boys on back to town.

"What do you think?" I nodded toward the ridge top.

"Someone spent a lot of time up there." He shaded his eyes as he looked into town from our lower level. "How long would it take to get from here to Seth's store, or to Tate's?"

"An easy five minutes if there's a car up here. No way to tell that now, too many of us driving and walking all over where a car could have been parked. Walking? Maybe eight to ten minutes."

"Walk off here, cross the creek on the bridge there at the trailer park, then straight down Main Street. Pretty visible most of the way."

"Come off the bridge, angle to the right, you're screened by the cedars in Memorial Park and by the statues. From there, it might be possible to slip unseen into the alleyway that runs parallel to Main Street all the way to the back of both stores. If you weren't running or making a show of trying to get somewhere fast, no one would take a second look."

"Watched. Waited. Walked down and shot them, walked out. Disappeared into town like nothing had happened." Yorke tapped his lip and reeled off the same probability line of events I'd been turning over in my head.

"But this doesn't help us, much, does it?" Yorke took off his cap and rubbed his bald head. "Damn. Wish there'd been more here. Would have been nice if the killer had left a clue."

"Pretty smart, whoever it is."

We stood there looking out into the blue sky hanging above town.

"You get a copy of the reports yet?" I asked him.

"I did."

"Read them?"

"I did."

"So what do you think?"

In a moment unbecoming of such an optimist, Yorke hesitated. "I think you've got a real problem on your hands, Tomas. If Rosemont is anything at all like Welling, there are a lot of black powder weapons out there, pistols and rifles. Knowing it was a probably a percussion pistol narrows things down, but not by much."

"We've got a bunch of cowboy shooters here as well. Love the competitions. I used to shoot them all the time."

"Rifle or pistol?" He asked.

"Eighteen sixty Colt Army, Civil War issue. Belonged to a Union Officer in the Twentieth Maine. Great Grandpa passed it down to

Aksel. He passed it to my dad. Now I have it. We all shot it. We keep it clean and in perfect working order."

Yorke whistled. "Can I get a look at it some time?"

"Sure. I keep it out at the homestead. Next time we run out there, I'll let you shoot it."

"Thanks. I'll look forward to that trip."

I headed for the truck and Yorke stepped to his cruiser. I hollered at him. "You got dinner plans tonight?"

"Taking the early evening patrol with Nathan, so yeah, a late dinner would be cool, if that works for you?"

"OK. Let's say The Cliff at twenty-one thirty."

"The Cliff it is. See you then. Bring my report copies with me?"

I nodded. "Take some time and go over more details. Maybe together we can sort out the nuances in the examiner's notes."

Yorke hopped in, gunned the Durango, and left a cloud of dust hanging over the stream.

I watched him leave. Once he was out of sight, I pulled my binoculars out of the truck, walked back up the ridge, and settled myself into the depression. I was comfortable within its contours. It almost fit me like a glove.

Glasses up, I watched Rosemont's afternoon people moving around our little downtown, all in their clumps of threes and fours, all trying to pay attention to their surroundings. As I watched, I wondered how long it would take until the tension wore down, the stress lessened, and the threat level decreased enough that they'd get tired and want to quit—likely just right before Rosemont's black-powder percussion pistol killer would strike again.

29

"Knock, knock."

I looked up from my desk to see Emery Burchfield standing in the entrance, pantomiming knocking on the door. In that moment I realized how impressed I actually was by our acting county attorney. For such a short man, he was highly skilled at looking down on people.

"Chief Arnesen. Got a minute or two?"

"Sure. For you, three minutes."

"Funny guy, Arnesen. Always the funny guy. Well, this isn't funny." He slid into the office space and tossed a file folder onto the countertop.

I didn't say anything because I knew he'd driven all the way from Welling, all thirty minutes, to talk to me about my incident with Mathiesen.

"I read Deputy Sheriff Yorke's report on your incident with Mr. Gregory Mathiesen. Want to tell me about it?"

I took a deep breath to let Burchfield know I meant business. "After he stumbled out of his house and figured out that Emily had escaped again, he almost slapped her right in front of me. He wound up, looked at me with an evil eye, and thought better about it. With his hand still in the air, he threw that evil eye at his wife. Yorke saw that and immediately stepped in and got them away. As I was following those three to the car, Greg called out my name. Soon as I turned around, his fist met my face. I let him have the first punch for free, but when he reared back and tried to land the second, I took him down."

Burchfield opened the folder, flipped back a couple of pages, and ran his fingers down a few lines of typing. His lips moved as he read through Yorke's notes for who knew how many times.

"So no excessive force?"

"Not sure what you mean by excessive?"

"How hard did you hit him? How hard did you slam him to the ground? How many times did you hit him, before and after you slammed him to the ground? That kind of excessive."

"Like I just told you. He hit me. Surprised me. I should have been prepared for that. I reacted on instinct at that point and slapped him. That slowed him up but not enough. He kept coming toward me, and that's when I backhanded him. That stopped him, for a second or two. But he didn't get the message, swung at me, I took his arm, pulled him around, and dropped him onto the porch deck. He hit hard."

"What then?"

Burchfield knew exactly 'what then' and wanted me to say it, so I obliged. "I slammed his head against the wood, twice, then a third time for good measure, I guess, to make sure he was paying attention. Then my dispatcher yelled at me to stop it. I stopped it."

"And?"

"And nothing. I cuffed him, stood him up, read him his rights. Had my paramedic take him to the holding cell to check him over and clean him up."

"What were the extent of his injuries?"

"He had a cut over his eye that bled a lot, like head wounds do. Redness on each cheek where I slapped him. And a pretty good shiner under his left eye from the porch. Nothing else of note. Like the unintended blessing of being drunk in a car wreck. Everyone else gets hurt or killed, but the drunk walks away uninjured."

"You saying Mr. Mathiesen was inebriated?"

"Drunk as a weasel, if weasels drink. Even his daughter knew he was drunk."

"Any proof?"

"Probably two hundred if I had to guess."

"Jokes, Arnesen?"

"The proof is right there in the report, acting county attorney Burchfield. He needed stitches. We had a lot of blood. He tested point one six, over legal limits, as you well know."

"So you don't think the head-banging on the porch a couple of extra times was excessive?"

"Mathiesen had physically threatened his daughter and his wife, hit me once, tried to hit me twice more, so forgive me if I decided to err on the side of making sure he wasn't going to keep trying to hit Emily, Estella, or me."

"Well, Arnesen, your version squares with Deputy Yorke's report and with his assessment of the situation, as far as Mathiesen's potential for continued violence against an officer. But don't for one minute think I'm going to just let this go as it is."

"I understand your position, Mr. Burchfield, and the position you want in the next election. I can appreciate your need to act and be decisive."

My mouth gets me in more trouble than my brain ever will.

"Chief Arnesen, I will make sure the Rosemont City Council has a copy of my notes on this incident. You might have some more explaining to do."

"Explaining is what I'm good at, Burchfield. At least it's one of several items on the 'Things-I'm-Good-at-List' that I keep in my top desk drawer right here." I pulled open the top left-hand drawer of my desk, reached in and grabbed a random piece of stationery.

Burchfield picked up the file folder, turned around, and walked out of the office. No comment, no pleasantries, no nothing.

I added another item to my 'Reasons-I'm-not-going-to-vote-for-Burchfield' list: impolite and doesn't know the proper etiquette for ending a professional interview, such as it was.

"Dispatch to Rosemont One."

"Why couldn't you have called me five minutes ago?"

"What?"

"Never mind. One, over."

"Estella is on her way to see you. Caseworker took Emily into state custody today until foster care can be arranged. Greg's still in jail."

"Do you know if Mrs. Stein has left town yet?"

"She's across the street in the Castle Motel parking lot."

"Stop her from leaving. Tell her I need to talk with her before she leaves. It's important. Ask her to come to the office with Emily. Then call Sylvi Nygaard. Tell her what's going on, see if she and Richard could get here soon. She and Richard used to be foster parents. Maybe we can keep Emily in town? Get over here fast. I don't want to be alone in the office with Estella."

"Ten-four, One. See you in a minute. I'll be there before Estella arrives."

"One, out."

"Dispatch, out."

Damn your pride, Arnesen. You lose your job and you're never going to find that killer.

30

True to her word, Kirsten came through the office door before anyone else we'd invited to the gathering. I wanted to leap across the countertop and kiss her until neither one of us could breathe. She must have seen something in my eyes, or my grin. The way I jumped up from my desk reaching for her might also have given her a clue.

She nodded and looked back over her shoulder. "Deputy Yorke, good to see you."

Yorke, uncharacteristically quiet, took his hat off and stood to the side of the door. His position gave him a clear line of sight down the street.

"I passed him on the way over and filled him in on the meeting. Sylvi and Richard were two aisles away from me in the store. They'll come, just needed time to talk this over since it's been a while since they had a foster child at the ranch."

Yorke stared out the door.

I hit the electronic latch to open the gate.

Kirsten came through, looked back at Yorke, leaned over the desk and kissed me lightly on the forehead.

Was that because Yorke was here or because she was just wanting to keep up appearances until this mess died down? Her kiss felt different, but it was enough to tide me over for the rest of the morning.

Estella, Mrs. Stein, and Emily arrived at the same time, mother and daughter crying and holding hands. Mrs. Stein held Emily's left hand, but Emily didn't seem to notice.

"Mrs. Stein, thank you for stopping by the office. I appreciate it, we appreciate it. I know you didn't have to come here."

"Well, Chief Arnesen, contrary to some people's ideas, we actually care about what happens to our children. I want Emily to be safe. That's my primary concern. I know you, of all people, understand that."

The barb stuck. My recent behavior proved that my personal default—protect the children—had been known to operate independently from my common sense and professional conduct codes.

"Why don't we go back to the conference room? Going to get a little tight if we try to stay in the office. Kirsten, would you take the ladies back there. I need to talk to Deputy Yorke for a second."

Kirsten knelt down and held her arms out to Emily, who jumped into them, away from her mother and Mrs. Stein. Kirsten smiled up at Estella and nodded at Mrs. Stein, who returned it. Carrying the still crying child, Kirsten held the gate open for the ladies, and they all walked back to our ten-person conference room, a fairly grand designation for space that once served as two closets and a sitting room.

"Is this a good idea, Yorke?"

"What do you mean?"

"I mean everyone in this room, including a distraught mother, saw the way you looked at Estella."

"Your point?"

"My point, Deputy Yorke, remains the same as it was the first day you saw them. She's married, albeit to a real SOB, and she has a lot going on right now: Prospect of losing her daughter, temporary for sure, permanent, well, that's up to the court. She's vulnerable. She's hurt. She's lonely. She'll become desperate if this gets worse, and it will get worse as soon as Greg makes bail. He's going to raise holy hell with all of us."

"I know, Tomas, I know all that. I know." His voice trailed off and he finally looked at me.

"That's the most pitiful expression I think I've ever seen on a man's face, Yorke. Just pitiful."

The ever-confident optimist shrugged his shoulders and slouched in his chair. With his head in his hands like a teenager about to ask a girl out for the first time, Yorke even sounded like a teen. "I feel like, like, I don't know what I feel like."

"It's one of two feelings, my friend: you've been run over by a truck and liked it, or you've been plugged into a light socket and every cell in your body has been lit up. Either way, you're a mess."

"Plugged in, then run over." He looked up, a wry grin escaping.

The gate was still open, so I walked out to him and shook his hand. "Congratulations, Deputy Sheriff Trooper Yorke. You are now an official member of the best men's club around, the *'I finally meet the woman of my dreams and can't do anything about it'* club."

He laughed. "That bad, huh."

"Worse than you can ever imagine."

"Does it get better?"

"Don't know."

"What do I do, Tomas?"

"You stay the hell away from her. You keep your distance. You bank the fire, and you bank it right now, get it covered and deep under the ashes. You do not let it get away from you. I've got your back on this, trust me. I know the territory. My second wife, well, I met her under similar, oh hell, you don't need that story right now. I got your back. Now get the hell out of here. Go patrol somewhere. Go find our murderer."

"I can't go back there and be supportive?"

"No. You can't go back there and be supportive. Jeez, Yorke. You got it bad." I grabbed him by the shoulders, turned him around, handed him his hat, and shoved him out the door.

He stumbled onto the sidewalk, put his hat on, an automatic impulse we all share, turned around, and looked at me.

I smiled, closed the door, and thought about locking it, but remembered the Nygaards were still out there—as well as my own dream woman, about whom I could do nothing about right now either.

But don't frustrated men find focus in their work?

But what if your frustration works with you?

❧ 31 ☙

I walked back into the conference room, bringing the population to five, but it felt like there were fifty of us crammed in there. The tears had stopped flowing, that was good, but Estella still looked scared stiff, white-tight-lipped drained of color, her glances going back and forth between Mrs. Stein and Emily.

Emily clung to her mother, umbilical reattached in the stress. When Mrs. Stein leaned toward the little girl to talk to her, to reassure her, Emily leaned away, tightening her grip on her mom's waist, fingers digging into the fabric of her mother's blue-checked jumper.

When I walked through the door, Estella looked up over Emily's golden hair. When she saw my face, she seemed disappointed somehow. *So the good deputy wasn't far off in what he was feeling*, I thought. Estella sensed the attraction as well. Now I knew I needed to make damn sure, at least for the time being, to keep the two of them far apart.

"Where are we?" I asked everyone in general and no one in particular.

"Waiting for you, Chief Arnesen," Mrs. Stein said.

"Getting to be a habit in these parts, for some folks anyway, waiting on Chief Arnesen." Kirsten looked at me.

"We're waiting for the Nygaards to get here. While we wait, I've got some thoughts on the situation." I looked at Kirsten, who took the clue and slipped out of her chair to stand at the conference door and watch for Sylvi and Richard.

"Mrs. Stein, you know the Nygaards, Sylvi and Richard. They've been foster parents for fifteen years, more than that, I think."

"I am well-acquainted with them, yes, Chief Arnesen. We were sorry last spring when they decided to opt out of the system."

"I understand. But if we can persuade them, in this instance, to opt back in. Would that be possible, say, on a short-term basis, for Emily's sake?" I watched her face for little telltales, indications if my idea was having any effect on her. She didn't look away from me or give me any other signs that she was going to get up right then and take Emily with her. I decided I would love to watch a poker game between her and our good newspaper editor.

"Let me see if you and I are on the same train of thought here, Chief Arnesen. You'd like the Nygaards to take Emily into foster care while all this gets sorted out. She can stay in her school with her friends, her mother could come visit, and an awful lot of people in this town who love this child would be keeping an eye out to protect her? Am I close?"

"Right on track, Mrs. Stein. Right on track." I smiled. She smiled back. Deal done. Except now we needed to convince the Nygaards. Plus, I still worried about Greg, but figured Mrs. Stein could handle him. The court order trumped all.

"I have two further stipulations, in addition to the obvious ones: that the Nygaards agree, and I get approval from Salt Lake. If we don't all agree on these two, I will take Emily with me this afternoon." Mrs. Stein's smile dropped.

"Let me see if you and I are on the same train of thought here," I said. "One: minimal contact with her father, and, two, if there is contact, it has to be well-supervised."

"Very well, *extremely* well supervised, if Judge Harvis grants any visitation rights at all. I will do everything within my power and that of DCFS to protect this child. Don't think for a minute I won't."

"We want to protect her as well, Mrs. Stein." I looked at Estella, at Kirsten, and back to Mrs. Stein.

Estella looked directly at the caseworker. "I will do whatever it takes to protect my daughter. If that means we both stay away from Greg, so be it. I don't want to put her in danger. After today, I don't want him in our lives. No more. I'm leaving him and filing for divorce."

The two women reached around Emily and held hands. Mrs. Stein's expression softened, and Estella started crying, harder this time, sobs racking her upper body. Emily, startled by her mother's sudden burst, began to cry again. Kirsten swooped in and gathered the child up, hugged her tightly, and walked to the door, murmuring to her all the way. Temporarily freed of that small bundle, Estella finally let it all go. Mrs. Stein held Estella.

I stepped out of the room to give them the time they needed to begin the tiniest bit of healing.

"So, Tomas, what have you concocted this time?" Richard held the office door open. Through it, I could see Sylvi, Kirsten, and Emily in an animated conversation. When Kirsten transferred Emily to Sylvi's arms and they all turned right, my heart skipped two or three beats.

"You want us to come out of retirement one more time, for Emily and for Estella?"

"Thanks, Richard."

"Did I say we would, yet?"

"Don't have to, Rich. They just answered the question for us." I pointed at the girls disappearing around the corner. Ice cream at Bjornson's Deli.

"State caseworker in there?" Richard headed for the conference room door.

"She's with Estella. Let's give them some time. I think Gregory Mathiesen is in for a big surprise. His domestic situation is about to change rather radically."

"Thank God and Greyhound. Answered prayer, Tomas, answered prayer." Richard clapped me on the back. "I'll call the Director in a bit, let her know what's going on, who the caseworker is, and that we would very much like to come back for this one assignment, in Emily's best interest. I think I want a chocolate latte," Richard said as we walked out to follow the ladies.

"Black cherry for me."

32

Five days passed. I could see the townsfolk losing their grips on readiness, hear their conversations veering away from the urgent purpose of patrolling Rosemont, feel their passion to protect each other fading by the day, by the hour, now by the minute. I had just stepped out of the office, trying to decide on The Cliff or Heavenly Grounds.

"Hey, Tomas. Got a second?" Trooper Yorke pulled up in his Durango.

"Sure. Want to come in the office?"

Yorke's typically deadpan face cracked a half-smile. He paused for a second too long. "Can't. Gotta go back on duty out of Welling for a while. Sheriff called me home. Said we couldn't afford to keep me down here any longer. Why, I only needed a second or two."

"Bummer. I like having you around, for some odd reason."

"Likewise. But I'll be a phone call or a ten-nineteen away from you. You holler. I come back. No questions asked. Be safe down here."

"You be careful out there among the heathens, my friend."

Yorke laughed, rolled up the power window, and drove away.

I wasn't surprised by the news. I didn't think they'd let him stick around here indefinitely. Two weeks on assignment took a decent-sized bite out of the Sheriff's Department's scheduling issues. Neither was I too surprised when I turned around from watching the Deputy drive off to see Mayor Emma Fosberg, councilwoman Freda Jacobsen, and the other town council members with Colin Parkin walking toward me up the street. It was the morning of the eighteenth day after Seth's murder, the fourteenth day after Tate's, the fifth day after my altercation with Mathiesen, and the second day following his release on bail. I still hadn't seen him in town.

"Good morning, Emma, Freda, Colin." I nodded at each. "What's up?"

"Can we talk inside?" Emma asked.

"Sure. But it's also nice out here in the morning sun, nice for mid-November."

They looked at each other, eye contact with me darting all over the place. Lots to say and not one of them knew how to get it out in the open. I decided to help. "I can tell you're all tired, and I bet I know why you're here too. It's been two full weeks with no incidents, no murders, nothing remotely suspicious at all, and you want to tell everyone they can 'Stand Down' now." Now I had their attention and direct eye contact, but still no relieved smiles. Those would come when they turned away from me to walk back to their offices and start getting the word out.

"Must be why we hired you for this, Chief Arnesen."

Since coming back to Rosemont, Freda had never once called me by my first name, even though she'd taught me in grade school. Once I had the job, ever proper, our beloved spinster teacher always used my title and last name. I respected her for her attention to such oft-forgotten courtesies. I tipped my hat to her. "Hope so. Although I haven't been too much out in front of these killings, have I?"

Emma said, "No one's faulting you, Tomas, for anything. We appreciate everything you've done so far, the way you and your team have handled this."

"Thanks, Em. I want to solve these cases more than anyone. We're doing our best with the evidence we have. There's not a lot to go on at this point."

"We understand. But you have to understand that all our folks are getting worn out traveling in groups. I feel like I'm on a special cut-rate tourist junket and this is our tenth country in three days. Does that make sense?"

"It does." I paused and wondered if she knew how many countries I'd metaphorically visited these last few days. Then I turned to Colin. "You here as Parkin's Store owner, former council member, Branch President or all three?"

He held up three fingers. "We do have some resources in the county that might be helpful."

"I, we, appreciate the offer."

Colin seemed genuinely eager for justice. "So? How can we help? What resources do you need?"

"Well, I suspected we'd be having this meeting sooner or later. We need people. New eyes and ears to pick up the slack from our overloaded Rosemonters."

Colin put his hand down and grinned at Freda. "Just like school days, eh?"

To her credit, she smiled.

Wanting to maintain his old teacher's approval, Colin continued. "Well, I took the liberty and called our Stake President in Welling. He's sending six three-person teams, two from each of the three wards. We also called the Branch president over to Ridgeway. They might be able to send a team as well. Welling teams left this morning, should be here any time. They'll stay with our branch families, so lodging won't be an issue, or meals. We'll just need to know their schedules once you get them organized. I'll let you know when and if the Ridgeway folks show up as well."

"Thanks, Colin."

"Hope I didn't overstep any boundaries here, Chief."

"Not a one. We all care about this place and our neighbors." I looked at my friends. "You all make me pretty proud right now. Well done."

I shook hands with everyone and held on to Colin's. "Send two or three of the new folks to my office when they arrive. I'll lay things out for them, duties, what to do, and definitely what *not* to do. This isn't about law enforcement. I want to make sure they understand. I need vigilance, attentiveness to their surroundings, and a willingness to hang out and help townsfolk as they move about their business, mostly in the evenings and early mornings. We'll let Kirsten schedule their watches. Might want to have a team or two staying central to escort folks here and there who might need to get out. And I'll want someone to keep watching over the Carlson sisters. Not obvious. They wouldn't care for that. From a distance, but twenty-four-seven."

Colin nodded and awkwardly pulled his hand away.

"One more thing," I reached out to keep Emma and Freda from walking off. "When you start getting the word out, remind folks they need to remain careful. Even if they aren't patrolling in teams, they still need to be aware of their surroundings and of the people around them. All that. If they see anything suspicious, they call me, Kirsten, Nick, or Nathan. Preferably me first. Also be very clear about the help coming from the Welling Stake."

Ever the community-builder, Emma asked, "What if we waited just a little while longer, until the teams arrive and call a quick special town meeting and introduce them. That way everyone knows they aren't strangers and no one panics." Emma shook hands with Colin. "Will you call me as soon as the Welling folks arrive?"

"Will do. Thanks, Freda, Emma." Colin waved good-bye and walked back toward the store.

Emma hooked arms with Freda. "Let's get the notification ball rolling for the meeting. You'll let your safety team know what's happening, of course."

I nodded. She hadn't asked a question. "Yes, Ms. Fosberg."

She laughed. At least some lightness had descended back into our fair town.

Before Freda and Emma walked away, I saw a couple of smiles creeping upon their faces. Whether it was the lame joke I'd just made, the fact that they had some actionable steps to take, or that they were seriously starting to think this plan might work out, I couldn't tell.

But their optimism gave me hope.

33

Still, I hadn't found my smile yet. Probably hidden behind the no-caffeine-yet morning jitters running through me. Next stop, Heavenly Grounds. I could sit in the front window setting Sarah had created: antique two-person settee, small oak writing desk, reproduction Tiffany floor lamp. I could enjoy the boost from my highly caffeinated morning special blend tea, see how long it took for the word to filter out, watch the shifting levels of street activity, catch the nods, glances, and maybe even have a few conversations with folks who'd see me in the window and poke their heads in the door.

The twinkles in her eyes belied her age. Sarah couldn't move quickly, but her mind was still as agile as ever. The morning blend of her kindness and caffeine had raised my spirits countless times before.

"Morning, Chief. Your tea's on the desk out there."

"Sarah. You're good. You are *very* good."

"And when I'm bad, I'm better." She laughed.

We shot those old Mae West movie lines at each other every time I walked into the shop. The special blend was always waiting for me, hot, either on the desk in the window setting or on the booth at the back of the room facing the front door.

"Thought you might want to watch the good citizens of Rosemont expressing their relief that the patrolling could end today." She saw my left eyebrow go up. "Emma stuck her head in the door as they walked away from their meeting with you. I figured you'd be in as soon as they got around the corner. She also said help was coming from Welling?"

"Colin called the Stake President."

"Guess we know what it means to have good neighbors, even if we have our religious differences from time to time."

"What can I say, Sarah, that hasn't already been said about you?"

"Not one blessed word more, Tomas Arent Arnesen, if you know what's good for you."

"Yes'm. Think I'll just go sit in the window with the best cup of tea in town, and watch the picture show out there."

"Just not the best cup of tea in the county, however. There's something even more special at the ranch. But thanks for the compliment. I always, well, most of the time, tell folks you're a smart boy."

"I try, Sarah. I surely do try."

"I heartily agree with that assessment, Tomas. Sometimes you can be very trying."

Of all the women in Rosemont I'd known growing up, Sarah Nelson O'Reilly was the one lady I thought Grandpa Aksel should have married after Gramma Julie died. Five years after Gramma's death, before I left to go to college, I thought about trying to set my Grandpa up with Sarah. I suspected Sarah would have been in favor of that but would never make the first move.

In their generation, and the code by which they lived—decency, courtesy, respect—the man *always* made the first invitation. If Aksel had shown the slightest indication of interest, well, who knows what might have happened. They had been and always remained good friends, but never anything more. Sarah, God bless her, had stayed with Grandpa the night he died. Maybe they'd shared a moment of grace and love then.

I looked back at her, brushing the gray hair out of her face, tidying the counter, getting the day-old doughnuts out in the wicker basket. She looked up and caught me watching her.

"Best views are out that window."

I took a deep breath and the words were out before I thought too much about asking the question. "Sarah, sitting here, watching you mind the store, I cannot for the life of me figure out why Grandpa Aksel never latched on to you after Julie died. After waiting a suitable period of mourning, that is."

"That's old history." She started to tell me to mind my own business. I read as much in her return stare. Then she softened and surprised me. "Old history, yes. But I did love Aksel, loved him from the beginning."

I turned to face her and sipped my tea, a smile slowly appearing with every sip. "Go on."

"When he came home already married to Julie, well, I cried a lot that night. Then I got over it. Good for Aksel! Good woman, beautiful woman. I got happy for them . . . finally. When she died giving birth to your daddy, I just about died myself. I ached for Aksel in so many ways. I wanted to hold him, let him cry in my arms, give him comfort."

I was shocked at how forthcoming she was being. Maybe the fog of mortality that had fallen over Rosemont was making her take stock. I had to let her know she couldn't have changed the past. "Grandpa wasn't that way. He kept it all inside. Wouldn't let anyone in to help or comfort. He had to find peace in his own way."

She began to cry ever so lightly. "He locked up your Gramma Julie's memory in his heart. He tried to love your daddy, but there wasn't much room left in there for Edward Tomas Arnesen. Lord knows Aksel wanted to love that boy."

She straightened up, pulled a day-old cake doughnut off the top of the basket, and threw it at me. "Enough of that old nonsense. You get back to watching the show, the new nonsense." She wiped a tear away and stomped back into the kitchen. I could smell the newest batch of brownies ready to come out.

She was right, of course. Old history in here. Much older than these doughnuts. Out there, maybe something new. Something better. Something—

"Want company?" Kirsten stuck her head in the door.

"Always." My smile nearly cracked my cup. "Taking your morning break early, I see."

"Is it a break if I'm coming to see you? You're my boss."

"Not if you're here in an unofficial capacity. And please tell me you're here in an unofficial capacity."

"I'm here in an unofficial capacity."

I exhaled. "Thank the Lord."

Sarah hollered from the kitchen. "I'll bring your latte up to you in a bit, dear. You sit down with that man of yours and enjoy the show."

"What show?" Kirsten sat down next to me.

"Sarah thinks we'll see some interesting sights as the word goes out about the patrolling ending."

"No doubt. What were you two talking about as I came in?"

"Old history, about her and my grandpa. Why they never got together after Gramma died. I wanted them to get married. Sarah's my favorite lady in town." A sharp little elbow in my ribs encouraged me to rephrase that observation. "Sarah's my favorite lady in town who I always wanted for an extra *grand*mother." If I put a little extra emphasis on the *grand* to make sure Kirsten wouldn't hit me again—sue me.

"Much better. Must have been some interesting history there, now that I think of it." Kirsten settled herself on the settee, more on my side than on hers. Even clothed, her body next to mine felt as warm as the tea in my hands, and I realized I was a lot further along in accepting this relationship than I thought. We were sitting—nearly cuddling—in the front window of possibly the town's most public place. *And I didn't care if anyone saw*. I also knew better than to speak my thoughts at the moment.

Lost as I'd been in my thoughts, Kirsten may have been talking for a while, but I only picked up the last part of what she was remembering. "Aksel used to tell me such stories about half the people who settled this place and made it what it is today. Well, minus the serial murderer. Stories about the attitudes that kept Rosemont alive and thriving, such as it is. I loved listening to him, the adventures, the way people helped each other, the times folks got in trouble."

Remembering, listening to the stories. Right there in front of me. "I am such an idiot." I slapped my forehead.

"I've known that for a long time, Tomas Arnesen. But why just now are you such an idiot?" Kirsten reached up and grabbed my hand, thinking I was going to smack myself again.

"History. Stories. We've been trying to figure out the link between Seth and Tate and there was nothing obvious there. But it might be there, less obvious. It *has* to be there."

"Where does it have to be?"

"Think, Kirsten. Think about it: history, events, attractions, happenings, natural disasters, crime. Where is it all written down?"

"Town ledger. Tomas, *the town ledger*. Why didn't you see that before now? Why didn't I see it, or Nick, or Nathan? What didn't anyone on the council see it?"

"Because we've been blinded by the trauma of the murders, that's why."

I turned and shouted to Sarah. "Later on the latte, Sarah. Sorry, we've got to go."

"Tell me about it when you can, Tomas. Bye, Kirsten. My, oh my, but do you two make a lovely couple."

I wasn't about to let her get the last word this time. I shouted back. "And you and Aksel would have made a lovely couple too, Sarah O'Reilly, who should have been Sarah Arnesen."

I grabbed Kirsten and pulled her up off the settee. "Quick. Let's go. Get out of here before she gets the last word or throws something at me."

We weren't fast enough. She flung a final Mae quote our way as we exited: "Just remember Tomas, 'Opportunity knocks for every man, but you have to give a woman a ring.'"

Kirsten grinned as we jumped into my Durango. "I like her."

34

"*History repeats itself. That's one of the things wrong with history.*" Clarence Darrow must have had a keen sense of his place in history's cycle. Probably saw too much of the worst of what history repeats.

As I opened the clasps on the leather-covered *Rosemont Town Journal*, I hoped he was right, that no matter how bad it might have been, I wanted—I needed—to find the history-repeating-itself information, a story or two whose details would lead me to a killer. My instincts, what few I'd honed to a blunt edge on the streets of Louisville, told me revenge likely motivated our killer. He or she fancied themselves an avenging angel. That I'd only now come to the journal stuck in my craw like a chicken bone that once got stuck in my throat. Getting it out was not pleasant.

"Where do we start?" Kirsten asked.

"Tough question. Something in the last, say, twenty years, linking Seth and Tate. If we find that, maybe we can start connecting dots?"

She didn't smile. "Otherwise, you might have to go back to the beginning and work your way forward."

I brushed the dust off the town's immense, informal history. "There's over a hundred and twenty years in this book."

"I know. We could take shifts, maybe? Work our way along, keep notes for each other? Copy sections and each of us take a pile of pages. You, me, Nathan, Nick. We could all help. That'd make discovery go faster. Ask Yorke to join the reading party."

I sat back in my chair, resting my hand on top of the first page. "I think I need to do this myself, Kirsten. Can't totally explain why. Since I don't know what I'm looking for, how do I tell you and the others what to look for? It might be there in one of your stacks and we'd miss it. Nope. I have to do this myself, page at a time, until I find the story."

"What if the story isn't written in there?"

"Then we keep on with the old-fashioned detective work, taking what we have and trying to make sense of it all." I shrugged my shoulders.

"Long days and nights for you, reading all this. You going to be able to take it, keep up with everything else around here?" She smiled at me now, more of a don't-wear-yourself-out grimace.

"Don't have a choice, do I? I gotta believe there's something here, something that will shed light on a puzzle piece, even if I don't get the whole thing."

"OK. You get started. I'm going to call Nathan and Nick with an update on the extra help coming from Welling and the town meeting tonight. Then I'm going to get my latté. Want anything else for now?"

"Something to eat later. Maybe lunch from The Cliff. I'll call." I was already tuning in to the handwriting on the first page.

Kirsten leaned over the desk and kissed me on the forehead. When I looked up, she kissed me again, on the lips. "Back to the store with my coffee. I'll check on you at lunch break because I know you're going to disappear into that tome and won't come out even if the building's on fire. I'll bring something with me. Later."

I waved at her, then read:

THE ROSEMONT DAILY JOURNAL, ROSEMONT, UTAH.
Incorporated July 2, 1879, a town in Engelmann County, Utah.

The earliest entries featured rather more ornate penmanship than I was used to reading. It took me a while to get my eyes and my cognition paths to connect so I could read the texts.

When Kirsten opened the door, I had no idea how much time had passed, but I could smell lunch: The Cliff's open-faced brown gravy roast beef sandwich with Caesar salad on the side, my favorite lunch of all time.

"You bring the tea?"

"Yes, dear. I brought your tea. In fact, I brought two, one for lunch and one for later, when I bring you dinner, whatever that will be, unless I can pry you out of that chair to go out and eat."

"Thanks."

"You're welcome. Now how about a little more enthusiasm with the thanks, like, maybe a kiss?"

I stood up but stopped halfway, hunched over like the old man I didn't want to admit to being. I rubbed my back before straightening up.

"You haven't moved in two-and-a-half hours."

"Guess not. This is fascinating stuff." I tapped the open book.

"OK. Walk it off, sit down over here, and eat with me, then I'll let you get back to the history lessons. But I'm going to call you every forty-five minutes and tell you to get up and walk around, go outside and get some fresh air. If you turn your phone off, I'm going to use the radio. If you turn the radio off, I'm going to call the Sheriff's office and file a violation of communication protocol against you. Got it?"

"Yes'm. I hear you, loud and clear. Coming over now to sit and eat with you."

We sat together at the conference table, thigh-to-thigh, occasionally brushing arms and whacking elbows. I was left-handed. She sat on my left side, on purpose I surmised, just so we would make more physical contact than usual. I have to admit: it was one of the more enjoyable meals I'd eaten in a while. Plus we ate in silence. She gave me the space I needed to digest my food as well as keep on sorting the town's history into categories that made sense to me.

"Good lunch, Kirsten. Thank you."

"Tony said he's got a great dinner planned for us tonight. But you will have to come with me in person to enjoy it." She smiled.

There's no arguing with that smile, none whatsoever.

"Dinner at The Cliff with the most beautiful girl in Engelmann County, in the state of Utah, a special dinner just for us? Call me foolish if I turn that offer down."

"Idiot and foolish? Sure am glad I'm getting your character defects out in the open before we get too much further along in this relationship."

I had my perfect retort right up to my lips but she ruined the moment by kissing me.

She collected the plates and tossed the napkins into the trash can across the room, a couple of three-point shots right on target. "Remember, I'm calling you every forty-five minutes. When I do, you will get up, walk around, go outside, and take seven deep breaths. Not one, not four, but seven complete deep breaths. I'll be watching."

True to her word, she called me every forty-five minutes. True to her instructions, I got up, went outside, did my deep breathing, holding a finger with each breath, until I got my seventh completed. I don't think she could see the finger-counting from up the street, but I wasn't about to take that for granted. The pauses and the breathing worked. I felt refreshed and clearheaded when I sat back down, and kept reading, turning pages in my bizarre treasure hunt for something long buried.

The day remained calm, quiet, and without incident. Our reinforcements from the Welling Stake arrived, settled into our temporary command post in the Civic Center conference room, and worked out their schedules with Kirsten for the rest of the day and that night. The stand-down notice for our folks got out, decently and in good order, like the rock-solid Norwegian stock from which so many of us sprang. I was thankful. I heard the radio squawk once but relaxed when I heard the call was for Nathan—a small accident at the schoolyard.

Kirsten walked into the office at 18:45. "Last call. Get up, walk away from the journal, take my arm. We will now stroll conspicuously down the street, hand-in-hand, so everyone can watch us go to dinner."

"Then what?" A mostly innocent question.

"Then I walk you back to the office. I go home. You go home. You go to sleep."

"And then?" A less innocent question.

"Breakfast tea, latte, and scones at oh-seven-hundred tomorrow morning at Heavenly Grounds. You go back to work on the journal. I go to work at the store." I felt the intensity of her stare riding the wireless connection. "That's your 'then what' for the next few days, or until you find what you need."

I closed the book, letting the top leather cover slap down. "Guess we're still on county time till we figure all of this out, Dispatcher Dyrdahl."

"Correct, Chief Public Safety Officer Arnesen." She pointed to the book. "How far did you get?"

"Just passed from nineteen oh six into nineteen oh seven."

"And?"

"And? And nothing. Fascinating what our history bookkeepers found interesting. A struggling town of a few hundred people trying to make a living didn't leave much time for anything other than a dance now and then. Good, solid Norwegian work ethic exhibited with intimate, detailed evidence. I know about every barn-raising in and around Rosemont, every new farm, every new birth, every sick or dead horse, what hunter came home empty-handed and who came home with the trophy buck. I know a lot about the supposed peccadilloes of a few 'women' of less than savory character who passed through Rosemont, trying to ply their wares to make enough money to get to the big city up north. Whichever city that was, the authors never thought to mention. Might be a fun thing to check out and see if their destination was Welling."

"Sounds like you'll need this evening break."

"No doubt. But there's also something compelling here. These writers cared about Rosemont. They were interested in everything about this town and its citizens. Last words from long-gone, good people. This is our history, and at some point I'm going to run smack into my family's story. And yours, and Nick's, and Nathan's."

"It's hard not to read ahead, isn't it?"

35

"Dispatch to Rosemont One and Two."

"This is One. Go ahead, Dispatch."

"Just got a report of a disturbance at the Mathiesen residence."

"Ten-four. You copy that, Rosemont Two?"

"On the way. Will wait for you, Chief. What's your twenty?"

"Three blocks out. Stay in your truck and watch. Do not, repeat, do not confront Greg. One, out."

"Ten-four. Two, out."

"Kirsten, call Nathan and have him stand by."

"Will do. Be careful over there."

"Promise."

I'd been waiting for this to happen. Released on bail four days ago, Greg had come home, found the empty house, started drinking, and, in short order, his anger must have boiled over. It was good news, in a twisted way, that the house, rather than Estella or Emily, was now taking the brunt of his rage.

Nick got out as soon as I drove up. "He's making a lot of noise in there, boss. Breaking things, probably doing a good job trashing his nest."

"His nest. He'll have to sleep in it." I looked at Nick. "You wait for Nathan. Both of you stay out here unless I call. I do not want this to escalate like it did the last time Greg and I . . . talked."

"Got it, Chief. Don't want to escalate the situation on Escalante. Kinda poetic, don't you think?"

"My, my, Nick. Unplumbed depths you have."

"Ya never know, Chief."

I walked up the front steps and stopped at the door. Greg had splintered the frame. Probably kicked it open. I waited until I heard the breaking noises stop.

"Greg. It's Tomas Arnesen."

"Go away. No one here called for you."

"Can't do that, Greg. You're out on bail. I need to talk to you about that. I have some papers for you. Plus, we have to talk about Estella and Emily."

Footsteps pounded hard to the door. I stepped back out of the door's swing path. It didn't swing open. Greg slammed what was left of the frame and the whole door fell onto the porch. Drunk, bleary-eyed, two days unshaven, an odor like rotting fruit rising up off him, Greg tried to face up to me but sagged against the splintered door frame. He held on with one hand, the other hand aimed in my direction, forefinger pointed right at my face. "Where are my guns?"

We'd taken those out of the house when we moved Estella and Emily out to the Nygaard's ranch. "Locked up in my office."

He stared at me, but the look had lost all its flavor. I felt sorry for him. Yeah, I know I shouldn't, I told myself. But I did. Been almost where he was right now, close, so I understood a bit of that wilderness.

"Where're my girls?"

"Gone. Safe."

A tiny light gleamed in his eyes, like a four-watt bulb coming on. "Safe from me, is what you mean."

"Exactly. Glad you understand that."

"Got the restraining order there?" He pointed to the papers in my left hand.

I handed it to him.

He surprised me by taking it, looking at it, and sticking it into his jeans' pocket. "Consider myself served, eh." His laugh covered the moment, but I heard hard bitterness when he asked, "What's next?"

"You stay here, in this house. You keep cool. No confrontations, no problems, no mistakes. If you want to stay drunk, fine. Just stay inside, make all the mess you want. We'll leave you alone until your court date."

"Not good, Tomas. This is not good." Greg pounded the frame behind him with his fist.

"I'm glad you understand, Greg."

"What can I do?" He kept pounding.

"Sober up. Clean up the house. Figure out how to live without the girls in your life for the foreseeable future, and make the best of a rotten situation." I paused for effect then spoke as clearly as I could. "This is your own doing, Greg."

The pounding stopped.

"You son-of-a-bitch. You did this."

"Well, I'm not sure your assessment of my birth status is accurate, but I'm sure nothing of your current situation sticks to me. I'm only picking up the pieces you leave behind."

"You don't pull any punches, do you?"

"Just the ones that need to be pulled in the line of duty. Someone needs to speak truth to you."

"Thought you church people supposed to be all lovey-dovey, preach us sinners some hope or something like that."

"Well, my head tells me I need to love you as one of God's black sheep, but I don't have to love your actions at all. Don't have much hope you'll change. But, yeah, I'll always speak the truth."

Greg stepped out of the door frame, held himself as erect as he could, and faced me, straight on. "Get off my porch. Get off my property. I still have some rights, almost-convicted felon that I am."

I held my hands up. "We still have a public safety obligation to check on you, Greg, to make sure you're all right. Your welfare is actually important to us."

"Arnesen, you're shoveling it, pure and unadulterated, as much as Charlie shovels on that ranch of yours. Just don't come back here yourself. Don't want to see your face again unless . . . ."

His voice trailed off.

"I'll send Nathan, then. That cool with you?"

"Nate. Cool. Yeah. Send him."

"Twice, maybe three times a day, Greg. Don't forget you also have to call your probation officer. You have to check in with the state boys. If you don't, then they call me, then I have to come out here, and then I have to arrest you. Again."

He patted the cell phone clipped to his belt. "Speed dial ten. Already checked in for today. No thanks to you."

"Then, happy drinking and enjoy the solitude."

"Glad to be home, Chief of Public Safety for the oh-so-caring burg of Rosemont, Utah." Greg spit to my left before he turned and stumbled back inside his house.

I listened for a few more moments.

"You still out there, Arnesen? I can hear you breathing. Get the hell off my porch!"

I got the hell off his porch, waved at Nick to leave, and keyed my mike. Nathan needed his new list of responsibilities. He needed to know to be careful. He needed to pay attention.

Greg was mad, alone, and likely to be drunk by morning—an unholy trinity if ever I'd seen one.

36

I knocked on the door at the Nygaard's house. A small voice on the other side of the door said, "Hi."

"Emily, this is Chief Arnesen. How are you?"

"I'm five."

"That's good. Is your mommy there?"

"She's crying."

"Did something happen?"

"Happy tears. Bye."

"Em—"

"Good morning, Tomas." Estella opened the door, wiping at her eyes with a napkin. Now that she'd gotten out from under Greg's control, she seemed, well, more beautiful than before, despite the redness in her eyes. I hoped Yorke wouldn't mind me thinking so.

"Oh, hey, morning Estella. You doing all right?"

"Fine, actually. Tears notwithstanding."

"Emily said they were happy tears?"

"That was my usual response in the bad times when Greg hit me and I had to protect her. Funny thing, this time I wasn't lying to her. These *are* happy tears."

"Being safe has that effect on people sometimes."

She laughed. If Kirsten hadn't already captured me so completely, I'd have considered giving Greg, Yorke, and anyone else a run for their money with her based solely on the sound of her voice. But I could feel the touch, the warmth, the subtle sultry promise of burned fingers if you got too close and weren't invited.

"Safe. Safe. Safe. I haven't felt this good in years, at least five, since Emily was born. I was sitting here in the kitchen, drinking this incredible coffee that Richard makes, watching Emily play with her dolls, and suddenly got overwhelmed by how much my life is changing. Has *already* changed."

"For the better, we hope, Estella. For the better."

"I know that, in my head. Don't know that the full impact has hit me yet."

"Remember, you aren't doing this alone. You and Emily have a lot of friends around here who will help."

She tried to hold back the new tears forming but couldn't. "Oh, Tomas. How can I ever repay you all?"

"That's easy, Estella. Keep Emily safe, start your new life, and enjoy every minute."

She smiled. Add another reason to the list—this was one special woman.

"I know, Tomas. It's hard to imagine getting through any of this, coming even this far, without all our friends here. I honestly didn't know so many cared."

"Greg did a pretty good job of keeping people out of the personal details of your family life, kept you away from people. A lot of us have wanted to help you at different times, but either didn't take the chance or have the courage to reach out."

Estella frowned.

"Sorry. Thoughtless of me to get that personal."

"It's all right. I did love him, once, at least enough to say yes when he asked me to marry him. Now that I can think clearly about our life together, things went downhill halfway through our three-day honeymoon."

Emily and Sylvi danced past the patio window, their laughter echoing off the ranch house's stone walls. Infectious, lilting, uplifting, the interruption seemed more God-sent than coincidence.

"But I have one good blessing from those seven years." Estella stood up, walked to the window, and waved at the dancers. They waved back and kept on dancing.

I watched Estella watching her friend and her daughter. It was better than any television show or movie I'd seen in a long time.

"Dispatch to Rosemont One. What's your twenty?"

"One to Dispatch. At the Nygaard's with Estella."

"Ten-twenty-one, Dispatch."

I wrestled my phone out of the holder that was supposed to be simple and easy to use and hit the number two. Kirsten answered before the first electronic tone ended.

"We've got major trouble, Tomas. Can you get out of there, like, right now, without letting Estella know where you're going?"

"Where am I going?"

"To the Mathiesens. Someone killed Greg. Shot him. You need to get over here now."

We don't get earthquakes in this part of Utah, but I could have sworn I felt the ground move beneath my feet. I placed a hand on the wall next to me to steady myself. *This can't be happening.* "You're there? Who else?"

"Just me and Nathan. Nathan came by to do the welfare checks you gave him. He found Greg."

"OK. On my way now."

I stood up, dropped my phone in my shirt pocket. "Estella, I need to run back to town for a while. Thanks for the visit. Let Sylvi know I had to go." She had to have known something was up. I didn't look at her when I spoke.

"Anything wrong, Tomas?"

"Honestly, I don't know yet. I just need to help Kirsten and Nathan for a bit."

I resisted the temptation to turn on the lights and the siren, but what waited for me didn't need announcing right now. From the Nygaard Ranch Road, I hit Sevier River Road, then turned left onto Escalante. I could see both their cars parked out front. No one else seemed to have discovered their presence. Or, if they had, they weren't paying attention except to look through their windows from behind the curtains.

Kirsten and Nathan stood at the bottom of the front steps.

I pointed to Nathan. "From the beginning."

"I drove up to make my check, as you requested, Chief. Greg didn't answer my knock. I walked around to the back to see if he was out there. Both front and back doors were closed, back door locked. I knocked again, then finally looked through the back door window. Saw him lying on the floor in a pool of blood. Called Kirsten to call you, went back out front to wait. She showed up in about three minutes. Then you."

"We're going in the front door. If he hasn't fixed it since yesterday, it'll fall open when I touch it. Let's go."

I stepped up close and looked the door over. It had been propped up in the opening to look like it had been closed. Did Greg do that, or did the killer? I grabbed the latch and the door indeed fell off its hinges. Inside, that singular mixed odor—blood and death—rode the silence around the house. It smelled fresh, still warm, and we'd probably find his body the same way.

We walked carefully through the house, checking the floors for any signs of traffic, blood trails, dust, some clue to what had happened in the house. We had to tread carefully through broken glass, displaced furniture, torn fabric, pictures either hanging sideways or shattered on the floor. I stopped at the kitchen door and took a mental snapshot of the scene.

Middle of the kitchen floor. Greg on his back. Blood pooling under his body, running down toward the back door. The floor wasn't level. I stood up on tiptoes to see the hole in the center of his chest. Dead like Seth and Tate, but not shot in the head.

"Take a look in here, you two. Tell me what you see. I waved Nathan and Kirsten to come stand in the doorway. I stepped into the kitchen to the left side of the door.

"Looks clean, Tomas. Not much here to see except for Greg." Kirsten said.

"What are we looking for, Chief?" Nathan looked puzzled.

"How would you describe the shape of things as we walked back here, through the house?"

"A mess."

"Yeah. Greg must have been really snockered to make this mess in his own place." Nathan still wandered in the dark.

"But the kitchen's not a mess." Kirsten said, stepping a little way into the light. When she did, I saw her ashen face clearly in the pale light. She may have just been putting on a good show for Nathan's sake, but she was unnerved. Heck, so was I, but this was the job.

"Oh, man, you're right." Nathan jumped on the bandwagon now.

"What do you think about that?" I prodded.

"Either Greg hadn't gotten to the kitchen yet in his drunken state or someone else cleaned this up after killing him." Kirsten answered.

"Which do you think is the more likely explanation?"

"Well, the obvious one is that he hadn't gotten to the kitchen." Nathan was doing his best to be a cop despite his training as a paramedic. He was better suited to work before a body was cold.

"Obvious. Yes." I replied. "Maybe too obvious?"

Kirsten turned around and looked down the hallway toward the front of the house. I had an inkling where she was headed.

"If the killer came through the back door, found Greg in the kitchen, shot him, cleaned up any signs of his presence, and left without seeing the rest of the house, he or she wouldn't have a clue about the mess Greg had made in the front of the house."

"Yeah, yeah. He wouldn't know the rest of the place was a mess and that cleaning things up out here would stick out like Chinle shale in Navajo sandstone."

"So where do you think I want you to go look for evidence?" I looked at Nathan.

"Back porch and yard area. Mark where I find anything."

"Good boy. Bring me the other camera before you do that. I want to get the pictures in here while you're outside."

"Got it, Chief. Back in a second."

"Nathan. Slow down. No need to hurry. Walk carefully back out. Just in case the killer did go out that way."

"Jeesh, Tomas. Sorry."

"No sweat. Just relax and take your time. I know this is not a regular part of your duty, but you have had training in this."

Kirsten stepped into the room and stood next to me, shoulder-to-shoulder. "When were you over here, Tomas?"

"Yesterday morning."

"Then where did you go?"

"Back to the office. Paperwork. Then dinner with you. Took you home then I drove out to the ranch. This looks to have happened last night or early this morning while I was at the ranch."

I caught her sideways glance at the body. "Kirsten. I did not kill Greg. I know it looks kinda bad. I did not do this."

Her perfect blue eyes locked onto mine. "I know. But Deputy Yorke is going to ask you those questions."

My throat did a half gainer into my stomach. *She's right.* "All I can do is tell the truth. Everything between Greg and me last week is public record. People are going to talk. People are going to wonder if Greg maybe wasn't telling the truth at the town meeting when he suggested I could be the murderer. There's not a damn thing I can do about that."

She held my hand. We didn't talk anymore.

Three minutes later, Nathan handed me the camera. "I'm going out back."

"Holler if you find something. Photograph it but don't do anything with whatever it is until I see it in place."

"Gotcha."

"Time to get all the wheels rolling. You call the Sheriff's Office, ask for Yorke. Tell him what's happened, that he needs to get down here, again. Then call Burchfield's office, then the funeral home. I want everyone in the loop on this. Nothing hidden. We run this investigation same way as the other two murders."

Kirsten hesitated, reaching for her radio mike and her phone. She reached out and patted my shirt front. "Good. Still wearing your vest."

"I promised. All the time. I get up in the morning, I put it on. Don't like it. Never have liked wearing it. But I promised you, so that's it."

"Sweet boy, you are." She hesitated again. "Will it be enough?"

"The vest? Or the truth? Both, I hope. The truth is all I have right now. All *we* have. But if you hesitate any longer making those calls, someone will indeed start asking other questions, like why it took us so long to notify other authorities, why it took us so long to get the information out, why it took us so long to ask for help."

True to form, she snapped into professional mode in the split-second after I stopped talking. She walked carefully down the hallway and I heard the radio call go out.

Of all things, Greg, why'd you have to do this *to me?*

37

Kirsten and I were typing our final reports about Greg's death and the crime scene. I was still cleaning up my typos. Her reports were usually letter-perfect first time out.

Yorke was not smiling when he walked into the office. But he did make direct eye contact with me, a good thing as far as I was concerned, even considering the circumstances. I was surprised when acting county attorney Emery Burchfield walked in right behind him.

Yorke was more curt than usual. "Interview room. Now. All of you."

"Good afternoon to you, Deputy Yorke, Mr. Burchfield."

Yorke shook his head, as though trying to warn me. I knew what he was doing and what he was trying to tell me, but it didn't matter. Burchfield was a small-town, tiny-county political hack with his eyes on some prize only he could see. Up to now, he hadn't involved himself for more than thirty seconds in two murders, didn't even seem interested. All of a sudden, here he comes, since an officer of the court might have been involved in a third murder.

Burchfield, slicked-back hair likely as black as his heart, stared at me. I think he meant it to be intimidating. It wasn't. But I decided not to press the matter. No point in attempting humor in this moment.

Burchfield was a black hole for anything remotely witty. It went in, never came out, and had no effect on him whatsoever.

"Through that door, good sirs." I replied.

"Lead the way, Arnesen." Burchfield held out his hand, inviting me to lead.

I led them into the room and stood to the side of the door as they entered. I waited for them to sit, curious to see how Yorke would play out the group's dynamics against Burchfield's presence. When the deputy sat down three chairs away from the attorney, I sighed as quietly as I could and sat two chairs away, opposite Burchfield, one chair away from Yorke. Kirsten sat down next to me.

Burchfield flipped open a folder, then pulled a pocket-sized digital recorder out of his pocket, turned it on, and set it on the tabletop, microphones facing my direction. Burchfield finally looked up at me. "OK if we record this interview, Chief Arnesen?"

"Yes."

Silence. Burchfield clearly had expected me to protest or say something funny or say no. He hadn't crafted a response for a simple yes. I chose not to break the silence. Next move was up to him.

"November fifteenth at thirteen-thirty. Rosemont, Utah. Interview room at the Rosemont Public Safety Office. Engelmann County Prosecuting Attorney Emery Burchfield conducting an interview with Rosemont Public Safety Chief, Tomas Arnesen. Witnesses are Deputy Sheriff Trooper Yorke, Engelmann County Sheriff's Department, and . . . ." He looked over the rim of his glasses at Kirsten. "What's your name, honey?"

I shifted in my seat, but she didn't flinch. "My name is Kirsten Dyrdahl, Rosemont Safety Team Dispatcher." Now she leaned closer to the microphone as if talking to a tiny office scribe inside the box. "And please, when you make the transcription of this recording, make sure Mr. Burchfield's sexist and demeaning attitude toward one of the witnesses is accurately reflected in the text."

That stopped Burchfield, but only for a few seconds. A barely audible laugh escaped his pursed lips. He recovered his balance, smiled at Kirsten like he was patting the head of a small wayward child, then turned to me, throwing the question at me to perhaps catch me off guard.

"Did you kill Gregory Mathiesen?"

I paused just to let Burchfield think he was doing something important. "No."

Silence. He stared at me, that not-intimidating stare. I stared back. Out of the corner of my eye, I saw a half-smile curl up Yorke's lip then fade away.

Burchfield ran both hands through his hair. "So, you didn't kill Rosemont City Council member Gregory Mathiesen?"

"No."

More silence. He looked down at the file folder spread open in front of him, shuffled two or three pages, then picked one out and held it up.

"The medical examiner's preliminary report places Gregory Mathiesen's time of death at approximately oh-four-thirty hours, Wednesday, November fourteenth. Where were you then?"

"Hanging out at my house on the ranch, probably asleep." I snapped my fingers. "Oh, yeah. At oh-four-thirty I was up peeing. Too much sweet tea with a late dinner."

"Mr. Arnesen, please don't make light of the fact that yet another man was murdered on your watch. Can anyone corroborate his story?"

"That I was up peeing?"

"That you were at your house on the ranch."

"I can. I was with Tomas at the ranch." I tried to make sure my face did not register surprise at Kirsten's announcement. "We drove out there in the late afternoon after I got off work. We spent the night together and drove back to town at oh-six-thirty. He went to the office. I went to the store to open up."

I watched Burchfield's face as he ran his right forefinger down another page, lips moving as he read the text. He frowned.

"When did you drive out to the Nygaard's, Arnesen?"

"Drove out there at about thirteen-thirty. Talked with Emily and Estella. Kirsten called me at fourteen-ten for my twenty and asked me to call back on my cell phone."

"Why on your cell phone?"

"Kirsten didn't want to take the chance that some of our listening ears might overhear the call about Greg's murder."

"Listening ears?"

Man, this guy was dense. "We have a lot of people around here who have scanners and like to listen to the calls. Their version of reality television, I guess."

"Ah. Well then. OK." He looked back down at his notes, like a poker player keeps peeking at his hole cards even though he knows exactly what the two cards are. "You left the house at fourteen-ten and drove straight to the Mathiesen residence?"

"I did exactly that."

"How long did it take for you to call for backup?"

"Didn't call for backup. Nathan and Kirsten were already there. We examined the scene, took photographs, did our preliminary investigations, got as much information collected as we could. While Nathan and I were conducting the first phase of the investigation, I instructed Kirsten to contact the Engelmann County Sheriff's office, specifically Deputy Yorke, then to call the funeral home. Deputy Yorke called the state boys to let them know what was happening. We had a state forensics team and deputy medical examiner helicoptered into Rosemont in three hours. They took over the investigation at that point."

Burchfield sat back in the chair and stared out into the space over the office table. He flipped the file folder shut, stood, and nodded to Yorke. "Serve the warrants."

Yorke shrugged his shoulders and stood up. He pulled two long pieces of paper out of his brown leather portfolio and handed them to me.

"Sorry, Chief. I don't have a choice."

I was reading the top paper while he talked. *Arrest Warrant: Suspicion of Murder.* Second and third were search warrants for the public safety office and for my home. I stood up and stared at Burchfield while accepting this ridiculous new reality. "I understand, Deputy Yorke. He's the legal officer and you uphold the law." I pointed at Burchfield. "In this case, as he sees fit to enforce it."

"Chief Tomas Arnesen, please place your weapons, badge, and

radio on the table. Then turn around with your hands behind your head, fingers laced together."

Before I completely complied with Yorke's orders, I tossed my cell phone to Kirsten. "Call Ryan McFadden, Salt Lake City, speed dial fourteen. Tell him what's going on and ask him how soon he can get down here."

I looked over at Burchfield. His smug expression had faded, and his eyes were a little wider than when he'd set my arrest in motion. That reaction seems to happen every time I mention Ryan McFadden's name, especially among prosecutors.

Once my fingers were laced, Yorke took my hands down, put the handcuffs on, and read me my rights.

Like popcorn kernels going off in the microwave, so many witty and trenchant words came to mind, but I wisely left them unspoken. That time. "What's next?" I asked Burchfield.

"What? You don't know how we do this?" Smug mask returned, the attorney took a tone like I was a six-year-old attending my first Law Day.

"We take you to the county jail and book you. Then you wait for your arraignment when the Sixth District Court's Judge Randell will advise you of the charges, make sure you understand your rights, and enter your plea: guilty or not guilty. I'm going to ask to expedite the process so we can get the date set immediately for the preliminary hearing. I'm asking for high bail given the nature of the crimes in question. At the preliminary hearing, if you've pled not guilty when I've presented the state's evidence against you, you will be bound over for trial for manslaughter at least, and first degree murder at best."

"Confident, aren't we? Maybe a little overconfident? You seem to be getting a little ahead of yourself, Mr. Burchfield." I tried to keep his attention focused on me for another few seconds.

"We'll see who's overconfident, Arnesen."

"Long as I get my day in court."

"You're going to get a lot more than your day in court. You better start thinking about your days in prison."

He turned to Kirsten and held out his hand. "I'll take that phone, young lady. That's evidence."

Burchfield, as always, underestimated Kirsten's skills. She'd found the number, memorized it, programmed her phone, and had her phone to her ear as she flipped mine to Burchfield. The way her cheeks quivered, I knew she was straining to keep her smile from getting too big and rosy.

"Be sure and tell Colin he can send the Welling watchdogs home."

"You sure about that, Tomas?" Kirsten looked surprised.

"Got a feeling we don't need them right now. Maybe not any more at all."

"Will do. Anything else I can tell Mr. Parkin?"

"Nope. Send them home with our thanks. Tell him I'll talk to him later. Thank him properly, in person, with a good handshake."

Burchfield couldn't resist a parting shot. "Kinda hard to shake a person's hand on the other side of the glass in the visiting room at county. Come on, let's get going. Sooner we get you into the system, the sooner I can get things rolling to keep you in the system."

Justice delayed is justice denied, so they say, whoever they are. In this case, I was entirely hopeful that justice expedited would turn out to be simply justice.

38

"So what do they have, and how do we take care of it?"

Professional to his well-paid core, Ryan McFadden wasted no time on courtesies. Probably one of the reasons I liked him so much. That he'd been voted the Least Likely to Amount to Anything in high school hadn't bothered him at all. Wound up graduating from the University of Missouri-Columbia, then Brigham Young University Law School. I was glad to have one of the best criminal defense attorneys in Utah sitting across from me in the jail.

"A lot of nothing. But there's one small potential hitch."

Ryan raised his left eyebrow.

"Kirsten lied during the interview. Burchfield has it on tape. She said she was with me the night Mathiesen was killed."

"So, you were alone. Where?"

"At the ranch."

Ryan did some quick calculations in his head. "Twenty minutes from town. Ten minutes at the scene. Twenty minutes back to the ranch. Lots of time on the road. Even late at night, someone might have seen your truck on the road. Know if Burchfield or his investigator has covered that?"

"Not sure. More than likely. The investigator on this is good. Deputy Sheriff Trooper Yorke, Engelmann County."

"But you didn't go out anytime, so no one could have seen you driving back and forth."

"Nope. I ate dinner. Mabel could give you the menu, exact times when she served it, and when, exactly, I left the main house for my cabin. If I had left, I'd bet you five hundred dollars she saw me go. Whether or not anyone could get her to say anything is another story. But since I didn't leave, you won't necessarily need her testimony."

"I'll talk to her just the same, cover all the bases." He twirled his black-and-gold Mont Blanc fountain pen in the fingers of his right hand like a baton. "Think Kirsten's story will hold up?"

"Don't know. She said no one saw her go home. She went in the back door, no lights on anywhere. Her porch light burned out last week. It's a quiet spot in the block."

"How about the next morning?"

"No one out. Townsfolk would assume I dropped her off at the store to open up, just like she said."

"We'll leave it be for now."

"If Burchfield does get something on this part of the story, you're going to have a much more interesting time defending me. And her."

"So I'd earn my princely fee in that case rather than the paltry sums I'm charging you?" He gave me a thumbs up, mostly for the sake of the jail officer keeping watch over us from a distance. "Burchfield, I heard tell, is requesting no bail, given the fact that you might be involved in three murders and could be a flight risk. He's playing this for all it's worth." Ryan started to get up.

"Leave it alone. He's already said he was going to request an expedited preliminary hearing in District Court. Judge Randell will be here tomorrow. I can handle jail until then. Burchfield wants the system to work quickly. Don't see too many felony cases like this down here. He's not going to want to mess things up by not getting things done in a timely manner." I laughed.

Ryan didn't. "OK. That way I also get to see what Burchfield has. You say he took weapons from the office and from the house?"

"Only from home, my eighteen-sixty Navy Colt revolver. He sent it to the lab for testing, powder residue, powder's chemical composition, metallurgy on the caps and balls, had it been recently fired, those tests."

"I'll get to see those. Anything else I need to know before I start my paperwork blizzard?"

"Deputy Yorke asked me if I killed Mathiesen. He was mostly sure I hadn't and almost positive I'm not implicated in the other two. I told him no way I'm the killer."

"How'd he take it?"

"As the truth. He's an ally. If you need something from inside, talk to Yorke. He'll help."

"Good to know. You still have two visitors, Yorke and Kirsten. Neither one will leave until they've had a chance to talk to you. Kirsten is being especially difficult. Sheriff said it was fine with him. Just don't take too long. Who's first?"

"Yorke first. Then Kirsten. Much better to end this day wrapped up in beauty."

Ryan nodded at the guard who opened the door. On his way out, he bellowed at Yorke and held up a hand to stop Kirsten from rushing into the room. "Gently, dear. A little more police work it seems, then he's all yours."

Yorke and I shook hands. "So what's up, my arresting officer?"

"Sheesh, Arnesen. Don't rub it in."

"Last time mentioned."

"Good. Now, here's some good news for a change. We might've caught a small break."

I sat up straighter. "Tell me more, you who are so gentle with cuffing a suspect."

"Ouch. Next time I'll ease up on the professional courtesy and treat you like a real suspect."

We both laughed. The tightness around my shoulders eased up. "So what's in the folder?"

He flipped it open on the table and tapped his finger at the bottom of the top page. "This is what's up. They found a thread on Greg's body that didn't match anything he was wearing when he was shot. Turned out to be a thread from a leather work glove. A real common type and impossible to trace, so generic. But it's still a lead."

I held up a finger and closed my eyes. *Leather work gloves. An overflowing mound of leather work gloves.*

"Got it. Have Nathan go to the Emporium. Seth has . . . had a huge bin of used work gloves. Have Nathan collect, bag, and tag every glove in the bin and in the store. Box them up and send them to state."

Yorke nodded ever so slightly. "Worth a shot. Maybe match something up or get another clue to follow. Sounds good. Will keep you posted on what comes out of the glove hunt."

"Thanks." We shook again. Yorke smiled as he followed my gaze toward the face glaring at him from behind the wired glass window. "I'll send her in now if that's good with you."

I didn't answer him and I didn't wait for her to sit down. "Well, offering an alibi for me wasn't too smart, was it?"

"I don't care, Tomas. Burchfield is not going to get any political leverage using you as his scapegoat or his ladder to new heights."

"Interesting reason for lying on the record, honey." I smiled.

"Good enough for me, sweetheart." She laughed, a lovely sound, one I needed to hear.

I could also hear tension in her voice, that question bubbling inside her, the big one I knew she didn't want to ask but needed to ask. I preempted her. "Do you trust me?"

"Implicitly."

I spoke directly and slowly. "I did not go back to Mathiesen's house after I dropped you off at home. And, just another reminder here, if anyone saw you go into your apartment at midnight, Burchfield can serve both of us on toast."

"No one saw me. Not on the street, not on the sidewalk. No one. But that's not all that's bothering you, is it?"

"Kirsten, Greg's murder doesn't fit the pattern. You know that. Shot in the heart, not in the forehead. It still feels deliberate. Cold-blooded for sure. Reptilian, in fact. Almost feels like, well, I can't get my finger on it."

"Maybe to throw suspicion on to you? Which it has in a major way."

"That thought scares me."

"Why?"

"Because it means whoever is doing this knows me, knows what's been going on in Rosemont, and, at the very least, has an ulterior motive involving me that I don't understand."

I hadn't put those pieces together until that moment. I stood up and walked to the back wall of the interview room. I stood there, looking over Kirsten's head through the glass window in the door. "It's like standing in my canyon. When I showed it to you, I hadn't noticed that back slot going up to the top. Never saw it until a new set of eyes opened the path for me. I can see this way right in front of me, the next few hours, next couple of days, but out there, beyond, this damn murderous highway is going to take a turn. I can't see beyond that curve yet, but I know the answer is around the bend."

"Then, when you get out, we'll work harder to solve these murders and stop whoever is killing our friends." She placed her hand on the glass plate in front of her.

I walked back over and did the same, covering hers with mine, feeling its warmth, or believing that I could. No way I deserved this woman. And no way did she deserve to have to defend me, to lie for me.

Fix it, Arnesen. Solve these cases or you could lose more than just your freedom.

39

"I can see where you'd think Mr. Arnesen had motive, Mr. Burchfield. But that motive is so slim we could probably hide it behind a rake handle." Sixth District Court Judge Ellis Randell looked over the top of his glasses at Burchfield, then held out an open palm toward me. "A decorated police officer, retired to his hometown, getting paid a pittance to help protect his friends and neighbors, kills another man to, what, protect his position, his status? Thin. Very thin."

"Given Mr. Arnesen's previous history? His suspension?"

"I am not terribly inclined to worry about Mr. Arnesen's previous history." Judge Randell pushed his glasses back up higher onto his nose.

Burchfield nearly shouted his reply. "But the record shows clear evidence of a proclivity to violence."

"*But* is the northbound end of a southbound mule deer, Mr. Burchfield."

"Your Honor?"

"Acting prosecuting attorney Burchfield, the defendant's prior record with the Louisville Police Department is not relevant to this proceeding. If anything, I am inclined to note that during his career with the aforementioned department, Chief Arnesen received nineteen merit awards and commendations, one medal of valor, at least forty-six letters of appreciation, the senders of which included the governor of the great state of Kentucky, four mayors, and eight prosecutors—not acting ones in a tiny county in Utah. Move on."

Burchfield gulped. He leaned over the podium, his hands gripping the smooth wood edges. His eyes surveyed the empty room, as if searching for someone to tell him what to do next. A low-level hum replied. I hoped he was hearing the swirling white noise of his budding career going down the drain.

"Well, as Chief of the Public Safety Detachment in Rosemont, Mr. Arnesen had the means at hand. Multiple firearms in his office as well as the one we confiscated at the ranch." Regaining a bit of his swagger, he pointed to my 1860 Colt Navy on the evidence table in front of the clerk.

"Yes. Means. A bit stronger than his motive. You recovered a revolver similar to the one the crime lab says was probably used to kill Mr. Mathiesen and the other two victims."

"Your Honor, might I request we review the crime lab's report on my client's weapon?" Ryan McFadden, my Salt Lake City attorney, stood and held out his copy of the report.

"Objection!" Burchfield shouted.

"Tsk. Tsk. Tsk. Mr. Burchfield. Remember? This is a preliminary hearing. We can be a little less rigorous, or zealous as may be the case. There's no one here but me. See? The jury box is empty." Judge Randell nodded at my lawyer. "Go ahead, Mr. McFadden. And might I say it is an honor to have you in my court today, the reasons notwithstanding."

"Thank you, your honor. We stipulate that this is the revolver Deputy Trooper Yorke, Engelmann County Sheriff's Department, confiscated using a duly executed search warrant. The chain of evidence has been maintained. In their investigation, the lab report states, and here I am reading directly from the text: 'This weapon has not been fired within the last several months. There was no powder residue, no inordinate amounts of cleaning materials used on the weapon's chambers or barrel. We tested the gun powder seized at the defendant's residence along with cap-and-ball ammunition. The powder's chemical signature did not match that of the residue recovered from the three murders, which we also tested. The ball ammunition also does not match those recovered from the crime scenes.' End of quote." McFadden held the report folder a little higher and smiled at Burchfield. "Here's the kicker, your Honor. The lab report reads, and again I quote: 'This weapon could not have been used in the three shootings in Engelmann County.' End quote. End report. End means."

"Mr. Burchfield? Did you recover any other black powder weapons, rifles, or revolvers from the Rosemont Public Safety Office or from Chief Arnesen's home?"

"No, Your Honor. We did not."

"Well, let's see what we have here. Thin motive hiding behind a rake handle. Means just unshot down, pardon the pun." Judge Randell cackled. "Is that about it? Oh, no, wait. I forgot. Means. Motive and, wait for it—opportunity. How about that, Mr. Burchfield?"

Emery Burchfield stepped back from the podium, his shoulders beginning to sag despite his best efforts to retain control. He held his case file folder in his right hand. It looked to me like he was signaling defeat.

"Oh, right. Now where is that deposition section? Ah. Here 'tis." Randell held up his papers and made a show of reading from them. "Unimpeachable witnesses. Solid statement. Corroboration, also on tape. Suspect was far away from crime scene at time of the crime. Yep. There it goes." The judge tossed the folder of papers off to the side of his desk. "Did you all see that?" he asked to no one in particular and everyone in the room. "Opportunity just flew away. No means. No motive. No opportunity."

I leaned forward in my seat, trying not to celebrate too soon, knowing how close Kirsten still skated to the edge of perjury, how close that could still bring me back to standing in front of Ellis Randell, me the one in handcuffs again.

"Case dismissed, with prejudice." He slammed his gavel down on the wooden block.

Burchfield jumped three inches off the floor, turned to stare at Kirsten then at me, then executed a pretty smart about-face, and pushed his way through the crowd.

"Just a moment, Mr. Burchfield. I'd like to see you in my chambers.

In addition to this superbly botched miscarriage of justice, there's a small matter of your sexist comments to Miss Dyrdahl in your initial interview with Chief Tomas. How very sloppy of you." Judge Randell got up from the bench and walked down to the door to his office. The bailiff held it open for him and waited for Burchfield to turn around and come back.

Burchfield dragged his feet into Randell's chambers like a schoolchild called to the principal's office for the first time. "This is not over, Arnesen. Not by a long shot," he muttered as he passed me.

"Excuse me, Mr. Burchfield. Are you, an officer of the court, threatening my client?" Ryan made sure everyone else in the room heard him. The bailiff and judge stepped toward us.

"I did nothing of the sort."

"Quote: 'This is not over, Arnesen. Not by a long shot.' End quote. Sounds punitive. I could construe it as a threat as well. Are you perhaps making this case more personal than professional?"

Burchfield glared at Ryan, who smiled and looked back without blinking.

I loved that Ryan was never really off the job. And that he knew every last inch of the law. The judge stared at our little tableau. He nudged the bailiff who walked toward us.

Burchfield saw the bailiff walking toward him. He held up his hands. "Apologies, Mr. Arnesen, Mr. McFadden. I meant no harm. The stress of this case seems to have clouded my judgment more than I thought."

"Well said, sir. Thank you." Ryan turned to the judge. "You will have the paperwork filed in a timely manner, Judge Randell, so my client can leave and get back to his home?"

"Within the half hour you can drive him to Rosemont, Mr. McFadden." Randell crooked a finger at Burchfield. "Step into my chambers."

40

True to his word, the judge had the papers taken care of and Ryan drove us back to Rosemont.

He glanced at Kirsten sitting in the passenger seat. "Given our success back there, young lady, I will not remonstrate with you about the foolish alibi you tried to give Tomas."

"I didn't want Burchfield to use Tomas."

"I understand that, Miss Dyrdahl. I'd heard a couple of stories in Salt Lake about the acting prosecuting attorney in Engelmann County. He didn't even manage to live down to those expectations in person."

Ryan glanced at me in the rearview mirror. "Your young lady apparently does not have much confidence in my abilities."

"My young lady didn't know you were my lawyer until I asked her to call you."

"So, Miss Dyrdahl, had you known Tomas had criminal representation of the caliber of one Ryan McFadden, would you have lied to the county prosecutor?"

She placed her index finger on her chin. "Probably."

"Probably? Why so?"

"Because I still wouldn't have had much to go on, except your reputation, and reputations can be misleading, or fabricated, or based on a single fortunate trial outcome which the attorney in question continues to use to pad his or her resumé."

"Ouch. Tell me more, young lady."

"My name is Kirsten. I'd rather you call me by my name. 'Young lady' reeks of Burchfield calling me 'honey' and some of the idiot, adolescent-brained Rosemont men who insist on calling me 'sweetie' when they come into the store."

"My apologies, Kirsten. I meant no harm. It won't happen again. Lawyer's honor."

Kirsten laughed. "Apology accepted, for that joke alone."

"Now, indulge me. Why would knowing who Tomas's lawyer was might not have changed your attitude about lying for him?"

"Again, let me repeat for the second time, the answer is simple. I didn't know you, Mr. McFadden."

"Reciprocity here. Call me Ryan."

"Because, Ryan, I make judgments about people's trustworthiness based on my personal interactions with them. We hadn't had any interaction, at least until I called you."

"Now?"

"I will not put myself or Tomas in jeopardy again, Ryan. I will trust you, as our friend and a pretty good lawyer, to take care of Tomas."

I waited for Ryan to react.

"A pretty good lawyer?" Wide-eyed, he stared at Kirsten. "Not great?"

Kirsten sighed like she was explaining how you make scrambled eggs to a five-year-old. "I don't know if you're great or good based on your reputation because I haven't seen you in action. Until now." She smiled.

Ryan's cheeks flushed. He fancied himself a ladies' man, a bachelor with a beautiful woman on his arm at every gala he attended. I knew he had no defenses against Kirsten's simple, clear beauty and that devastatingly real smile.

"I bow to your insights, Kirsten. Thank you for your honesty. I think I may have to come down here more often to visit."

"You're welcome to visit us any time, Ryan."

"Us. Not you?"

I smothered a laugh and failed, choking on my laughter. This was going to be fun.

"Why, Mr. McFadden. I think you're flirting with me right in front of my boyfriend. Shameless. What will your girlfriends say?"

"I won't tell them if you won't."

"But I might." I leaned my head between their two seats. "Ease up, Ryan. She is totally, completely, and in all other ways out of our collective reach."

"Why, then, is she reaching back to hold your hand at this very instant?" Ryan grinned.

"If I had a reasonable answer for that question, my good friend, I'd be both satisfied and wise. She tells me she loves me, but since I don't have a clue why, I plan to do my best to enjoy it and not mess things up."

"Not mess things up too badly, that's the subtext behind your claim to uncertainty." Ryan laughed, and the Mustang swerved onto the shoulder of the highway.

"Careful there, mate. I've never known you to be distracted by a lady. Watching you struggle with my Kirsten is a new and rather fascinating event for me."

"Never met someone this distracting. Smart. Beautiful. Wise beyond her years. How'd you do it, Tomas?"

"He didn't, Ryan. I did. If I'd waited for him to make a move, a first move, any move, I'd still be waiting." She squeezed my hand.

"I think we are going to have to have a few brews at The Cliff so you can tell me exactly what it is about Tomas, I mean, the whole story, from the beginning. Where does it begin by the way? Give me a hint of the rest of the promising and rich fable you will spin for me over dinner and ambers tonight."

Kirsten looked at me, then gazed forward, looking back through time. "I was nine. He was twenty-nine, home for a visit. I followed him around town for three days, watching, listening. He never told me to go away. Every once in a while he'd stop and talk to me like I was a real person, not some gawky, pig-tailed brat making a nuisance of herself. I could see how much he loved the people here, how much they loved him in return. Everyone wanted to spend time with him. Me included.

That's when it started. I went home and told my Grandma Astrid I knew who I was going to marry when I grew up. She asked me who the lucky fellow was. I said, 'I'm going to marry Tomas Arnesen.'"

Grandma didn't blink an eye. 'That's a perfect choice, my dear. Are you going to tell him?'

"I said, 'Not right away, Grandma. I'm going to give him some time to get used to the idea.' So I gave him time."

Ryan was staring at me in the rearview mirror. He shook his head, slowed down, and pulled the Mustang off to the side of the road. Engine idling, Ryan faced Kirsten. "This is too much. How about you get out and get in the back seat rather than climb over. Although that would be enjoyable to watch in the rearview mirror. Hang on now."

Ryan McFadden, bachelor king of Salt Lake City, got out of his black Mustang GT, walked around, and opened the passenger door for Kirsten. She got out. Ryan flipped the seat forward and she slid into the back seat next to me. "Buckle up, kiddies."

"Thank you, Ryan McFadden." She held her hand up to him. He took it, bowed over it, kissed it, then passed her hand to me so we could continue holding hands.

Back in the driver's seat, looking and speaking straight ahead, he said, "This will be the last time I play chauffeur for you, Tomas Arnesen. Kirsten, however, I will drive you any place, any time, with or without him."

"Thank you, good sir." She looked at me as Ryan gunned the engine and spit a gravel contrail behind us as he hit the highway again. "He doesn't give up easily, does he?"

"Nope. He doesn't. However, in your case, in our case, he will. Won't you?"

Ryan answered by running the Mustang up to seventy-five, holding it there, fueling the supercharger with more raucous laughter as the highway rolled up behind us into Rosemont. His amusement continued over dinner which included more than a few ambers. We left the Mustang parked at The Cliff. Kirsten and I carried Ryan back to my office and deposited him on the cot.

"He's a good friend, isn't he?" Kirsten said as she pulled the blanket up over him.

"Right up there on the trophy shelf with Seth. He came out to Kentucky during my hearings and trials as moral support. My union lawyer deferred to him several times during the processes. Yeah. A good friend. Maybe even a great friend."

Kirsten nodded through a yawn.

"You need to get to sleep as well. Been a long few days for us." I led her toward the door. "Want to walk or shall I drive you home?"

"Let's walk. It's cold, but I want to walk, look at the stars, and not think about any of this ugliness around us, just for a little while. Can we do that?"

"We can."

I held the door open and walked her home. We both stumbled a few times trying to look up at the stars, sideways at each other, and ahead into the darkness. At her apartment door, we stood like two high schoolers on their first date, smiling like a couple of naive kids who didn't know how much harder life could get. In our just-inebriated-enough states, the tragic events of the last month were blurry, peripheral issues to the only thing that mattered to us right then: each other. Though my world had been the size of Rosemont ever since I'd moved back, that world had quickly shrunk to just enough space to wrap around Kirsten Dyrdahl and myself. I knew there was so much else that mattered right now, so much I had to do to seek justice for my town, for my friends, but when I got honest with myself, she was the only one that mattered. I was going to find this killer because I wanted to look cool for a girl. Was is that simple? Maybe. Maybe not. All I knew is that on that doorstep, on that night, with that woman, I longed for this moment to never end. I wanted her with me, always. I wanted her to—

Kirsten kissed me.

"Good night, Mr. Thinks-Too-Much-And-Acts-Too-Late. See you in the morning before work. I'll come by the office."

I'm certain I've never worn as stupid a grin as then. "Roger that. Come early enough for tea, coffee, and scones at Heavenly Grounds. My treat."

"Yes. Your treat. Night."

I waited until I heard the locks click and saw the porch light out and the living room lights on. She stood in the window and waved.

By the time I got back to the office I was chilled through and through. Ryan was snoring louder than the Mustang's engine winding out to max rpms, so I went into the conference room, grabbed another blanket and three pillows on the way, and crashed there. It wasn't the best night's sleep I'd ever had, but dreaming about Kirsten helped.

41

The moment he awoke, Ryan mumbled, "Need coffee."

I walked with him to Sarah's. Kirsten met us on the way. No one said much until after the first cup. Ryan tried to sneer at me when I ordered my Earl Grey but failed.

Kirsten laughed, and that made Ryan hold his head and moan. "Hurts because you feel guilty about last night," Kirsten said.

"Guilty? How you figure that?" he muttered.

"Look at me. Look at Tomas. No hangovers. We drank as much as you did. Do you see us suffering?"

Ryan glared at us through one barely open eye. "No. You suffer from the disease of morning insufferableness or unsufferability or something like that. There's something disturbing and very wrong about your cheerfulness and vigor."

She patted him on the hand, and he pulled it back like she'd shocked him. "We don't have hangovers because we don't feel guilty about drinking. Pure and simple."

"Hogwash. Old wives' tale." Ryan still couldn't get the morning fuzz out of his vocal cords.

Kirsten plowed on, ignoring Ryan's humbuggery. "Question that concerns me is why you feel guilty for drinking like that. Must be something back there in your past? We could help you discover that, perhaps, help you get rid of it. Then you can drink yourself silly and wake up next morning with nothing in your mouth that feels like you gargled with steel wool."

Ryan took a deep breath. "I need some air. Too much philosophizing for this hour of the morning."

The coffee shop doorbell jingled. I looked around. "What's up, Emma?"

Our mayor had only cracked the door open. She didn't come in. "Tomas? Can you come over to the council chambers?" Her well-rehearsed poker face, useful for all things political, wasn't working on me.

"Sure. When?" I donned my best poker face too. I doubt she fell for it either.

"Now. Please."

"OK."

She didn't wait to see if I would follow, just turned and walked out and back down the street.

"Mayor Fosberg is requesting my presence in the council chambers. Want to come along? Hopefully I won't need your kind of representation when I'm there, but who knows."

Ryan tried to blink away his hangover. "Sure. Moral support?"

"Not sure. Back of my neck is tickling me. Something about this does not feel kosher."

We walked into the council chambers. Ryan, two full cups of coffee warming his insides, seemed to get steadier with every step. He went through the door first and slid to the right. He held his hand behind his back and motioned me to come in slowly. I did.

The Rosemont Town Council members sat in their large black and very expensive conference room chairs. Emery Burchfield sat in Gregory Mathiesen's chair. I looked across the countertop at Lukas Sogard, Freda Jacobsen, Reinert Tonnessen, Anborg Laake, and Mayor Emma Fosberg. I ignored Burchfield. He glared at Ryan, who smiled back.

"Tomas. Please. Come in, take a seat." Emma pointed at a single, small-backed desk chair sitting in the middle of the floor where the podium and microphone usually sat. I walked toward it then decided to sit down in the first row of chairs where the good citizens of Rosemont sat. Nathan and Nick were sitting in that same row. Kirsten followed and sat down next to me.

"Arnesen—" Lukas Sogard pointed to the chair again.

By this time, I'd started to get fed up with their disrespect. I was still an appointed official. "Chief Tomas is fine. Chief Arnesen is better. If you can't summon up the courtesy to use either of those titles, Mr. Arnesen also works."

Burchfield rocked back and forth in Greg's chair, an ugly little smirk running back and forth on his face.

"Not for long, you ain't no Chief." Cowboy Reinert, Lukas's lapdog and partner in crime, bounced up out of his chair.

"Shut up and sit down, Reinert." Emma put on her mayoral manner and voice. "Chief Arnesen, the Engelmann County prosecuting attorney—"

"—you mean *acting* Engelmann County prosecuting attorney, don't you?" Ryan spoke.

That made Burchfield stop his rocking, but the springs on the chairs were so strong it almost popped him out onto the council tabletop in front of him. He had to catch himself with his hands.

"You're making this terribly hard, Tomas," Emma said.

"I'm not making anything here, Mayor. You invited me. Remember? Like about eight minutes ago?" I held a badge better than I could hold my tongue sometimes.

"The Rosemont Town Council has decided to terminate your services as Chief of our Public Safety Team due to the suspicious nature of recent events and your involvement in them." Emma never wasted any time getting to the point.

I rose to defend myself, but Ryan waved me away. "Let me see if I have this straight." He walked to what would have been center court, had we been in an actual courtroom. And when Ryan got to work, you'd hear it in his cadence and the way he'd stress exactly what he wanted his audience to hear.

"Mr. Burchfield can't find *anything* wrong with my client's alibi for the time when Greg was murdered. All the information we gave him, quite openly I might add, checks out. He has *no solid leads* to connect Chief Arnesen to *anything* involving Greg's murder. The charges against Tomas have been dismissed *with prejudice*, meaning, for you laypeople present, *acting* prosecuting attorney Burchfield cannot recharge my client with murder in the case of Gregory Mathiesen. No motive. No means. No opportunity. This little gathering has a distinctly punitive feel to it. Burchfield over there got his proverbial fanny kicked in court so now he's resorting to intimidation to get his way. Our lawsuit against him, the county, and the city of Rosemont is going to bottle you all up for a long time."

Emma respected Ryan's reputation. "Now, Mr. McFadden, there's no need to threaten us."

Ryan's eyes were now fully open. Apparently there's no better hangover cure for a lawyer than a good argument. "Respectfully, Mayor Fosberg, it's the council who's threatening my client, so we are given no recourse but to threaten in return. That *idiot* is so devoid of conscience that he's at a city council meeting, sitting in a dead man's chair in a city office to which *he has not been elected*. He thought he had a juicy series of murders involving an officer of the law to spice up his political fortune. Only yesterday, he discovered that he's got nothing but his own hot air to show for it. Now, in a purple snit, he's using you, the high and exalted Rosemont Town Council, to fire Chief Arnesen *without cause*. Oh, yes, indeed, Madam Mayor, there is *plenty* of need here."

The silence that followed was revelatory, as in straight out of the book of Revelation. After an angel opens a seal in that book, there's silence for about half an hour. It wasn't half an hour of silence, but it felt like it. I enjoyed every second of it. I didn't count it off or count it down, but I sure counted them out, even knowing what they were going to go ahead and do with me.

"The city council decided to take this action on our own," Emma said, stone-faced as ever.

"Well, you will all get your days in court. I'm sure we can sort it out. Expect a summons soon, all of you. Including you, Burchfield." Ryan pointed at the acting prosecuting attorney.

Emma sputtered, "These murders are getting Rosemont bad press.

Television stations sent reporters after the first two went into the public record. More are on the way or are already here because of Greg's death." Emma leaned out over the desk.

"We can't afford to have our main spokesperson be a person under suspicion." Lukas growled from his pushed-back-against-the-wall spot, as far away from me as he could get.

"How, exactly, did I become a person under suspicion?"

More silence in heaven as from the Revelation of St. John the Divine.

"What have you done to solve these crimes, Tomas? That's what they all want to know, out there. Citizens, news media people, us, the ones who hired you." Emma sat back down.

I could see she'd made up her mind before I'd even walked into the room. But I wasn't going to make it easy on them. "I'm doing everything possible to solve these crimes."

"Not enough, not enough." Lukas really hated me and was letting it show.

Emma turned to him. "Stop it, Lukas. We don't need any more animosity than we already have."

"Oh, no, Madam Mayor. Let the man spout and spew." Ryan held up a pocket recorder. "His comments will play nicely when we come to court."

More silence, but Emma kept her game face hard and bright. "Mr. Tomas Arnesen, Chief Public Safety Officer of the fine city of Rosemont, Utah, you are terminated immediately. Nick Lowrance is now Interim Chief. You are to turn in your badge, weapon, vehicle, and radio and remove yourself from the investigation immediately."

Kirsten grabbed my hand.

I thought I heard Nathan—or maybe it was Nick—gasp.

I stood and bowed to Emory. "Nicely done, Burchfield."

"You answer to me, Tomas Arnesen—to us, not to him," Emma said.

"I'm not answering to you or to anyone else. You just lost any hold on me you had." I pulled my badge wallet out of my pocket and tossed it onto the table in front of Emma. "I just got this back yesterday afternoon at the jail. Here it goes again." The radio followed. The gun went last. I walked up to her and set it down on top of the wallet

Lukas stood up and came to the table. "Now get your ass out of here."

Ryan walked up so close to Lukas he could have kissed him. "Mr. Whoever-you-are, I'm going to enjoy taking you apart on the witness stand and exposing your lack of professionalism as an elected official. I also hope the day never comes when you need assistance of any kind and look around to see me standing there. You will be out of luck. Tomas, however, will always be ready, willing, and able to help people in need, even idiots and bigots."

"Good luck with things, Emma, Reinert, Lukas, Freda, Anborg," I said. Neither of the two ladies had looked away from me during the lynching. Red flushes rode high on their cheeks.

Quietly, Anborg said, "Just so you know, Tomas. The vote was not unanimous. Emma forgot to mention that you do have support on this town council. Just not enough this morning to stop this hell-bound train." She rose to face Emma. "Shame on you, Emma Fosberg. Shame on all of you." Then she and Freda linked arms and walked out of the chambers.

"Thank you, ladies, for your support. I appreciate the effort." I hoped my shouted thanks got down the hallway to them. I decided enough was enough so I turned to walk out.

Kirsten unclipped her radio, pulled the satellite phone out of its cradle in her fanny pack, and pulled the Safety Team's cell phone out of her pocket. All three accompanied her badge wallet to the table where she stacked them neatly next to my pile. She and Ryan followed my exit without a word.

I couldn't help but smile at her pretty-much-expected show of solidarity.

But then Nathan followed suit, which did surprise me—a little. He laid out his badge wallet and First-Aid fanny pack, then joined our quiet rebellion in the doorway.

Nick hesitated, took two steps forward, one step back, one more forward, then stopped.

"It's OK, Nick. Someone has to pay the piper for their sakes, no matter how shortsighted and ill-advised they are. You stick."

He nodded. I saw his shoulders slump a bit followed by a huge, deep breath. He knew, or at least I hoped he knew, none of us would truly abandon him.

Trying to perform his newly acquired duties while still being a friend, Nick asked, "OK if I see you out?"

"Sure. Join the good-bye party."

❧ III ❧
VISIT THE INIQUITY OF THE FATHERS

42

If Grandpa Aksel told me once, he told me several hundred thousand times, "Tomas, it's not what comes at you that makes you or breaks you; it's what you do with it when it arrives on your doorstep." His words echoed in my mind as I faced two of the people I trusted most in Rosedale.

"Listen, Nathan, Kirsten. You two go back in there right now, pick up your badges and apologize, lightly, for walking out."

"But—"

"As someone once reminded me, dear heart, butt's the south end of a northbound donkey. No buts here. This is not about me, although I appreciate the show of solidarity. This is about what's best for Rosemont. You doing your jobs as always is best for the town right now."

Neither of them moved.

"Nathan. Go back in there. Now. If you don't want to do it for your neighbors, since you walked out for my sake, walk back in there—for my sake. Do it. Please."

"Put that way makes it hard to refuse, Chief."

"Good. Don't refuse."

He held out his hand. We shook. He went back into the building.

"You too, Kirsten. Sooner rather than later."

She stood there and looked at me for a long time. Then she smiled, reached out and took my face in her hands, and kissed me lightly on the lips. "Yet one more reason why I knew loving you was the right thing to do."

Nick had that sour look on his face again as he watched Kirsten and me. He tried to smooth it off, but managed only a grimace followed by staring at the floor.

Kirsten turned me loose and headed for the door. "What are you going to do now?"

"I'm going to say good day to Ryan, then head out to the ranch. Get some steak and eggs. Breakfast in the evening has always been a favorite meal. After that, choose a particularly refreshing blend from my tea stash, then relax and see if I can turn my brain, if not off, then at least down a notch or two. It'll keep on running no matter which tea I drink, no matter how many aspirin I take. My subconscious battery will try to connect the dots, cross the tees, follow the path through the maze. If I get some sleep—good, sound, or otherwise—tomorrow I'll ride the ranch's backcountry to see if, while perusing the landscape, that background bubbling shoots anything to the surface."

"Call me every once in a while so I know you're all right."

"Will do. You and Nathan keep Nick here from doing anything silly or rash. We all know he gets a little headstrong." I looked Nick straight in the eyes and spoke directly to him. "Good instincts, but you don't always seem to think things through. Try to do less of that while running the show. OK?"

"Will do." His answer was monotone, but at least it was in the affirmative. Nick placed his hand on my shoulder. "Guess I'll go back in there and make sure they do the right thing, take Nathan and Kirsten back into the fold."

Kirsten held the door open for him. Nick walked through and scraped his shoulders on the jam trying to stay as far away from her as he could. She let the door swing shut.

"I'll call you tonight. Late. You can tell me how the rest of this interesting day turned out, if it got any better or not."

"Please. Call. Late as you want."

I took my time driving out to the ranch. The shock of what had transpired settled into the passenger seat beside me. *You just lost your job, Arnesen.* I rolled a window down to drown out the thought, but the thought grew louder.

As familiar with grief and loss as I was, I knew that what I was feeling would pass soon enough, that grief progresses in stages. I was also old enough to know that getting through all the stages wasn't the end of grief. Once you got to the end of it, it'd just start over again. Grief was cyclical, and if you ever wanted to get free of it, you had to do the work to get through as many cycles as the depth of grief required. So I welcomed shock as a long-lost friend, hoping to push him out of the truck so his big brother anger would show up when I needed him to.

First time you've been fired in a long time. That means you're free to do whatever you want and kiss whomever you want, though we both know there's only one whomever you want to kiss. Now you can without even having to worry about all those city eyes. Even better, you don't have to worry about whoever's hunting Rosemont anymore. That's not your job.

Technically, I was right. It wasn't my job anymore. But I wouldn't quit doing the work of the job even if I was comatose. If brainwaves could be literally interpreted, they'd surely attest to me working out the who, when, where, and whys of this case. My moral compass—at least what I hoped was still a functional moral compass that could align itself with a True North—wouldn't let me drop this case. When I checked my motivations, that inner compass pointed toward the people of Rosemont, then recalibrated to drunk, foul-smelling Greg, then switched to Seth's favorite coffee, then finally settled itself on the real reason I needed to find the killer: Kirsten. I would protect her at all costs. There are worse things than justice and the love of a good woman for a man to die for.

The panoply of faces that had resurfaced during my drive abated the anger I knew was hiding within. It was just a matter of time. As a longtime officer, I knew emotion would trump proper detective work. Even though I was too close to the case, I had to find objective distance—and that meant trying to separate what had just happened from what needed to happen in the immediate future. Though I didn't want to admit it, any anger directed toward those who'd just canned me would have been put to ill use. Instead, I piled that anger onto what I already felt for the person responsible for this entire series of messy, murderous, callous events: Rosemont's first serial killer since who knows when.

After I pulled into the ranch, I grabbed half-a-dozen folders containing my personal copies of all the reports and files from our three murders. Mabel had my dinner on the table when I walked into my little house. After stuffing myself on her steak and eggs and oven potatoes, I sat down on the porch, watched the evening sky shift into night, stars beginning to wheel overhead, and leafed through the reports, page after page, hoping I'd missed a description or a summary, anything to shed light on our killer.

Clean crime scenes, the third one a little too clean compared to Seth and Tate, but that in itself gave me nothing to hold up to the light.

Two head shots. One to the chest. Common denominator? The black powder cap-and-ball revolver. Seth, Tate, and Greg had known their killer.

One of our own.

I'd said that out loud soon after we'd found Tate's body. Now it echoed around in my head like I'd shouted "Fire!" in the town auditorium.

The November cold drove me back inside the cabin. I lit a fire, gathered up the files, sat down in my father's ancient leather chair, and poured another cup of Silver Needle. Thirty or forty more times walking my eyes down these black lines, I knew the answer would jump off the page and yell at me, "Here I am. I did it."

I woke up smelling bacon, biscuits and gravy, and another steak. And coffee—steaming, hot, strong, Norwegian egg coffee, one of the liquids that I'll sometimes gladly allow to replace my breakfast tea. I don't drink it that often.

I tossed off the blanket Mabel had pulled over me sometime in the night and got up to see if I could catch our Spirit Woman before she went back to the main house. No such luck. I did see her tiny form slip into the back door. "Thanks, Mabel," I hollered at the closed door.

An excellent breakfast made most of what I didn't know fade into the background. I kept the echoes rolling around as I walked down to the barns, saddled Chance, and hollered at Charlie.

"Going on for a ride. Back by evening."

He gave me a thumbs up.

I closed the last open gate and rode up into the back third of the Arnesen property, taking my usual circuitous route to the spring where I could leave Chance while I soaked up some energy in the solitude.

43

The immediacy of my new status as an unemployed citizen of Rosemont faded with every mile Chance's trot took me across the ranch. I let all those loose ends quiver in the breeze, like the two or three remaining leaves on the aspens through which I was riding. But nothing about the three deaths faded completely away. How could those images disappear from my head?

I'd seen a lot of mayhem, brokenness, the ugliness embedded in what one human being can do to another. I'd been able to put it away at the end of a shift, pick it up next shift, and keep right on working to solve the case. But I hardly ever took anything home with me, to either wife, to the rest of my bachelor days before, in between or after.

I was close with Seth. I'd worked with Tate. I knew their families back three generations. We shared history. These killings had been personal, no matter what else we knew. The killer had stood right in front of his victims, put a gun to their heads—to Greg's chest—and pulled the trigger, cold and remorseless.

I blinked.

Chance stood over me. I had one rein still clutched in my right hand. I was on the ground. Something hard had struck me in the chest and knocked me off the horse. I heard thunder rolling far off. Couldn't focus.

What the hell happened?
Get your head working, Arnesen.
Long way off.
Gunshot?

Noise and those reverberations specific to a high-powered rifle finally wormed its way past my pain receptors. Definitely a gunshot. I did not move, tried to catch my breath, worked to get my head to clear. I ran my right hand slowly over my shirt front, then slid it out to catch a look in the corner of my eye. No blood.

Stay still.
Don't move.
Long distance shot.
Sniper, but with a very loud rifle, or power load?
Center mass. Not a head shot. Why I am still alive?
Wait.
Wait.

Chance shuddered, fell to his knees, then toppled over, wheezing heavily as he fell. His head landed on my legs. I heard the report but still couldn't tell where it had come from. At least six hundred yards or more. Well off the top of the ridge opposite us. Two or three breaths, another shudder, and he lay still.

Son of a horse-killing bitch!

Whoever had shot me either figured I was done with and shot my horse for the hell of it or wasn't taking any chances. Killed my horse to make sure I'd not get out of here too easily. *Make me walk out wounded?* No. If I stayed here much longer, I'd be victim number four. Five if you counted Chance, which I did.

In that instant, my head cleared. Adrenaline rush pushed me into high gear. The shooter—it had to be our killer—could easily drive or ride down to make sure I was dead, and if not, finish me with a shot to my forehead.

The canyon entrance was a quarter mile away behind me. I'd fallen into a shallow draw that channeled some of the spring water back down through the ranch toward the creek, then to the river. Chance's bulk still sat slightly above me, covering me, a protector even in death.

I moved a little, tensed, waited for a third shot. Moved a little more. Still no response. I kept sliding backward and away until I pushed myself into the aspens, which, even as bare as they were, provided modest cover.

My chest hurt like a circus roustabout had hit my breastbone with a sledgehammer instead of hitting the tent stake. Hunched over, I stumbled. I needed to get better footing and head to the canyon's entrance.

I stopped every fifth or sixth step to listen and watch my back trail. No indication the sniper was following or tracking me.

Carefully, I kept telling myself. *Carefully now, leave no sign, leave no mark. Get over the rocks, get into my canyon.* Once in there I could defend myself, to a point. I had three or four good hiding places: modest breaks in the wall from which I could spring out and smack the attacker with a big piece of rotten firewood. Or throw a rock at him. Or curse him for killing my horse while I threw rocks at him. Or beat him to a pulp until I thought justice had been rightly served for the devastation he'd brought upon my town. My adrenaline surged.

I slid down and squirmed through the small opening. Every muscle protested as I lay on my back to get farther up and in. Twenty feet inside and around the first wall, I sat down to rest. I took off my jacket and shirt to look at my vest. I could see the impact spot. Gingerly, I removed the vest, then fingered the bruise starting to show on my sternum. Center mass, an expert shot, especially if the weapon were a muzzle-loader, which I suspected. I wasn't exactly sure why I suspected that, but it felt like a reasonable assumption given the other murders. The sound a muzzle-loader makes has a quality unto itself, not the same sound as a regular hunting rifle.

I looked back toward the landscape now hidden from direct view. Only one place the shooter could have used to make that shot. *Whew. Damn.* Twelve-hundred yards from the Cold Creek tipple, right at the top. Only place along the ridge with that clear of a line of site to where I rode toward the spring. Twenty yards more and I'd have been inside the tree line and covered.

No water. It was going to get much colder. I slipped my vest, shirt, and jacket back on. I had the means to light a fire but didn't want to take the chance the shooter had come down, watching for a sign that I might still be kicking. Well, shuffling along may be the better phrase. I may be old—and I knew this was certainly the case whenever Kirsten and I passed by our reflections—but I wasn't going to go down as a shuffler. *I will shuffle to heal, to escape, but once the advantage is mine, killer from on high, you'll be put low. I'll see to that before I shuffle off for good.* I kept losing myself in what I wanted to do instead of what I needed to do.

Think it through, Arnesen. Charlie would watch for me. He'd call Kirsten or Nick when I didn't return by sunset. So he'd have called them by now. He knew the general direction I'd ridden and Kirsten would know where to look for me: up top on the mesa, the place she'd scampered off to during her first visit to my invisible canyon.

I walked back up to the canyon's hidden entry passage. I stood there for five or six more minutes listening for pursuit. Hearing nothing at all, I made up my mind, headed to the back of the canyon, and started climbing the chimney. Slow going. Every time I lifted an arm to pull, my chest burned like someone'd lit a camp fire inside it.

But I kept on going, my breath beginning to file my throat raw, whistling through my nose loud enough I knew the killer would hear my wheezing. I inched my way up, knowing I was losing options by the minute. I kept praying that Kirsten had gotten the call, or at least had relayed it to Nick and Nathan, that they'd be waiting for me when I climbed out. Maybe she'd tell them about the three small stones, one of them as black and round as a marble, that she'd set as a marker back during our first mesa-top rendezvous. Then again, she'd have to explain *why* she'd been there with me.

God, I pray I get to see her just once more.

Full dark when I pulled myself over the lip of the chimney's cut. No one showed. I saw no lights, heard no voices, engines, or neighing horses.

I unclipped the penlight from my vest, knowing the battery might last another two or three hours, but any distance I could travel back toward the farm road would cut down the time I'd be exposed.

One foot. Two feet. Walk. Watch for holes.

More canyons. Since Kirsten and I had walked some of this, I felt semi-comfortable in the dark. As long as I took it easy. But cold seeped into my hands and feet.

Can't stop. Don't stop. Keep going. They are coming.

Someone must have gotten the word. Charlie called it in.

Keep going.

Look down.

Pay attention.

I didn't feel my footing change. One step, then the ground rose up hard and sharp, straight into my elbows, and then pounded my chest, again, for good measure. That took what little wind I had left and sent it flying out into the dark.

I tried. Gave it a good run. Would've liked to get the SOB who did this. The one who killed Seth, Tate, and Greg. Would have loved to have gotten him.

I let the silence and dark wash over me, rolled over on my back, and watched the stars sharpening into brilliance. Out here on the mesa, no light pollution of any kind, I turned off the flashlight and enjoyed the show.

Sleepy.

Wake up.

Turn on the light.

Shine it.

Wave it.

Don't shuffle off yet, Arnesen.

"Hey. I see something. Over there."

Voices out of the dark. Off to my right.

"Tomas? Is that you? Wave your light."

Kirsten's voice. What does she want me to do?

"Wave your light."

Wave my light? I didn't have a light, did I?

Oh, yeah. Little one. Wave it!

In seconds, she launched herself into my arms.

I grunted from the impact. Maybe even fainted it hurt so much.

"Tomas? Tomas. Look at me. It's Nathan. Look at me."

I looked.

"Here. Only a taste. Only a taste. Get your lips wet first. Don't gulp it down."

Water. Cool and quenching.

"Good. Are you hurt?"

"Bullet. Chest." I held up my vest. "Center mass."

Nathan knelt down to open my jacket and shirt. He shined his headlamp onto my chest. "Whew. Center mass is right. That's some bruising you got there. Going to get worse."

Kirsten pushed Nathan away with a gentle force. She wrapped a blanket around me and held me tight.

"Charlie called me when you didn't come back. I called Nathan. We came looking for you." I could have died a happy man with the way she was looking at me.

She pointed at Nathan. "Go get the ATV. He can't walk out to the road. I'll stay with him."

Nathan shot us a thumbs-up and ran to the ATV.

The ride back hurt. Every bounce, hole, and lurch went right to the center of my body, inside and outside. I cried from the pain and didn't worry about the tears. Kirsten had already seen those.

I sat on the exam table in Rosemont's two-room medical facility. Nathan, as thorough as ever and surprisingly gentle as well, wrapped me up and medicated me. My breathing normalized and the pain wasn't as body-shattering as it had been. I couldn't stop playing with my vest, fingering the damaged spot through which the bullet did not shred my heart.

I looked up to see Nick in the doorway, staring at me. I smiled and held up the vest. "Pretty damn close, don't you think, Nick? Too damn close."

Nick walked up and took the vest away from me, examining the dent. He handed it back to me. "Yeah. Damn close, Tomas. Good thing you were wearing the vest." He looked back out the door. "When did you start wearing it? Should we be wearing ours?"

"Started wearing it after Tate was killed. Promised Kirsten."

Nick nodded at Kirsten. "Smart woman." He looked at his shoes, then glanced at his watch. "Chief, I'm really sorry about this, but I gotta get some work done. I'm not used to this Chief stuff yet. Feel better soon, boss." Nick's cheeks reddened. "Old habits."

"Die hard. Don't worry, Nick. Nothing to be sorry about. Go on. Get your report filed. I'll talk to you tomorrow."

44

Confucius said, "You cannot open a book without learning something." At least, someone who was around at the time remembered him saying something like that and wrote it down. Whether the old philosopher actually uttered those words or the scribe put them into his mouth doesn't really matter anymore. Does it? The wise guy had it right.

Off the job, convalescing from my near-death experience, compounded by my fortunately brief November exposure, I had time on my hands, on my feet, pretty much time all over the place.

Kirsten and I had been scheming what we could do to make everything right in Rosemont again. I cautioned her, "If you can get the ledger, well and good. But be careful."

Kirsten held up a matching ancient leather-bound volume, twin to the ledger. "Found this in Seth's office, buried under a pile of old books and papers. No one is going to notice, at least not for a while. I switch them, out in the open, and we're home free."

"Let's hope nothing more exciting happens for a while here in our fair city." I held her hand.

"Well, nothing so exciting it has to be written down by a town official." She squeezed my hand, leaned over, and gave me a peck on the cheek and headed for the door.

"Kirsten. Be careful. If you get time, look and see what there is on Averil's suicide. See if they kept any notes or a file. If so, copy them or get them somehow."

"Why those? Can't do you much good now, can it?"

"Don't know that I can explain the why." I twirled my right forefinger around in a circle off my right temple. "My Fourth of July sparkler of a brain lit up a notion that I needed to look at whatever those folks wrote about Averil."

"OK, love. You got it. What Tomas wants, Tomas gets."

I slapped her lightly on the butt as she completed her turn out the door. "Well, that's not totally true, is it?"

She laughed. Tossed it back over her shoulder at me. "But it will be." Down the walk to her car, she stopped and shouted at me. "Eventually."

As good to her word as Russian sage in full-blue bloom, she smuggled the town ledger out of the office. The replacement sat in its spot on the top shelf behind the radio console and desk. She had also pulled what few notes we had on Averil's suicide, leaving in their place blank sheets of matching gray manuscript paper she'd found in a bottom drawer of the dispatcher's desk. She left the manila folder with the nearly illegible LOWRANCE, AVERIL on the peeling label.

Ledger, suicide files, free time. Luxury. I read through the suicide notes first since there were only four pages.

No surprises jumped off page one, two, or three. But page four unloaded on me.

I stared at the single, hastily drawn image, Averil lying on the floor, looking for all time like a gingerbread man. My brain ticked into high speed. The image, so familiar, filled my vision. I thought I was going to faint.

Ding. Alarm beeping. My notes from Seth's and Tate's murder scenes.

I laid them out in a line on top of the dining room table.

Averil's.

Seth's.

Tate's.

Three gingerbread men.

I pulled Greg's file just to make sure I hadn't overlooked anything. His outline didn't match the other bodies.

Even though they were not to scale with each other, I held Averil, Seth, and Tate up to the lamplight and laid them over each other, one at a time. Even accounting for the slightly different scales, the positions matched closely enough. Not an accident. Not the result of a gunshot, then falling down. Seth and Tate had been *arranged* to match Averil's suicide position. But who would have done such a strange thing? It was an answer, but it wasn't *the* answer.

Two mornings, two afternoons, two evenings, and well into the third morning later, I still hadn't found so much as a jot of an inkling. My mother used to call me Mr. Persistent when I got my head wrapped around a project or an idea. I tended to get obsessive. Well, tended isn't exactly right either. I flat-out got obsessive, every time, every idea, good or bad, every project I ever undertook in school. Maybe that's one of the reasons I did pretty well as an investigator for the Louisville PD once I got the badge.

Kirsten brought me lunch, again. "Anything turn up yet?"

"Only the fact that Seth and Tate were posed to match Averil's suicide scene." I held out the three drawings. "Other than that, the trail has not only gone cold, it has disappeared into the rocks. I'm beginning to think there's nothing here except neighbors complaining about neighbors' dogs barking at night, someone reporting they saw a figure at their window, and a pretty steady stream of people worried about their relatives and asking for welfare checks. Plus the usual lineup of adolescent shoplifters and their rites of passages. Rosemont has never been a very exciting town."

"But your instincts are still telling you there's something useful here?"

I thought about her question. "The hairs on the back of my neck stand up every time I think about Seth, Tate, and Greg. There's something here." I tapped the ledger and slapped the three drawings down on top of it.

"Well, then, you'd better get back to it, hadn't you?" She leaned over and kissed me.

"You know, this kissing me good-bye is becoming a regular part of my day. When do you think you might kiss me hello?"

"Oh, you never know about us girls. But think of this as anticipatory socialization."

"Anticipatory what?"

"Socialization. I'm helping you get ready, get socialized in other words, for what's to come."

"What's to come?"

"Kissing hello, perhaps, if you're good." She slapped my hand away, pointed at the journal, and laughed. "Read on, MacDuff. Read on."

"Aye, aye, sir." My reward for that was another light slap on the back of my head.

I read. I read on and kept reading until later that afternoon: *Rosemont Town Ledger*, the entry for October 12, 1931, neatly written in tight print and signed by one Ulysses Grant McFadden, then town councilman, grandfather to one Salt Lake City big-time criminal lawyer of my intimate acquaintance:

TRAGEDY STRIKES ROSEMONT

> In what we are calling a terrible accident, Birgit Lowrance has been killed in a fall at her home. Her husband, Averil Lowrance, reportedly was inconsolable in the hours following the accident. Good friends stood by to help Mr. Lowrance, including Archie Ramsey, Tate Thoresen Senior, Astrid Dyrdahl, and Aksel Arnesen. Mrs. Lowrance's fall and subsequent death seemed suspicious to the county investigator, but the unassailable testimony of the above-mentioned witnesses left him no room for any other conclusion, hence, no charges were filed against Mr. Lowrance, and no further investigations were deemed necessary.

Ramsey. Thoresen. Lowrance. Arnesen. Dyrdahl.

Five names. Two related to our first two victims. But no Mathiesen there.

I had three puzzle pieces connected on the table, but those didn't give me much of a picture. Where's the box top when you need it?

I pulled out my cell phone and dialed.

"Nels here."

"Afternoon, Nels."

"Tomas. How the hell are you? I heard what our town council did to you. Are you ready for your rebuttal interview so we can get all sides on the record?"

"Not why I called, Nels. I need your exhaustive and encyclopedic compendium of Rosemont history. I need to know everything you can tell me or find in the Republic's archives about Birgit Lowrance's death, October twelfth, nineteen-thirty-one. Think you can help me out?"

"When do you want it?"

"Now. Yesterday's even better."

"You're kidding. No, check that. You're not kidding. Where are you?"

"I'm at the ranch, recuperating, in a manner of speaking."

"Want me to come out there, or do you want to come into town?"

"Out here, please. Better to keep the townsfolk out of the loop for the moment. Too many prying eyes. I don't need anyone to notice me at the moment."

"Gotcha. How about I call when I'm on the way there?"

"Works for me. Get me something more than this town ledger entry, will ya?"

"I'll do my best, Tomas."

I decided to keep reading, but now that I had what I thought was the main connective tissue, my restore point as it were, I tuned my eyes and brain to seek keywords while I skimmed the entries. I covered four decades much more quickly than I had up to this point.

ROSEMONT ROCKED BY ANOTHER TRAGIC DEATH

October 13, 1971. Averil Lowrance committed suicide yesterday. His grandson, Nicholas Lowrance, discovered the grisly scene when he went to check on Averil. Mr. Lowrance had shot himself in the head with his grandfather's Civil War revolver. Nicholas did not want to comment when asked about his grandfather.

I dialed Nels quickly. "You still at the paper?"

"Almost ready to go. What's up?"

"Can you also pull the paper with the story about Averil Lowrance's suicide? There's not much in the ledger about it. Did the paper get more story?"

"Funny you mention that. I have that edition sitting on my desk. Was rereading it last night. You think there's a clue in these stories?"

"I'm not sure, Nels. But one thing I can tell you is that there *is* a connection between these stories. You knew Averil at the end, didn't you?"

"Last couple years, yeah, I knew him. Wasn't much fun to be around, that's for sure. Only one who could tolerate him and that he tolerated was Nick." Nels coughed. "Hey, I got a notion. Going to call Colin and Stig. See if they can shake loose and come up with me. They've been around a lot longer than I have. Might know stories, or at least parts of our history that didn't get written down."

"Sure. Bring 'em up. Thanks. See you in a few?" I asked.

"On my way soon as I call the boys."

I called Mabel on the house phone and asked her to bring coffee and doughnuts for four.

"Who's coming?"

"Editor Nels, Colin Parkin, Stig."

"Editor, now he likes cinnamon buns. I'll pop some into the oven. Stig and Colin eat pretty much whatever's to hand. So, hot buns, lots of 'em, hot coffee ready when they arrive. Oh, there's a UPS package for you, from some law enforcement supply company."

"Yes'm." So, my new low profile vest had arrived. Thinner, less visible, slightly less stopping power, but could still save my life.

At the house, waiting for the boys, as only Nels could get away with calling them, I slipped the new vest on and put one of my uniform shirts over it. Checking myself in the mirror, I could still see an outline. I put on a thicker T-shirt, then topped that off with a denim work shirt. Much better. If you weren't looking for it, you probably wouldn't see it.

The boys sipped coffee and ate at least six of Mabel's cinnamon delicacies while I skimmed the paper's coverage of Averil's suicide, again picking out key words: *Gunshot. Forehead. Many years despondent. Lost land, property.*

Averil had lived in his original homestead cabin on the back edge of the Dyrdahl property, which had once belonged to the Lowrance family. Only Astrid Dyrdahl's kindness had kept the old man from starving, freezing to death, or dying of exposure. She'd kept a roof over his head and, with his grandson Nick helping, kept the old drunk fed, as much as he'd accept help or food.

Averil repaid their combined kindnesses by shooting himself in the main house, in the room where he and Birgit once held dances and fine dinners, the living room where Nick found his grandfather's lifeless body that morning.

I was so entranced by what I was reading that I didn't notice all eyes on me. I looked up. "So who can tell me about Averil's last years?"

Colin set his coffee cup down. "He was angry and drunk. All the time. I never once saw him sober. Never once said hello to him that I didn't get a string of profanity in return. The only person he treated with any civility was Nick. I don't know what they talked about, but Nick spent hours with him and they seemed to get along just fine."

I prodded. "He ever say anything at all about Birgit's death?"

Colin shook his head. "Not to me. Not to anyone else I know of. But I did overhear him one day, spewing vile abuse on his long-ago friends."

I nodded. "Thoresen, Ramsey, Dyrdahl, and Arnesen. Seth's, Tate's, and my grandparents." I sat back in my recliner and scratched at the now receding bruise on my chest. It itched, deep inside where I couldn't get to it, as my body slowly reabsorbed the hematoma that had formed around the impact site.

Stig took up the tale. "He sure hated them all at the end. Couldn't figure that one out. I mean, every one of them stepped up over the years to help Averil. Fed, clothed, housed, visited him both times he got locked up for being drunk and disorderly in public. Astrid didn't have to give the man one inch of ground after the bank foreclosed on the property and she bought it. Deeded the bastard five acres at the back of the property, including the original cabin. She didn't have to do that. He lost the property himself. No one to blame. But, for some reason, he blamed them."

I looked back to the paper and ran through the article again. "Nothing here about a suicide note."

Nels answered my indirect question. "They never found one. Don't know that they looked real hard though. Everyone stayed in shock for weeks, especially Astrid and young Nick. For a couple of years, he stayed withdrawn, spent most of his free time after school at the cabin. Astrid let him come and go like it was his. Turned out, it was. Old man quitclaimed the cabin and acreage to Nick. Just forgot to tell anyone else about it." He took another sip and two more bites.

I felt like we were getting somewhere, but the fog of the past was still too dense for me to see how then connected to now. "Nick found Averil first, says here. Who came next?"

Nels set his cup down. "Astrid. She'd been up to Salt Lake to see a cousin. Nick must have been sitting there staring at his grandfather's body, all the bloody mess, for an hour or more when she walked into the house."

No one spoke for a beat.

I summarized our collective retelling of what should have been long-forgotten history. "So Nick finds Averil. He goes into shock. Astrid finds the two of them and she calls the authorities. After that, it would be zoo-city. Sheriff's office, county attorney, funeral home, newspapers, maybe television news, a free-for-all in quiet little Rosemont, Utah."

"Sounds about right, Tomas. Listen, you need me anymore? I've got some more work to do on the paper yet tonight. Kinda like to get it done before the clock shifts to a.m."

"Thanks, Nels. Yes. I think you've given me plenty of help and some new directions to follow." I pointed to the papers he'd brought. "Can I keep these for a while longer?"

"Sure. I know where you live. I'll want 'em back for the archives. For now, they're yours. Try not to spill tea on them."

I raised my mug. "Won't spill the Glenlivet on them either. Cheers."

Nels scurried out the door, tipped his hat in the direction of the picture windows on the back of the main house, as though hoping Mabel might see his offered courtesy.

I sat there in the quiet with Stig and Colin. I needed to confirm my suspicion that Averil's body had been moved. "So, no suicide note?"

Stig shook his head. "We all thought that was peculiar. Averil liked to talk about everything and all the time. You'd think as much as he liked having an audience, even his audience of one with young Nick there at the end, he'd want to leave something behind. But maybe Averil thought most people would just understand that he was tired of living such a rough life. Maybe he'd already spoken to Nick before he, you know. Maybe he didn't need to leave a suicide note because he'd already said his piece. But, yes, they never found a suicide note."

That made the hairs on the back of my neck come to attention. I'd have to follow that thread to see where it would lead. That lost filament, while not glowing brightly, now cast the tiniest glow over the landscape of our murders. There was light there. I could see my next step. "Thanks, you two. If you think of anything else, let me know."

"Don't have to ask, Tomas. We're going to check with Tollef and see what he remembers as well. Something comes out into the light, we'll holler."

Well, Confucius, I guess you were right. I've opened a few books and I've learned more than I ever wanted to know.

45

I needed my dad and my grandpa and they weren't here. Next best, depending on your perspective, would be to go where they'd lived. Especially Grandpa's part of the house. I could walk now without every step sending packets of pain signals out of my chest, through and through, into my lower back, down my arms, into my abdomen. I finally felt almost back to whatever passed for normal.

I hadn't been in the old part of the house for years. Exactly ten days after Grandpa Aksel's memorial service, my dad closed off that section of the homestead and the rooms in which he had grown up. He shuttered the windows and brought darkness over the spaces in which I had played while growing up with a doting grandfather. My father spent much of his time running the ranch's ever-increasing business enterprises. I know he had moments, probably daily, when he wondered if his son was ever going to measure up to the Arnesen standards. To this day, I'm still not sure if I have, or ever will, measure up. Best I can think to do—in the middle of this mess we're in—is stop worrying about that and measure up to Aksel's opinion of me.

Dust lay everywhere. The chinking in the old logs had dried out long ago. The gaps and holes had had lots of years to let in critters, light, and dust. I stopped counting my sneezes at twenty-three.

Grandpa's bedroom had always smelled of cinnamon. He loved it. Had sticks of it lying everywhere, stuck one in his coffee, and in his later years when the doctor cut him off the coffee, he made sure he could keep his spice habit for the no-caffeine teas he learned to drink. It also had a tang, like Bay Rum or Clubman, scents I remembered from visiting Maiseland's Barber Shop with him. I took a deep breath, sucked in half the dust in the county, and my sneezing storm broke out again. In the aftermath, so faint it hardly registered, swam the cinnamon and the Bay Rum.

"Miss you, Grandpa. Miss you a lot."

I sat down in his rocking chair, closed my eyes, and rocked. There he was, sitting on the bed opposite me, letting me work that cedar rocker back and forth, grinning up at me every once in a while, writing all the time in his leather journal.

"Whatcha writin', Grandpa?"

"About my day. What I saw. What I heard. The people I talked with, the things I thought about."

"Can I read it?" the eight-year-old me asked him constantly.

Every time he'd shake his head no and say, "Someday I'll let you read a page or two, when you're older, maybe wiser, although sometimes you make me wonder about you gaining any wisdom."

That young boy had already started drifting off the topic by the time Grandpa got to "older, maybe wiser" and went back to rocking the chair to see if he could scoot it off the braided rug onto the wood floor. On the wood floor, he could rock it clear across the bedroom. Looking back now, Grandpa had probably put that exercise on the "my-grandson-will-never-get-wiser" list.

I stopped rocking to look around the bedroom. I hadn't seen his journal for years. Dad never mentioned it.

"Where would you put it, Grandpa, when you weren't writing in it?"

Nothing on the old oak roll top desk. I opened every drawer, even clicked open the secret compartment in the back.

"OK, Grandpa Aksel, you're rocking, you have an idea you need to get on paper, you need your journal." I dropped both hands over the arms of the chair and let them dangle, running my fingers over the cedar worn smooth with years of his hands, and Grandma's too. My left hand fingers touched something under the chair's seat.

"Well. What's this?" I got up and turned the chair over. He'd built something under the seat, a drawer front-recessed six inches from the chair's front edge. I'd rocked in this chair for hours and hours over the years and never knew the drawer was under my butt. With the chair set back on its rockers, I reached under, touched the small knob, and slid the drawer open.

"Right here in plain sight. Pretty sneaky, Grandpa, pretty damn sneaky."

First surprise? Finding the journal. Second surprise? When I pulled it out, there was a card with my name on the envelope taped to the front with brown packing tape with barely any adhesion left. When I touched it, the tape crumbled into dust. The card fell to the floor.

I left it there on the floor, staring at it for a long time. The urge to leave it there with the past faded from the urge to know, to have one more conversation with him. I followed my internal voice's advice, picked it up, then opened and read it.

Tomas: Desperately hope you never read this. As strange as it sounds, I also hope you find it. I hope you read this, sitting in my bedroom and trying to rock the chair off the carpet. I know you know the conflicting hope I have expressed. It's just not possible to explain the confusion, unless you keep reading.

I left you a view of life on Arnesen Ranch. Read them on vacation. You can also learn more about your father and mother, and what happened to him after your mother died. That can help you.

My confession begins on page 78, toward the back of the book. Read it. Forgive me if you can. If not, I would understand if I was there in the room with you. I want you to ride out the storm of anger and disappointment in me.

All my love. Grandpa

I started sneezing again and decided to go back into the main house, find Mabel, get some tea with cinnamon sticks accompanied by my favorite bendable sugar cookies, then settle down to read my grandfather's confession. Whatever it was, I'd already forgiven him.

By the time I found Mabel in the kitchen and had asked for the tea set up, I'd begun to hear his voice growing clearer and clearer. I thought I'd nearly forgotten what he sounded like, that long East Texas drawl he brought with him to the homestead, the three syllables he routinely managed to pull out of a one-syllable word, the faintest whisper of a lisp, noticeable when he grew tired.

Tea steeping, cinnamon stick soaking up the water in the cup, journal open in my lap, I heard him telling me the story on the pages. As I read it, the room faded away and time settled back onto the dust motes circulating around the room.

He was there with me. He was so tired. I heard his voice, the lisp prominent. Clear as daylight reflecting from ripples on the Sevier River, I heard Grandpa Aksel.

46

E ven before I began reading what my grandfather had penned so long ago, the names on the page grabbed at my still-healing chest wound:

I've never looked twice at Birgit Lowrance, at least not after I met your grandmother. Did not need it. But Averil Lowrance got it into his stubborn brain that she and I had an affair, even after I married Julie.

I guess one night demons got him tight. They had an argument over me and her. She kept telling him there was no "me and her," but he would not listen. Finally, he beat her, then beat her with fist. When she fell, she hit head on the iron stove, on the temple. She died, I think. I pray instant.

Astrid Dyrdahl, Archibald Ramsey, and Tate Thoresen. We all friends, family, attached. You know what it is down here. We had been riding and stopped to water horses, check on Averil and Birgit. Astrid first to find them in kitchen. Birgit dead on floor, pool of blood around her. Averil sit in chair, stared at her. We came when she called us.

"I killed her. I'm going to hell. I killed her."

She turned to us. "Aksel. Tate. This was accident." Here she took the coffee pot off the stove and spilled it all over the floor, sprayed a little on Birgit shoes.

"She spilled coffee, slipped when she tried to clean up, and hit her head on the stove. It was an accident."

Both of us stood there and looked at her.

"An accident. You both hear me? I do not want this family gone through fire and storm that will entail. Bad enough we have to bury our dear Birgit, bad enough Averil must live with this. I do not want him to live that life in prison."

Tate and I were still in shock. Astrid gave us time to recover our wit.

"Tate. Can you do that? Can you be the first to tell the story?" She asked him. "You go into town, get a call to sheriff. We have a death here. Tell them where. Do it now."

Tate cleared his throat, straightened up, as Astrid looked in his eyes. He said nothing, nodded, turned and walked away.

She beckoned me over. "This will take us both."

"Averil. Look at us. See. At. Us." Astrid hit every word hard and sharp.

He looked up at us.

"Listen to us, Averil. Listen to your life. When Sheriff comes, we tell him it was an accident. We will say we found you right after it happened. He will ask us if we saw it. We will say, no, but you told us what happened."

I pick up new story. "Astrid is correct. It was accident. That is all you need tell to the sheriff. When he asks you what happened, you say it was accident. You spilled coffee. She reached for the towel to clean it up, slipped, hit her head on stove. That is what you tell the sheriff."

He looked on, blinked around the room until he saw Birgit. Then he began to cry. "I did not mean to do it."

"Did not do what, Averil?" I asked.

Through his sobs, he said. "I did not mean to spill the coffee."

It is the story he told the sheriff. Maybe sheriff suspects something else, but he had no place to go, no evidence suggesting murder or assault. Accident. That's what he wrote in his report. We verified. There is town council member writing in Rosemont's Journal.

It should have ended there. Did not. Averil began to drink himself to early grave. Angry, bitter, he got worse. Someday he turned the story backward. Me, Tate and Astrid. Three of us responsible for Birgit's death. The more he drank, more truth fell off down the path.

When Averil hung on brink of losing house, Astrid purchased all property and house, to help him. She deeded him five acres of rear property, where Rock Creek flows out. Averil drank himself resentful. Mad at Astrid for charity. Only person he could bear, only person who tolerated him, his grandson, Nick.

I guess we leave him. It hard to love a friend determined to hate you. We tried, over years. Tate Senior died. Averil killed himself. Astrid had stroke. Doc Guudemann gave me a year or two. I knew then, time to let go.

Could we have done more by Averil or done other? Let him go to prison? Let truth out? Maybe. Probably. I taught your father, know he taught you Arnesen motto: No such thing as Coulda, Shoulda, Oughta. Do best we can with what we have. But now to write this down here, black and white in the journal for you to read, hoping you read it, praying you do not ever find it. I think there was more I could have made Averil. More. I should have done more, done as a friend, as moral human being.

I take all with me to my grave, praying for, oh I cannot find the English now, *en smak*, oh yes, now there it is, a taste of *tilgivelse*, yes, of course, I can say it, forgiveness.

When I see Tate Senior, Astrid, Birgit, and Averil on the other side, I hope we shall be friends again, nothing more and nothing less. I hope, Tomas, you know. *Fare deg godt.* Farewell.

"Tomas, what's wrong here." Mabel stood in the doorway to the living room.

I wiped the tears off my face. "I found Grandpa Aksel's journal. Reading pieces of it brought back so many memories."

Mabel subtly nodded then spoke with the kind of warmth this Ranch used to be known for. "We all miss him. Your daddy missed him as much as you did, I think."

"Hard to know with Dad. I miss them both, to tell the truth."

"Leave all that past back there where it belongs."

I closed the journal, got up, and walked over to this tiny brown lady of completely unknown ancestry, this rock-steady wise, funny, and powerful woman who'd taken care of three generations of Arnesens. I swept her up in a huge hug, twirled her around and around until we almost fell over. She started laughing, and I couldn't help but go with her.

"Lord a-mighty, Mr. Rosemont Chief of Safety. I think you twirled me backwards like a time machine. I feel years younger. Now you put that sad book away. Don't read it no more, less'n you've stored up a big batch of joy. You go out there, wrap up that dark-haired Kirsten Dyrdahl and do not let her go. Yessir, Tomas Arnesen, you do that right now." She poked me in the ribs with one hand, then touched my face. "When you're done kissing her, make sure she knows old Mabel told you to do that."

I leaned way down and kissed her back, lightly on both cheeks. "That is one order I will obey."

I heard her laughter follow me through the front doors all the way to the truck.

As I drove into town, on the road for the first time in days, I had two sources now for the one story. I had connections. I had linkages. I had a list of names. I didn't have the whole picture, but the image was forming in my subconscious. I was content to let it grow in there until I could take it out for everyone to see.

To our mini-courthouse annex first. I'd sneak in the side door to talk to Lynette Farrow, if she'd talk to me. Maybe she could give me some hints about Astrid's final years, anything at all along that thread line so I could tie it up. If she couldn't, I knew Cathrine Varland, unofficial town historian and family-tree researcher, had a lot of family histories at her fingertips.

Second order of the day?

Follow Mabel's clear instruction concerning an encounter with a young lady at Parkin's Store.

47

Unfortunately, one murder is good business for a small town. Two murders mean the town gets all sorts of publicity, warranted or not. Then business improves even more for a longer period of time. Three murders lead to the biblical equivalent of a flood: trailers, trucks with antenna arrays, SUVs, all emblazoned with company logos, slogans, radio, television, newspapers.

Radio and newspaper reporters tend to be more low-key and less visible in terms of their arrivals but have the same instincts and tenacity the TV crews do. Sometimes they're more interested in getting the whole story rather than a sound clip or a much-edited interview with a local for that touch of color, as they say.

Local reporters from two counties away came over after Seth Ramsey's murder. They came back, along with multiple crews from Salt Lake, when we announced Tate's murder. Once Greg's murder leaked, we had local, state, and national coverage. Exactly what we wanted.

Nels, however grim the circumstances, held his own with everyone, including the national reporters from NBC, CBS, ABC, and FOX. Yeah, we were now on the map for three unfortunate reasons.

They ate in our restaurants and bought fancy coffees at Heavenly

Grounds and daily essentials at Parkin's, Thoresen's, and Mountain Harvest. Producers and crews booked up every motel room and cabin. A few enterprising families—the end result of our entrepreneurial and enterprising Norwegian stock—quickly turned spare bedrooms into Bed and Breakfasts, charged a premium, and didn't blink an eye while writing out their deposit slips. Some provided space for fifth wheels.

Sure, they made nuisances of themselves while trying to do their jobs, but since I wasn't in charge anymore, I wasn't on their radars, especially once they found out I wasn't going to give them anything. Even though a few had thought me a suspect, my alibis checked out. I was just the former Public Safety Officer of Rosemont run out of his job during the most murderous times our town had ever faced.

Nels checked in with me periodically, asked if I'd learned anything new. A reporter from the *Cedar City Daily News* and one from KCSG-TV also checked in. They both were particularly interested in the local connections, more interested than the "big boys and girls" from state and national.

I was trying to slip unobtrusively down the back way to the courthouse when I overheard Lukas Sogard talking to Hal Leonard, the newspaper reporter from Cedar City. I'd been laying low for a few days, trying to heal.

"So, do you have any theories about why these three men have been murdered?"

Lukas faced away from me. I stopped and stepped around the corner. Neither he nor the reporter could see me, but I could hear them.

"I think it certainly has something to do with Tomas Arnesen's coming back here to Rosemont."

"Why would you think that?"

"No troubles here, ever. Rosemont's a quiet place. None of this started until Arnesen came home. And then that fight with Greg Mathiesen? Something's wrong there."

"But I saw the report from the investigation. It cleared Chief Arnesen of any suspicion in Mr. Mathiesen's death. The judge dropped the case with prejudice."

Lukas spit, then let out a dry laugh. "Yeah, right. Cops and judges covering for each other if you ask me."

I stepped out and walked around the corner. "Morning, gents. How goes the news today?"

"Pretty quiet, Chief Arnesen," Hal replied.

"He ain't no chief anymore," Lukas muttered.

"Well, Lukas, you're exactly right."

Lukas spit again. "Voted to kick your ass out of Rosemont's what I did."

"Again, that's not what you voted for, Lukas. You voted to fire me as Chief of Rosemont's Public Safety Team. That's all. I mean, you need to make sure you get the facts clear. You of all people must appreciate that, getting the facts straight, don't you, Hal?" I turned to the reporter and left Lukas alone.

"Facts are my business, Chief. Get 'em wrong and you pay for it. Get 'em right and they pay you for it."

Lukas snorted and walked away.

Hal waved to Lukas, then looked me in the eye. "He surely doesn't like you, Tomas. Not one bit. If it was colder you could see the venom steaming out of his ears."

"Mostly hot air if anything, Hal. Lukas is a coward. Operates best when he's got a captive audience or when he's with his buddies."

"Like Burley Wilkes and Reinert Tonnessen?"

"They don't call you Cedar City's best reporter for nothing, do they?" I laughed.

"Don't know about that but you better not turn your back on those three if you're out alone around them. What's with the enmity there?"

"Old Norwegians never die, it seems. They just pass their prejudices on to the next generation, or two or three. Grandpa Aksel kicked Sogard's granddad off the ranch for stealing feed. My dad bought a hundred acres for the ranch that Reinert's dad thought belonged to him by divine right, or something. Now Burley, well, he's not smart enough to have an original thought. He picks things up from whomever he's around at the moment. He's been around Sogard and Tonnessen for the last ten years or more, so I'm not surprised by his attitude either."

Hal looked down at his long, skinny reporter's pad, ripped some pages out of it, and tossed them into the trashcan behind him. "Not much useful information from him now that I've seen his willingness to play fast and loose with the facts." He looked up at me. "I know you're fired, but what's happening?"

"Off the record?"

"Completely off." He struck his hand out waiting for me to shake it.

"No need for that. I trust you. Off the record, I'm fired, but I'm still going to do everything I can to figure this mess out. My accomplices keep me informed."

"Nick, I mean Chief Lowrance, is not saying anything to anyone. None of us can get more than 'No comment' out of him. Sometimes he'll hold up the 'on-going investigation' sign just to spice things up, I guess."

I didn't say anything.

"So Nick is not one of your accomplices, I take it?"

"No comment." I grinned.

"You have a direction? Anything connecting the victims? Other than they lived in Rosemont, of course."

"I'm reading through the town ledger. City fathers have been writing down everything of note and a lot of nothing worth noting. I keep hoping to find a link, find any clue. So far? Nada."

We stood there on the corner, silent, looking up and down the street and the people and cars passing by.

"If you get something, think you might let me in on it before it gets to the big boys?"

Now I struck my hand out. "Wouldn't have it any other way, Hal."

Hal said, "No need," but we still shook hands.

"Something breaks, you get it as soon as I can bring you into the loop. You first."

Hal nodded in appreciation. "You might think about talking to Nick about his townspeople. A lot of them doing a lot of talking with us news types. I'm hearing piles of crap, speculation, bullshit up to your knees, and your name keeps coming up."

"Don't I know it. But since I'm fired, I'm also off the daily list of interviews, just the way I like. I plan to stay away from Nick as well, let him run the show now that he's Chief. But as long as the talking heads don't get in the way of my investigation, I'm going to let it go."

"Your investigation. I like the sound of that, Tomas, I mean, Chief Arnesen."

"Thanks, Mr. Leonard. For the support and the title. Guess I'm still performing the duties, title or not, fired or not."

"What's best for the people of Rosemont is what I'm hearing. When I get the chance to print that, you can bet your ass I will."

"You're a good guy, Hal Leonard. We probably need to break this up. Too many people have started watching us in the last five minutes. No need to give anyone more fodder for the manure spreader. Don't want to imperil your mortal reporter's soul."

Hal placed his hand to his heart. "Too late for that, Chief, but, yeah, I think I need to get a bite at The Cliff and listen to the table talk. See you later."

"Try the New York. Best steak in Utah."

He waved at me over his shoulder and walked down the street.

I watched him go and saw the people on the streets trying to keep eyes on both of us. Well, with two eyes in each head, maybe they could pull it off? But it wasn't anything I needed to fret about. Not when I had more pages to read.

48

"Hey, Chief. Hold up."

A white GMC Sierra 3500 HD pulled up alongside me. The black logo on the driver's door read S-TECH Security, the company watching Cold Creek Mine.

"I'm not the chief anymore. If this is official, you'll need to talk to Nick Lowrance, Acting Chief."

"Can't find him. Been trying. Saw you and, well, you may not be chief anymore but you might know what to do about this." He gestured over his shoulder. I looked in the window at three teenagers huddled together in the back seat.

"Found them jumping the fence around the tipple, running away as fast as they could go. They seemed more scared or upset by something behind them than of being grabbed up by us."

They didn't look happy. This rite of passage would lead them straight to their parents' displeasure and about twenty-five hours of community service, the going rate for trespassing in a closed coal mine.

The burly ex-miner-now-security-guard in the passenger seat leaned over toward the driver's window. "They didn't resist when we invited them to get in the truck here, and they haven't said a word all the way down the hill."

I looked closer. "Hey, Karl. You OK?" I recognized Karl Iverson Junior. His dad owned the Wood & Wire Hardware Store. I didn't know the other two, but the girl looked a little like Silje Erickson. "You're Silje's little sister, aren't you?"

"Yes. I'm Erica. I know Charlie. He works for you, doesn't he?"

"He does. Good guy."

"I like him. Silje really likes him."

She started to smile but abruptly stopped and looked at her friends and at the security guards in the front seat staring back at her.

I grinned. "That's good, cause I think he really likes her too, but he's a cowboy, you know? Might take him a while. Tell Silje that Chief Arnesen suggests she might want to make the first move."

This time she laughed.

I held out my hand to the driver. "I'll take them off your hands. Unofficially of course, if that's all right by you."

We shook. "Fine by us, Chief Arnesen. You seem to have a touch with them." He turned around and nodded. "We're dropping you off with the Chief here. Do us a favor and stay away from the mine. I know you think it's something you just gotta do before you turn sixteen or something, but the place is still too damn dangerous for people to be messing around in. Understand?"

"Yes, sir," all three of them answered.

Driver, who had still not given me his name, pushed the door lock button.

I opened the crew door and all three teens slid out as fast as they could and stood behind me. I looked at Driver and his oversized passenger. "I'll need your names when I write up the report for Nick when he gets back around the office."

Driver spoke. "J. B. Scanlon. He's Lee David. We work out of Rock Springs, Wyoming, mostly. We drew the short straw last time for our month of duty down here. Need anymore, you have the company's phones, right?"

J. B. Scanlon didn't wait for my response. He rolled up the window and drove off.

I turned to the kids. "So what do I do with you three?"

They weren't talking. Faces covered in just enough soot to be noticeable, they all stared at the ground, likely believing they were about to get into more trouble with me. I was the least of their worries. And even though what they'd done was technically breaking the law, it was a rite of passage that had existed ever since the coal mines had closed.

"You guys thirsty?"

They nodded.

"Good. I am, too. Let's hit the deli for doughnuts and something fizzy."

They brightened up a little. By the time we all had a couple of cake doughnuts and they were on their second refills, the mood had shifted. Even if I had tried, I couldn't get them to shut up.

"So tell me what happened up there—the truth—and no one else has to know about this. Oh, yeah, and you promise me you will never go up there again unless it is a supervised school trip on Cold Creek Mine Memorial Day."

They looked at each other and nodded. Then one by one they stuck their hands out for me to shake.

"So, no pinky-swear or stuff like that?" I laughed and they did too.

Karl Junior started. "We got inside the fencing around the tipple and were trying to figure out if we could climb it, get up inside to the top, see how far we could see."

Erica made sure to justify their actions. "No one that we know who's been up there has ever gone up to the top of the tipple. We thought it would be the best. You know, get photos of us climbing, the view from up there. The best."

Karl's dreams of fame seemed to float in front of him. "You could change the whole scene for everyone else who ever followed."

The other young man nodded. "Yeah. We'd be the ones. The first ones."

I finally placed the third kid. "Ah, Elvin. Your dad would be well and truly ticked off about this, wouldn't he? I mean, County Judge and all."

Elvin lost his grin, faded away as quickly as the last color leaves an aspen leaf.

"What spooked you?"

Elvin paused and stared directly at me. "How'd you know something did?"

"I've been at this a long time, son. You didn't look like you were spooked by being caught by those two rent-a-cops. Something else."

Erica resumed their story. "We were halfway up inside the tipple, working our way up a conveyor belt. Some coal chunks started falling down on us."

"I thought I heard someone cough or sneeze," Elvin said.

Erica said, "We decided it wasn't the wind playing tricks on us or the setting, with all that black and dirt and darkness. Someone was up above us. We climbed down and out and ran back for the fence. We didn't look back or nothing. We just got out of there. That's when the security guys grabbed us and tossed us into the truck and drove us back to town."

"That's it?"

"That's it, sir." Junior was adamant. I could tell from the way his voice started breaking that he was telling the truth.

"You are, all three of you, positive someone else was in the tipple above you."

They all nodded.

"OK. One of your cars is still up there, isn't it? Probably parked just down from the last turn before you hit the main yard, back off in that cutout?"

Three sets of wide-open eyes stared at me. "Like I said, I've been doing this a long time. Whose car?"

Junior raised his hand.

"Here's the deal. You two go home. I'll take Junior back up to get his car and I'll look around. You don't tell anyone about what I'm going to do and I won't tell anyone about what you just did. If a story about the three of you does leak out, your parents and I will have a nice long chat, which will pretty much guarantee twenty-five hours of community service—minimum. And it will not be easy community service if I know your dad, Elvin. And I know your dad, Elvin."

I walked them to the door. Elvin and Erica waved at Karl Junior and took off for home. Both would have pretty good walks.

Karl and I walked to my truck. I got in to drive, then flung the passenger side door open. Perfectly framed by the open door, Karl stood with his hands in his pockets and his eyes on the ground.

"C'mon, Karl. We need to get back out there. Maybe whoever was there is still there and I can see for myself. Get in."

Karl didn't move.

"Is something the matter? Is my ride not cool enough?"

At least that elicited a quiet, quick laugh. "It's not that, sir. It's just that . . ."

"Karl, we're wasting time."

"I know! I'm sorry. It's just that I didn't tell you everything in there. They didn't see it."

"Didn't see what?" For the first time in days, my healing chest wound made itself known. "Can you at least get in here to tell me?"

Karl climbed into the cab and shut the door. "I saw a clear set of bootprints on one side of the conveyor belt, clear as day." Karl waved his arm back and forth. "Had to be fresh the way the wind was blowing. I could see the dust moving inside. They were fresh. Someone was up there above us, sir."

"Think that person saw you three?"

"Don't know. Don't think so. Pretty dark, and when we left we ran out the other side from where we entered. There's no opening on that side of the tipple, not one top to bottom. They'd have to come down and out the way we went in."

"You looked back, didn't you?"

Junior dropped his gaze and hesitated.

"But you didn't see anything."

"Not sure, sir. Just not sure. But I know someone was there."

I thought for a while. "I want the three of you to stick together these next few days. Stay around adults as much as possible when you aren't in school. Anything or anyone makes you feel strange, you call me."

Karl had turned white.

I grabbed his shoulder. "Karl, listen to me. You guys are going to be fine. Just do what I ask for the next few days. When things settle down, I might have a good story for you that will, like, totally change your adventure and turn you three into awesome heroes."

"No shi—I mean, no kidding, sir?"

"None at all. Now, let's go get your car."

Once we arrived at the coal mine, Karl wasted no time in getting into his car. I'd thought of looking around, but night had fallen and surely whoever had been there had left once the kids had been picked up. Before turning back to town, I looked up at the coal tipple top. If someone could get up there, that'd be quite a nice perch, just like the kids had said. A great view of the town. Heck, even a great view of ...

Sometimes you're not altogether that bad of a former chief, Arnesen.

I estimated that from the coal tipple top to my spring was a little over twelve hundred yards. Long damn shot, just like I'd thought. But makeable with a Sharp's Berdan. Distance plus center mass plus less powerful round than a modern sniper rifle.

That was the solution to the equation and the question, "Why am I still alive?" Another piece of the puzzle on the board. But I didn't know where it fit.

I followed Karl's beat-up red Honda Civic back to town. Next stop, Lynette at the courthouse.

49

Our courthouse, an extension to the Stordahl Civic Center hall on the opposite side of the building from our public safety office, never ran to the busy side of a legal day. Just not that much happened in Rosemont. At least till my short tenure. It wasn't hard to find a slack time to slip in the side door, go around one corner, and walk into Lynette's office. She worked for the Engelmann County Recorder's office in Welling, lived in Rosemont, and kept daily office hours even though she was part-time.

I didn't make a sound until I spoke. "Good day, Lynette."

From behind decades-old glasses, Lynette squinted at me. "Why, Tomas Arnesen. I did not see you come in. Can I help you with something?"

"You mean you're not going to send me out and call the Acting Chief of Rosemont Public Safety?"

"Why would I do that? We all know some of the town council members are basically cowards who don't want to mess with their cushy monthly stipends for serving our city's needs. What is it now, all of fifty bucks a meeting?" She laughed. "Look, Tomas. You never come in here to pass the time of day. You do one of two things: walk past or stick your head in, say hi all nice and polite-like, and head on out to do whatever it is you do out there."

"Oh?"

"When you come all the way up to my desk, as you did just now, you need information. Every time, without exception. Oh, you're still very polite, but usually what you need from me overrides your inclination to engage me in significant conversation. But I will credit you this, when you do ask me how I am, even from the doorway on your way somewhere else, you stop to listen, if and when I tell you how I am. So thank you for that, Tomas Arnesen. Now, how can I help you?"

She would have made a keen detective. "I need to know everything you remember about Astrid Dyrdahl's final years. Don't need anything confidential, just your memories."

"Is this related to the murders?"

"Yes." No sense in trying to sidestep her.

"Good. I knew you wouldn't quit working just because those idiots in the next room can't find their way out of a foot-deep gulley."

"Thanks."

"Sit down. I'll tell you what I remember. You tell me if it helps. Deal?" She stuck out her hand. We shook. I sat down.

"Well, first off, about Averil committing suicide in Astrid's living room. Don't care if it was his house before, it was still unkind of him to do that. She never got over it. I know that. Three days before her stroke, she came in here, filed some papers for her and Kirsten. We talked. She cried. Still hurt her deep inside, that man did. If he hadn't shot himself, I might have been tempted to do it myself." The color rose in her cheeks, perfectly matching her red hair, pulled back in a bun, and spoke a lot about her temperament.

"How long did she live after the stroke?"

"About six months. It was massive and left her completely bedridden. Kirsten, God bless that child forever, stayed with her grandma night and day. She moved back into the house. Cooked, cleaned, and cared for Astrid when the home health folks couldn't get there. She worked her jobs, kept the store straight, kept the dispatch going for the Safety Team. She's a trooper, Tomas Arnesen."

Lynette pointed a gun-like finger at me. "I promise you one thing:

you hurt that young lady in any way, I will do to you what that failure Averil Lowrance did to himself. I will shoot you dead. You hear me?"

Heck, with the seriousness she shot at me right then, she could have been a mercenary. "Loud and clear. That's also the consensus of every lady in Rosemont when the subject of me and Kirsten comes up, which seems to come up a lot lately, for some odd reason."

"Well, the two of you together does add up to one odd reason, don't you think?"

I nodded. "Even if the conversation is about the weather, it'll wind its way around to the two of us: how I'd better be treating her good, how much trouble I'll be in if, in your words, I hurt that young lady in any way."

Lynette started to respond, but I held up my hand, politely. "Let me say three things in my own defense: I am more surprised by her attention than anyone else in this county. Two, I am hopelessly in love with her. Given the aftermath of both of my failed marriages and the accompanying grief, I will not put another human being through that, much less go through it myself. Third, I can almost completely assure you, Kirsten Dyrdahl is no longer a young lady. She is a grown-up woman."

Now, since I couldn't keep the smile off my face, I knew she was going to either throw me out or throw something at me. I stood up and headed for the door.

She threw her pencil sharpener.

"Ouch. Good thing that wasn't your chair."

"Remember what I told you, about Astrid and about Kirsten. You mess this up and you'll be running from a bunch of us old ladies. You won't like what'll happen to you if we catch you."

"Thanks for the information. It helped."

"Remember, Tomas Arnesen. We know where you live. I bet Mabel would be in the lead!" Her shout echoed out into the short hallway as I exited the building.

50

Kirsten had what I needed, both in terms of information and morale-boosting. I certainly needed a hug and a kiss, or two or three, in public if necessary. My chest still hurt a little when I walked, but it was the good kind of hurt now, the itch that spoke of healing, the reduced level of ache that reminded me how close I'd come to not being here, to not being period.

When that realization hit me, and it had smacked me several times a day once the initial shock and shakes wore off, I started looking for Kirsten. Called her. Found her at the store or went to the house or the apartment. The first time my mortality ran up and barked at me here in Rosemont, I wanted Kirsten. When the panic receded and I had time to think about the response, I knew I'd changed. The old Arnesen, when confronted by his own mortality, would head back to the station, close the door to his little detective's office to drink Glenlivet for an hour or so, off-duty, usually.

The fast, bumpy walk to the store did all my aching good, inside and out. Anticipation is a powerful drug. I was licking my lips and checking my breath half-a-block away. The hug and kiss deposited atop the aching exceeded my expectations. It did that every time, which was another reason I knew Kirsten had me, that I belonged to her, that she was not going to let me go as promised.

Sometimes it's easy to be a coward, to hang back from acting because you're afraid. I'd spent plenty of hours avoiding confrontations with my ex-wives, hours at the station pretending I had a case that was keeping me over time, or that a buddy needed assistance. Easy to hang back and live off my excuses until both wives gave up and walked away.

I stood on the sidewalk, looking into the store's front plate glass windows. All four of the registers lined up across the front expanse, two of them with their lights blinking. Janny worked Number 1 and Edie sat back and monitored the two self-check registers. Soon after Tollef decided to modernize the store, I tried to use the Do-It-Yourself lines and screwed up a simple four-item transaction. Now I go to Janny's register when she's working.

I knew Kirsten watched the registers and the front entrance to the store from her perch in the office behind the long two-way mirror window that everyone knew was a two-way window.

"Afternoon, Chief." Tollef Varland sidled up to me, which is a hard thing for him to do, weighing in at a healthy three hundred pounds.

"On leave, Tollef. On leave."

"Aw, dritt, Tomas. Town council asking you to step down doesn't mean anything out here. We know you'll watch out for us no matter what."

"Nick will do just fine."

"Oh, come on, Tomas. That pup couldn't find his head with a GPS unit, map, or compass."

"Tollef, Tollef. What do you have against the youth of our fair community?"

"Not a dang thing. Except their lousy attitudes and even more abysmal work ethic."

"How's Cathrine doing these days?"

"Still working me over to lose weight. Last week she bought me one of those walking machines that talks back to you. This week looks like I'm going back to those watching people and getting weighed, in private, but it's still kinda in public too. How's that for how she's doing?"

"Well, as long as you know she still cares, Tollef."

He laughed and slapped me on the back, knocked me three steps into the store's entrance. "Sometimes I just wish she didn't care so dang much, Tomas. But I do love her."

"How can you not love a North Dakota Norwegian pig farmer's daughter who thinks you're the best thing since lutefisk?"

"Yah, sure. Dat's the trut." Tollef could exaggerate his accent when it suited him. "You going in to see Kirsten?"

Here it was. Go back to the excuses or get on with the riskiest move I'd ever made. "Yep. Going to walk in there, wave her to come down, and," I tapped Tollef on the shoulder, "you probably don't want to get too far away for this. I'm going to pick her up, swing her around, and give her the biggest, longest kiss she's ever gotten. At least I hope it's the longest one."

I didn't wait for Tollef's response. I walked into the store, waved up at the two-way mirror for Kirsten to come down. She did, and I kept my promise to Mabel and Tollef. With Lynette's admonitions and threats ringing in my ears, I fell completely off the wheel.

After what seemed like a minute-long kiss but felt like a blissful glimpse of eternity to me, Kirsten pulled back, her eyes wide. She took a deep breath.

Maybe I'd literally taken her breath away.

"What was that for, Tomas Arnesen? Aren't you worried about what they're all going to say?"

"Not anymore. Everyone in this town has given me advice about us. I decided to take all their advice."

I didn't get on my knee. This wasn't a formal proposal, more like the prelude to a proposal. Going back through my grandpa's dusty room, I'd found the single pearl ring he'd given grandma, his promise to her that one day a diamond would take its place.

"This was Gramma's ring. Aksel gave it to her as a promise ring. He promised her a diamond to replace it. Gramma told him she didn't need a diamond. Probably lose it working on the ranch, and then she'd feel real bad. The pearl, she said, was beautiful, soft, pale ivory white, and she'd wear it and be proud. I want you to wear it now."

Kirsten started to tear up, and I did too. "Tomas? Are you sure?"

"As sure of anything as I've ever been in my life. You having second thoughts about sticking with an old man?"

She slipped the pearl onto her right-hand ring finger. A perfect fit. "No, Tomas Arnesen. I am not having second thoughts. I am having third and fourth and fifth thoughts, all about life with you, about the bedroom when we get there, about children, about how good you and I are together."

The flush reached up out of my collar and ran all the way to my cheeks, ears, and forehead.

Kirsten giggled, held the ring up to the light, and twirled around.

Janny, Edie, Tollef, and the five other shoppers started applauding. I noticed nothing but the sparkle in Kirsten's eyes. "Hey, Tollef. Can I borrow her for a bit?" I called out.

He was going to say something risqué—probably overheard the bedroom remark—but chose to pass the opportunity and took a different road. "No sweat. Go, go, go. Just have her back in a half hour."

We sat in the front corner of Heavenly Grounds, heads together, holding hands, talking softly about nothing and everything.

"Tell me about Astrid. What was she like in those last years when you lived with her?"

She looked at me for a long two or three seconds. "Something's going on, isn't it? You know something new."

"I don't know if I know anything new. But I have some threads I need to connect. You can help."

Kirsten sighed, then looked beyond me and into her past. "My grandmother seemed sad. Lost a husband, then a daughter, then a friend when Averil killed himself. Sad. Lonely. But never dispirited, never depressed. We talked all the time about the ranch, about how she worked side-by-side with grandpa, how much she loved the land and this place, her friends, Rosemont. All of it. One time, right before the stroke, she had one of those moments I hope we all have once in a while."

I must have had a puzzled look on my face.

"You know, when for no reason you can think of you feel like dancing naked in the moonlight or singing at the top of your lungs in the middle of the street. Like Scrooge must have felt when he realized he hadn't missed Christmas after all. Giddy. All silly and unable to keep still. I watched her go from clipping sheets to the clothesline to wrapping herself up in one and dancing all over the backyard. Half-an-hour she danced. I couldn't look away. She radiated love and wonder and hope. It was one of the best afternoons I've ever had."

I crooked an eyebrow.

She leaned over and kissed me on the top of my head. "Until today when you came to the store."

"You aim better with a gun than you do your lips. Sure hope it improves in the next few weeks."

We sat there smiling at each other like two teenagers discovering what they think is love, trying to figure out what to do next: hug, kiss, or just sit there and stare at each other some more. We opted to kiss again. She got closer to my lips, right smack on them as a matter of fact.

"Good. You're a quick learner."

Kirsten sat back and smiled. "After her stroke, it was so hard watching all that life and energy fade away. She fought hard, but in the end just too much damage had been done for her to fight back. Funny thing though, right at the end. A few minutes before she died, she got agitated and kept rolling her hand over and over, kept pointing a finger across the room. We played the oddest game of charades ever, me trying to decipher what she wanted. I thought maybe she saw something or someone outside, looking through the window."

"Did you decipher it?"

"No. After a while she stopped and looked at me with these huge tears in her eyes. Two more breaths after that episode and she was gone. I looked out the window again. Maybe she saw the angels coming for her? I felt awful that I couldn't break through with her and help. To this day I still wonder what was happening in her head."

"Where were you? In the house, I mean. Where did you have her bed?"

Kirsten cocked her head and gave me that what-on-earth-does-that-have-to-do-with-anything-I've-been-telling-you look.

I raised my left eyebrow to reiterate the question.

"Oh, we had her hospital bed in the living room, on the short wall right under Grandfather's portrait."

"What was across the room? What was on the opposite side of the bed? Where might she have been pointing?"

"Desk. Table and chairs. The old secretary Grandpa made for her. Oh, my goodness. The secretary? Was that it?"

"I don't know, but I'd like to go check it out if that's all right?"

"OK. Don't know what you'll find, but go ahead."

I kissed her again. "If I find something important, I'll call you right away. Now, scoot back to work. Tollef's been tolerant enough today."

"Scoot? *Scoot?* I'm not twelve anymore."

I kissed her again as we stood up, turned her around, and gently swatted her lovely behind. "I'm ancient, what can I say? You're stuck with all those colorful, outdated expressions for which we old people are justly famous."

She laughed. "Famous old man grabbing my behind."

Expecting retaliation of some sort, I got in my truck. I could walk to the house, but the way my brain was clicking off ideas, I needed to be standing in the old house's living room as quickly as I could get there. I needed to stand in the space where two souls had died—one righteously, one troubled and lost.

51

Kirsten had sketched out a map of the living room as they had set it up when her grandmother became bedridden. I wandered around the room for a while, holding the map, turning it, orienting myself to the bed's spot, the windows opposite, the front door, the kitchen off to the right. Once I had it set in my head, I stood as close to where Astrid's head would have been.

Sure enough, the desk and chair fit neatly beneath the window. The White Oak secretary Averil had made stood next to the desk, on the right side of the window, fitting neatly into the space between the desk and the wall, custom-crafted for the exact measurements of the corner. A precise fit, with a quarter-inch on each side.

I had nothing to lose and felt a certain tingle run through my shoulders. *OK. Now we play, "What if?"* What if Gramma Astrid had been pointing at the desk or the secretary? What if she'd wanted Kirsten to look there? What if she wasn't seeing Averil out the window coming for her?

I took the desk first. Every drawer, every paper, every envelope. Kirsten followed her mother and her grandma in the way she kept her life organized, at least the paper part of her life. Neat, clean, file folders, every expense, every bit of income, all right at hand. I resisted the temptation to delve too deeply into Kirsten's life on paper, despite knowing she couldn't care less if I saw it or not. It left me feeling a bit voyeuristic. There'd be time to learn about each other's financial habits later.

I looked for older papers, letters, a different handwriting. The desk yielded three items other than what belonged to Kirsten: a letter from her dad to her mom dated April, 1944, a high school graduation card from Astrid to Kirsten, and the funeral home register from Kirsten's mom's services.

OK. Nothing helpful in the desk. On to the secretary.

I opened the center drawer and found five calendars from Parkin's Store, 1956 through 1960, three different-colored sets of elegant, lace-trimmed, heavy stationery, several fountain pens, a pearl-handled letter opener, and a pile of letters tied up with a green ribbon. The letters were addressed to Astrid Haaland, her maiden name. The return address consisted of the ornate Victorian initials D. M. over a post office box in San Francisco. The writing looked decidedly feminine. I didn't open them, but counted twenty letters. The first postmark showed August 15, 1930. The last one was dated August 15, 1950. Twenty letters, one a year for twenty years. I started to untie the package then stopped. *D. M. San Francisco. A long time ago. A feminine hand. Leave it alone.* I put them back down in the drawer and closed it.

As I pulled the top open and down, two wooden sides slid out of their pockets on which the top came to rest. I looked at the top row of three large drawers, square fronts with rounded knobs, hand-forged, no two matching. The second row held three more large drawers with expertly rounded drawer fronts, rounded to fit the side curves of the desk. My estimation of Averil's talents as a woodworker continued to grow.

Eight small square drawers, four on a side, flanked two open shelves in the middle of the back. I took out my notebook and inventoried the drawers.

Top drawer, left side: sewing thread, needles in paper packets, assorted thimbles.

Center drawer: more sets of unused stationery.

Top right drawer: black-and-white and sepia photographs of Astrid in her baptismal gown and an older couple—not Astrid and Everall, perhaps one of their parents—and several images of different and very severe unsmiling ancestors.

The three middle drawers produced a small mound of clippings from the *Rosemont Republic*: social events, who had relatives in town from faraway places, dinner parties, guest speakers at church banquets, missionary visits, children's plays, and a photo of nearly every new business ribbon-cutting for the last thirty-plus years.

The eight small drawers yielded more knick-knacks, broken jewelry, three fabric-measuring tapes, a pocket watch that worked when I wound it, and a vast assortment of business cards from all over the world. Who knew Astrid collected these? I wondered if Kirsten even knew about them.

I found a copy of Astrid's Last Will and Testament in the top center shelf. I set that aside to read when I finished the search. Maybe there was a clue in there.

The bottom shelf held both blank and handwritten recipe cards, some with Astrid's handwriting, which I recognized, and many others I didn't know but suspected came from the kitchens of Rosemont women and women around the world, just like the business cards.

Nothing else of note. I sat back, disappointed, then leafed through the few pages of Astrid's will. It didn't take long. What little she had at the end, the property long since given over to Kirsten, went to charity and to an orphanage in Peru, of all places. If nothing else materialized, I'd learned a little more about the surprising Astrid Haaland Dyrdahl's life.

I leaned back too far and the chair nearly fell over.

In the flash of realization that I was going down, as my face came level with the desktop and before the chair and I hit the floor, an anomaly registered. Then I hit the floor. Fortunately, the impact didn't jar the anomaly out of my brain.

I got up and leaned over the desk, fingering the bottom of the lower shelf. The bottom stood a fingernail or two proud of the frame. I grabbed one of the fabric tape measures. The top shelf was three inches tall. The bottom shelf was a full quarter-inch shorter. I'd missed that until the chair went backward.

I slid the tip of the letter opener into the line at the bottom of the shelf, turned it, and the shelf bottom popped open. I held my breath as I pulled the shelf all the way out of the desk, then looked down into the hidden compartment and saw one final hope: a sheet of elegant blue stationery, folded in half.

Something saved and hidden. A paper toward which a dying lady had pointed, trying to pass its presence on to her granddaughter. I'd left the letters unread. I could not leave this document in the same condition.

52

I knew from my grandfather's journal the truth of that fateful night. He and their friends had covered for Averil. How could Averil ever think Aksel would have an affair, with anyone? Grandpa was completely lost the first time he saw Ingrid Winther walking across the campus at St. Olaf College in Northfield, Minnesota. Being second-generation Norwegian-American, my grandpa always joked about how he had to go back to the homeland to find a wife.

I had my list. I had my suspicions. So close to the truth now it scared me. I reached for the radio mike clipped to my shoulder. It wasn't there.

You're fired, ex-chief Arnesen. Remember?

My cell phone rang.

"Ex-Chief Arnesen." I said it before I realized what I'd said.

"Chief Arnesen. This is Engelmann Dispatch. The sheriff asked me to contact you. We haven't heard from Deputy Yorke in several hours."

"I haven't seen him in a couple of days."

"He left this morning to see you. Had something come up he wanted you to see but didn't want to do it over the air or by phone. He'd been on the phone most of the day yesterday with the Salt Lake forensic team that had worked on the Rosemont cases. Seemed pretty excited about it."

"What time did he leave Welling?"

"It was oh six-thirty when he called in to tell us he was on the road."

The hairs on the back of my neck prickled. "OK. I'm headed back to town. I'll start checking, see if anyone has seen him or the Durango."

"Please check, Chief Arnesen. We don't like our officers being off the air for any length of time. If you locate him in the next hour, Sheriff Consolves is going to send a lot more troops your way."

"Copy that. I'll have to call in on my cell phone since I don't have access to my radio at the moment."

"No problem. We understand up here. Stay with it, Chief. And call as soon as you know something. Oh, Chief. Did you get the forensics report from the state lab? We got a copy late yesterday evening. That's what put the fire under Deputy Yorke."

"Who got the original?"

"Sent to Acting Public Safety Chief Nicholas Lowrance."

"Will do." Now the hairs on the back of my neck were dancing. If they started doing the twist, well, when that happens I'm usually in the middle of something messy.

Speed dial Kirsten's phone.

"Hi. This is Kirsten. Can't answer now for any number of good reasons. Leave a message at the beep. Thanks."

"Hey, love. Tomas. Have you seen Yorke? Call me as soon as you get this."

My message was short enough that I was sure she wouldn't be able to hear the growing fear I was trying to stifle. Then again, my call sounded urgent because it was urgent. She'd know.

Once in town, I drove straight to Parkin's, where I stuck my head in the door and waved at Cathrine.

She looked up from scanning groceries for a customer, then swatted a stray strand of wiry gray hair away from her forehead. "Hey, Chief. What's up?"

"I'm trying to track down Kirsten. Got her voice mail just now and I can't use the radio because, well, I don't have a radio anymore."

"Stupid, fraidy-cat council. I know. But she's not here. Came in, I assume, soon after you two had your chat. She got a phone call, asked if she could leave for a while. Haven't seen her since. Thought the call was from you. We all like that you two are spending time together, so I haven't thought anything else about it."

Yorke's AWOL. Now Kirsten too? Something's not right. Something's very not right.

"Hmm. What time did the phone call come in?"

"About an hour ago. She hadn't been back in the office very long."

"Did she walk or take her Jeep?"

"Took the Jeep. Saw her leave. Got out of the parking lot pretty quick too. Never saw her drive that fast before."

"If she calls you, tell her to call me as quickly as she can."

"Now you've got me a little scared, Tomas. Is something wrong?"

"I honestly don't know, Cathrine. I don't know. I'll check with you later."

I drove back to town, my brain working over several scenarios, sorting, filing, accepting, rejecting, moving the pieces around on my mental chessboard like knights and queens. I had my backup office key in one of those little metal magnetic boxes stuck inside my toolbox. I'd get on the radio, suspended or not, and start tracking my people down.

The radio was turned off. It's not supposed to be turned off. Ever. Now my dancing hairs stood at full attention, unmoving even with the slight chilling breeze that'd just come through.

"Rosemont One to Dispatch."

Silence. Static. Nothing.

"Rosemont One to Dispatch. What's your twenty?"

Static.

"Rosemont One to Safety One."

"Safety One. Go ahead."

"Nathan, what's your twenty?"

"At the school. Another monkey bar incident. One of the Opland kids took a header—"

"Sorry to interrupt, Nathan. Have you seen either Kirsten or Deputy Yorke today?"

"Saw Kirsten a while ago, driving the Jeep down Main Street. Haven't seen Yorke in a couple of days."

"Thanks. When you get done at the school, stick close to your radio and your phone, for me."

"Got it, Chief. What's up? What's going on?"

"Like I told Cathrine a minute ago when I talked to her, I don't know. We have two people missing at the moment. I need you to stick close to that radio, keep your full EMT kit handy, and definitely get the ambulance ready."

"Chief. You're not making any sense."

"Copy that. Just get yourself and everything medical ready. When I need you, I'm probably going to need you to come running to wherever I am. Got that? I know I can't give you orders, being fired and all that, but right now I don't much care about all those boundaries. Do it for Kirsten, if for no one else."

"Will do. Let me get going."

"Rosemont One to Rosemont Two."

Silence.

"Rosemont One to Rosemont Two."

"Two here. Go ahead, Tomas."

"Nick. I'm looking for Kirsten. Have you seen her?"

"Should you be using the radio? What's your twenty?"

"I'm at the office using the radio and I don't give a damn whether I should be using it or not. Have you seen Kirsten? Why is she off the air? She's never off the air."

"Uh, well, no. I haven't seen her. I had her shut the radio down this morning so I could work on the antenna. Just haven't gotten around to it yet."

Turn the system off? Fix the antenna? What the hell was he doing?

"Seems to be working fine, Nick. We're talking. Have you seen Deputy Yorke? County dispatch said he left to come down here early this morning. They haven't heard from him since. They're getting worried. If we don't find him, a whole bunch of the Engelmann County Sheriff's Department will be headed our way in less than an hour."

Silence.

"Two, you still there?"

"Oh, I just remembered. Yeah, I did, I saw the deputy this morning around seven-fifteen."

"And?"

"Well, we talked for a bit, then he said thanks, said he was going to go on over to Springville then back to Welling. Wasn't too clear on his reasons. Think it was about follow-up with some NTSB folks about the senator's plane crash."

"Nick, what's your twenty?"

"Oh, hey, Tomas, I gotta go now. I'll get back to you."

Click.

I know the sound when the person on the other end of the radio turns it completely off.

Nothing in our conversation added up. Well, it didn't add to a number or to anything else as definitive as an answer. What it did add up to was a huge sense of misgiving which the hairs on the back of my neck confirmed. They felt like they were about to leap out of my body.

I dropped the mike, took two deep breaths, and stopped moving. In the calm, I'd realized several things: I had time. If Nick wanted me there for some kind of payoff, I had time to think this out.

I looked through every folder on my desk, on the counter, everywhere, looking for the forensics report. Not here. Checked the trash cans. Nothing there. Then I tossed the shredder can's contents on the countertop. Red paper, manila folder, pieces of a metal clasp. No entry in the log. Could have been anything, but I knew if I put these shredded pieces back together, I'd be reading that report from the state lab.

Sheriff's department business line. I knew I had to check out the details with them and knew I was beginning to run up against a time barrier. I didn't wait for the dispatcher to get out her excellent phone response.

"Can you read me the highlights of that forensics report?"

"Uh, sure, Chief. What's up? What do you need?"

"Just run over the big things, any conclusions, anything that sticks out."

"Hang on, please."

Two clicks, a hum, then Emilio came on the line. "Tomas. What's going on?"

"Emilio, I don't have time for this. I need information from that forensics report and I need it now. Please. I'm running out of time here."

"Yorke involved?"

"Yes. We're getting to life and death I'm afraid."

"OK. Nuff for me. Let me look over this again."

Fortunately, Emilio didn't take long as my blood pressure was pushing me to say something I'd regret.

"Says they matched three sets of prints at all three crime scenes: the victims, Nathan Bronstad, and Nicholas Lowrance. Said your prints showed up at the third crime scene only. Note here kinda scolding you for that lapse."

"Anything else of note?"

"Not that I can see. Does that help?"

"Does. I think you need to get your troops rolling now, Sheriff. Don't wait. I'll call in a few more minutes with more specific directions for you. Sheriff, this is a ten-thirty-nine, and I hope to God not an officer-down call."

I hung up, knowing Emilio would understand, and the call was even now hitting the airwaves.

53

Where are you, Nick Lowrance?

Not in town. Not at home. Wasn't at or around the Dyrdahl's house, which had once belonged to his grandfather.

The cabin. The original dwelling. He had to be there.

The back of my neck burned like it was on fire. I wanted the events unfolding in front of me to unfold in slow motion. I wanted the clock to stop so I could catch up.

The homestead cabin was five miles beyond Rosemont, fifteen miles from the Arnesen Ranch. If I went home, changed, picked up a horse and trailer, I'd lose some of that time slipping through my fingers. I called the ranch phone.

Charlie answered. "Hey boss, what's up?"

"Charlie, I need you to saddle Reckless for me, get him in a trailer. Meet me on the road to the Dyrdahl's main house as soon as you can. Drop everything else. Stick my Winchester in the boot. Bring the forty-five as well. There's a vest on my bed. Bring it and one of my denim work shirts. Probably lying in a heap where I left them the other day."

"See you there in about twenty minutes, or less."

One of the many things I liked about Charlie: he never questioned an order, just got it done. He'd beat me to the intersection if I knew anything about him. I unlocked my safe and took out both my S&W Bodyguards, clipped one holster to my belt in the small of my back, the other wrapped around my ankle. I took off my T-shirt and slipped on a long-sleeved thermal hunting shirt.

I called the Sheriff's Office non-emergency number before leaving the office. "Sheriff Consolves. I know where Yorke is and am headed that way now."

"Understood. I'll be on the road in ten minutes with at least three deputies. Highway Patrol is sending at least two units as well."

"Great. Come to the Public Safety Office here. Charlie Dupree will be waiting for you with directions to where I'll be. He'll get you up there quietly. Last part of the trip is horsebackm so you might want to let the troops know."

"Good luck, Tomas. Be careful out there."

"Roger that, Sheriff. Will do my best. Bye for now."

Good thing I didn't bet anyone on Charlie's punctuality. He waved as I drove up to the intersection. Reckless was saddled, rifle in the boot, ready to go.

"Thanks, Charlie."

Charlie tipped his Stetson and waited. Not quite out of high school, it looked more like he was mimicking every tipped-hat scene from every Western he'd ever seen. Still, the kid was loyal and smart. He'd worked around me long enough to know there was more to come.

"I need you to get back to the ranch, saddle at least six, no, make it eight horses, then have Bud and anyone else around trailer the horses back right here. Once you get Bud working on the horses, I want you to wait in town at the office for Sheriff Consolves and the officers he's bringing with him. Bring them here, get them mounted, then lead them to the aspen grove just east of the old Lowrance cabin, the one that sits against that basalt flow ridge at the back of the Dyrdahl's property. You know it?"

"Know it well, Boss."

I enhanced my wardrobe before mounting. I pulled the new low-profile vest over the thermal crew, the old denim work shirt over that.

I loosened the straps on the spare bulletproof vest and wore it outside, visible. I checked my arm movement. The thickness restricted me somewhat, but I could still get to my weapons. I clipped the .45 holster to my belt, toward the front, out in the open. Nick would see it. I pulled on my riding gloves and swung up into the saddle. Reckless danced a little bit, anxious to be on the road.

"Let's get to it, Charlie."

"Damn straight, Chief." He smiled and tipped his hat again. First time he'd ever called me anything other than Boss.

I rode off into the afternoon light, letting Reckless generally choose the path as we rode northeast. I planned to circle around the open front of the cabin and try to come up from the forest side, unseen for as long as possible.

When Averil Lowrance had proved up his homestead, he knew exactly what he was doing. Backed up against a large mixed grove—mostly pinyon pine, Douglas fir, juniper, and aspen—he used the timber he'd cut to construct the twelve-by-twenty starter home. One side of the grove ended against a sharp basalt flow ridge. The cabin backed up against the ridge leaving Averil a 270-degree view from his front porch, his five acres spread out in front. Anything moving across the flats, animal and human, had come under his watchful eyes. If he didn't want to visit with his visitors, he'd slip out the back and disappear into the forest.

It was nearly impossible to approach the house from straight behind. You'd have to climb a series of treacherous ridges and valleys to get to the cardboard-edge thin ridge above the house. From there, if you could balance yourself long enough, you could look down onto the roof, about a hundred feet below, think about sliding down the ridge slope, only about three degrees off vertical, or decide the smartest thing you could do would be to turn around and climb down, up, down, up and out. Well, smartest at that moment if you considered the lack of good judgment shown by starting out in the first place. Nope. Getting at Averil from behind was never an option.

More than once, my grandpa had told me that Averil had always been a bit paranoid. "Came from his war experiences, that's what I think," he told me, when I asked why his friend seemed to like being alone. "Had his whole unit wiped out in Germany. Surprise attack from behind. He played dead, two of his buddies lying on top of him, their blood all over him. Relief troops found them the next morning. He never told me directly how he spent the night, but I expect he stayed under them buddies until help came. Experience like that gotta impact a fella's psyche, that's for damn sure."

Every time I sit down in a public place with my back to a solid wall that I've checked out, I understand a piece of Averil's psyche.

Charlie would bring my backup this same route. He'd know how to help the sheriff get everyone in position. I just wished I had a clue how I was going to let them know what to do, and, more importantly, when to do it, whatever it was and whenever I thought of it.

I could see the cabin now and figured I'd been spotted if anyone was in there and they were watching. But I moved slowly, riding just inside the tree line. Averil had thinned out the aspens in this part of his property years ago, so there was more space through them than you sometimes find.

Smoke rose from the chimney. Someone was home.

Well, I wasn't going to figure this out or get any closer to finding Kirsten and the deputy if I waited.

Time for action.

Time to do something.

Time I knew was running out.

I spurred Reckless and laughed at my bravado in giving him that name. He whinnied in reply and broke into a trot as we escaped the tree line. I rode straight up the trail toward the cabin, and the dusty black Rosemont Safety Team SUV was parked off to the side.

I reined Reckless in and stopped about fifty feet from the front door.

54

When Kirsten opened the cabin door and stepped out on the porch, I almost stopped breathing. The front of her jacket was covered in blood, her hands and cheeks also smeared. But she looked otherwise all right and seemed to be standing and walking with no problems.

Not her blood.

I breathed a deep sigh. Having Kirsten come out alone was a smart move on Nick's part because those seconds were just long enough for him to step from around the side of the cabin, between the log wall and the side of his truck.

I didn't look away from Kirsten and kept Nick in my peripheral vision. I waited. He was going to have to break the silence.

"Hey, Tomas. Glad you could join us." Nick walked out two steps and two steps more over toward the porch and Kirsten.

Her eyes darted back and forth, but I couldn't tell what she was trying to tell me. She backed into the doorway.

"Ah, ah, ah. Stay out here on the porch Kirsten. Stay right there." Nick walked farther into my field of vision, the muzzle of the long-barreled Sharps Berdan unwavering from its aim: center mass again, right in the same hole he'd tried to bore into me before.

I held my hands up. "Nice shot, Nick. Thought it would be something like that. If I check out the Cold Creek tipple, I'll find evidence of your presence at the top, won't I? Whew. That's an award-winning shot for sure."

"Twelve hundred yards, Chief! Should've gone for the headshot. Lot riskier than the center mass shot I took. Too bad you were wearing the vest." He smiled.

This was not his usual goofy smile that had made us laugh just a few weeks ago. The tight-lipped grimace that narrowed his eyes and pulled down the corners of his mouth spoke volumes—anger and hate with a little malice thrown in. I'd never seen that expression on his face.

I smiled back. "You're good at this, Nick. Very good. Had us all fooled, running around in circles."

"Thought you had figured it out a while back. That's why I took the shot when you were out riding. Sorry about that."

"Sorry about my horse?"

"Nah. Not really. Thought if I'd only wounded you, you didn't need means of getting yourself out of there to safety. Shooting the horse was a spur of the moment decision."

Reckless snorted.

A glint off the Sharps barrel caught my eye. Nick had flinched. Arms still raised, I hadn't moved. Nick hadn't given me any instructions yet, so I stayed still. *Go ahead and tell me your story, kid, preferably before you flinch me off this earth.*

He obliged. "Took me quite a while to find your slot canyon, Chief. I thought I knew this country, including your ranch, better than most. You're pretty good at hiding signs you know, for a city boy."

"A city boy who grew up on that ranch. I still know places you've never seen out there and never will."

Nick shrugged that off. "Well, guess it doesn't matter since I've got you all here."

I smiled at him, deciding to take a risk and maybe, just maybe, throw him off kilter the tiniest bit. "You, me, Kirsten, and Deputy Yorke."

Nick's eyes widened just a fraction, but the motion registered for me. Now I knew what had happened to Yorke. Just not if he were dead or alive. It was likely Yorke's blood on Kirsten.

"How'd you know that?" he asked.

"Deduction, good guesses, and a tad bit of information. Kirsten should have been on the air this morning. I called Nathan. Then you. You gave me that cock-and-bull story about the transmitter, then essentially hung up on me on a pretext. Not even a good pretext, just, 'Oh, hey, I gotta go.' For a killer I thought you'd be a better liar."

"How'd you know about the deputy?"

"Didn't, until now. But the sheriff's office called earlier asking if I'd seen or heard from him. He came down here to tell me something that would help the case. Guess you got to him first."

"I did. About ten miles out of town, he saw me putting Kirsten into the back of my truck. How unlucky for him that he was even on that back road headed this way, searching for you. Guess he noticed Kirsten's hands were tied. When he got out of his Durango, I shot him."

"Is he dead?" I tried to say it as steadily as I could.

Kirsten's head shaking side-to-side answered my question before Nick did.

"Nope. Guess one of the requisite qualifications for the Engelmann County Sheriff's Department is a hard head. Bullet ricocheted off his badge and clipped his head, skin wound, but it bled like crazy, knocked him back, and that gave me all the time I needed to get him in cuffs and into the truck with Kirsten."

Kirsten pointed back into the cabin. "I stopped the bleeding as best I could with my jacket. He's inside, resting, I hope. A little more with it, but I'm sure he's got a mild concussion."

I nodded toward Kirsten, then stared at Nick, hoping he'd see the menace deep within my eyes. "Now we add assault on a law enforcement officer to the list."

Nick shrugged and grinned at me again.

I should be afraid of him. Facing it right now might help me think more clearly later.

"You got something going on in that head of yours, Tomas. Tell me what it is." Nick inclined the aim of the Sharps a few inches above my center mass.

My face flushed.

Kirsten's eyes darted nervously to me, then steadied.

"Not much, Nick. I just decided I'm scared of you. Maybe I should've been for a lot longer considering you've killed, what, three people so far? I'm fearful for what you might do to Kirsten. And you've already upped the ante by shooting Yorke."

"Well, that's a good thing. A very smart thing, *Chief* Arnesen. You surprise me. I figured a big-shot, former city detective wouldn't be scared of too many things in this life."

"Man'd be foolish not to face his fears, get them out in the open so he can deal with them in a useful and appropriate manner."

"Shit. You do talk funny sometimes. Most of the time. I never understood half of what you said to me. I hate those corny old sayings you tossed around like Mardi Gras necklaces."

I shrugged my shoulders and remained silent.

In less than two seconds, Nick registered his displeasure by filling up the space with his noise. "No corny sayings now, huh, Chief? No goofy insights passed down from your grandfather or your father? Thought so. There's nothing clever in your mouth when you're facing the muzzle of a large rifle that'll finish that hole I almost put through your chest."

So silence bothered him. Noted. Win with silence or let silence force him into a false move, a mistake. There was nothing to talk about in this moment except the weather. I wasn't going to bring it up unless, for some odd reason, he chose to make an observation.

He walked in front of Kirsten and spoke over his shoulder to her. "Move over to the swing there. Sit down in it and start swinging and don't stop until I tell you to stop."

Once she had the swing in motion, Nick stepped around so he could see me without looking through the horse. "Step down out of the saddle. I want to see your hands all the way. Make sure you don't get too close to your holster."

It's more than a little awkward to dismount holding your hands in the air, but I managed. I did as Nick told me to do. No more, no less. Dismounted, I stood still and waited some more.

"Jeez, Tomas. Do I have to tell you every little thing I want you to do?"

"In this situation, Nick? Yes. I don't want to assume anything. I don't relish making a mistake that'll get someone else shot."

"Smart. I like that about you, always thinking. Even thinking you can use silence, making me tell you everything I want from you. Guess that could be a weapon of sorts." Then, as if to refute my deduction, Nick stared at me eyes-wide and released an unholy scream into the night.

If I wasn't afraid before, well, I'm man enough to admit when I'm no longer dealing with a man.

As if nothing had just awoken every bird from here to the next country, Nick then spoke in a soft, measured voice. "Take the rifle out of the boot and toss it to me. Try to make it land right here at my feet. Use your left hand only. Do it. Now."

I pulled the Winchester out, grabbing onto the stock, and flipped it in Nick's general direction. It landed off to one side and not at his feet.

"Missed it by a little there, Chief."

"Hard to do one-handed."

"Whatever. Now, take the Colt out of the holster, two fingers, and toss it here as well."

I complied. So far, so good, but I was only passing the fifth-floor window and we had a long way to fall.

"Now the holster. Unbuckle and flip it over here."

Still good.

"Take out that thirty-eight you always carry on your ankle."

"Shit," I said, out loud with as much emphasis and surprise in my tone as I could muster.

"Ha! You didn't think I ever noticed how you got all armed up when you were going on duty?"

"Guess not. You seem to have a lot of this covered. Been thinking it out, planning it?"

Nick's grin pulled so wide I thought his cheeks were going to recede into his forehead. "For a long time. A real long time. Now, shut up and walk to the doorway, Chief. Stop when you get there. When I say go you walk into the room, right to the middle of it. Don't go left or right. Don't do anything stupid. Kirsten will be right behind you and the Sharps will be right behind her in the small of her back. Got it?"

"Got it."

"Walk into the doorway."

I walked into the doorway.

"Now into the room."

I walked into the center of the room and stood there. I saw Yorke curled up on a cot in the far corner but didn't move my head to look his way.

He sent a quick thumbs-up that he was doing all right, then let his hand drop back onto the blanket as feet shuffled behind me.

So far, so good. Second floor down and counting.

"Turn around."

I did so and Kirsten fell into my arms. I held her tightly and hung on until further instructions arrived from Nick. To her credit, she wasn't crying, but she was calm, in control, and watchful.

We must have given each other some kind of knowing look because Nick screamed again. "Enough! What you see in this old fart is beyond me, Kirsten. If we had more time, I'd let you explain it to me. But we don't have a lot of time. Both of you, go sit over there in those chairs. Sit by the cot so I have all three of you in front of me."

So far, so much better.

The old handmade wooden arm chairs were sturdy and unimaginative but functional. Single-wide top brace, leaving a lot of space open above the seat. I drug one around for Kirsten and put it at the foot of the cot. I pulled mine to the middle of the cot, leaving Yorke's face exposed but covering his hands and midsection.

When I sat down, I managed to point toward the small of my back.

Yorke coughed, once, twice, then moaned.

Kirsten asked, "Can I get him some water? Please, Nick?"

"Carefully."

She leaned to her right and pulled a canteen off the floor. She handed it to me and I held it back for Yorke.

He took a long pull then handed it back to me.

"Mind if I take a hit as well? Got a bit thirsty riding up here," I asked politely.

"Go ahead."

Sweet cool spring water. In this moment, it tasted like the water of life from the Fountain of Youth. I handed it to Kirsten. Just as she reached for it, I dropped it. It bounced and rolled away from me, water gurgling out.

Kirsten gave a little cry and grabbed it.

I slid my chair back two inches while Nick's attention shifted to Kirsten picking up the canteen. Three long seconds later, my back felt lighter, my holster and .38 now safely under Yorke's blanket.

"I suppose you're all wondering why I've called you here?" Nick laughed, no, squealed. High-pitched, unhinged. It was ugly and mean and in woefully bad taste, like a barbecued armadillo still roasting on a spit. "Let me begin by sharing my favorite Bible verse with you."

Nick and the Bible, in the same sentence, in the same place together? Nick, who professed his Catholicism but never backed it up with action?

He laid the Sharps down on the small table next to him and picked up the 1860 Navy Colt that had killed three Rosemont men. He held that on us. It was a heavy revolver, but his hand was steady. One-handed, he flipped the Bible open to a bookmark, held it up, and proclaimed, "From the Book of the Exodus, chapter twenty, verse five. 'You shall not bow down to them or worship them; for I the Lord your God am a jealous God, punishing children for the iniquity of parents, to the third and the fourth generation of those who reject me.'" He sighed, then threw the Bible across the room at me.

I didn't flinch. The Good Book hit me squarely in the chest with a dull pain.

"Center mass again. No damage I can see. None at all. Damn, but you're good, Arnesen. Take off your vest. Drop it on the floor. Kick it over here."

I did so.

He picked it up, hefted it, then tossed it behind him. "So now you'll want to know the whole story, won't you? I'll tell you the story. You can even ask questions. Once we're done, I'll shoot you all. Perhaps I'll even get wounded myself in all the melee and wind up a hero."

"A hero? How do you figure that, Nick?" Kirsten asked.

"Well, Mathiesen gave me the clue at the town meeting. I was trying to figure out how to pull off the final act when he accused you oh so slyly of being the killer. I thought right then that was brilliant. I set out to make it work out that way."

I nodded. "So Mathiesen was part of your next setup, changing your plans on the fly."

"Yep. Worked out beautifully. Better than I hoped. Fighting, angry words, confrontations in public, investigations, the city council sacking you. That was so sweet. I tried to be so noncommittal when they asked me what they should do. Now I'm the Acting Chief of Public Safety for Rosemont, Utah, soon to be a hero."

I laughed.

Nick's grin became a sneer.

Seems mockery bothered him more than silence. I should've known. Big egos are just empty containers for insecurity.

I finally saw what he'd been trying to set up all this time. "You caught me, the killer, trying to cover my tracks. Kirsten and the deputy were collateral damage, killed in our gun battle or shootout, whatever you're going to call it. Be interesting to see how you stage this. Our state lab guys and investigators are pretty good."

Yorke finally spoke up. "A shootout in a rotten wood cabin'll make sparks, which'll make fire, which'll burn evidence."

Nick nodded the gun at Yorke. "If your county guys are this good, maybe I *should* be afraid."

55

I'd about had enough but knew I needed to tread lightly around this Nick I'd apparently never known. Not a clue from his outward behavior that his mind worked like a sieve—the truth simply ran through and drained out the bottom.

"Well, Nick, my man, you sure been playing us well. All of us. In fact, you snowed the entire town of Rosemont and everyone along the way—police academy troopers, college shrinks, friends. You are good."

Nick sneered, "Better than you ever were, Mr. High and Mighty Chief."

"I didn't know you wanted the job that much," I said.

"I wanted it, a lot. But then I heard you were retiring and coming back to Rosemont. Knew the council would offer you the job. Just didn't think you'd want it."

"Disappointed you, did we?"

"For about a minute. Until I figured out how to get all this started. Been thinking about this for a long time. You came back and there it was, all laid out in front of me."

"What was laid out in front of you?" Kirsten asked. "Nick, I don't understand any of this. What do those Bible verses have to do with anything, with us?"

Nick's eyes glazed over, like he was looking at something far off. I thought about moving then but he snapped back.

"By no means clearing the guilty, but visiting the iniquity of the parents upon the children and the children's children, to the third and the fourth generation."

"Averil was the first generation. You're the third generation. Kirsten is a third generation. So am I for that matter." I thought the observation might prime the story pump. It did.

Nick pointed at us and swirled his index finger. "*These* are the sins of the fathers visited on the third generation, in your cases, well, except for Mathiesen and Deputy Yorke over there. Payback for what your grandparents did to my grandfather."

"What did they do to Averil?" Kirsten sounded truly puzzled.

"They killed him, sure as I'm sitting here."

"He killed himself in my mother's living room, in my grandmother's house." Kirsten challenged Nick, sitting forward in her chair, her arms locked against the chair's, ready to throw herself at him.

"Easy, Kirsten. I was planning to shoot you first and let Tomas watch you die before I finished him off. Relax."

"Kirsten. Sit back. Listen. Please." I held out my hand and she reached over to hold it.

"Ain't that sweet."

"Go on, Nick. I want to know why we're here. Why Seth Ramsey and Tate Thoresen are dead. Why you kidnapped Kirsten and went to all this trouble to get me here."

"Grandfather told me the story about how all your grandparents, Seth's and Tate's included, caused my grandmother's death, how they conspired to keep it a secret. They all agreed to tell the same story—that it was an accident. They covered it up."

"Did he ever tell you exactly what happened? How they killed Birgit?" I asked him as gently as I could. His answer might reveal more than he intended.

"No. He always choked up then, broke down and cried, every time. After a while I quit asking because it hurt him so much just remembering."

Now I was the one interrogating him. "OK. What's next?"

"He gave me a list of names, former friends he hated, the ones who caused all his pain and suffering, those who drove him to drink."

I wanted to remind Nick that no one ever drove anyone else to drink. They always drove themselves.

"Tate Thoresen Senior. Aksel Arnesen. Archibald Ramsey. Responsible for Grandmother Birgit's death. Astrid Dyrdahl, who stole his land, his house, his life, and left him nothing."

"So you checked a Thoresen and a Ramsey off the list. Threw in Mathiesen for the sport of it, to further your plan. Now you have an Arnesen and a Dyrdahl in your hands. Tie up your revenge and clean up the family honor in one shot—or maybe three or four more. That about it?"

"That's it exactly."

I shook my head. "No, Nick. That's not it exactly. In fact, it's not even close. Your sins and your story are, to borrow another biblical image, as far off as the east is from the west. You've killed three people, tried to kill me, wounded a deputy, kidnapped Kirsten, and got me to come and play with you. Tragic, son, incredibly tragic. Killing people for no good reason. Seeking revenge on descendants of good, solid, honest people. You've killed for a lie. Your Grandfather Averil lied to you those last years while he drove himself into the bottle until he disappeared. The man who shot himself no longer resembled Averil Lowrance in any way."

Nick stood up and pointed the Navy Colt at my head.

The black hole of the barrel seemed to grow as I stared back at it.

"You lying son of a bitch. You'll say anything to save your hide you selfish bastard."

I stood up and faced him. "You got to dump your grandfather's hate and grief on us. Least you can do is be man enough to hear my story—to hear your grandfather's story. The real one."

"And you just happen to know it. Isn't that convenient?" Nick's disdain dripped along with the sweat on his brow.

"No. I have your grandfather's words, his writing, his confession, the truth about what happened. Are you game enough to listen to it?" I held up my hands. No sudden moves. "I have his confession here in my pocket. Can I take it out?"

Nick's eyes flashed to my pocket.

I could see yearning in his eyes. For all his anger, I wagered he needed to know what I had. At least then he could justify shooting us.

"Go ahead. Slowly. Carefully. Two fingers only."

I complied, unfolded the letter, and held it up. "Averil Lowrance's handwriting."

"You could have forged it." Nick resisted looking closely.

"And when exactly could I have done that, especially since I didn't know until today that you were the killer? How would I know you were trying to clean up what you thought was Averil's legacy? Trying to exact revenge on the people who tried to help him, who tried to save his life? Come on, Nick. Think about it."

Nick still hesitated. Time to toss out my next-to-last option to see what happened. "So, Buddy-boy, what are you going to do now?"

"*What* did you just call me?"

"Buddy. Boy."

Nick looked even more unsettled now. He licked his lips, shifting his glance from me to Kirsten, then back to me holding up the letter. "No one knows me by that name. *How do you know that name?*" His voice cracked and went up an octave and a half.

"I told you, Nick. It's in the letter. I suspect it's what your grandfather always called you. So? Do you want me to read it to you? Or do you want to read it yourself?"

"You'll try something, I know you will. I start reading it, lose my focus, you'll try something."

"My word. I will do nothing, make no moves, until you read the letter."

"Give it to Kirsten. She'll read it."

"You got it, Nick." I handed it over to her.

"Tomas, sit down," he commanded. "Kirsten, read the letter."

56

Buddy-boy. So much to tell you.
Forgive me.
I killed Birgit.
My friends covered up for me.

The guilt ate me up, hollowed me out so I drank to fill the empty. Couldn't do it. Drank to forget. Never forgot. I drank to stop seeing her face, all the blood. I tried to stay awake and never sleep because her face, blood, blood all I could see when I closed my eyes.

The guilt, did I say that? Can't remember. I tried to kill myself, gun misfired. Sobered me up right away. Sit in my old living room, belongs to Astrid and her granddaughter, Kirsten. Going to finish this I started soon enough, this house we used to call home, your grandmother and I.

Tell Astrid I'm sorry, once you read this letter. I, guilt never left. Had to rewrite history, so's could live with myself, tolerate my presence the least bit, shove guilt away, keep it at arm's length.

Who better to take blame than friends? Blamed them. Told the story long enough that they were responsible until I believed it. All those years I hated them out loud, you listening, my grandson who didn't know the truth, never knew the truth, the ugly awful truth of your grandpa, the murderer. I got mad drunk. Knew she was having an affair with Aksel even when I knew it weren't jot of truth. I believed my lies, told those lies to you. Wanted you to hate them. Didn't think I could live it out, alone with hatred and anger, bitterness.

But truth told, I didn't hate them. Don't now in this moment. Love 'em. All my friends. They never stopped loving me, never stopped trying to help me. I rejected them, their help, their love. But I never stopped loving them.

I drank the land up. I drank the house away. I drank my life, swallow by swallow until there was nothing left but Astrid's charity and then Kirsten's. I took it. I took it all, every kindness, every gentle gesture, each hopeful action, each honest word. I took it all and gave back blood. Forgive me.

Now have one clean moment before I bring the darkness down onto myself, before I leave the light behind. Throw my lies away. Purge hate for my sake. Leave it all go.

I'm sorry, Buddy-boy. Truly sorry.

Grandfather Averil

57

Nick stared at me, the flush on his face fading into gray then white. He took three, four, five very deep breaths.

I thought, or hoped, really, he was going to pass out, but the gun didn't waver one inch away from another center mass shot.

"Not true. *Not* true. *Not true!* Can't be true. Grandpa would never lie to me." Nick spoke through gritted teeth, his pallor reddening with every syllable.

Sometimes the line between Public Safety Officer and counselor was fine indeed. "Nick. Your grandpa didn't lie to you so much as he lied to himself. He created an alternate reality of sorts, then pulled you into it, pulled you into the fantasy he created because he couldn't handle his guilt."

"No. You did—"

"—did what, Nick? What could I do? You've been watching us. You've been in my back pocket all along, seen and known every move we've made."

"Didn't know about the vest."

"Kinda glad you missed that one myself."

Nick chuckled, but there was no warmth in it.

I didn't see any other way out of this but through it. I had to keep pushing his buttons. "Nicholas Averil Lowrance, you have to know in your heart there's no way I had anything to do with this letter from your grandfather to his *buddy-boy*."

"Stop calling me that. He called me that." Nick emphasized every word with a thrust of the gun toward our faces. "You don't get to call me that."

"OK. You've been smarter than us this whole time, so that gives me a little hope you'll realize the truth. The letter is genuine. Your grandfather wrote it, for you. If Kirsten's grandmother hadn't had the stroke, you would have gotten the letter a lot sooner and none of this would have happened. No one would have died."

"Coulda, shoulda, oughta. You aren't one for living that way, Tomas. I know that from hanging out with you. You can't rewrite history." Nick shrugged his shoulders.

"I understand that. Wish we could get those three deaths off the record, but we can't. You'll have to answer for them. Answer for shooting Yorke here. You know that. We could probably make the charge for kidnapping Kirsten and Trooper disappear. We will help you all the way, like Averil's friends tried to help him. Maybe we can do better at that than our relatives did."

Kirsten shot me a look as if to say, "You're pressing too hard."

I paid no mind, the only time in recent memory I'd so quickly dismissed her glance. I squared my eyes on Nick and spoke with all the confidence of a man who didn't want to die and didn't want his girlfriend to either. "But you gotta know . . . you won't walk from this."

Nick's eyes brightened. "Well, Mr. Big-shot-I-used-to-be-a-detective, like I told you earlier, Mathiesen was right at the town meeting. You are the killer. I'm the hero."

"Hmm. Good story. You'll have to go to some lengths to get that Colt's gunshot residue on my hands before you shoot me. If I shoot two other people, there'll be a lot of powder flying in the air."

"I can handle that."

"But how will you explain the evidence we collected? The copies of all the letters, pages from the town's journal, evidence reports, all sent to Sheriff Consolves, and, for clarity's sake, copies of the letter from the deputy that investigated Birgit's death where he speculates that it was not an accident? We also have copies of the drawings from Averil's suicide and the matching images from Seth and Tate with the way you staged them."

"That's all you got?"

"Actually, no. We have your fingerprints at all three murder scenes. We have the leather gloves you used with all three victims' blood on them. You didn't handle things as carefully as you thought you did."

Yorke spoke from the cot. "You were smart to put the gloves at the bottom of the glove bin. Would have been better to have burnt them. And you left the latex gloves inside the leather ones. Guess you figured no one would ever go through the bin until much, much later. You know, you sweat in those gloves." The deputy's voice faltered. He coughed.

I took over. "Takes a while, but we'll get DNA from the gloves and the DNA will be yours. Three victims' blood, your DNA. We gotcha, Nick. No matter what happens here, you're done."

"You're bluffing."

"You've been around me enough in the last few months to know I don't bluff. Not any time under any circumstance."

"You could say that so I'd think you weren't, but you really are."

I laughed and shook my head. "Now you're confusing me. You're reaching for connections that aren't there."

He stayed silent.

I looked at my watch. Big mistake.

Nick's eyes widened. "What are you up to?"

"Nick. We can help you. We *want* to help you. There's no reason anyone else has to die today. Give me some time to work this out so we all walk out of here, alive."

"Sheriff's coming, isn't he?"

He'd correctly interpreted my glance. Might as well tell him straight up. "Probably riding up to the cabin. Could even be out there for all I know. They don't waste time when a ten-seventy-eight shots-fired call goes out."

"How would they know where to go?"

"Charlie. I told him where I was headed."

Nick glanced toward the front window then jerked his head back around to glare at me. He stepped back out of view. "So you put it all together. Finally. Smart move coming here, so you thought. Not such a smart move now, eh."

Nick looked at me, at Yorke, then at Kirsten. He lowered the Colt to his side. Something passed over his face. If we'd been standing outside I would have said it looked like a shadow from a cloud or a raven flying between him and the sunlight. But we were inside in dim light with nothing to cast a shadow over his face—nothing but his own resignation.

The hairs on the back of my neck extended themselves out from my body. He'd made a decision. His face shapeshifted into an unreadable façade, with no indication of what he was thinking. I could observe none of the usual signs I'd learned to read: nostrils flaring, eyes crinkling tighter, beads of sweat forming at the hairline, lips thinning out or almost disappearing, jaw muscles working, nails turning white. Nick disappeared. Any semblance to the human being I'd known vanished. In front of me, a powerful weapon at his side, daring me to make a move, stood one of our own, but he'd transformed into a killer intent on erasing the past by eradicating his present. Nick's hollow eyes told me our time was short.

I tensed, then willed myself to relax, then got up on the balls of my feet ready to throw myself either at him or to jump in front of Kirsten. It all depended now on where he aimed the gun when he moved again. I knew he'd move. I hoped Yorke had my Bodyguard ready. Even a small diversion could be the difference between any of us getting out of here alive. Chances were better than fifty-fifty more than one of us would come out in a body bag.

Then a distinct, official, yet welcome voice blared from outside. "This is Sheriff Consolves. I want everyone in the cabin to come out slowly, hands up. Do it now."

The sheriff's voice rasping through the bullhorn galvanized Nick. He brought the Navy Colt up, bringing his left hand into a two-hand grip, turning his body toward Kirsten.

I shouted, "Kirsten. Down!" I threw myself between her and Nick.

As soon as I cleared the space in front of the cot, Yorke took his shot.

In that nanosecond, time stopped as Nick pulled his trigger.

The cap and ball round ricocheted off my right shoulder. The impact knocked me backwards. I hit the floor and rolled to make sure Kirsten had scrambled behind me. Only then did I look back toward Nick. I felt blood flowing from my shredded shoulder. For a few moments, I knew the adrenaline rush would keep my head clear. But after that?

Yorke, shaky from blood loss and exposure, going for center mass, had hit Nick in the left shoulder, an impact right on the collarbone.

"Push me up toward Nick," I whispered to Kirsten.

She didn't hesitate. She grabbed my belt, pulled me up, and pushed me toward Nick in one motion.

Nick's legs had buckled from the impact, but he didn't go down. He slumped back against the wall, still with a solid two-hand grip on the Colt. Being shot has a way of slowing a person down, but he wasn't out. When he raised the Colt, toward me this time, Yorke's second shot hit him in the fold between his groin and upper thigh. That one put him down. Nick dropped the gun and used his free left hand to try to steady himself as he slid down to the floor.

As I pushed myself closer to take the Colt out of his right hand, Nick raised it and waved it back and forth as if to say no, no, no. Then he rested the gun in his lap and looked around the room.

"We're coming in," the sheriff called.

"Hold up, Emilio. Hold up. Wait!" I shouted. "Hear me? This is Tomas. Hold up."

"I hear you. We'll hold up but not for long. If there are any more shots, we're coming in hot."

"What about it, Nick? Any more shooting?"

Nick panted as he tried to speak. "Where was the other gun?"

"My back. You never saw me carry that one, did you? Yorke took it when I dropped the canteen."

"Good move, Chief."

"Nick, let the Sheriff come in. Nathan's out there too. We can get you help."

"Nah. I think Yorke's a better shot under the circumstances than I expected. I'm pretty sure he hit the femoral."

"Not too late. Let me call them in."

"Please, Nick. Let them help you." Kirsten had her hand on my shoulder to put pressure on my wound, which was also bleeding profusely.

"Appreciate the offer, you two. No. I think it's better this way. You know, like grandfather like grandson." We all shouted in the same instant as Nick raised the heavy Navy Colt, placed the barrel center-on against his forehead, and pulled the trigger.

Before the report died out, Emilio and two deputies burst through the door, weapons ready.

I had one hand in the air.

Yorke had both his hands up, dropping the S&W Bodyguard onto the cot so no one would mistake him for the shooter. He was, but in this case we didn't need any additional misunderstandings, not with loaded weapons pointed into the room.

Emilio looked around, saw the blood everywhere, and spotted Nick lying against the wall. "Stand down. Get Nathan in here. Call Air Rescue. We'll need the helicopter to get these people out of here. We have two officers wounded."

The room starting fading in and out on me as white noise whistled around and through my ears. I tried to move my head to get more of Kirsten's face into my field of vision. I tasted something acrid in my throat. Kirsten's lips on my forehead was the last sensation I felt.

Not a bad way to go if this was it, but damn, I didn't want to go.

The white noise reached its crescendo then burst open, a tiny black hole sucking everything into it.

58

When I woke up in my room at Utah Valley Regional Medical Center, Kirsten held my hand. She was asleep with her head on the edge of my bed. Nathan stood behind her, smiling. I wiggled my fingers and she woke up as quickly as she answered the radio or the phone, mid-first ring. In this case, mid-first wriggle.

I thought she would kiss me, but she didn't. She kept hold of my hand and stared at me like she was taking inventory at the store, cataloguing every detail. But she did smile at me while looking me over. That was almost as good as a kiss.

"She didn't leave your side," Nathan said from behind. "She bullied her way into the OR and watched the surgery in scrubs from behind the anesthesiologist. I tried to talk her into resting while you were in recovery, but she gave me that look. You know the one I mean."

I nodded. I'd been the recipient of her icy stare on several occasions. It turns men into five-year-old boys.

"How's Yorke?" Those were the words I formed in my head. What came out sounded more like, "Sork?"

Kirsten reached for a cup of ice chips and fed me a spoonful. Funny how ice chips can feel so sweet melting in your mouth and how soothing the coolness can be running down your throat.

She then interpreted and answered my still dry-mouth mumbling. "He's recovering. Next room over. Doctors said you can see him later."

"Good." That came out much clearer. I tried more, but slowly. "Call Hal Leonard and Nels. Promised them story. Hal first."

"They're both waiting in the cafeteria. Have been most of the day. You feel up to talking to them now?"

"Some more ice chips, maybe some red Jell-O. I'll be good to go for a while."

Nathan said, "The Sheriff and Burchfield want to talk to you as well."

"They can wait. Hal and Nels first."

I closed my eyes for a second and heard Kirsten tell Nathan, "Give us about fifteen more minutes, Nate, then bring Nels. Better yet, bring them both. Let Tomas tell both of them."

"No. Not together. Promised Hal," I croaked.

"Tough. I'll tell Nels and Hal that they get this exclusive together or they get nothing at all. I am not going to jeopardize your recovery."

I opened my eyes again to receive the icy stare full-blast. "OK."

"Good boy." She patted my head with one hand while she fed me another spoonful of ice chips.

Surprisingly, or not, Nels and Hal had no problems with Kirsten's decision. They understood and had been talking about such an eventuality in the cafeteria. They'd worked out their angles to the story and were going to share the byline. Best thing was, all the state and national reporters were going to have to go through the two of them to get all the good, juicy, rather sensational details.

Kirsten made me take a nap after giving Nels and Hal their exclusive. She stood outside my room, door closed, and refused entrance to everyone except hospital staff—and said staff members had to give her damn good reasons why they needed to interrupt my sleep. Two nurses decided they didn't need to check my blood pressure and ask five more questions about pain levels and comfort or discomfort if it meant another tangle with my guardian.

The nap proved refreshing and put about a quarter charge into my battery. But the late afternoon session used up every bit of that recharge and then some. When I completed dictating my report to Lynette, I was soaked in sweat and my shoulder felt like someone had stuck an icy-hot ice pick into it. Sheriff Consolves, Emery Burchfield, Ryan McFadden, Trooper Yorke in a wheelchair, and Kirsten attended the session. The hospital staff grumbled about the roomful but decided not to make an issue of it.

But I got the story straight, made sure every detail got into the record. Burchfield didn't come out smelling too good, as if I cared about his status in the first place. OK. I did, because I always think about how events might affect the other person, tend to give them some benefit of the doubt. In this case, I may have given the acting Engelmann County prosecuting attorney about a 5 percent break. I also made sure Yorke, Kirsten, and Nathan got more than their fifteen minutes of fame, as did several other Rosemonters. By the time I'd signed the transcription, the official record matched, in every detail, the stories Nels planned to serialize in the *Rosemont Republic* and those Hal would feature on his *Investigative Insiders* program.

Kirsten wiped my forehead and literally shooed everyone out of the room, using her hands like she was herding sheep.

I wanted to laugh, but every movement sent that ice pick deeper into my shoulder. I croaked as she took hold of Yorke's wheelchair.

"Nope. Stay. Second."

She wheeled him around, without question or argument, and rolled him up to my bedside.

"Thanks, Yorke. You going to be okay?"

He took my offered hand, offered at great pain, which I refused to let get in the way of this gesture. Anything less would have been completely unmanly. We shook.

"I've been out of it lately for some odd reason. What were you coming to town to tell me? Dispatcher said you were pretty excited."

"Lab found some threads stuck in Greg's shirt. Type-specific to leatherwork gloves, common enough around here. But Greg didn't have any in the house. I went back and checked. Won't need it now but I'll bet if we go through the glove bin at Seth's we'll find a pair with more trace evidence left on them."

"Sneaky. Nick probably grabbed a pair going in to Seth's, used them in all three murders, then dropped 'em back in the bin at some point."

"Might want to check it out just to tie up a loose end."

I nodded and the action used up every bit of the energy I had left. I found strength enough to raise my left eyebrow at Kirsten and ask Yorke, "You going to be all right?"

He winked. "*We'll* be just fine. Plan on having a time at the ranch with you and Kirsten."

Kirsten tilted her head toward the open door where Estella Mathiesen stood. "Good for you," I croaked. Now I was done.

Yorke smiled and waved at Estella to come in. She leaned down and kissed me gently on the forehead. "Thank you, Tomas. For everything."

Kisses from two beautiful women in one afternoon, and I could not enjoy the aftermath. My eyes closed without my permission and I drifted off, listening to Kirsten whispering to Yorke and Estella over the rubbery hum of his wheelchair rolling out the door. Then? Nothing until dinner, when Mrs. Way-too-cheerful-nurse brought my soft-food diet to make sure my next round of pain meds didn't go crazy in an empty stomach. When she left after depositing the tray on my table, pointing vigorously at the tiny white pill cup, pantomiming me popping those pills into my mouth, Kirsten burst into laughter. "The look on your face when Nurse Berg comes into the room is priceless, Tomas. Priceless. You look like a deer in headlights."

"She is simply too damn cheerful. Unsettling in this place."

"Well, you won't be here too much longer from what I hear."

We kept the banter going meal by meal until I was eating solid food, or what passed for that from the hospital cafeteria. Kirsten completely ignored visiting hours and no one on the staff challenged her.

And on the sixth day, God breezed into my room hidden in the guise of my orthopedic Doctor, Elliot Karstun. "You ready to go home?"

"Been ready, Doc, pretty much since I got here."

"Ah. A policeman's bravado. Sure you were. You didn't even know up from down for the first forty-eight hours. But, OK. I'll give you a break on that." He leaned down and checked my bandages, the arrangement of my shoulder and arm in the sling. "I will see you in a week, check the incisions, take some X-rays to see how the bones are knitting, make sure none of the screws have shifted, that sort of examination."

"I can handle that. What's the prognosis for use of my shoulder?"

"Too soon to tell. I did a dang fine and thoroughly professional job getting everything screwed and wired together. I'm still worried about that sponge we haven't been able to find. It'll turn up somewhere."

"Good one, Doc. You play that for all your patients?"

His smile was far too straight for me to tell if he was truly joking. "Nope. Only the ones who get shot trying to save people's lives."

"And after next week's visit?"

"A lot depends on how much you want to participate in your healing and restoration. You work it, put up with the pain, I think we can get you back to ninety percent, maybe more."

"But I'll always have some restrictions and won't be able to do everything I used to before the shot tore it up in there?"

"What do you want to do after recovery that you couldn't do before?"

I had to stop and think. It was my right shoulder. I shoot left-handed, so that wouldn't be an issue. I shrugged my shoulders, then immediately winced. He hadn't left a sponge. He'd left the ice pick.

"Don't do that." Doctor Karstun frowned.

"Yeah, I think I figured that out."

"When you come back for your appointment, we'll get your physical therapy scheduled. It's not going to be fun for the first month or so, but I'll wait to lay that on you."

"Thanks, Doc. I appreciate your honesty. I'll work as hard as I can to get back as far as I can go."

"I'll go sign the papers to release you. They'll come get you in the wheelchair and roll you out. Who's taking you home?" He followed an exchange of glances between Kirsten and me. "Ah. Yes. Very good." He took Kirsten's hand. "If you ever need a position managing an OR, let me know. Shoot, I'd give you the whole hospital to run."

"Thanks for the offers. But as of now it looks like I have two full-time positions, work and him."

"I know which one will be the hardest." Elliot still held her hand.

"I'll take good care of him, Doctor Karstun. See that he gets his rest, stays quiet, and shows up for his appointments, all of them."

"Good! Thank you. I know you will."

Karstun, *still* holding her hand, gave Kirsten a hug—a hug I thought lasted a tad too long. Then I realized that if I kept getting upset by every man who took advantage of enjoying a hug from Kirsten, I'd not have much extra time to enjoy her hugs myself.

59

Now that we were finally and blessedly alone, I asked Kirsten, "So, tell me what's been happening in our fair little town?"

"Let's get you home first. I saved the latest issue of the *Rosemont Republic* for you. Nels did a great job with the first installment of the story. You'll absolutely love the editorial pages."

"What did he wind up using for the headline?"

"One of Our Own."

I laughed. Everything hurt, but it didn't matter. Then I stopped laughing and looked up at Kirsten. "Sorry. Inappropriate response."

"But understandable in the circumstances. No one else is listening." She leaned down and kissed the top of my head. "Oh, and our presence is requested at the courthouse next Tuesday morning. We are character witnesses for Estella and Emily at the hearing. Full parental rights restored seems to be in the wind."

"Anyone else at the hearing?" I smiled.

"Deputy Sheriff Trooper Yorke will be attending as a disinterested third-party. In court, that is."

"And out of court our good deputy sheriff is a most interested first-party." I laughed again. It still hurt. "Well, I hope they take their time and that we get an invitation to the wedding."

Kirsten patted my hand and kissed the top of my head, again.

This time I said something. "Doc didn't do anything to my lips you know."

"I know, love. I do want to kiss you, now and forever. But as soon as I lean down to kiss you, you're going to want to hug me. You'll raise your arm instinctively to wrap me up, and it's going to hurt like fire. Then you'll start crying because it hurts so bad, then I'll start crying because you're hurting. That's the precise moment when the hospital staff will wheel the chair in to take you back. I think we'll wait a little while longer for that particular form of endearment."

I sighed. *Why did she always have to be right?* She patted my head this time, laughing. *That blessed sound will heal me ten times faster*, I thought.

On the way out to the car, riding in my silver-black, high-wheeled chariot, Kirsten dropped some community news on me. "When you get back to work—"

"Who said I'm going back to work?"

A quick laugh escaped her lips, as if she couldn't believe I *wouldn't* want to go back to work. She abruptly stopped our forward momentum, spun my wheelchair around to face her, set its brake, crouched down, and looked me in the eye. "We all say, Tomas. So don't fight it. The good news is you will probably have a new city council. We're circulating a recall petition for the mayor, Lukas Sogard, and Reinert Tonnessen. I told Emma it's not personal with her, but it is for the other two. She feels horrible about what happened and will probably resign before we hold the election. Freda Jacobsen and Anborg Laake will continue. So, yes, you will go back to work as the Chief of Public Safety for Rosemont, Utah. *After* you're fully recovered."

"Yes, ma'am." I saluted her.

She raised up, spun me back around, then lightly slapped the back of my head.

The sting felt comforting somehow. I got settled into the front seat of the Rosemont Safety Team's Special Service Tahoe.

Kirsten slid into the driver's side, made sure I was buckled up, and that the large foam wedge on which my arm rested was indeed wedged under my arm and against the door. She started the engine, then turned to look at me. "Where to from here?"

I knew what she meant but chose to give her a literal answer first. "Back to the ranch. Mabel will have afternoon tea and scones waiting for us on the veranda by the time we drive up."

She smiled, reached over, and patted my hand again, then shifted into gear and pulled out of the hospital patient loading zone. "It's all right, Tomas. I'm not sure where to go from here either. Sounds like back to the ranch for tea and scones is a good next step."

"A good next step *for us*," I added.

The laugh with which she rewarded me went straight out into the afternoon, racing ahead of us into the clear, crisp November light. The reddish-pink-orange tint that colored the streaming clouds overhead made it hard for me to tell if her face only reflected the sky's hues or if she was blushing.

In either case, my view of her rose-tinted profile made for a fine ride home.

ABOUT THE AUTHOR

This photograph of James H. Drury was taken by his nephew, Blake Atwood, on an unforgettable road trip in 2009 from Price, Utah, to Healdsburg, California, where Jim picked up his first custom-made, twelve-string guitar crafted by McKnight Guitars.

To see and hear him play this magnificent instrument, visit https://youtu.be/CkJt958DnWs.

BLAKE ATWOOD is James Drury's nephew. He is an author, editor, and ghostwriter who can be contacted through BlakeAtwood.com.

IN MEMORIAM

THE REV. JAMES HUGH DRURY of Ascension St. Matthew's Church passed away April 7, 2015 in Salt Lake City at the age of 67. A beloved husband, father, brother, and son, a respected community leader, and a compassionate pastor simply known as "PJ" to most, James was born in 1948 in Lexington, KY to Hugh and Betty Drury.

A self-described Air Force brat, James attended 13 different schools throughout the U.S. in his first 12 years of education, including three years of high school in Misawa, Japan. In 1970, he graduated from California Baptist College in Riverside with a B.A. in English Literature. In 1977, he graduated from Lutheran Theological Seminary in Gettysburg, PA with a Master of Divinity. In 1990, he graduated from St. Mary's University in San Antonio, TX with a Master of Arts in Communication Arts.

James then poured his robust life experience, considerable education, and capable spiritual leadership into the lives of thousands of people in multiple congregations. His first pastorate was Peace Lutheran Church in Lompoc, CA, from 1977–1982. He then led Christ the King Lutheran Church in Universal City, TX from 1982–1992. He then moved to Alaska to pastor Sitka Lutheran Church from 1992–

IN MEMORIAM

2008. In 2008, he moved to Price, UT to pastor the Lutheran-Episcopal congregation at Ascension St. Matthew's Church.

James met his beloved wife Linda during his time in Sitka and doted upon her as well as her grandchildren and grown children.

Like his father before him, he was a man who loved to help people. He strove to help both his local and spiritual communities thrive through the constant volunteering of his time. He played in various bands for local events throughout his life and enjoyed many different civic volunteer opportunities, like being the Board President of The Island Institute of Sitka, AK. He thoroughly enjoyed being the Volunteer Director for the Keet Gooshi Heen Elementary School's annual fifth-grade Shakespeare production. In addition to shepherding his flock, he was a clergy member of the Diocesan Council of the Episcopal Diocese of Utah, assisted the Evangelical Lutheran Church in America (ELCA) on many communications projects, and was an Ecumenical Officer for the Utah Conference of the ELCA Rocky Mountain Synod.

James was also a restless creative. Over the course of his life, he was a jovial broadcast radio personality, a knowledgeable adjunct professor, an accomplished guitarist, and the skillful author and poet of the books *A Sharpness of Grief*, *Do Not Dismiss What Is*, and *Let's Go Walking*. These works are currently being republished in a collection of his poetry as well as his devotional works.

However, his favorite passion project was likely "How Everything Works," an album of children's songs he wrote, played, and recorded as a fundraiser for his grandchildren's school.

Singing to Jesus as he passed from this life into the next, his final words were a lasting testament to his unwavering faith in God.

Made in the USA
San Bernardino, CA
21 January 2019